In that half-second, while both sprawling hijackers were scrambling to bring their rifles to bear, Sheik Ahmed drew his sword. It flashed twice like summer lightning, and two heads bounced like bowling balls with the roll of the ship. The headless bodies spouted red lava over the deck.

I looked at Ahmed. As he met my gaze his nostrils flared and his grip tightened on the sword hilt.

He was daring me to say something, so of course I said it. "If you mess up my clean decks that way again, I'll throw you off the ship, Harvard or no Harvard, so help me!"

The fierceness became absolutely blank. He lowered the smeared sword, threw back his head and shouted a laugh.

"Bennington warned me about you," he chortled, his eyes glinting, "but he didn't tell the half of it!"

ANALOG BOOKS

— Series Editor: Ben Bova —

SF

CAPTAIN EMPIRICAL

SAM
NICHOLSON

SF
ace books
A Division of Charter Communications Inc.
A GROSSET & DUNLAP COMPANY
360 Park Avenue South
New York, New York 10010

An ACE Book by arrangement with
Baronet Publishing Company

Cover art by Vincent Di Fate

First Ace Printing: January 1979

Printed in U.S.A.

Captain
Empirical

Chapter 1

The Q-Pod Tape Begins

The first snag in sending the mining expedition to the Asteroids was that everybody wanted to get into the act.

I had foreseen the snag, of course. Since I am taping this report for the Company's files, I will mention that their Rec-Paks confirm I warned Mickleberry in Operations—and Executive Director Holloway at the Company's subsidiary, Space Mining, Incorporated—that the bureaucrats and grifters would be swarming aboard.

Nobody listened. During the following months I worked on a troubleshooting job with the Company's sea-going fleet . . . and you goddamned Company bastards know I am a blue-water master mariner who wishes to hell . . . *erase tape . . . resume . . .*

. . . with the Company's sea-going fleet. Mickleberry summoned me to New York and said that the Company's Board of Directors, at Holloway's recommendation, wanted me to head the Asteroid Expedition. The Headquarters Wheel was in Moon orbit—the personnel were arriving at Moon Residence—the stores canisters were lifting off daily from Space Mining's Assembly/Launch Complex at Cape Canaveral.

It all sounded great until I asked. "How many freeloaders?"

Mickleberry got his thin, pinched-nose expression. "In a project of this scope, Captain Schuster, it is customary for certain scientific observers to accompany—"

"Such as?"

"NASA naturally wishes to be included."

"Uh-huh. And—?"

"Several courtesy passengers from Space-interested nations."

There was a pause that hung too long. I repeated, "And—?"

He coughed. "The United Nations Space-Sharing Committee wishes to check on our ore assays—"

"Over your dead body, Mickleberry, does that double-dealing guru Fakey Atur come aboard the Space Mining Wheel!"

"Khadir Fai k'y Atur will remain in New York. The UN committee is sending a technical staff."

I reflected that I would be at least two years with this egghead menagerie—six months out, a year there, six months home. I said, "I don't want the job."

Mickleberry leaned back in his chair. "In that

case we will have to call our Director Emeritus, Dr. Jardin, out of retirement—"

"What! That fog-bound theory-splicer?"

"Director Holloway cannot be spared from the ALC."

We eyed each other. It was a stand-off. My sea-lawyer brain got up steam. I said, "Look, Mickleberry, the expedition has two distinct parts, right? The research—and bringing home the bacon. Okay, let Jardin have the eggheads, and give me command of the Assay Q-Pod and the four Space Tugs."

He hesitated. "You anticipate no—uh—conflict of interests?"

"Overlapping of spheres? In a way," I admitted. "But I don't care about status. Let Jardin parade around the Wheel—and let me be in charge of the mining. The important thing is to strike paydirt up there."

Of course, the deal was not decided until all aspects had been discussed. I insisted on complete mining autonomy. Knowing how slow Jardin was on the uptake, I did not want to be dependent on the Wheel in case of emergency. In particular, I wanted the Q-Pod and the Tugs to carry at all times enough Vita/Carbo rations to last until a rescue craft could come out from the Moon.

I won my point. A couple weeks later we spun out of Moon orbit on the Wheel—a first-class Space safari.

The six months went faster than I would have thought possible. The Wheel community settled out into the theorists and the mining gang, but there was room for everybody. We had our own fields of training and research. Every day was different—*how* different, we found out the hard way.

As the Wheel approached the relevant Asteroid sector, various regular measurements were made along a specific course—somewhat like gradually blowing up the enlargement of a photograph. The nearer we got to the Asteroids, the more these superimposed readings took on a sort of shimmy.

Maybe I can explain better by an analogy. The southeastern corner of England is in the process of sinking—a slow process, of course. However, the downward tilt has now reached the stage where an unusally high tide coming up the Thames could flood vast sections of London. This tilt is imperceptible in daily terms and must be seen over 2,000 years of intermittent human measurement.

But let us say that a Spaceship was approaching Earth over a period of six months, and highly sensitive geological instruments measured southeastern England every day of the approach. The sinking would be detected—maybe only as a shift at the end of thirteen decimal places, but as a shift nonetheless. If the Space explorers had a preconceived notion that the Earth was, in fact, a solid blue-white marble, they would probably write off the shift as an effect of their own approach.

That is what happened on the Wheel. Convinced by relatively few years of observations (speaking cosmically) that the Asteroid fragments moved in a fixed, unchanging pattern, the theorists and that goddamned fathead . . . *scrub tape . . . resume . . .*

. . . unchanging orbit, Dr. Jardin and the theorists disregarded the shimmy. If I had been running the expedition—well, I don't wanta hold a *post mortem*. Dr. Jardin did not inform me of the peculiar readings, and the Q-Pod subsequently plunged blindly into disaster.

The Wheel established her Asteroid position, and the ore prospecting went fine, at first. Aboard the Q-Pod I had a bright young astronaut, Lieutenant Worthing, a middle-aged ores analyst, Dr. Loft, and his assistant, a young chap named Grimes. As per agreement with the UN, we shot electro-pitons into the spheroids we were claiming, gave their positions to the Wheel, and held off calling a Tug until the Space Sharing Committee's analysts could come out and check our assays.

This meant waiting around for the UN grifters to get off their duffs . . . *scrub tape* . . . *resume* . . .
. . . waiting around for the UN analysts, so I told the Wheel we would jockey the spheroids into towing formation.

We made a swing around the group—and for the first time were aware that something had gone haywire. The spheroids had shifted bearings. Astronaut Worthing said, "I think it's the effect of shooting pitons into them, captain. We've been playing billiards and nudging all the spheroids into the same pocket."

"Yeah, maybe," I said doubtfully. To me, the spheroids had over-reacted. I wondered if we had miscalculated mass. I did not like the feel of the whole situation. I added, "Let me do the maneuvering, Lieutenant." I knew I had had more experience in handling a vessel among reefs and shoals. Space is too empty for practice in Fancy Dan figure eights.

I began herding the spheroids into formation, always keeping to the outside, with the stern tube and stern maneuvering jets clear.

It happened so damned fast—like being vacuumed into quicksand. One moment, the clustered spheroids were a point off our bow—the next, an avalanche rolled over the viewscreen.

Our forward jets were plugged—the Q-Pod would blow up if I tried to reverse. I coded *Mark* on the Chart Reader, *Interpolate* on the Thrust—and blew full power through the stern tube and stern jets.

There was a choked splutter—my throat went dry—then the blast blew clear. We had power and limited steering.

Lieutenant Worthing looked poleaxed. I had no time to snap him out of shock. I stepped to the computer and began figuring our heading by dead reckoning, since our electronic sensors had gone deaf, dumb, and blind in that peculiarly sticky tension of fifty thousand tons of adhering/cohering spheroids.

Our heading could have been better—but it also could have been worse. I rectified with the jets and steadied us on the new course, with a new *Mark* on the Chart Reader.

When I stepped back from the navigation consoles, I could feel the sweat running under my shirt. Dr. Loft and Grimes were standing at the control room hatchway. Grimes was in pale shock, like Worthing, but Dr. Loft seemed to have his emotions under control. He asked, "Sending us back to the Wheel?"

"No. Blind as we are, and pushing that mass ahead of us, we could destroy the Wheel. Besides, whatever strange force we've run into, we've got to get away from it. To the best of my ability, I've headed us for the Moon."

Worthing said huskily, "The—Moon?"

"That's right," I barked, "and I want us to arrive there shipshape and Bristol fashion. There will be no letdown in discipline or morale! And now, lieutenant, prepare a Mayday tape and start transmitting.

"We can't send anything through this mass!"

I did not think we could, either, but I had to find something for him to do. I said sternly, "I gave an order, lieutenant!"

He looked relieved, as if glad somebody else had the command, and moved to the tapes.

Grimes said, "My God—it'll take a year for the Q-Pod—we can't—we can't—"

"We can shut off the ore centrifuge and the assay burners," said Dr. Loft briskly. "Come, Grimes—to work! If Captain Schuster says we're headed for the Moon, we'll get there!"

He coaxed Grimes into the lab. I was glad for his vote of confidence but doubted that I could deliver the goods.

Worthing came back, licked his dry lips and said, "Shouldn't you deal out the cyanide pills? You know damned well we're in our coffins!"

"Oh? How come?"

"Blind   reckoning   can't   hold   true   over 250,000,000 miles!"

"Depends on who's doing the reckoning. Besides, you don't think Mickleberry is gonna let an expensive Q-Pod stay missing!"

"But if the Moon looks for us, they'll be looking for a Q-Pod, not for a clump of—of perambulating ore! We don't have a chance!"

"Pipe down, mister. You sound like a Cub Scout lost in the wilds of Bay Ridge. Just do as you're told, and keep your lip buttoned. And *that's* an order."

He knew I meant it, so he piped down.

But he had been right. The navigation would not hold. And only close scrutiny by another spacecraft—of which there were none, at the moment—could detect our presence in the ore.

The longer I thought about it, the madder I got. It was obvious to me that those adhesion/cohesion forces must have registered on Jardin's screens— and he had ignored them.

If I could have had five minutes on the Wheel with that conceited over-educated fathead . . .
erase tape . .

Chapter 2

January 2 . . .
Meanwhile, Back At Operations

Ms. Delaney absent-mindedly took a pencil from her desk tray, poked the pencil through her blue-white chignon and surveyed the expanse of railed-off enclaves in Operations.

In all her thirty-six years with the Company, she had never seen the Operations floor so quiet. The lull was more than the usual post New Years let-down. There was not much typing, not much talking. The computers were silent. Even the telex seemed muted.

She sighed and looked at the small key lying on her desk blotter. The faded tag looped to it said. *Nr. 042 717 (Capt. Schuster).* Who would use the key next? Ace trouble-shooter Schuster—or his executor?

She adjusted eye range in her bifocals and glanced at the clock above the wall-long black-board upon which the schedules of the Company's ships continued faithfully to be chalked, despite the Insta/Data screens. The Board meeting had been going on for an hour. Had Mickleberry remembered that Second Mate Fiske was coming at three o'clock?

She twirled the pencil in her chignon and wondered what the Board would decide. Was Schuster alive or dead? A terrible fate for a man who loved the sea—if he really had died in the bleak expanses of the Asteroid Belt.

Ms. Delaney had always disapproved of the Company's financial takeover of Space Mining, Inc. It never could have happened while old Alderman was Board Chairman. What business did a shipping company have in Space?

The new Board—Bennington and his men— had changed everything. The coziness was gone, somehow. Fewer ships—highly specialized ships —everything automatic, computerized—

Bennington had put the Company in Space. In fact, the Space Mining Assembly/Launch Complex on Cape Canaveral was now considerably more important than the sea operations. And if any one man had been responsible for Space Mining's success, it had been Captain Bob Schuster.

Of course, he had been a world of trouble to Mickleberry in Operations, reflected Ms. Delaney. Schuster was a roughneck, loudmouthed and short-tempered. But so very smart.

An elevator door slid aside. A tall, silver-coiffured girl emerged, a black caped jacket over her blue divided skirt. Blue gaiter-boots were silver-buttoned to her skirt hem. She was admitted past the receptionist's railing, threaded her way through the small enclaves and presented herself at Ms. Delaney's desk.

Ms. Delaney came out of her musings and said, "Oh, Ms. Fiske. Mr. Mickleberry is at a Board meeting. Could you wait a few minutes?"

"You're damned right I'll wait." The girl sat on the bench that lined the fence of Ms. Delaney's bailiwick. She drew a gold snuff box from her coat pocket, inhaled a pinch of Drenalin and asked, "Any news about Schuster?"

Ms. Delaney said cautiously, "It's not officially released, but the Wheel has given the Q-Pod up for lost."

Ms. Fiske sneezed and dabbed a tissue at her nose. "Who's being tapped to replace Shuster?"

"No one," sighed Ms. Delaney. "Men like Schuster come once in a century."

"Why didn't Space Mining put a base on Mars?"

"Mars is off limits, Ms. Fiske—under UN protection because of possible bacteriological intelligences. I must say the UN is making it as difficult as they can for us—and demanding a percentage besides! Space Sharing! Blackmail, I call it! Schuster was livid about the whole thing!"

There was a silence. Ms. Delaney swung her chair to face the typewriter extension. The letter in the machine was half-finished—a query about a drydocking estimate. She fingered out the rest —*presto, staccato*—flicked the Discharge lever, and watched the pages slide into the Ready tray, with the envelope that had been photo-addressed from the letter heading.

Ms. Fiske said impulsively, "Ms. Delaney, won't you level with us? Which of 'em has been keeping women out of the top command posts—Mickleberry or Schuster?"

Ms. Delaney swung to face the question. "I honestly wouldn't have the least idea. It's the Board that ultimately—"

"Nuts. It's Operations."

"Does it make any difference *which*?"

"Yes—because we can't fight a faceless, anonymous policy that slithers through loopholes and pretends no issue exists! We have the same technical training as the men—"

She stopped. An elevator door had slid open, and two men were emerging—a spry, parched, elderly man with white hair, and a rather small, slight man who looked like a bookkeeper until his expensive tailoring was taken into account.

Ms. Delaney gave another twirl to the pencil. If Mickleberry was bringing the Company's top legal expert, Hope could be Abandoned.

Ms. Fiske rose as the pair approached. The elderly man—coolly formidable in close-up—shook the girl's hand and said in a precise voice, "Second Mate Fiske. Thank you for being prompt." He gestured to the panelled door at the rear of Ms. Delaney's enclosure, and Second Mate Fiske preceded him into the office.

The well-tailored legal lion stayed beside Ms. Delaney's desk and said, "You have Schuster's key? Can you brief me on his files?"

"Oh, yes, Mr. Xavier." Ms. Delaney picked up the key, rose from her chair and led Xavier into an ell that bordered Mickleberry's office. She paused before the filing cases and blurted out,

"But it's only been a month, Mr. Xavier, and the

Q-Pod has full rations for five months more! Why, they could live a year—! A month isn't long, in the Asteroid Belt!"

"At the speeds and distances involved, a month is a very long time, Ms. Delaney. It's not that we're writing Schuster off—we sincerely hope he and his team turn up eventually—but there are legal aspects to be considered—the *mesdames* Loft, Worthing, and Grimes, for examples, who must have legal presumption of death in order to collect insurance, sell property, and so forth."

Ms. Delaney went to one of the battered old green filing cabinets. She turned the key in the lock and pulled out the bottom drawer. It was a hodge-podge of dog-eared files. "He hated paperwork," she murmured. In an involuntary tidying motion she pushed the files back on their track. There was a clunk, and a bottle of Scotch tumbled into view.

Ms. Delaney burst into tears and the pencil fell from her chignon. "It's as if he were lying there, large as life," she gasped, blotting her face with her handkerchief. "It's silly of me—"

Xavier tactfully turned his attention to the files while Ms. Delaney pulled herself together. After a while he commented, "None of this seems to be current business."

"Let me see, counselor. I'm more familiar with—"

Xavier stepped aside. Ms. Delaney, once more her competent self, flipped the files in review. Suddenly she stopped and said, "My goodness!"

"Something wrong?"

"Why, I didn't know Captain Schuster kept any

Rec-Paks here! But there's a stack of Rec-Pak shells behind the last file!"

"What usually happens to his recorded reports?"

"They're filed in the shell slots under subject matter. Or the Rec-Pak cartridges are erased and re-used in the department."

She took out a small black casing. "Here's a label—*Personal Memo*—and a ship and a date. Whatever—?"

Xavier took the other shells out and counted them. "Seven—eight in all."

"Do you think they're—important?"

Xavier eyed her with humor. "Considering that Schuster knew where the bodies are buried around here—having buried a few himself—these tapes are probably so important that they ought to be dumped into the nearest compactor."

"Not without hearing them, surely!"

"That's up to Bennington, as Schuster's executor." Xavier replaced the shells and closed the drawer. "Until the probate formalities are concluded—and having determined that no current business is involved—we can lock the file."

Ms. Delaney obediently locked the old cabinet, and they returned to the main Operations floor.

"Better not leave the key lying around," advised Xavier. "I'll be in touch."

He smiled and was whisked away by the elevator.

Schuster had made *personal* tapes! Ms. Delaney sat at her desk in a daze. Had he—perhaps—mentioned *her?*"

A button on her keyboard flashed urgently. She lifted the handset, pushed the button and said crisply, "Operations—Ms. Delaney."

A supercilious Oxbridge/English voice, with a hint of Third World drawl, said, "Please connect me with Mr. Mickleberry. This is Fai k'y Atur, Khadir of Bungl'a Cush, chairman of the United Nations Space Sharing Committee."

Of all the nerve! thought Ms. Delaney. *Without UN graft, he'd be sitting under a nutmeg tree, turning a prayer wheel! Always boasting about ten thousand years of culture—and can't even earn a living! And he presumes to demand Mickleberry!*

She said aloud, "Mr. Mickleberry is in conference, Khadir. Perhaps you are not aware that this office deals only with the sea fleet. All Space operations are handled by Space Mining on Cape Canaveral."

"I am aware, dear lady," came the voice, with ineffable contempt, "that the late Captain Schuster was a tool of the New York Board of Directors. The United Nations cannot waste time with underlings such as Executive Director Holloway of Space Mining. Mickleberry, please!"

"Mr. Mickleberry is in conference," repeated Ms. Delaney, who could be fairly ineffable herself. "If you care to leave a message—"

"Have I encountered the immovable secretary? Very well. I wish a personal interview with Mr. Mickleberry to discuss Captain Schuster's blatant fraud with the mineral asteroids."

Good for Schuster! thought Ms. Delaney. She said sweetly, "May we have a telephone number that will reach you?"

The Khadir obliged, and the conversation was terminated.

Second Mate Fiske came out of Mickleberry's

office, an angry red over her cheekbones. She smiled wryly, "We're not through with that bastard yet!" to Ms. Delaney, and left Operations.

Ms. Delaney buzzed Mickleberry, who responded, "Yes?"

"Mr. Mickleberry, the Khadir of Bungl'a Cush has phoned for an appointment to talk to you about what he claims is a blatant fraud by Captain Schuster. I'm sure there's some mistake—"

"Obviously. Schuster's frauds are never blatant."

"—but will you see him? He refuses to talk to Holloway."

"One moment."

During the wait, Ms. Delaney could visualize him hemming and hawing over his desk calendar. Finally he said, "Get it over with. Tomorrow at nine."

"At nine is Mr. Pruitt, the shipyard consultant."

"Who will be on time? Bungl'a Cush can only with difficulty separate B.C. and A.D."

He clicked off. Ms. Delaney giggled, sent three letters gliding from the typewriter to the Ready tray, and admitted three more appointments to Mickleberry. At ten minutes to five she phoned the number that Khadir had given her, was handed off to a male secretary as supercilious as his boss and relayed the nine o'clock appointment.

Five minutes to five. A pimply youth guided the electronic Letter Opt-Code Operator from an elevator. Starting at the receptionist's desk, LOCO hummed around the enclaves on fat rubber wheels, slurping letters, Rec-Paks, data tabulations, and memo sheets into its maw and fast-shuffling them into Interdepartment, Mail Class, Foreign, Domestic (Local and Out-of-Town) and Reject.

LOCO was a busy, tubby, popular machine—in direct contrast to its lackadaisical, hollow-chested human guide.

"You're late, Howie," said Ms. Delaney, as the ill-matched pair arrived at her desk.

"Basketball pools," explained Howie Lind, scooping up Ms. Delaney's Out mail and pitching it to LOCO. "Methuselah got anything?"

Ms. Delaney buzzed Mickleberry. "Would there be anything more, Mr. Mickleberry? Any mail for LOCO?"

"No to both questions, thank you. Run along, Ms. Delaney."

Howie guided the busily-ingesting LOCO away.

Five o'clock. The railed enclosures emptied. Ms. Delaney remembered Schuster's first visit to Operations—a tough young junior officer he was then, fresh as a sea breeze. He had looked at the large department and said, "Like sheep pens, ain't they?"

And she had said, "Why, Mr. Schuster, what an odd comparison for a seaman to make!"

"Oh, I'm a country boy," he had grinned, his blunt, homely features lighting up in a way that had made him almost handsome.

Strange, that she should remember it. She had seen him only when he had reported to Operations, throughout the years. Unlike the other officers back then, he had never tried to date her. At first she wondered if she would meet him on one of her vacation cruises, but he had remained a cargo man on the non-passenger cargo ships. He had never married.

Well, there were enough girls in every port. Ms. Delaney sighed, took her purse from her desk drawer—and remembered Xavier warning her about Schuster's key. She dropped the key into her purse, slipped the hood over the typing unit—

What had Schuster recorded?

Quietly she edged into the file room. She unlocked the old cabinet, pulled out the drawer—how loud the *screek* sounded in the emptied department!—snatched the topmost shell, dropped it into her purse, closed and locked the cabinet and edged out of the ell.

Nobody had seen her.

At the Security desk the guard said, "Mickleberry working overtime again, Ms. Delaney? Maybe expecting word about Schuster?"

Maybe, she thought to herself. Maybe the old boy *was* lonely.

* * *

Later that night, after she had cleaned up her small kitchen, readied her clothes for the morrow, double-checked the night latch and chain and the window grid, she snuggled into her sofa-bed and snapped the Rec-Pack into her bedside Rec/Radio/Clock. The shell label had said *Ocean Wanderer*—Schuster's one flyer into the cruise world. Her cheeks became pink and her breath quickened. Maybe romance *had* touched his life, after all!

The tape began playing, and a low pleasant voice (that perhaps had gone husky with the years) said, "Throughout my life at sea . . ."

● ● ●

THE FOURTH-STAGE POLYGRAPH

Throughout my life at sea I have been known as a cargo man. This does not mean I dislike the cruise trade. An old yarn-spinning bastard like me can always use a captive audience.

However, during the years when I was coming up in the officer ranks I did not have the background or education for more than the rust-bucket jobs the Company gave me. To compensate, I suppose, I made myself an expert on cargoes and on the tough jobs a better-educated man would not have had to accept.

So I did not know what to make of it when Mickleberry in Operations ordered me off a container ship, then transiting the Panama Canal, and pulled me back to New York to sign on as relief skipper of *Ocean Wanderer,* the Company's newest cruise vessel.

I was tired from three days of bad weather and the jet trip home, and I sat in Mickleberry's office as if I would need a derrick to get me out of the chair.

I was miffed, too, having sat in the same chair the year before and warned Mickleberry that the *Wanderer* was headed for the rocks with Lover Boy Tressingdale as skipper. Some years previously the guy had sailed as one of my mates. He was clever enough, but he had a slick, apple-polishing manner and the morals of a tomcat.

Mickleberry had brushed my warnings aside. He said Tressingdale was ingratiating, educated, refined—I liked that 'refined', having sailed with the guy—and his morals were, after all, none of the Company's business.

"A guy who cheats with women can just as easily cheat with Company assets," I told Mickleberry. "Be careful who you put aboard as chief steward with Tressingdale. Ship's stores are highly negotiable in the Third World areas where the *Wanderer* will be cruising."

Mickleberry had not listened. As Tressingdale's chief steward he had chosen another refined gentleman, named Bruner—the kind of alcoholic who tanks up on vodka and imagines nobody will notice his fusel-oil breath, pouchy eyes, or unsteady hands.

And now I had to sit and keep my mouth shut while Mickleberry put his thin fingertips together and explained in his precise voice that *Ocean Wanderer's* cost sheets were unsatisfactory.

"We have transferred Captain Tressingdale to a less—ah—vulnerable ship, but we have left Steward Bruner aboard pending fuller investigation," he stated.

Even for Mickleberry, this was stupid. I said, "Bruner is a crook. All he'll do for an investigation is bolix it up."

"Bruner is a sea-lawyer who intends to fight to the last ditch for a cushy job. Our legal department wants evidence of criminal guilt, so we can get rid of him, once and for all.

"To assist you, Captain Schuster, we will have aboard as passengers—" he picked up a Xeroxed passenger list from the desk, "—Mr. and Mrs. Borg-Cohen. You know, of course, about Borg-Cohen's sensitive work."

I did not know. I raised my eyebrows and Mickleberry explained, "Mr. Borg-Cohen manufactures what are crudely known as lie detectors. The machines actually measure the tell-tale physical reactions—"

"Okay, okay. I know what a lie detector measures."

"Mr. Borg-Cohen extended the basic polygraph to detect the intention of wrong doing and prevent it. That is why he is best known as the Shopping Cart King."

I thought Mickleberry was high as a kite. "Shopping Cart King?"

"He manufactures a supermarket shopping cart with sensors inside the push-bar which detect a guilt reaction from hand pressure—as, for example, from a person intending to push the cart beyond the prescribed area. Upon which, the cart's wheels lock. This single device has saved supermarkets thousands of dollars formerly used for the collection of strayed carts and the replacement of stolen ones."

"What's the customer reaction to the monitoring?"

"Generally favorable. Honest people get fed up with chiselers who increase marketing costs. Mr. Borg-Cohen has employed the same mechanism for industrial tools liable to be borrowed or pilfered by plant employees. The guilt-detecting sensors render the tools inoperable if misappropriated."

"Yeah, but there's all kinds of guilt," I objected. "Suppose a guy is operating an electric drill. He starts to worry whether his wife knows about his girl friend. His hand sweats, the drill freezes and a thousand-dollar hunk of steel has to be scrapped."

Mickleberry pyramided his fingers again. "That is why I called Mr. Borg-Cohen's work sensitive. His sensors can distinguish between personal-emotional guilt and offenses-against-property guilt. His mechanisms can stop a man from stealing a lawn mower—but not from killing his wife."

"What's this got to do with nailing Bruner?"

"Mr. Borg-Cohen, taking the basic polygraph a step farther, has developed an inhibitor. When the subject steps through a frame like an airport metal-detector, his guilt intention can be measured and, if necessary, blocked out."

"Remote control lobotomy?"

Mickleberry pursed his mouth. "I would not say so, no. It is a specifically limited barrier. It brainwashes only as a padlock brainwashes a thief away from a door."

He paused and added, "Steward Bruner's troublemaking can, we hope, be nullified by the installation of the inhibitor."

Oh Jeez, I thought. I asked, "When do I go aboard?"

"A car is waiting to take you to the pier. Is your suitcase in the outer office? Good."

I hauled myself to my feet. Mickleberry said dryly, "Remember, captain, your cargo is passengers, not containers. Captain Tressingdale was, despite his faults, a charming, popular man. Try to emulate those traits. If possible."

I could have busted him one and quit, but I knew he had been pressured by the top brass into putting me aboard. It kinda amused me to irritate his ulcers.

Ocean Wanderer was a sleek, compact cruise ship, but as soon as the car dropped me at the pier I could see the result of the Tressingdale-Bruner rip-offs. The rust on the ship's hull had been dabbed at, not painted. Rust streaks on the upper deckhouse also showed poor maintenance.

I knew the chief mate, a solid competent man named Alcott. I did not hold him responsible for the neglect. Tressingdale had tried to balance the milking of the steward's department by cutting down on the deck expenses.

I grabbed my suitcase, dodged the forklift trucks and started aboard. I got no farther than the top of the gangway, which was half blocked by gray metal cases stamped FRAGILE—TEMPERATURE-SENSITIVE APPARATUS—THIS SIDE UP.

The junior third mate was coping pokerfaced with a man and a woman standing beside the cases. My first thought was that they were a genuinely nice middle-aged couple.

The man was a wiry type who had rounded somewhat as life had slowed him down, but he was still in good trim. He had a mop of iron-gray hair, bright eyes and a ruddy, peppy-looking face. His clothes were lived-in but of good quality, as if a tailor got a chance to work on him now and then.

The woman was an old-fashioned, real woman. Her own graying hair was braided around her head. Her face was plump and relaxed, with a good, soap-washed complexion and clear hazel eyes. Her clothes had quiet style. I thought, there's a lady.

The watch officer saw me and said, "Captain Schuster—Mr. and Mrs. Borg-Cohen. There's been a misunderstanding about—"

The couple looked at me, and I could see myself in their surprised glances—travel-rumpled, unshaven, probably smelling like a goat. I set down the suitcase and shook hands with them reflecting that Tressingdale would have been more charming.

Borg-Cohen said to me, "Mr. Mickleberry assured me, captain, that my equipment could be stored in a room with temperature control, but this officer—"

I had not bothered to argue with Mickleberry, but my first resolve had been to throw Borg-Cohen and his spy machine off the ship. Now the job did not seem so agreeable. I said to him, "Come up to my quarters—you and your wife—so we can figure this deal out."

The officer spoke up, "Mr. Alcott has been called ashore, sir, but he left the keys to your quarters with me."

He took the keys from his pocket, and I accepted them without comment, although Alcott should not have handed them off. He could not have taken them ashore either, of course. Under Mickleberry's coaching, the team never knew who was carrying the ball.

I grabbed the suitcase again and led the Borg-Cohens through the alleyways. The damned floating hotel was as unfamiliar to me as it was to them.

The skipper's quarters were aft of the bridge. I latchkeyed my way into the dayroom and stopped as if I was an intruder.

The quarters were clean and shipshape, but Tressingdale was still in the atmosphere. The dayroom stank of hair oil, scented cigarettes, and women's perfume.

I waved my guests ahead of me. "Sit down and take the weight off your feet."

They smiled at each other and moved to the settee. I lumbered after them.

"What would you like to drink?" I went on, opening a bar cabinet that lit up like a pinball machine and ruined what little was left of my ingratiating manner.

Mrs. Borg-Cohen began to laugh—a nice understanding laugh.

"Too much has happened too fast, captain, yes?" she said in her warm voice. "It should be Captain Tressingdale here, and you have had to substitute in a hurry. The plane trip you are feeling yet, with maybe tiredness before that. I see by your eyes you have not slept. Now don't worry about Poppa and me. Take a good shower and feel better before you worry about Poppa's inhibitor."

"That's the most sensible talk I've heard all day," I told her.

I telephoned the messman to bring us a tray of coffee, picked up the suitcase and dived into the bedroom. I showered, scraped my face and pulled on a uniform instead of the khakis I usually slopped around in.

When I came back to the dayroom I felt more like myself. The tray was on the table in front of the settee. I sat down, accepted a cup of coffee from Mrs. Borg-Cohen and explained as tactfully as I could, "The trouble with shipping companies is that they are run by bankers and accountants who never try to learn about the sea.

"Mr. Borg-Cohen, I can understand why your machines go over big in supermarkets or industrial plants, but the seafaring unions would never in a million years tolerate that kind of monitoring.

"Why, if the crew realized what your boxes contain, I would have a mutiny on my hands. Regardless of what those front-office dummies cooked up, I can't allow you to operate any polygraph machine on board."

Mr. Borg-Cohen rubbed his unruly mop of hair and gave me a shrewd look. "You, personally, do not want the inhibitor on board."

"Frankly, I do not. A robot has no place in a ship's chain of command. Only human judgment is flexible enough to react to sea conditions. A master who cannot size up and get rid of a crooked officer has no business commanding a ship."

Mr. Borg-Cohen turned to his wife. "So, Momma, we can take the inhibitor and go home."

She was struggling not to let the tears spill out of her eyes. It was easy to guess that this cancelled cruise was only the latest in a long line of similar disappointments. I said quickly. "Stay aboard, Mr. Borg-Cohen. The Company wasted your time. They owe you and your wife a cruise."

His wife pleaded, "You made the arrangements already, to take the time, Poppa."

He smiled and patted her knee. "Well, all right. A cruise could maybe be interesting."

He glanced around—at the bar cabinet still lit up like a pinball machine, and at my ugly mug. Something seemed to strike him funny. He repeated, "Interesting," and the couple got to their feet.

I rose also and said, "I don't know what air-conditioned stowage space may be available, but temporarily we can stow the inhibitor in the pilot's cabin on this deck. The ship won't be using—"

I stopped and muttered, "Oh, cripes."

They looked at me. I explained, "You won't believe this, but I don't know where the hell this cruise is supposed to go. I never asked."

Well, they leaned against each other and howled. Finally Mr. Borg-Cohen took a bright-colored folder from his pocket.

"In case you don't find out, I give you the cruise brochure," he said.

I thanked him, and they left. I glanced at the Azores-Casablanca-Maderia-Canaries-St. Thomas itinerary, chortling to myself. I shut the bar cabinet, shifted my coffee cup to the desk and telephoned the orders about Borg-Cohen's boxes.

As I sat down behind the mess of sailing papers on the desk, I heard a knock at the opened day-room door. It was Chief Steward Bruner with a passenger list in his hand.

Bruner was heavier and yet more drawn than the last time I had seen him, as if the vodka had sagged to his belly and pulled his jaw muscles down with it. He said sourly, "When Tressingdale was axed I might have known Schuster would be put aboard to go through the ship."

"Like a dose of salts, Bruner."

"You don't scare me. Your loud mouth won't last

a week on a luxury cruise. When the passengers start complaining, your head will follow Tressingdale's."

"Don't bet on it. If that's all you have to say, get out."

He flapped the passenger list at me. "Who do you want at your table?"

"The Borg-Cohens. Otherwise I don't care."

Female voices yapped shrilly in the alleyway, and a pair of bewigged, bedaubed, pantsuited dames hove into view. They hailed Bruner like an old pal, but their mouths fell open when they saw me behind the desk.

"Who are you? A relief skipper?" demanded one of them, round-eyed under sticky lashes. "Well, of all the nerve! The passenger agent promised us Tressingdale!"

It was a tough broadside to meet, even if I had been braced for it, which I was not. While I was forming and deleting a comeback, Bruner slid an arm around each female and eased the pair into the alleyway. Before the voices faded out I could hear Bruner telling them, "Steer clear of Schuster. He opens bottles with his teeth and eats passengers for breakfast."

If I was in a competition for passenger favor, I sure had been left at the post. I hoped eventually to beat out Bruner, but meanwhile I had to get the show on the road.

My luck running true to form, we sailed out the Narrows and into a fogbank. Visibility lengthened as we moved away from the coast, but it was well past the dinner hour before I felt justified in leaving the bridge. The evening being half shot, I decided to spend the rest of it conferring with

Chief Engineer Haines and Chief Mate Alcott. I told the watch to locate them, and I went to my quarters.

The two officers arrived a few minutes later. Being old shipmates we had a couple drinks while we chewed the fat, but it was more than a get-together of old buddies. I am not a polygraph lie-detector. To find out if a guy is on the level, I have to sit down opposite him and listen to what he tells me.

The conference satisfied me that Haines and Alcott were as straight and dependable as I had remembered them, and it cleared the decks for my fight with Bruner.

The next morning I decided to open the Bruner offensive at once. I drank my morning coffee on the bridge while I checked with the navigation officer. Then I went below and began my inventory of the steward's department. I did not know how Brunner and Tressingdale had been smuggling the stores off the ship. In phony laundry bags? In emptied crates returned to a crooked ship chandler?

One fact was certain from the audit. They had been running a neat little racket with sacks of American flour, cases of coffee and canned meat, cartons of cigarettes.

I worked all day inventorying the lockers, storerooms, freezers. I made sure a day-to-day use-record would be kept. Bruner trailed around after me, giving me the needle.

"You can raise hell for one cruise, Schuster," he taunted me. "I can wait. You won't be here for the next."

What he said was true. If he kept his nose clean

this voyage how could I get the goods on him?

At the end of a hard day I realized I had to put in an appearance at dinner. I cleaned up and went down there. Late, I admit. The sudden chill in the dining room hit me like a wet fish.

Two VIP couples and an enamel-faced harridan were at my table, in addition to the Borg-Cohens. I said, "Good evening," as I took my chair. I was trying to be high-class, but the words sounded short and unfriendly. I could have skated on the looks I got. A couple of women-folk started speaking across me.

"Well! I was wondering if we had a captain! Weren't you?"

"Oh, no. Only the captain could have called Mr. Haines away from seven No Trump, doubled and redoubled."

I thought, *Jeez, I put my foot in it again.* Naturally Chief Haines had come immediately at my summons. For all he knew, the ship could have been going down for the third time. I should have made clear to him and Alcott that it was no Mayday.

Mrs. Borg-Cohen was saying, "A captain must first do his job."

"My dear, the passengers are his job! Otherwise he's a figurehead. The officers do all the work. A modern ship runs itself anyhow. Doesn't it, Captain Schuster?"

"Why ask me?" I deadpanned. "I've never been to sea before."

"You've never been on a cruise before!" was the crowing answer. "Mr. Bruner says you've always been a cargo man. And when a passenger spends absolutely thousands for a month at sea, he wants more talent than a cargo man!"

I almost told her to get out and walk, but Mr. Borg-Cohen's clear eyes were begging me to keep it cool. I said heartily, "The Red Sox look pretty good in training, don't they?"

Borg-Cohen fielded this ball and the dinner proceeded without mayhem.

After dinner I said to hell with the cruise entertainment and went to my quarters. I unbuttoned my collar, poured myself a scotch and wondered if I could learn the cruise technique soon enough. Bruner obviously had sold the passengers a bill of goods on my incompetence. I meant well, but I certainly had started out on two left feet.

The telephone rang. It was Borg-Cohen. "Captain, if you have five minutes—"

"Sure. Come on up."

He came promptly, opted for bourbon and ginger ale and faced me across the dayroom table. He began, "Captain, you do not know what it is like to be a mad scientist."

I had to smile as I agreed that mad scientists were a closed book to me.

"It is always, one invention has to follow the next," he went on. "From the basic polygraph comes the shopping cart. From the cart, the inhibitor. From the inhibitor, a fourth stage. You see how they are all stages of the same thing?"

I hesitated, and he spoke more slowly, tracing invisible diagrams on the table. "The polygraph measures if a person is comfortable with what he is saying. Is his discomfort embarrassment or guilt? If guilt, what kind? High-peak love-hate guilt? Or low-tremor sneak-and-snitch guilt? You follow?"

I nodded and he continued, "The second stage is to use the guilt to trigger a mechanism. An industrial worker thinks, 'I will steal this power tool. The insurance company pays.' But the low-tremor guilt is in his touch. The mechanism is released, and the power is cut off.

"For the third stage the guilt does not trigger another mechanism. It is turned back against the person and cancels his impulse to act. Cancels only that impulse. As, for example, the sight of an armed policeman might cancel out a thief's impulse to snatch a purse."

"Or might not."

"True. Human motives are complex. A thief might very well kill a policeman because hate or vengeance overrode the desire to steal. The inhibitor cancels only property-guilt impulses.

"But we will forget the inhibitor. I came tonight to tell you that a fourth stage is nagging to get out of my mad brain. By chance, I can experiment with it on board because I brought along extra modifiers for the inhibitor. I hope I can work while Momma cruises."

"As long as the experiment does not distort the readings of the ship's instruments, you can work as much as you please. Do you need work space?"

"The pilot's cabin is sufficient. But I need a subject. For only twenty seconds a day. Would you be so kind, captain? Look, I set up the frame right here, in front of your bedroom door. Twice a day as you pass through the frame you put your hand on a metal plate and count to ten. Couldn't you do so much?"

I considered. If I refused he might buttonhole a crewman and land the Company in trouble with the union. I said, "Okay, I'll do it. Is the frame the whole works?"

"I would like a sensor in the main lounge—very small, like a thermostat."

"What's this fourth stage all about?"

He shook his head. "The guinea pig must never be told. The knowledge could affect his reactions. May I set up the frame tomorrow?"

I thought it over. "All right. I'll have to pay an electrician full wages while you work, but you can settle the bill with the Company."

"Of course." He finished his drink and stood up. "I have now a request from Momma. You could maybe come and play bridge? Momma would like a partner who is not such a mad genius that counting trump is beneath him."

I laughed. Momma knew I had made a mistake, walking out on the entertainment. I downed the scotch, rebuttoned my collar and said, "I haven't played bridge since Culbertson was a pup, but I can finesse with the best of 'em."

The card game broke the ice just fine. I still was not Tressingdale, but I was learning the ropes.

The next morning after breakfast Borg-Cohen began setting up the frame for the new machine. The standby electrician became the nucleus for a group of kibitzing officers who came and went as the watches changed. I encouraged this open curiosity. I did not want the crew to think I was trying to put something over on them.

In the afternoon I asked Chief Haines for his opinion about the fourth-stage purpose. He said slowly, "It sounds crazy, but I believe the lounge sensor is taking a subvocal Gallup poll and feeding the information to a small computer in the pilot's cabin, which in turn sends the information to the frame. I can see a pattern of intake-analysis-output. But intake of what, or output of what, is beyond me."

Shortly before dinner Borg-Cohen finished assembling the gadget, and everybody cleared out. Feeling kinda foolish, I stepped into the frame, put my hand on the plate and counted ten seconds.

Nothing happened. I passed through to the bedroom, gussied myself up and beat it to the dining room.

I reflected that we had a real friendly crowd this voyage. As I sat down I said, "Hello, folks. You can blame Mr. Borg-Cohen if I'm late. Now I'm a guinea pig as well as a figurehead."

It got a laugh. Bruner was pussyfooting among the tables, and I saw him staring at me as if there was something he did not understand. I figured I could forget about Bruner, now that I was really beginning to hit my stride.

I do not remember too much about the first part of the cruise, except that we had perfect weather and I was seldom at the bridge. I checked at noon and midnight, but otherwise I left the running of the ship to the officers. She was a good little ship and practically ran herself.

The cruise director reported to me every morning with a list of the day's activities, and I spread myself around as much as I could. My shuffleboard scorched the decks, and by the time we were island-hopping the Azores I was the terror of the dance floor. I always did like that rock beat.

Sometimes I was so busy with social activities that I barely had time for those ten-second pauses in Borg-Cohen's frame.

The only thing that puzzled me was that Mrs.

Borg-Cohen was very quiet and did not seem to be enjoying the cruise. It was a shame, a good-looking woman like that. If she had bought a classy wig and used a little makeup, she would have been the prettiest woman there.

We docked at Casablanca early one sun-drenched morning. The tour buses were, thank God, lined up and waiting at the pier. I had heard that King Hassan was running a tight ship. In Morocco the buses reported on schedule, or else.

My head was none too strong after the previous evening's party. With relief I saw the last mooring line secured and ordered, "Finished with the engine." I went to my officer to dispose of the shore brass.

By the time the officials and agents and peddlers had been swept out of the corners, the passengers had disembarked for the day's tour and I had the ship to myself.

Not to myself. I heard a light knock at the opened dayroom door, and one of my dancing partners sauntered in. Claudia, or maybe Sylvia. A swinger but cute.

"Stop slaving over a hot ship, captain," she smiled. "Come ashore. Take me to the Casbah—if this cement oasis has a Casbah."

"If it hasn't, we'll build one," I smiled back. "Wait'll I change into my shore duds."

There was no harm, I reflected, in a shore trip with a cute girl. It was not that I was dumb enough to go overboard about women, like Tressingdale. I walked through the frame, absently resting my hand on the plate.

A shock jarred me to my back teeth, and I

jumped back. The frame panel split open and sprayed tiny particles over the carpet.

For a moment I was completely disoriented. I could not figure out what I was doing or why I had that cheap hustler in my room.

The girl looked at my face, gave a yip and ran out.

Borg-Cohen. I had to talk to Borg-Cohen. But he was probably on the shore tour.

Wait a minute. Would a nice, middle-aged Jewish couple be touring an Arab country?

I telephoned their stateroom. No answer. I telephoned the watch officer, "Find Borg-Cohen and send him here pronto."

My knees were still numb from the shock. I folded onto the settee and wondered how I would feel after the numbness wore off.

Mr. and Mrs. Borg-Cohen came into the dayroom. They paused when they saw the broken frame. Mrs. Borg-Cohen said to her husband, "So! It happened, just what I told you!"

I said gruffly, "Never mind, Momma. I won't keelhaul him."

"You are you again! I am so glad!" She burst into tears.

They sat down. I asked Borg-Cohen, "What was the fourth stage?"

"An on-the-job training machine." His face was paler and not so peppy. "As you maybe have read, the difficulty in training unskilled workers is not the teaching of the job itself, but fitting an unskilled worker into a sophisticated environment.

"There seems to be a psychic block that is removed only as the worker becomes used to the environment. When the block is removed, he learns quickly. Before it is removed he cannot learn even to throw a switch.

"The on-the-job trainer translates the atmosphere in the shop—and atmosphere is only what emanates from people in their sense-reactions—into impulses which are fed into the subject's nerve centers. He absorbs the atmosphere quickly—the motions of the job come natural to him."

"So you were keying me into the passenger atmosphere?"

"Bruner was out to get you fired. I do not like such slimy crooks. I put a sensor in the main lounge to pick up the pattern of what the passengers expected of a captain, and I set up the frame to make you receptive to those wishes.

"Almost immediately you became more congenial. The life of the party, even. But I forgot two things. The environment consensus had no real understanding of your job. And second, there was a basic ethical conflict. The machine had to break. Even under hypnosis a person cannot be compelled to act against his ethical convictions. Next time I experiment with the trainer—"

"I told Poppa," interrupted Mrs. Borg-Cohen, "you were too nice a man to do what those women wanted you to do. Never could you be so low."

"I'm not sure about that," I teased her. "I was thinking about how you are the prettiest woman aboard."

She laughed and shook her head, and Borg-Cohen said it was lucky for him that the machine blew up when it did, as any woman would prefer a captain to a mad scientist.

After they left I went out on deck to get my

numb thoughts working again. I ambled to the bridge wing and looked down at where a ship chandler's truck was unloading seaweed-heaped cases of live lobsters.

Bruner! I thought, my God, I muffed that play completely! Half the voyage gone, and I had forgotten why I had been put aboard.

Bruner was standing alongside the ship, looking over the cases as they came off the truck. He groped a small canvas sack from a mass of weed and threw it back onto the truck. The driver shoved the sack into another case, so fast that it was almost sleight-of-hand. He jumped from the truck and slung the case on top of a pile of other cases waiting to be lifted aboard in a cargo net.

Bruner moved, but he was too late. The net tightened around the cases, and they rose in the air. Bruner clasped his hands nervously as he watched.

Casablanca. A port for the Turkish heroin traffic. A small sack that Bruner did not want? Why? Because Tressingdale was not there to hide the sack in the ship's safe? I should have realized that guys who smuggled stores would have no objection to smuggling dope. And now Bruner was finding out the hard way that you do not say No to dope pushers.

What would he do? Find the sack and ditch it? Try to run it into New York? Somebody would be waiting for it. Somebody who would not take excuses.

As I paced the deck a peculiar thing happened. I seemed to hear Bruner say, "Schuster!" and begin cussing. I heard "meat freezer" and I saw a jerky series of mental pictures zero in on a locker of pre-cut and wrapped beef ribs.

I realized that the shock from Borg-Cohen's machine had stripped my brain paths raw. Now that the numbness was wearing off, I was hearing half-vocalized thoughts the way a guy with a hangover hears noises. A ticking clock sounds like a boiler factory.

I waited an hour, my head bursting with voices like Times Square on New Years Eve. I guess I was picking up every subvocal emanation within a sea mile. It killed whatever interest I might have had in telepathy, believe me.

When the torment had ebbed off, I brought Alcott as witness and went below to the main galley, where the cooks were ankle-deep in seaweed and bad-tempered lobsters. Bruner was there, talking to the head chef.

He went pasty white when he saw that Alcott was with me, I said, "Bruner, the heroin is in the meat freezer. With the beef ribs."

His eyes rolled up and he crumpled onto the seaweed. All hell broke loose. The lobsters were strictly sea-to-customer, with unwired claws. They swarmed over Bruner. Alcott and I waded in to haul him free, while the chef shook his fists and hollered at us in French.

I dragged Bruner into the alleyway, found his ring of keys, tossed it to Alcott and told him to bring the contents of the sixth locker—contraband, that is—to my office.

Wanting to deal with Bruner while he was still groggy, I shook some life into him, hoisted him to his feet and propelled him ahead of me.

By the time we got to my quarters his nerve was coming back and he was threatening to sue. In a few minutes Alcott walked in and laid a stiff canvas sack on the desk. His ears, nose and fingers were shiny from frost. He said reproachfully, "You didn't tell me which end to start counting from, Captain"

I pried open the sack. It held small fat plastic bags.

"You can't prove anything," Bruner blustered.

"I don't have to prove anything," I shrugged. "I can just call the Moroccan authorities, tell them how I saw the sack come on board, and let them take you away. I don't know Hassan's punishment for heroin pushers. I understand thieves get their right hands chopped off."

He went to pieces again. When he was too worn out for more cussing or whining, I said, "I'll make a deal. Resign from the Company. I'll have the Casablanca agent arrange your plane ticket to New York. The heroin goes overboard as soon as we are at sea."

"But you can't continue the cruise without a chief steward!"

"I'll wire Mickleberry tonight. He can fly a steward to join the ship at Las Palmas. Make up your mind, Bruner. The resignation—or Hassan's cops."

"If you hadn't seen—hadn't guessed where—! They ought to burn you at the stake, you damned mind-reading devil!"

I sat at the desk and typed his resignation. After he had signed it I said to Alcott, "Confine Bruner to his cabin until the agent can take him off the ship."

Alcott dragged him away. I thought, another dirty job done. And this time it was more good luck than good management.

The telephone rang. It was Mrs. Borg-Cohen. "Captain, I was thinking. It is not that these women on cruises are so bad. It is that they are lonely. So very lonely. You will remember—and not get impatient or think ill of them?"

"I'll always remember, Momma."

She said, "Good!" and hung up. I suddenly felt very lonely myself.

Well, the agent put Bruner on the plane in Morocco, the new chief steward came aboard in Las Palmas, and the voyage circled back to New York without incident.

Naturally I was summoned to Operations to enlarge upon my Voyage Reports. When I was through explaining, Mickleberry put his fingertips together and said, "You have a choice of assignment, captain. You may stay aboard the *Wanderer*, provided you smarten your appearance, tone down your language, and learn a dance step slightly more modern than the Lindy Hop."

"Oh cripes. What's the alternative?"

"You can fly to Baltimore, where *Bulk Trader* is in drydock and needs a skipper to take her out."

"When does the Baltimore plane leave?"

"This evening." He held out an envelope. "The plane ticket—and your bonus check."

"Bonus?" I took the envelope and stood up. "After I scuttled the installation of the Borg-Cohen inhibitor?"

He got his superior expression. "The difficulty with running a shipping company is that the ship

personnel are stiff-necked diehards who never try
to learn about scientific progress."

I thought never the twain . . . Mickleberry
added, "However, we are pleased that you rid us of
Bruner, by whatever methods. One cannot teach
an old seadog new tricks."

I let it go at that. I had learned a lot in the cruise,
but I was not going to share it with Mickleberry.

Chapter 3

January 2 (cont.) . . .
What Happened When the Lights
Went Out

Howie Lind guided LOCO into the mailroom
and called it a day. Postage meters and PO/
Intake/Dispatch Conduits were not his thing. The
Company had hired his brawn (such as it was).
They were not gonna get his brains for nothing.

He stood a moment in the mailroom doorway.
The odds were that Schuster would not make it.
Howie wondered who would get his dough. The
guy must have been loaded—he had big money
and never spent it. And probably most of it was
stashed away where the Revenue bastards—

Stashed away. Howie recalled that Schuster had
a filing drawer in Operations. It was where Ms.
Delaney held his mail when he was someplace
beyond a forwarding address, like the Moon Residence. Howie had often seen Ms. Delaney reach

into her right-hand desk drawer and take out
Schuster's key. It was a key to one of the older files.

Maybe Schuster had tossed some expense
money there—spare cash he did not want to carry
around. Maybe it was still there.

Howie peered into the darkened corridor. The
only light was from the occasional glow at base-
board level. At the other end of the corridor a
night Security guard was leading a police dog on a
leash.

Howie slipped into the corridor and sneaked to
the stairs. He opened the fire door and raced up
the cement well. On the next floor he stepped out
of the cement and into Operations. The big lights
were doused, as on the floor below. A gleam came
from Mickleberry's half-open door.

Suddenly the telex began to chatter. The gleam
widened. Howie ducked below the outer railing as
Mickleberry headed for the machine. The chatter
stopped. Howie cautiously raised his eyes above
the railing-level and saw Mickleberry return to his
office.

All quiet. Howie walked quickly and noiselessly
to Ms. Delaney's desk. He took from his pocket a
pencil flashlight that had been useful on previous
similar occasions, and he opened the right-hand
drawer. He saw at a glance that the old key with the
faded label was no longer there. This confirmed
his belief that the files held something valuable. He
closed the drawer and walked into the filing room.

A minute's search revealed the card *Schuster* on
a lower drawer. The cabinet was locked. Howie
again had recourse to his pockets and came up with
an illegal assortment of keys. One of them un-

locked the cabinet, and Howie pulled out the drawer —not with a hasty *screek*, but as a man who knew how this sort of thing should be done.

The whiskey bottle went under his sloppy wool pullover, and he could get down to a serious search. No money. His cheeks burned, as if the Old Man was laughing at him. But there had to be *something*—

Like Xavier, Howie was well aware that Schuster knew where Company bodies were buried. He came upon the Rec-Pak shells. *Personal Memo*, huh? There might be Top Secret Info.

But the guard must be through with his patrol of the lower floor. Howie stowed a Rec-Pak shell beside the whiskey bottle, re-stacked the others, closed the drawer and returned to the main office.

He listened—and crouched behind Ms. Delaney's desk. The fire door opened and shut. There was a soft *gr-r-r* that caused the hairs on the back of his neck to rise. A flashlight beam exploded in the direction of the desk, but Howie did not move.

The beam snapped off, and the guard's voice said, "It's only Mickleberry working overtime. Come on, girl—you know Mickleberry."

The dog was coaxed away. Howie sneaked into the stairwell again and descended to the locker room reserved for non-executive C-3 personnel. He transferred the whiskey bottle and the Rec-Pak shell to the shabby briefcase holding the basketball slips and payments, donned his leather jacket and cap and left the building in the straggle of other employees.

The night was cold. He walked briskly south and

turned east. Midway in a block that was a short, smooth slot between avenues, he paused before a dingy window labelled *Parts & Service.* The window was dark, but when he rapped on the door beside it, the door was (as Howie expressed it) opened unto him.

He followed a blubber-fat unshaven man to a back office where a gooseneck lamp lit a scarred desk top. The man sat at the desk, and Howie took what Xavier would have called the *res* from his briefcase. The man tallied the betting slips and the cash, grunted and said,

"What else you got in there?"

Howie brought out the Scotch. "Just a Christmas present Schuster forgot to give me."

"Yeah? You bin cleaning out Schuster's locker? What's this?"

The blubbery fist dipped into the briefcase and pulled out the Rec-Pak shell. Howie protested, "Hey, I ain't selling that! I'm just gonna listen and put it back. I mean, Mickleberry won't miss a bottle of Scotch, but if he finds a Schuster Rec-Pack gone—!"

"Cool it. Siddown."

Howie sat uneasily on a rickety chair on the other side of the desk. The man took a Rec-Pak unit from a drawer, inserted the Schuster cartridge, switched the tape on, at low volume, and listened with the unit against his ear.

A couple minutes of auditing was apparently enough. He switched off the tape, shook with gurgling laughter, pulled the desk phone toward him, thumbed a number and waited, wheezing chuckles.

"Aggie? Yeah, look, I got a Schuster tape that'll double your circulation overnight . . . Schuster, the Space captain! . . . Sure it's genuine! A Company label on the shell, handwritten . . . Sure you can look at it! But you gotta record it tonight and lemme have it back . . . How can he sue? It ain't copyright, and he's dead . . . Well, okay, he'll be dead in six months. Don't publish till then . . . Look, if you don't want it— . . . Okay. Sure."

He hung up and said to Howie, "Pick the shell up tomorrow morning. He brought a thick roll of bills from his pocket, peeled off a couple and added a couple more. "Easy does it. There won't be no stink."

Howie accepted the bills, feeling it would be unwise to question manna, however sparsely it descended.

He was in a cheerful frame of mind as he slouched from the dingy shop. He was scheduled for supper with his sister in Brooklyn—and now had a bottle of Scotch for his brother-in-law. After he had tagged along to the ceremony awarding his nephew Mervin the brown belt in Judo, the evening would be his own. He had not sketched out how he would spend it, but he thought verily, verily, he could afford whatever Temptation was lurking in his way.

And he had been spared lifting the Top Secret dirt from Schuster's Rec-Pak. Cerebral activity was not Howie's long suit.

Chapter 4

January 2 (cont.) . . .
Mickleberry Works Late

Mickleberry worked steadily until eight o'clock, making the decisions he had been forced to postpone during his appointment-filled day. He was an electric-crisp presence in the age-blurred office. His eyes were clear aquamarine, so sharp that they seemed to glint with facets. He exuded an astringent tang, like menthol or peppermint or expensive after-shave. In his neat, old-fashioned script he was jotting notes on letters to be answered, indicating to Ms. Delaney the nature of the reply.

When his desk was clear, he stacked the letters and took them to the *In Process* tray of Ms. Delaney's typing unit. From habit he gave a tug at her desk's top drawer before returning to his office. The drawer opened, and he felt (for the nth time) extremely irritated. For thirty-six years he had been telling Helen Delaney to lock her desk before leaving. An unlocked desk cast unfair suspicion on the cleaning staff, in the event that a valuable object disappeared.

A natural association of ideas reminded him that Xavier had wanted to investigate Schuster's files. Since nothing further had been said, he assumed nothing important had been found. However, perhaps he should take a moment—

He swung his office door wider to increase the beam of light, opened Ms. Delaney's right-hand drawer—and like Howie, saw at a glance that Schuster's key was gone. Mickleberry assumed Xavier had taken it, and he felt further irritation. Xavier should have realized the old cabinet held other files which might be needed.

He stood uncertainly a moment, closed Ms. Delaney's desk and returned to his office. From a long (and imposing) mahogany breakfront jammed with volumes (legal and nautical), he rummaged a dilapidated cardboard box heavy with duplicate keys. He selected several which seemed to be the right size and vintage and walked briskly into the filing ell. He turned on the light—having no reason for concealment—and began fitting keys into the relevant cabinet.

The third key fitted smoothly, and his fingers gave an automatic counter-clockwise twist. The key did not move. A clockwise reflex—and Mickleberry heard the distinct click of locking levers.

The cabinet had been unlocked!

Astonished disbelief rooted him to the spot. Neither Xavier nor Ms. Delaney could have been so careless. Perhaps the old lock was defective. He turned the key back and forth several times before admitting total bafflement and opening Schuster's drawer.

The disorder did not surprise him, nor the insignificance of the files. When he discovered the Rec-Paks, his eyebrows lifted. Like Ms. Delaney, he had not known that Schuster had recorded *Personal Memos*.

He pinched his ear and considered. If Schuster were available for consultation, the tapes would be inviolate. Listening to them would be tantamount to reading private mail—a deplorable act Mickleberry would not for a moment commit.

However, under the circumstances—! He selected three shells that seemed to date back some years, shut *and locked* the cabinet and took the shells to his office. He keyed the phone into an outside line and, a few seconds later, was talking to his man Ames. "You may bring the car now, Ames."

Mickleberry noted the time on his wristwatch and thought about the ships mentioned on the shell labels. An idea struck him. He tapped the tune of another outside number, waited and said,

"Good evening, Cartwright. Is Mr. Bennington at home? . . . Is Captain Turner still staying—? Excellent. I have a couple Rec-Paks for their— uh—listening pleasure, one tape dating from Mr. Alderman's days as Board Chairman. Ames will bring them up to you on our way home . . . Thank you, Cartwright."

He cradled the phone, locked his desk and flipped the page on his appointment calendar. The Khadir of Bungl'a Cush. Who would deal with these bumptious beggars for him, if Schuster was dead in the Asteroid Belt?

Ninety minutes later Mickleberry, refreshed and renewed by a tepid bath, and clad in pyjamas, dressing gown and slippers, was seated in his study. His evening meal was on the gateleg table beside his comfortable leather chair. Oatmeal, whole wheat toast, prunes, and Postum.

He relaxed with the righteous well-being of a man who has earned his day's wages, and pressed the control button beside his supper tray. From a bookcase across the room Schuster began to speak, in a gruff but humorous tone, "As a seaman, man and boy . . ."

● ● ●

GET THE LEAD OUT

As a seaman, man and boy, I figured I had sailed aboard every type of ship, but old Mickleberry in Operations gave me a jolt when he said he was recommending me as skipper on a nuclear vessel.

It was mid-afternoon, in his office. I thought somebody had been spiking his martinis at the Athletic Club. The nuclear *Savannah* had made a promising start, but union trouble, exorbitant wage demands, and radiation hysteria had scuttled commercial use of nuclear power at sea.

On the off chance that Mickleberry was sober, and remembering that the *Savannah's* personnel had studied three and a half years under the supervision of the Atomic Energy Commission, I asked, "When does the job start?"

He picked up an airline folder. "You're cleared through to Basra on tonight's flight. A Qamat plane will meet you on arrival."

I searched through my mental atlas. Qamat was a small sheikdom south of Kuwait on the Persian Gulf. I had loaded oil there but had not got beyond the steel-fenced dock area. Qamat was fanatically Moslem and was closed to foreigners. In some surprise I asked, "Have the Qamatis a nuclear ship?"

Mickleberry allowed a smile on his parchment mouth. "A few years ago Sheik Ahmed was up to his neck in cheap oil. Now he has more money than he can spend. Among his first purchases were a lab of American physicists and a Japanese shipyard. He has just taken delivery of the world's only nuclear-powered yacht."

"Sounds dicey to me," I commented. "The Japs tried a couple nuclear cargo vessels last year, and, according to the newspapers, they sprayed radiation like a leaky hose nozzle. How does the Company come into it, anyhow? Qamat has a bunch of Scandihoovians running its supply ships."

"Apparently the present officers do not meet specifications. Sheik Ahmed was a Harvard classmate of Mr. Bennington—" a salaam in the direction of the Boardroom, "—and has asked him for the loan of a master mariner. Since a courtesy reduction in the price of bunkers oil was mentioned—"

"An under-the-table deal, hey? Why me? You guys fire me every time I open my yap."

His thin nose quivered. "Personally, Captain Schuster, I would send you to a hotter place than Qamat. However, your—un—outrageous resilience was a factor in Mr. Bennington's decision."

He held out the airline folder. As I accepted it he added, "Watch your step. Sheik Ahmed is not a typical Harvard man."

"Fine. Maybe I'll be able to tell him something."

Mickleberry coughed. "Good day, captain. Safe voyage."

On the flight to Basra I was too preoccupied to do my usual grousing about triple-seat leg cramp and cabin headache. Atomic power and civilian shipping were like oil and water. I felt that the physicists were mostly to blame.

Radiation danger was not the basic stumbling block. Statistically nuclear power had a remarkably safe record. It was flogged-up alchemist *mystique* that scared authorities into closing seaports. Shades of alchemist glory had inspired seamen to demand astronomical sums for routine work.

If you want a statistically lethal energy source, in contrast to atoms, take North Sea natural gas. At regular intervals it blasts a street in England or Scotland to matchsticks. Does anybody squawk? Of course not. They scrape up the bodies, fill in the bomb holes, and a guy in blue overalls and a cloth cap reconnects the pipes.

The gas inspector is a regular Joe, like you or me. The guy who pokes rods in and out of a reactor pile is a white-coated Superman. A sorcerer's apprentice.

I blamed the physicists for more than the *mystique*. I had been waiting maybe twenty years for a bucket-seat sports car that refueled biannually. Nuclear power plants and Naval vessels were great, but where were the consumer items?

The usual answer was: hung up on the problem of shielding. But the hang-up had lasted so long that I suspected atomic theory was hardening into dogma. Research is like glue. Unless you apply it when it is fresh, it hardens and only makes more work for the next guy.

As for shielding, I had a couple ideas on that score, myself. Why the hell nobody had picked up that old Rutherford experiment—!

At Basra I assumed I would be transferring to one of the thirty-year-old DC 4's that still spin their props in remote areas, but I was directed to a sad-eyed little Arab in a black suit.

He bowed and said, "I am Hassan. His Excellency sends a plane."

I thanked him. He latched onto my suitcase and led me to a white-and-gold VIP Cessna. In guard-formation at the boarding steps were four human hawks swathed in white burnooses, the hoods thrown back to show gold-corded white head-scarves. Lashed over the burnooses were cartridge-ribbed bandoliers and rifles.

Had I been the sheik, I would not have trusted those cold-eyed thugs with a bean shooter. I ignored them and boarded the plane. It was like a private club car, except that gold gleamed where aluminum or brass usually sufficed.

We strapped into the roomy chairs. Hassan spoke into a hand mike, the pilot revved up and we eased into the traffic pattern. When we were airborne a steward came with a tray of scotch-and-soda for me and cokes for the Arabs. I asked Hassan,

"What size is the yacht? Who brought her around from Japan?"

"She is three hundred feet long, captain. She came under tow. The Japanese would not allow atomic sailing. During long stretches at sea, of course, the ship was under her own power, and the scientists have certified that she is in order."

A thought occurred to me. "Who are the engine crew?"

He looked surprised. "His Excellency's two chief physicists and their staff. They are not your concern, captain."

That was what he thought. I had no intention of sharing my command with court alchemists or allowing a caste division on board.

Having followed the Gulf's west coast, the plane sat down on Qamat's white-dust landing strip. A jeep took me to the steel-fenced dock area, bypassing the town.

The ship was good-looking, I had to admit. Brilliant white. Flared bow, low-profile streamlined deck house. A red-carpeted gangway led up to a sideport you could drive a camel through.

The white-uniformed third mate was lounging in the air-conditioned jet stream at the top of the gangway. He straightened up as I approached with the jeep driver lugging my suitcase after me.

Before the officer could speak, a bulky sunburned man wearing a flowered sports shirt over gray shorts came forward, shook my hand and said, "Welcome to the club, captain. I'm Beckwith."

In almost the same motion he took a small

namecard from his pocket and hooked it into my lapel. I saw that he, the third mate and the seaman taking my suitcase from the jeep driver had similar cards.

I knew the blank film under the name was a radiation monitor, but I growled, "What's this? An Elks' Convention?"

I saw the officer's face brighten. Beckwith stared at me. He began, "But Captain Schuster, a safety precaution—"

"Yeah, yeah. How much radiation did she leak from Japan?"

"Leak? Why none. The Japs did a superb job. But, of course—"

"You've got a dozen monitors on every deck, right? Is a guy's lapel gonna register anything more? If the ship is seaworthy, she's seaworthy. If she's not, we'll all get off instead of playing with a pack of cards.

"The sea always has had hazards," I went on, "but crewmen and passengers don't wear life jackets the whole damned time a ship sails, do they? The airlines lose a plane now and then, but a fat lot of business they'd get if every passenger had to wear a parachute.

"When are you atom scouts gonna grow up?" I pursued. "Safety is one thing. Mumbo jumbo is something else. This is not a lab or a club, but a ship. If you're not clear about that point now, mister, you'll be clear after I get through with you."

Before he could hinge his jaw up again I told the third mate, "If the chief mate is aboard, I want to see him in my office."

I barged after the seaman, trying not to look

impressed as he led me through the deep-carpeted
alleyways. The interior of the ship was what
Paradise would be, if Nieman-Marcus was furnish-
ing it.

My quarters were a piece of the whole. The
office/dayroom stretched from Monday to Friday,
and the bathroom had gold where there usually
was chrome.

I changed from my shore suit to khakis. When I
came from the bedroom I saw that Beckwith had
brought the other chief alchemist into the dayroom. The two were standing on the middle of the
bulkhead-to-bulkhead Sarouk.

The second chief kinda interested me. He
looked fresh and quick. He had tousled sandy hair,
grainy cheeks and broad hands. He wore a seer-
sucker suit that was fifteen years old, and his
glance put a question mark on everything. It
asked, "What if—?" His radiation card was labeled
Winters.

Beckwith was preparing to sound off, but I said
mildly, "Sit down, gentlemen. Mr. Beckwith, you
thought I was pretty rough, didn't you? With
crewmen present, I had to slam you down hard.
When I give an order from the bridge, I can't have
a man answer, 'Wait till we check with the scientists.'"

Beckwith seemed easier in his mind. Winters
looked like a terrier cocking an ear at a ball game.

Beckwith began, lowering his bulk to the settee,
"Captain Schuster, it's obvious you have had no
briefing for this job."

"Briefing how? To me, that atomic pile is nothing but a power source for steam turbines, which I

have encountered before. I don't give a damn what stokes the furnace—coal, oil or radioactive pellets.

"It's about time the atomic establishment recognized the three phases of any invention: Creation, which takes genius; construction and repair, which take training; and everyday use, which takes only enough brains to push knob A while keeping the mitts off lever C.

"Henry Ford and his ilk were geniuses. The guy who repairs auto transmissions is a trained mechanic. Any ten-year-old kid can get behind the wheel and drive. That's exactly the way an invention ought to progress to be of any use. If every automobile had to come equipped with a graduate engineer, we'd all be shoveling manure."

Beckwith blustered, "That's the wildest exaggeration I ever heard!"

"Stick around. You've only known me five minutes."

There was a knock at the open dayroom door, and a rangy rawboned man came in. He was wearing khakis and had an envelope in his fist.

"Torgessen, chief mate," he said in a closemouthed manner.

He had shoulders like a blacksmith and arms like a boilermaker. I had sailed with his sturdy type before. He was a squarehead who shipped out from November to April and farmed potatoes the rest of the year.

He handed over the envelope. I took it and told him to sit down.

Somewhat hesitantly he sat near the scientists. I opened the gold-monogrammed envelope. In a handwritten letter Sheik Ahmed was informing me that he would be boarding the vessel at 0800 the next morning for the shakedown cruise.

I passed the order along to my guests and asked Torgessen if he had been aboard from Japan.

"No, captain," he answered. "We were hired later. The tugboat company had their own men on the bridge. But I spoke to the tugboat captain at the dock canteen, after the ship arrived, and he said she was very stiff despite the stabilizers and tended to broach with a following sea. He said if you couldn't hold her to the wind in a heavy blow, you'd be in trouble."

"That damned shielding!" I muttered. "If it's up to the *Savannah's* standard, there's a thousand tons of lead and cement putting the ship out of whack."

I turned to Beckwith. "If you whizbangs would stop repeating rituals and take another look at that simple experiment by Rutherford—"

Winters recocked his ear. Beckwith opened his mouth, but I said, "Later. If we're sailing tomorrow, we have more to do than chew the fat," I asked Torgessen, "Ordered any boat drills?"

He rubbed his hand over his graying head. "No, sir. Only the deckhands are seamen. The Steward's department are Arabs and don't understand what we tell them. And the engineers—" he looked doubtfully at the physicists "—don't take orders."

"We'll see about that. Go up to the bridge and ring the alarm."

He left the dayroom. The physicists looked comfortably amused. I said, "I'm not kidding. Report to your boat stations. The sea is still bigger than all of us."

Beckwith flared up, but Winters towed him away.

The alarm clanged its raucous signal. I went up to the bridge and looked down from the wing. There had not been so much chaos since the Six-Day War. The locally-recruited messmen and cooks ran out of their sandals getting ashore. The European seamen straggled to their stations, and the alchemy staff flapped around the decks.

I said to Torgessen, "We'll repeat the drill until it goes smoothly, if it takes us all night."

It nearly did, at that. Before we started we had to send a party ashore to shanghai the native crewmen. Most of them had legged it all the way to town and had to be pried out by the constabulary.

Still, by 0800 the next morning I figured we had a passably disciplined crew for Sheik Ahmed's inspection. I was wearing my least wrinkled whites and was hoping my face did not show my opinion of Harvard men.

We were ready to cast off, the line-handlers at their stations, the quartermaster behind the wheel and the third mate on the bridge. From the bridge wing I could see a motor procession raising dust on the way from the town.

Two jeeps loaded with soldiers were fore and aft of a solid-gold Rolls Royce. On the dock the Rolls swerved alongside and the jeeps closed ranks between the Rolls and the spectators in the canteen area.

The vehicles braked with a flourish. The four guardsmen piled out of a jeep and lined up at the rear door of the Rolls, which opened to emit Hassan. He proceeded up the red carpet. Finding no booby traps, he turned and bowed. A guardsman swung the Rolls door wide. The sheik stepped out and stood motionless.

Sheik Ahmed was in native robes, tall and ramrod-straight. Against the white of his flowing head scarf, his face was strikingly dark and sharply modeled. From where I stood, he looked in the prime of life, though he would have to be over fifty if he had been a classmate of Bennington.

A small curved sword hung on a wide belt under his burnoose. When he moved, the dazzle of gems on the belt, sword hilt and scabbard nearly knocked my eyes out. In the morning sunlight the jewel facets blazed like a welding torch.

Looking neither right nor left Sheik Ahmed strode up the red carpet, his bodyguard falling behind. At the top of the gangway he gave an order. Two of the guards bowed and retired. The other two exchanged a look, threw themselves on their knees and emoted as only Arabs can emote.

I watched them wailing and pointing to the ship. I thought, *Uh-oh. Any time a couple of privates volunteer for duty, they're up to no good.*

Hassan now added his palm-raised entreaties. The sheik assented and the party disappeared into the ship. I walkie-talkied the second mate to close the sideport.

In a few seconds Sheik Ahmed strode onto the bridge alone. He paused, gave me a short nod. "Captain Schuster," I drew myself to attention and responded, "Sir." He smiled, ordered, "Cast off the lines," and we were in business.

I had no complaints about the way the ship handled in calm water. The bridge had every instrument I needed, plus one I would not have installed on a bet, like the true-position radar. I knew my true position and course. I did not need it repeated on an instrument.

We could have done 30 knots without exerting ourselves, but we took a full day to mosey down the Persian Gulf and turn the other sheiks green with envy. I was enjoying myself, except for my mistrust of the two guards. At our exclusive supper that first night in his dining room, I said to the sheik,

"You know your own men best, of course, but generally it's a mistake to allow weapons aboard."

He looked up from his shrimp cocktail. "As you probably saw, captain, I dismissed the men. But Auda and Ali have been with me since they were boys. They are feudal in their loyalty. The ship represented a danger they would not let me enter alone."

I thought *Oh, yeah?* but I did not pursue the matter further.

All day an escort of various boats had trailed after us, at distances which accorded with the owner's radiation fears. They came out to look us over and turned back after their curiosity was satisfied. Both Torgessen and I noticed, however, that one powerful motor launch had been pacing us since Qamat. He asked.

"Who can it be? News media or Russians?"

I thought either possibility was unlikely. "The media would be coming alongside for an interview, and this yacht has nothing to interest the Russians."

The next day we turned south in the Arabian Sea. There was no wind or swell of any consequence, but the ship began a fast, jerky roll. As far as I could, I quartered the waves. We had no particular destination, and I could adjust the ship to the sea.

The launch continued to pace us, just below our

visible horizon but keeping a constant distance on the radar screen. I began to get leery. To follow us beyond the Gulf, he must have stowed considerable extra fuel aboard.

In the late afternoon I pushed the yacht to 30 knots. The launch slowly began to close the distance. The ship was steering on the gyro, and there was no quartermaster in the wheelhouse. At that moment except for Sheik Ahmed I was alone.

Ahmed had been on the bridge most of the time, after one escorted tour to the white-banked nuclear pit. Beckwith pussyfooted around down there like a high priest before an altar, but for my money the place was as exciting as an empty swimming pool. Equipment is only equipment. If it works, use it. If it don't work, scrap it.

When I saw that the launch did not mean to be outrun, I said to the sheik, "We can continue south at full speed and possibly exhaust his fuel, or we can turn and chase him down."

Ahmed drummed his steely fingers on his jeweled sword hilt. "Why did he wait so long to overtake?"

"We're out of the main traffic stream. Maybe that's—"

I heard a startled "Hey!" from the chartroom, where Torgessen was plotting our position. A scuffle. Torgessen came out with two rifles at his back. Ali and Auda were on the operative ends of the rifles.

One guard left Torgessen and prodded his rifle against Ahmed's chest. I thought, *So much for Feudal Loyalty.* The guard said to me,

"I want the fuel pellets, in a shielded container.

Also, the money in the ship's safe. You will do it thus. You will ring a boat drill."

He paused to give me a hyena's grin. "You have perfected all crewmen in the boat drill. While they are on the outside decks at their stations, you and Ali will descend and obtain the fuel. Then you will help us to board our launch."

I had a millisecond to decide whether to go along or run a bluff. I looked at the fierce contempt on Ahmed's face and chanced the bluff. I knew Torgessen would catch on and follow through.

"Okay, okay, you can have the damned pellets." I growled. I walked boldly to the heat-and-smoke sensors and clicked a switch.

"What's that?" demanded the guard, by deduction Auda.

"You want a boat drill, don't you?" I barked, "My God, this is a nuclear ship! You can't have a boat drill at full speed! Do you want us to blow up from here to Karachi?"

I continued along the consoles, going Flick, Press, Shift as I passed the instruments. The guards looked nervous, awed, unsuspecting. The nuclear *mystique* had its uses, after all.

When I came to the gyro pilot I reached down briskly and released the gear. In the same second I grabbed the wheel and pulled it a quarter turn.

As the shielding-weighted ship broadsided the waves, she gave a sharp lurch. The guards were jerked off their feet.

Torgessen had been braced for the stunt since the moment I had clicked the sensor switch. He hooked a size 12 brogue around Ali's sandal as he made a flying tackle that pinned Auda to the deck.

In that half-second, while both sprawling hijackers were scrambling to bring their rifles to bear, Ahmed drew his sword. It flashed twice like summer lightning, and two heads bounced like bowling balls with the roll of the ship. The headless bodies spouted red lava over the deck.

Torgessen turned greenish-yellow and shuddered to his feet as a head wobbled into his lap. I said quickly, "Mate, set the course and instruments again."

He pulled himself to the gyro pilot and held onto the wheel a moment before correcting the course. I looked at Ahmed. The feudal anger of a double-crossed despot was giving way to afterthoughts even more dangerous for anyone presuming to criticize. As he met my gaze his nostrils flared and his grip tightened on the sword hilt.

He was daring me to say something, so of course I said it. "If you mess up my clean decks that way again, I'll throw you off the ship, Harvard or no Harvard, so help me!"

The fierceness became absolutely blank. He lowered the smeared sword, threw back his head and shouted a laugh.

"Bennington warned me about you," he chortled, his eyes glinting, "but he didn't tell the half of it."

Whatever that was supposed to mean. He went on, "I'll send Hassan to jettison the bodies and clean up. In case he needs an object lesson. Come to my cabin as soon as you are free."

He wiped his sword on his burnoose, sheathed it and strode off the bridge. I said to Torgessen, who was still doggedly setting switches, "Go below and take a whiskey. I'll hold the fort."

He mumbled thanks and hurried away. I chose a couple flags at random from the flag locker and covered the bodies, retrieving the heads and assigning one to each. The wrong one, probably.

I saw on the radar that the launch was coming all-out to catch us. I reduced speed. They would be coming alongside just when Hassan would be heaving their buddies overboard. I figured they needed an object lesson, too.

In a few minutes Torgessen returned, in a clean uniform and with a healthier color on his face. I went to my quarters and knocked back a half glass of scotch. To be honest, I had not liked those rolling heads any better than Torgessen had. After changing my spattered clothes I went to the sheik's cabin.

He was immaculate and dazzling again. He told me to sit down and asked me what I was drinking. I said scotch and he took drink fixings from a gold-trimmed mahogany cabinet.

"When I asked Bennington for a trouble-shooter," he smiled, "I didn't foresee that kind of trouble."

"Frankly, there's no need for me here," I replied. "Torgessen can handle the ship just as well. He understands the structural defects. The only thing I would like to persuade you to accomplish is to replace Beckwith's staff with seamen.

"There's too much exaggerated complexity about nuclear power," I went on. "Seamen went easily from rigging sails to stoking coal to being oilers and motormen. They can go just as easily to packing pellets into steel tubes.

"Sheik, you have no union problem in Qamat. You can train men in a straightforward manner, as they are trained on Naval ships, and assign them to jobs without being pressured into paying them ten times what the job is worth."

"Winters has asked to be released so that he can go back to research," said Ahmed. "I'll bring a chief engineer from one of the supply ships and have Beckwith train him for Winter's place.

"But I hope you'll stay on for the rest of the season, captain. I want you to take the ship around Africa to the Mediterranean—Monaco."

"Rainier is not gonna let you within fifty miles of his gambling den," I predicted.

We puttered around the Arabian Sea for a week and returned to Qamat. Winters resigned from the ship, but he came to my quarters one evening before he went ashore. He sat on the dayroom settee, his eyes asking "What if—?" as he looked at me.

"Captain," he said, "you expressed an idea about shielding. What was it?"

With that keen terrier cocking an ear at me, the idea suddenly did not seem so hot. But I began.

"I wanta explain why I thought of it. In my experience the first solution to a technical problem is seldom the best. If it were, aviation would not have got beyond the Curtiss Jenny.

"But a wrong solution can persist a hell of a long time. Take my own field. For centuries— millennia—the dummies hung square sails athwart the ship and could sail only before the wind. In the last breath of the sailing ship's history, some genius rigged a ship fore-and-aft, so she could tack.

"It may take millennia before the lead-shielding syndrome is licked. But I think the answer was already given at the turn of the century when Rutherford found that a magnet could divert the radiation from a piece of radium. That basic experiment has been used for doing what-all to radiation—except disposing of it."

I fumbled to explain better. "Look. It's like a rancher building a three-foot-thick wall around his spread to stop stampedes, when all he has to do is get on a horse, turn the direction of the stampede and get the critters milling in a circle."

Winters said smoothly, "Super-conducting magnets could be light enough and strong enough to deflect the alpha and beta particles, but gamma radiation is electromagnetic energy and not bendable by magnetic fields."

"Okay, so gamma rays can't be bent. But don't talk as if that was the final word! A few giants did some basic work in the field, and you guys are resting on their laurels. How do you know for sure that magnetic fields can't be rigged to weaken or damp down or block out gamma radiation? Has anybody done any serious work in that direction?"

"Calm down, captain! Don't blow a fuse," he smiled. "All right, let's assume the gamma radiation could somehow be blocked. What would you do with all those milling particles?"

"Aw, have a heart!" I protested. "If I was that smart, I wouldn't have to work at sea!"

Winters laughed as Ahmed had done. When he could listen to me again, I said, "The important thing is—"

He grinned. "The important thing is to get the lead out."

Winters was an inventor. Beckwith was an ossifier.

As I had warned the sheik, we were not allowed in any Mediterranean port. We only barely snuck past Gibraltar. We had plenty of company on board, though, as the yachts of millionaires and ex-crowned heads came out to us. I had a good time. Once in a while at dinner I grabbed the wrong fork, but otherwise I figured I was a credit to the Company.

At the end of the season I quit the sheik and returned to New York with a nice bonus check in my pocket. I was feeling on top of the world, but Mickleberry was as crabby as ever. He asked me.

"After your term of service aboard a nuclear vessel, Captain Schuster, does E still equal mc^2?"

"Why sure," I told him. "For the time being, anyhow."

Chapter 5

January 2 (cont.) . . .
Bennington At Home

Shortly before midnight John Bennington, his wife Trudy, and their guest Captain Ralph Turner entered the deep-carpeted, marble-faced lobby of an apartment building overlooking Central Park. They paused before a private elevator. Bennington unlocked the door with a key, and the trio entered the mirrored/plush/gilt cage.

Even in the bright, reflected light, a patina of wealth and breeding softened their handsome faces—deceptively, in the case of John Bennington. At the time of the Space Mining takeover a Briton who had come to New York for the negotiations had wondered how this amiable aristocrat had succeeded so well against the financial sharks and gnomes. Then he had happened to see Bennington's face in sharp profile—the line of chin and nose unexpectedly razor-keen, the glance hooded—and he thought immediately of an eagle poised, with zest, for the kill. He remembered the power surge that had dizzied him, as it dizzies all visitors, at his first sight of Manhattan's sky-scrapers—exciting, inexorable power.

Captain Ralph Turner—square of face, solid of build, healthily tanned by outdoor sun—had a different kind of strength. He neither stalked prey—nor turned from attack. It was not so much that he considered problems to be interesting opportunities for new solutions—it was that difficulties did not impress him. Nothing—in this world or the next—really impressed his balanced, ironical mind. If somebody admonished him, *This place is holy ground,* he just said *Nuts* and walked over it.

Trudy Bennington, who looked the most delicate and decadent of the three, was perhaps the cleverest. For twenty-five years she had, like Scheherazade, held her Sultan's amused interest—and the worldly emoluments pertaining thereto. Eternal Eve—who never worries about the stars going out, because she has only to say, *come hither* and they glow again.

She now pushed back the hood of her voluminous mink cape, admired the mother-of-pearl accents in her pale gold coiffure and said to the sun-bronzed Captain Turner, "There's not a show worth seeing nowadays. Jack and I should join you on Tahiti."

"And be equally bored by the Tahiti Hilton," smiled Turner. "Take a shuttle to the Moon Residence, Trudy."

They paused to adjust to the internal hump they felt as the swift elevator braked to a stop. The door opened, and they stepped into a panelled foyer with an intricate parquetry floor and oriental rugs. Trudy said vaguely, "Poor Schuster!"

Bennington latchkeyed their way into the penthouse. The inner foyer was dark except for a tall lamp that burned on a marble table. Two black Rec-Pak shells and a carved-ivory-encased unit were at the foot of the lamp.

Trudy said, "A nightcap, Ralph? Cartwright always leaves a tray for us in the den."

Bennington had tossed his brimmed hat on the table and picked up the ivory Rec-Pak unit. "Listen to this!" he interrupted. A correct voice was saying, ". . . delivered the two Schuster shells this evening. Mr. Mickleberry thought they would be of especial interest to Mr. Bennington and Captain Turner."

He flicked off the unit. The others came to the table. "What on Earth—" murmured Trudy. "Or should I say, what on the Moon—?"

"They're apparently Earth tapes," said Bennington. "Xavier must have found them in Schuster's Operations files today. Ralph, this shell has the name *Miss Jane*—bring back memories? And—oh, Lord! *Duwayo*—that's for me!"

He tossed a shell to Turner, and his wife took the other from his hand. "*Personal Memo!* I can't wait to hear the captain's non-Company remarks! Coming, Ralph?"

"Trudy, I'm not used to the bright lights," Turner smiled. "I'll have to thank you for a pleasant evening and hit the sack. With a bedtime yarn by Schuster."

"You can find the headboard Rec-Pak unit, can't you? Slide the stereo panel—"

"I know. I found that panel when I was hunting for the phone."

His hosts wished him 'Good night', and Captain Turner retired to his electronic jungle.

"Poor Schuster—I hope he won't haunt us for prying into his secrets!" breathed Trudy. She swished through the softly lit penthouse, doffing her mink on the way.

She threw the mink over a den chair on her course to an antique credenza, lifted up a panel in the credenza top, inserted the shell, and headed for the round ebony table on which a tray of bottles, Vacu/Ice, glasses, and plastic-wrapped sandwiches had been set out.

Bennington had followed at a slower pace, and she asked him, "What would interest you about the *Duwayo?*"

He laid his overcoat on top of his wife's mink cape, settled into a tapestried sofa and replied, "You remember Vaughan, the officer who married Comptroller Barnes' daughter?"

"Of course. An Adonis in uniform," she commented, unpeeling a ham-and-swiss sandwich.

"Barnes asked Mickleberry to do something for Vaughan, and Mickleberry put him on Schuster's ship."

"Oh-oh."

"Yes. Vaughan was young and cocky and thought his marriage had exempted him from the rules. Schuster caught him Under The Influence on the bridge and not only fired him but put him off the ship—which at the time was all hell and gone from New York. The repatriation was a considerable item, and Mickleberry called Schuster on the carpet for it—for the whole incident. It seemed to him that Schuster was working a chip off his shoulder—using a minor lapse to humiliate Vaughan because the kid was young and handsome—"

"Strangely unperceptive of the old maestro," said Trudy. "As long as Schuster holds the reins, he doesn't care if the stallions are young and handsome."

Bennington smiled and repeated, *"Holds* the reins—. Feel that he's still alive?"

She stood, sandwich in hand, and cocked her head. "I don't feel that he's gone—and I *would* feel it, I think. He's the keystone, isn't he? You, holding one side of the arch—and Mickleberry holding the other. And between you, the keystone. Oh, yes, I would *feel,* if he were gone. But about the *Duwayo*—"

"Well, Schuster was sore about being asked for an explanation of the Vaughan incident. He blew his stack, and Mickleberry fired him."

". . . never means anything," mumbled Trudy through the sandwich.

"Not usually. But that time Schuster steamed out of the building and ran into the charterer's agent Rondane Smith, who snapped him up for a Singapore consortium. Hence, the *Duwayo*."

"You say that with such finality, darling—but now I realize what happened *after* the *Duwayo*. It was then that Vaughan went berserk in a drydock and cost the Company God-knows-what in damages—"

"Trudy, we had to act upon the available evidence—"

"—and you and Mickleberry got down on your knees and begged Schuster to come home. *That* was the finality."

"Do you want to hear the *Duwayo* story or don't you?" Bennington leaned forward and picked up the control cube from the coffee table. "Bring me a Scotch with a dollop of ice."

"Yes, master." Trudy brought the drink, plumped herself on the sofa and said, "Do you suppose it begins 'Once Upon A Time?'"

"It won't begin at all unless you shut up."

Trudy bounced up to kiss her husband's ear. Thus mollified, Bennington took a swallow of Scotch, flicked a control bead, and Schuster's voice—as warmly real as if the Old Man were in the den—began, "When I met Mr. Lee Soomb at a jungle port in Sumatra . . ."

● ● ●

A RAT OF ANY PSIZE

When I met Mr. Lee Soomb at a jungle port in Sumatra, I had no idea of the later significance of his weird machines to food production and city engineering. I was relief skipper on the *Duwayo,* a supply vessel chartered to an international food corporation that was trying to build a coconut oil refinery in the jungle.

I do not know if the refinery even got off the ground. Indonesia generally has done a great job of lifting itself by its own bootstraps, but like most developing countries it has primitive areas where civilized rules do not apply and the devil takes the hindmost.

The food corporation had the bad luck to choose one of those wild areas. The building supplies ran into the sand. What was not pilfered from the *Duwayo* was stolen from the building site or ripped bodily from the construction work.

The food corporation's losses were no skin off our nose. The *Duwayo* had been chartered at a fixed monthly fee which should have given a profit to the Singapore consortium that owned her. However, the ship also began replacing stores and equipment at a puzzling rate. Her skipper was pulled off at Singapore by the Operations chief, Lin Wu, and I was sent aboard.

I was known to be Lin's hatchet man, and I did not make myself more popular during the short haul up the Malacca Strait, I inspected the officers' quarters and found enough canned food to stock a supermarket, plus items stolen from the paint locker, rope locker, engine room, and bridge.

The *Duwayo* had white officers and Chinese crew. The Chinese were old hands, reliable from the consortium's viewpoint because their gambling and smuggling were financed by their own wages. There was no question of their doing the stealing.

The white officers were another matter. Most of them had drifted east of Suez because of trouble in westerly waters, and the jungle bay of Sumatra presented irresistible temptations. The native girls, like the wily savages they were, came to the ship and enticed the officers home with them, and the village fastened onto them like leeches.

Being disinclined to spend their own cash, if

they had any, the officers had begun to scrounge from the ship to satisfy their girl friends. By this time, too, there probably was uglier pressure from the male family members who had muscled into the racket.

After we had docked at the jungle base and the cargo was discharged I let the officers go ashore as usual. If they wanted to support a gang of pack rats with their own money, I hoped they had a nice day for it.

One officer remained on board, the second engineer. I had found no loot in his cabin. He was a Midwesterner named Gavan, a round-shouldered string bean with blunt-tipped fingers. He had signed a two-year contract because the money was good, and I knew he was sending almost every cent home.

That afternoon, since we were the only officers on the ship, I invited him to my quarters for a drink and tried to sound him out. A shipboard racket usually has a ringleader. Gavan kept his lip buttoned. I could not decide whether he was afraid of reprisals or really did not know which bastard had egged everybody on to plucking the ship bare.

When our second drink was watering down in the heat, the Indonesian watchman, a seedy-looking Malay, tapped at my opened dayroom door and waved a white business card at me.

Wondering if the visitor was food corporation brass, I took the card and read, MR. LEE SOOMB, MOUNTAIN COFFEE ESTATES. Coffee? I handed the card to Gavan and asked, "Do they raise coffee in this overgrown swamp?"

He studied the card. "I believe a British outfit is

developing the highlands to the west, captain. The name Soomb doesn't ring any bell, though."

I told the watchman to send the guy up. After a moment a slight, white-suited figure hugging a wicker basket stood in the doorway.

Mr. Lee Soomb was light-skinned and sandy-haired like a Malay and had a touch of Chinese ivory.

He set the basket carefully on the deck and bowed at us both. "Whom have I the honor of addressing Captain?"

I did not get out of my chair. For all I knew, he could be a local con man. I said, "I'm Captain Schuster. You have business with the ship?"

"Am in need of technical advice not forthcoming, alas, from construction engineers with own problems. In remote fastness, how to wire an electrical system correctly? After desperate trip to coast, ship is last resort."

I decided he was legit and invited him to sit down. "This is Mr. Gavan, second engineer," I added. "What's the difficulty?"

Mr. Soomb perched humbly on a chair. "In tropical agriculture, difficulty is fertilizer. Food crops quickly drain nutrients, and soils do not have natural renewing action of frosts and snowfall."

Gavan interrupted, "But you have volcanic soil for the coffee, don't you?"

"Yes. Coffee estate is well started. It is not as Estates manager but as private individual that I am seeking advice."

He paused as if he was not sure I would deal with a private individual. When I said nothing, he went on.

"Under Indonesian law I personally can own twenty hectares of dry land—dry as opposed to wet riceland. I have bought this acreage in the valley adjacent to the Estates. I hope to grow the new cereal grains, which need much fertilizer. I have no money for import. Must devise fertilizer locally."

"Out of what?"

"Jungle compost and overabundant bone-and-protein source. Rodents."

I had not thought of rats in that connection, but from our Chinese crews I had heard how Red China processed human bodies. Probably ton for ton both rats and men reduced to the same fertilizer components.

The snag occurred to me. "How can you catch enough rats?"

He dragged the wicker basket towards him and opened it. Inside was the oddest-looking contraption—! Seeing my surprised glance Mr. Soomb hurriedly drew out a coarse, smudged paper and closed the basket. He held the paper out to Gavan.

"Please. Engineer's opinion of better rattrap? Electric current is generated on Estates. Direct current as on ship."

Gavan's face lit up with interest. To me, the diagram looked like a kid's backyard slide, with the ladder stanchions stuck inside a barrel. Mr. Soomb explained, moving his finger up the slide, "The rising approach ramp can be anything, of course. At top is an electrocuting grid and conveyor belt depositing dead rats in container."

"You don't need a conveyor belt," said Gavan immediately. "Put a back-slant on your ramp, with an isolated live-plate. The rat climbs the ramp, continues over the bend to the plate, gets the wattage and slides by gravity into the barrel.

"But why a barrel?" he went on. "Use a trash compactor. The compacted blocks can be sliced into the vegetable compost. And why a ramp, if it comes to that?"

Mr. Soomb hesitated. "Universal constant in rodent psychology. Height acts as magnet."

I felt this was true. Like what the mountaineers have said about Everest. They climbed it because it was—no, wait a minute—

Gavan was asking, "And suppose you run out of rats?"

"Impossible. Rats are an absolute infinity."

Gavan grinned. "Like marching the Chinese Army four abreast past any given point?"

"No, no. I should have said, cosmic infinity."

In that split-second I heard—sensed— movement in the alleyway. I yelled "Watchit!", lunged low from my chair and slid out of sight behind the desk.

The air whined, and a knife handle quivered at heart level in the upholstery of the chair I had been using.

Mr. Soomb and Gavan had been too startled to move. But now the slight, white-clad figure charged into the alleyway, angrily yelling a spate of native words.

Gavan sat still, with a tight look that said he knew more than he thought was safe to tell me.

I got to my feet, came to the chair and pulled out the knife. It was double-edged, with a runnel cut down the center of the blade. A real killer.

Mr. Soomb came back, breathless. "Watchman

reports assailant has dived overboard into sea. Do you wish the police?"

"Hell no," I said. "We can't tie up the ship in red tape." I added to Gavan, "I should have foreseen that backlash."

I kinda admired the gutsy way Mr. Soomb had run out to counterattack. I put the knife in a desk drawer and asked him, "Would you like to stay aboard tonight, Mr. Soomb? The pilot's cabin is available. Mr. Gavan and bosun Wong can knock together a rattrap in the tweendeck, and we'll see how it works. The ship needs a deratting anyhow."

Color came into Mr. Soomb's ivory cheeks, and his caramel eyes glistened. "Thank you. I will, of course, reimburse the ship for the costs."

I waved this aside. "Dicker with Wong about smuggling a trash compactor next trip."

Gavan protested, "How can Wong smuggle anything as big as a trash compactor?"

"Wong could smuggle an elephant into an igloo. Don't ask me how he does it."

Mr. Lee Soomb hoisted his mysterious basket, and Gavan led him below.

I phoned down to the watchman and asked him to come to the office. His story of the man diving into the sea had been pure malarkey. We had heard no splash. A moored, empty ship is a sounding-board magnifying even the plop of a bottle into the water.

Moreover, the knife-throw had come from a blind angle. Only one man would have known where I was sitting.

The watchman slunk into the doorway, with the

bold look of a guy who thinks he is getting away with something. I grabbed him by his greasy hair, punched a fist into his belly, threw him to the deck and bent over him. The knife-sheath was strapped under a pant-leg.

I let him go, and he sat up. His eyes were not so cocky. I said, "Tell your pals the good times are over."

He crawled to his feet. I took the knife from the desk and motioned him ahead of me, out to the dockside boat deck. I flipped the knife overboard. It fell in a bright flash and stuck in a dock piling.

"Get off the ship and stay off," I ordered him. "If I see you in the dock area, I'll beat you to a pulp."

He scurried to the deck ladder. A few seconds later I saw him run down the accommodation ladder and jerk the knife from the piling.

He was one rat I should have compacted, I guessed. He would be laying for me if I went ashore. Maybe some of the officers also were laying for me. I had no illusions about the spot I was in. Skippers who break up shipboard rackets tend to be lost at sea.

I ordered supper for Mr. Soomb, Gavan and myself to be served in my dayroom. It was not a very coherent meal. I was preoccupied, and the other two were jawing about the automatic feed lines and photoelectric cells.

I still could not figure out where the necessary tons of rats would come from. I asked Mr. Soomb what he meant by a cosmic infinity.

He pushed his plate away and began, "As you know, captain, this planet has gone through several distinct experiments in life energy, from the trilobite to the Tyrannosaurus to present-day species. This creative force is resident solely in the cosmos and is not within human manipulation."

He explained further. "When I say present species, I mean that this is the Age of Rats. Within the Age, the rats are infinite because they are, in fact, the current experiment in life energy."

"Just a minute," I interrupted. "This is the Age of Mammals. A rat is only one kind of mammal."

He smiled. "No, no. The rat came first, captain. All mammals are only different kinds of rats— some nearer the original strain, some further removed, all sharing the same Rat characteristics. There is an immense fluidity among the species.

"Not as to physical interbreeding, of course," he continued, "but as to the psionic impulses forming mental patterns. Personality interplay ranges over the entire spectrum."

Gavan translated, "He means, that's why people look like their dogs. There's no real difference in mental characteristics and like attracts like."

Mr. Soomb nodded. "The essence of Rat is a common pool shared by all mammals."

I had to admit I had been thinking in terms of human rats, but this blurring of species was too deep for me. I asked how the rattrap was working out.

"Shall we go below and see what we have caught?" asked Mr. Soomb.

Well, the damned trap was as lethal as it could get, and Gavan had posted signs, KEEP AWAY— LIVE WIRE. Basically it was a wooden mock-up of the playground slide, with the back-slant Gavan had suggested and an exposed wire rigged over a piece of metal scrap.

A beer case had been dragged up to represent the compactor. It was already full of electrocuted rats. I looked to see what bait had been so effective. There was no bait. Had height alone drawn the rats?

I noticed Mr. Soomb's wicker basket lying open behind a pile of dunnage. I investigated.

Here was the odd setup I had glimpsed briefly when Mr. Soomb had taken out the diagram. In the middle of a square shallow box was a free-standing sphere of copper wires. Concentrically from this sphere were two circles. The inner was a clear plastic ring over what seemed to be scraps of writing. The outer ring was of double-decker isinglass sandwiches. That was all.

I demanded. "What's the big idea? What's that a model of?"

Mr. Soomb explained, "It is not a model. It is a working psionic machine."

That word psionic again. I growled, "The Russian telekinesis rip-off?"

"Psionic waves are genuine waves, captain. Obviously the brain's psionic energy must be emitted on measurable wavelengths, like electromagnetic energy but beyond it.

"Try to understand my problem," he went on. "Rats, like other animals, have their hunting areas. To catch them in the necessary quantity for fertilizer, I needed to control them over long distances, miles beyond the limits of their natural senses. By what means could I broadcast to them and make them assemble at a collection point? On what meter band would they receive me? Again obviously, the mind-to-mind, the psionic."

He smiled, "Fortunately psionic waves can be

harnessed more simply than electromagnetic ones."

I indicated the transmitter. "How does it work?"

"First, the brain is a total energy field, not a mere network of here-to-there relays." He pointed to the wire sphere. "My concentration transfers my psionic field to this sphere, which selectively transforms field-level energy to wave-level. Originally I built only the sphere and the outer circle of identity contacts—rat blood and brain tissue layered in mica cubes.

"However, I could not be continually present to concentrate on the sphere. I needed a kind of storage battery for my field energy, to transfer my concentration to the machine. I transcribed my mental pictures into written words, defining the essence of Rat, as if the words were a printed circuit."

I asked, naturally, what his definition was. He said, "The cunning and slyness; the omnivorous, ruthless feeding habits; the gnawing in secret dark places; the boldness of the pack and treacherous cowardice of the lone individual."

He turned again to his psionic machine and continued, "I glued the word-tracers under a plastic ring between the energy sphere and the contact cubes. To stop the machine, I need only lift off the ring."

While we talked, a dirty gray rat drifted towards us, its tail sculpturing the dust-layer on the deck. The rat was soaking wet. Apparently it had swum to the anchor chain and climbed aboard through the hawse pipe. We had rat guards, of course, on the mooring lines.

The rat nosed aimlessly to the psionic sender, then fixed its beady eyes on the ramp. It scurried up—went over the top—stiffened and tumbled into the beer case.

I had seen it, so I had to believe it. I remarked, "That's a dangerous sending pattern. I don't know how you measure psionic waves, but a whazzahertz one way or another and you might get human beings climbing that ramp."

"No, no, captain. The transmitter is fine-tuned to the *rattus rattus* thought-structure." He paused a moment. "Of course, an incidental side effect could be a transformation of total energy an another receiving animal."

I looked to Gavan. He translated, "Well, captain, a rat and a weasel are pretty much alike and have similar thoughts and behavior. If a rat signal took over a weasel brain, the weasel might simply turn into a rat."

"Why?"

"The brain is the control center. We are what we think."

"I think you guys are bananas."

I left them discussing how to shield the live-plate, and I went to my quarters. I was concerned about that wet rat. Apparently, in deratting the ship, the psionic machine would derat the entire coast.

I hit the sack with the personnel question still unanswered. Lin Wu wanted to salvage what officers he could. Men who went to pieces in a jungle could still be usable on trade routes where the environment provided the discipline they lacked.

Between the personnel uncertainty and the

muggy jungle heat, I was restless. About midnight I got out of the bunk, pulled on my pants, scuffed my feet into sandals and went out on deck.

Because of the pilfering, the *Duwayo* was fully lit with deck lights, spotlights, cargo lights. I went up to the bridge. Gavan's string-bean figure was draped over the dodger. He turned and frowned absently as I stepped up to him.

"I was worried, captain," he said.

"About what?"

"That psionic machine. It may be fine-tuned as Soomb says, but it is tuned to the mental, not physical, essence of Rat. It could attract and transform weasels—or monkeys—or men."

"Oh, sure. Now tell me how it could turn a two-hundred-pound man into a two-pound rat."

"We know psionic waves have the speed and penetration of cosmic rays, but all measurement has been along that one dimension—an outgoing, positive dimension. No one has experimented with an inward, inself-directed, negative thrust. Psionic waves can do—and undo."

He hesitated. "Have you ever thought about the function of the neutron in the atomic nucleus?"

"I don't lose any sleep over it, no."

"Because the neutron has no electric charge, should we assume it has no charge whatsoever? What if it has a positive psionic charge?"

"For one thing, the hydrogen atom would be out in left field psionically."

"Maybe not. We don't know the possible psionic functions of the neutron. Hydrogen could be a stabilizer in that instant when the brain's negative thrust was pulled to psionic-positive neutrons—a thrust that could infiltrate and short out the non-hydrogen-atoms' electric paths, dissipating all sub-atomic particles.

"From which particles," he said slowly, "a psionic signal could form a two-pound rat."

"And the remaining hundred ninety-eight pounds of man?"

"Well, that would recombine its molecules around the hydrogen base and become water, mostly, with a few mineral salts."

He brooded. "I ought to warn Soomb not to use a live wire on the rattrap. If water hit it, he could blow every fuse on the Estates."

The ship's lights went dead. We were standing in blackness.

With Gavan at my heels I barged off the bridge, into my quarters, and fumbled a couple of flash-lights from the desk. We beat it down to the tween-deck.

We noticed the air, first. The tangy ozone smell of a lightning flash. The deck was wet. The steel of the hull and the overhead beams dripped as if from a heavy dew. The insulation around the live-wire was scorched away.

Gavan unplugged the cable to the trap. I saw him pause, play his flashlight on an object, lean over and pick it up. It was the watchman's knife.

"My God!" he cried.

He rushed to the mound of rats overflowing the beer case. "They are here, captain!" he yelled hysterically. "They sneaked on board—probably to kill you—and the machine got them!"

I thought he had found electrocuted human bodies. I went over to him. He was directing the flashlight onto the rats.

"Don't you recognize him, captain?" he babbled. "The chief mate—that rat over there, with crooked teeth and scarred nose. Oh, he was a real *rattus rattus*, all right! The Old Man was scared to death of him. We all were. I never would have dared talk about him while he was alive, but seeing him dead—him and the watchman—"

I liked Gavan too much to belt him one. I took a deep breath and tried reasoning. I said, "Clothes."

"What, captain?"

"Those guys weren't running around nude, were they? If the psionic signal transformed them into rats, what happened to their clothes?"

For a moment a kind of sane relief brightened his face. Then it clouded over and he said, "Clothing is only an extension of personality. In a total energy transformation it would be incorporated into hide and hair."

He looked at the knife he was still holding and murmured, "Maybe some objects have their own psionic life."

"And maybe some men overwork on two-year contracts," I said gruffly. "Gimme that knife. Go fix the power blackout—and forget this whole conversation."

He pulled himself together, handing over the knife and left.

I turned my flashlight on the rats. To me, they were only rats. Of course, there was the mammalian link. I could understand how a vivid imagination could turn rodents into pseudohumans. Like

Mickey Mouse. Or that crooked-toothed mate over there, his spikey tail lying across the seedy-looking—

Wait a minute—I was off the rails again.

I walked over the wet deck to the psionic transmitter and lifted off the plastic ring. It tingled, a moment before it went cold. Whatever the machine was summoning, I wanted no more of it.

The officers came back to the ship the next day, their spree having turned sour. The chief mate never came aboard. The watchman was never seen again, either.

I had to report the mate's nonappearance to the local authorities, and they held the ship a week while they investigated. Gavan was like a cat on hot bricks, half convinced he had participated in psionic murder. He would have spilled the whole crazy story if Mr. Soomb and I, for different reasons, had not stifled him.

Although the ship was losing no money by the delay, the time passed heavily. Mr. Soomb, after an earnest conference with bosun Wong, went ashore with his psionic machine and a reluctantly-given wiring diagram from Gavan for what Soomb and Wong were now calling the deratting station.

In his wicker basket, Mr. Soomb also had the watchman's knife, which he begged of me. A kinda morbid souvenir, I thought.

Unsatisfactory though it was, that seemed to close the story of Mr. Soomb. When the *Duwayo* finally returned to Singapore and I had delivered my report to Lin Wu, I was transferred to another ship needing a troubleshooter, and I never saw the *Duwayo* again.

For three months Lin kept me on the Borneo-to-Japan oil route. Then I got a letter from my former employers in New York. The issue upon which they had fired me—my attempt to dismiss a drunken officer with Company pull—had turned out as I had predicted. The guy had gone berserk, and the Company had a mess of damage suits on their hands.

In apology—though they did not express it that way—they were offering to reinstate me in my former command. I figured I ought to accept, although I liked my work with the consortium.

Lin Wu understood my reasons for quitting and we parted good friends. In fact, I owed to Lin my knowledge of what happened further to Mr. Lee Soomb, his psionic machine and his deratting station.

About a year after the episode on the *Duwayo* I got a letter from Lin enclosing a clipping from the Asian edition of a news magazine. The headline was SEA FARMING. I began to read.

"The engineering research firm of Soomb & Wong—"

Soomb and Wong? I laughed at the way bosun Wong had parlayed a smuggled trash compactor into a partnership. I read on:

"—are supplying rat-based vitamin-enriched food meal for a projected fish hatchery now under construction north of Timor. Cheaper than netted plankton, the rat meal has proved satisfactory for hatchling growth."

The article reviewed the "fertilizer processing which Soomb & Wong have done on the larger Indonesian plantations" and came to a further most interesting point:

"A by-product of the extensive deratting necessary to the fertilizer is a drastically-reduced crime rate. Environmentalists interpret that as proof that a clean rat-free community induces healthier mores."

I wondered how Gavan would interpret the reduced crime rate, wherever he was. He would say that Rat-essence thieves were not healthier—just reconstituted into a couple pounds of rat meal and varying amounts of water vapor. The *Duwayo's* tweendeck had been sopping wet for no good reason, that was for sure.

Although Soomb & Wong were increasingly in the news, I did not give them serious thought until an incident several months later.

The ship was alongside a New York pier. The watch said a guy from the Sanitation Department wanted to talk to me. I figured a messman had dumped a pail of garbage overboard and I would have to wangle us out of a fine.

But the Sanitation guy turned out to be a wheel in the planning department. I could not understand what the hell he wanted with me. However, I shook his hand and offered him a drink, and after a while we got down to cases.

"Quite by chance, captain," he began, "in a social conversation with one of your Company executives, I found out that you were working for a Singapore consortium about two years ago."

I admitted the fact. He asked, "Did you ever meet up with the firm of Soomb & Wong?"

I hesitated, and he went on, "They have approached us with what seems on the surface to be a workable recycling project combining deratting stations and the collection of vegetable discards."

What he meant, I supposed, was that Soomb wanted to clean out the market district and restaurant alleys for processing materials. I still did not comment, and the guy continued. "We like the proposition, and we like what we hear of the results—a cleaner city, less crime. But we're trying to corroborate the facts. We need a report from nearer home. The Orient is—well, the Orient."

I saw his point. I said, "I wouldn't believe any statistics from that area, myself. But all I can tell you is that Soomb and Wong set up their first deratting station aboard my ship, the *Duwayo*."

"Was it efficient?"

I wondered if I ought to tell him about the psionic-positive neutrons and the drenched tweendeck. New York City kept pretty accurate vital statistics. If the deratting stations really began disposing of every sly, thieving, ruthless, secretely-gnawing Rat in the five boroughs—

At last I said, "Efficient, yes. The machine did not leave a Rat of any psize."

The Sanitation guy seemed satisfied, so I let the matter rest. As far as I know, it is still resting.

Chapter 6

January 2 (cont.) . . .
Captain Turner Remembers

Ralph Turner was propped up in the satin-
canopied bed. The satin-quilted headboard was
keyed to a soft glow, and Schuster's Rec-Pak was in
the proper audio slot, but Turner's mind was miles
away.

Only business could have dragged him back to
New York. His present life was so different from
his past that New York made him feel like a
Jekyll/Hyde. He was now a marine biologist. His
command was a research vessel. His colleagues
were the French scientists on Tahiti and Noumea.

When he had been born, another course had
been laid out for him. As the grandson and only
heir of Josph Alderman, he had been destined to
take over the Company and the rest of the Alderman empire. It had not occurred to him to
protest—in those days, kids had family pride, per-

sonal pride. All that he had asked was to be allowed to earn his own way to the top.

After graduating from King's Point, he had sought work on the West Coast and had stayed with a Pacific shipping line for ten years, until the Company had bought financial control of a Far East line. He could work for the company in the Far East without risking the nepotism charge that might have come if he had sailed out of New York.

When old Alderman died, that family obligation somehow had died with him. Turner supposed that he could have fought Bennington and his adherents among the stockholders, but he had no ground to fight upon. He had no ideas for expansion—no interest in office work. He might have fought a chiseler with no more qualifications than himself, but Bennington was an exceptional man who deserved a chance at the Company. Turner had backed him with the Alderman voting stock—and had never regretted it. Bennington had put the Company in Space.

Bennington, Mickleberry and Schuster had been a good triumvirate. Schuster's loss would be a blow because he was the action man. Look at this arrant nonsense of the UN bleeding the Company white with their so-called Space Sharing. If they wanted a share in Space, why the hell didn't they go up and take it, instead of whining for *baksheesh*?

The world was crazy. Thank God he was a marine biologist and not Company Board Chairman.

But he was still proud of his career at sea. He had earned his master's papers and been given a command through merit. Nobody in New York had known who he was. Not even Schuster.

He smiled and activated the tape. A well-remembered voice began to speak, bringing back the past—the stinking hot rustbucket decks—the copra, and the clouds of tiny black devils.

"I will be brief about how I happened to find myself on Singapore Harbor's outer roads . . ."

● ● ●

THE COPRA POPULATION

I will be brief about how I happened to find myself on Singapore Harbor's outer roads, loading copra from one old rustbucket into another. The situation was this:

A Greek sailing from Indonesia with 7,000 tons of copra for a coconut-oil refinery in the Philippines had decided to put his ship on a reef for the insurance money. He did not shave her close enough the first time and got cold feet about a second try. He plugged the gash in her bow with cement and limped into Singapore, where the authorities held the ship on a hatful of liens.

The owners of the cargo naturally wanted to trans-ship, and the nearest available cargo vessel was the old *Miss Jane,* under the command of Skinny Eggerton, who had just left off a cargo of Swedish nitrate at Madras. When he was ordered to Singapore, he duly chugged east at his top speed of twelve knots. The copra receivers thought the deal was set.

But did he pick up the copra? No, he did not. He shot off messages claiming the transfer could not

be made. The Greek's derrick's were unusable—
his own booms could not be rigged—the Greek's
starboard list was an insurmountable obstacle—the
currents and winds were contrary.

When this dither reached the wheels of power in
New York, they grabbed their push-button tele-
phones and asked each other, "Which of us last
fired loud-mouthed Schuster? Who's got the Flying Dutchman on his payroll?"

At the time they found the answer, I was on the
North Sea, sitting on a naphtha tankship in a
bottleneck of fog outside the western end of the
Kiel Canal. The radioman said New York wanted
to talk to me, and I ambled off the bridge and took
the call.

My current Owner began. "Captain Schuster, we
have an urgent assignment for you. The skipper of
an old C-1a in the Singapore roads is having trouble rigging his booms to take aboard a copra cargo
from another ship."

"What's the matter? Didn't he do his King's Point
homework?" I growled. "Do you want me to draw
him a picture?"

Muffled haws in several overtones told me I was
talking into a multiple link-up. The first voice to
recover belonged to a charterers' agent I knew
pretty well.

"Captain, this is Andrew Clark," he said. "The
problem is that Skinny Eggerton is dragging his
feet about taking aboard 7,000 tons of copra bugs,
cockroaches and rats. You know Skinny's war with
the vermin kingdom."

"Yeah, he's saving the planet single-handed
from a takeover."

"Well, his efforts are not appreciated at the moment. Could you fly out there as supercargo, get the copra aboard and persuade Skinny to deliver his copra population to Legaspi?"

"Sure, Mr. Clark. If it's okay with my owner. When do I start?"

"We have the Kiel agent on another line. Could you be ready to leave in the Canal? Your chief mate can take the ship into the Baltic."

Another voice cut in, "And, Captain, that Greek has sure as hell been selling the cargo piecemeal in the roads. Don't let him con you—"

A general horse laugh interrupted him, and the line went dead.

I left the radio room, told the chief mate I hoped he was ready to solo, packed my suitcases and waited for the fog to lift.

In four hours we were at Bruensbuettel, and the Kiel agent and the German police took me off the ship. The agent gave me a plane ticket, a hundred American dollars and a sheaf of Telex data.

In twenty-four hours (elapsed time) I was in Singapore, suffering jet-lag, cabin-headache and triple-seat charley horse. I picked up a launch to the *Miss Jane,* loosened my necktie and shirt collar and hoped Skinny would buy me a drink.

I got a laugh out of the set-up. There was the Greek, red with rust and listing heavily to starboard, like a blowsy madam three sheets to the wind. The *Miss Jane,* primly black of hull and white of superstructure, was anchored a cable length away, like a schoolmarm drawing her skirts aside.

Skinny had been notified I was coming, of course, but there was no welcome mat on the accommodation ladder. I lugged my suitcase up to the deck. A well-built kid wearing khakis and an officer's cap came out of the closely-screened cargo office, shifted the toothpick in his mouth and said,

"You Schuster? You gotta put up with the pilot's cabin. Bunk, washbasin, towel, no air conditioning and Eggerton ordered the topside wooden slats removed this morning. You like hot sun on bare steel? Or shall I call the launch back with a toot on the tooter?"

Shall I? I was about to ask him if he had brought his governess along. I took a second look at his strong jaw and hard, callused hands and decided his grammar was none of my business. I set down my suitcase and realized Eggerton had check-mated me on the *Miss Jane*.

The kid had not moved. He was sizing me up and chewing the toothpick. I said, "I want to go over to the Greek."

"Free-style or back stoke? I can lend you a life-jacket. Our boats are temporarily out of commission."

"They float, don't they?"

"If you want to stick your big toe in the drainage hole. Eggerton took the corks."

He was keeping a straight face, so I didn't crack either. I said, "Captain Eggerton is on the premises?"

"He left orders not to be disturbed."

"Until when?"

"Until the receivers admit there is no way the copra can be salvaged."

Without seeming on the muscle he was still blocking me out. He was in his rights. Eggerton did not have to take me aboard. I knew I could stand

and jaw at the kid all afternoon without advancing an inch.

The man I needed was the chief mate. I was about to ask for him when I caught an amused look from the kid's eyes—from his fatigue-reddened worry-smudged eyes. The young shoulders in front of me were bearing the weight of Eggerton's war on the vermin kingdom.

"Okay, Mister Mate," I smiled. "You can stop covering for Skinny. I know him."

That I had called the turn so quickly shook him out of his poker-faced irony. He took the toothpick from his mouth, opened the screen door, heaved my suitcase into the cargo office and said, "Come up and have a drink, Captain."

Over the years Eggerton had made considerable interior alterations on the old ship. I saw that the chief mate's quarters were two staterooms combined to give an office, bedroom and small bath.

"Sit down. I'll get some ice," the young mate said.

I sat in the chair beside his desk. The quarters were neat, shipshape. He came back with a bowl of ice, set the bowl on the desk, rubbed his wet hand across his shirt and said, "My name's Turner."

I should have placed him, then and there, but I had worked for a lot of owners and charterers, and Turner is not an unusual name.

We shook hands, he brought Scotch, soda and glasses from a locker, and we had a drink. I noted that he barely colored the soda and ice in his glass.

"I gave Eggerton sleeping pills," he began, after I had downed a hefty slug of my drink. "I didn't know what else to do. He goes crazy, multiplying bugs. He was ordered here from Madras, so he had to come, but he was under a strain. It lifted somewhat when he thought he had persuaded the receivers that trans-shipment was impossible. When he got the message you were coming, he went to pieces."

"He must have known somebody would be sent to investigate."

"When he panics over vermin, he pushes facts away. He goes quietly berserk. Like the orders he gave about your accomodations. That was okay by me." He smiled a little. "Giving the hotfoot to an unwanted supercargo was within my scope.

"But sabotaging the lifeboats was too much. I took barbiturate from the medical locker, and slipped it into his noon tea." After a pause he continued, "Eggerton is a good skipper otherwise. It's just the vermin."

"He must have hauled copra before. Your fine-mesh screening is not new."

"Fresh copra, yes. It's not bad when it first comes on board. You can be a week at sea before the bugs swarm out of the ventilators. And they're only minor vermin, being totally dependent on copra. Of course, Eggerton goes after them. I've seen him use a whole can of aerosol spray in his dayroom, until the bugs were ankle deep on either side of his screen door.

"But, you understand, the Greek has been sitting there for weeks. His cargo is rotten. He is alive not only with copra bugs but with cockroaches and rats. Eggerton is right about one thing—the cargo is not worth salvaging."

"Nuts. Legaspi can squeeze the oil of out of the roaches instead of the coconut."

He pushed the bottle toward me again. I said, "Not right now, thanks. Why won't the Greek trim his list?"

"He claims he has to keep his portside damage above the waterline. Nonsense, of course. There's no sea to batter his patchwork. The fact is, he's been embezzling the cargo and doesn't want a surveyor reading his load lines."

"We have to put him on an even keel before we can come alongside. Plug up a lifeboat and lower it for me."

Turner shook his head. "When the Old Man says no boat, it's no boat. He wants no contact between the *Miss Jane* and the Greek. You can order the shore launch, of course."

Of course. And once I was in the launch, the accomodation ladder would be raised and I would not get aboard again. The kid should not have let me get my foot in the door. Now that he had taken my measure, he would not be making any more mistakes.

I got up. "Okay, forget the boats. Where's the Black Hole that Skinny has prepared for me?"

He escorted me to the small airless cabin aft of the chartroom and said he would send up my suitcase. I climbed out of my shore clothes, and a seaman brought the suitcase. I asked him, "Is the bosun on deck? Tell him to come here, will you?"

By the time I had my khakis and work shoes on, the bosun was in the doorway. He was a small, knobbly man in paint-stained denims, with a sheathed knife on his belt.

"Bosun, you must have a small flatboat or raft that you lower for work on the hull. Put it in the water on the lee side, with an oar."

"I'd have to ask Turner, sir?"

"Have to? A bottle of whiskey might change your mind?"

"No, it would not, sir." He gave a hitch to his belt.

Just my luck to run up against an honest man. I said, "Bosun, I have about twelve hours to save Skinny from being relieved of his command. You and Turner are trying to save him by being loyal. You're just cutting his throat."

I saw doubt come into his expression, and I went on, "Do you think the copra consortium cares about loyalty? Don't kid yourself. All they care about is their damned dollars. Sure, Skinny has been running a profitable ship. But the minute this present delay cancels out his past usefulness, he'll be fired.

"And Turner will be keelhauled because he should know better. I haven't quite placed the kid yet," I added, "but I will. No matter how smart he was about getting his licenses, he would not have a chief mate's job so young unless he had shipping connections—connections who will give him hell for being loyal to a vermin-crazed skipper when he should have been wheeling and dealing with Schuster.

"Now, what I want to do is to save Skinny—and to give Turner a lesson in how not to deal with the kind of low-down conniving son-of-a-bitch his relatives send out to do their dirty work. If you don't cooperate, so help me, I'll take your head to New York on one of Turner's silver platters."

He hitched up his belt again. "Why didn't you say so, Captain Schuster? Was there anything besides the flatboat?"

"Yeah. I was just about to render inoperable the winch for the accommodation ladder. You can take care of that little detail."

He smiled, nodded and left.

I gathered up the Telex data and went to Turner's quarters. He had cleared away the drinks and had a Deck Stores tabulation in his typewriter.

"Check this info for me, will you?" I said, offhand.

He took the sheets with a preoccupied air, and I beat it down to the main deck. The small flat was being lowered aft of the starboard lifeboat. I climbed inside when it had reached the rail and was lowered into the gray current.

Skinny had anchored above the Greek, so all I had to do was sit tight, using the oar as a rudder, and let the current carry me.

The delusions people got were funny, I reflected. Vermin systematically destroying mankind. I wondered idly how many rats there really were to every human. Ten? A hundred?

I oared myself around the Greek's tilted, grass-grown bow. When I came to the rust-eater accommodation ladder, I saw four grinning piratical faces looking over the rail, the remnant of the personnel. I knew better than to try climbing the in-tilted ladder. I took the flat's bow line, made a monkey fist at the end and sent it whirling over the rail. A couple guys caught it and called down, "Okay, it's fast."

I climbed up. The guys hooked their arms under mine and heaved me over the rail, into the sour miasma of rotting copra.

A laugh rumbled and a big, broad-faced man with beard-stubble held out a grimy hand. "Cap'n Schuster. I am Karos. Come have a drink."

I followed Captain Karos into an up-slanting alleyway. The ship was incredible. Filth, grime and rust. Tiny black bugs dripped from the bulkheads. Shiny three-inch cockroaches clitter-clattered ahead of us. Going up the companionways was like climbing the tower of Pisa, but we finally reached the boat deck and Karos' quarters.

The mixture of smells in that dayroom was nearly too much for me. Garlic and strong tobacco, greasy bunk covers and urine, and the overall sourness of the cargo.

I sat down on a straight wooden chair, and Karos brought a bottle and a couple cloudy glasses out of a locker.

"The consortium, they should take the insurance money," he said, sitting at the desk. "You tell them, yes? The copra is a dead loss. You see how it is—my grabs are rusted. Eggerton must use coolies in the holds and slings on his booms. He cannot even come alongside, with our list."

I took the half-glass of paint remover he poured me. "You can trim the list."

He shrugged his shoulders and turned up his palms. "With my portside damage? I cannot compromise the seaworthiness of the vessel. When the Singapore agent tells me you are coming, I say, 'They can send a dozen Schusters. The job is impossible.'"

I managed a gulp of the booze. "How much copra you got left?"

He showed yellow teeth in a sly grin. "You know copra deteriorates. I got maybe 5,000 tons, maybe less."

Two thousand tons was considerable deterioration. I was about to say so when I noticed a change come over Karos' face. His eyes brightened and his mouth half-pursed in a tender expression.

"Leda, my little sweetheart! You have come to meet Schuster? Come, come—you are hungry, yes?"

I looked around for some sort of female—not a woman in this pigsty, but maybe a dog, cat or parrot.

Crossing the threshold of the bedroom was the biggest cockroach I had ever seen. Fully six inches of coppery armor. The creature paused, twiddled its feelers and advanced.

Karos opened a desk drawer and brought out a breadcrust. The cockroach clicked over the linoleum-covered deck, scuttled up his body and walked down his arm to the crust.

"Beautiful, isn't she?" mooned the Greek. "And she keeps everything so clean for me. Do you see copra bugs up here? Not one. All day long, she eats. All night long, she eats. Even my toenails she cleans for me while I sleep."

It was a near thing, but another gulp of paint remover settled my stomach. I put the glass down on the deck, to get the fumes away.

The crust did not hold Leda's interest. She walked across the desk and twiddled at me, flaring her shiny wings.

I unconsciously drew back. Karos laughed in a way that made me remember he had been sitting on a half-wrecked ship for weeks. Stir-crazy. He said to me,

"Don't hurt her feelings. She is human, like you or me. Only beautiful, like we are not. See that shine on her wings! See her color! She is the most beautiful thing on this ship!"

It could be true, but it was not saying much. I pulled my handkerchief out of my pocket and wiped the sweat from my neck. The roach was still preening on the desk, and I got an idea.

I gritted my teeth, threw the handkerchief over Leda, swept her up and tied the handkerchief ends tight.

Karos sprang up. I said, "Careful! Leda goes before I do. Sit down."

He sat down slowly. I dangled the squirming cloth and said, "Leda is a hostage until you bring this ship on an even keel and open the hatches. I'll keep her on the *Miss Jane* until we have the copra."

"She will starve! She will be poisoned! Eggerton's ship is no place for a cockroach! Steel washed down with lye soap! Look, I promise—if you like, I write—"

It occurred to me that I did not want to babysit a cockroach. I said, "Come there with me. We'll be back alongside as soon as your crew has trimmed the ballast tanks. Both you and Leda will get better food on the *Miss Jane*."

He rubbed his knuckles over his stubble. He was watching the handkerchief. "She will break a leg! Wait—I find a box—"

He opened a desk drawer and I prepared to

dodge a knife. But he only took out a cigar box. He dumped the cigars and pushed the box across to me. "Please!"

I saw that sweat was streaming down his face. I said, "Put the breadcrust in there, while you're at it."

He scooped the crust into the box. I put the box on my knees, loosened the handkerchief and gently laid the mess inside, closing the lid.

I stood up. "Let's go."

"We lower a boat," he said. "I do not take Leda on that wooden crate."

We went out to the starboard boat. I stood at the rail with Leda while he issued orders that were Greek to me. The two of us and a seaman got into the boat and were lowered to the water. The seaman started the motor, paused to take the flatboat under tow, and we went dead slow, back to *Miss Jane.*

The accommodation ladder was still in place. I had half-expected to see it being hoisted up by muscle power, with Turner sounding the yo-heave-ho. Apparently he had conceded that round to me.

The seaman brought the boat alongside, and Karos preceded me up the ladder. Turner was waiting for us, the irony on his face again. I said to him,

"Captain Karos has ordered his ship righted. We can shift over there in a couple hours."

The Greek ignored Turner and begged me, "Now, Schuster, you will let her out! My poor Leda!"

I handed him the cigar box. He opened it. Leda

had passed up the breadcrust and was chewing her way through my handkerchief. Turner raised his eyebrows at me. I explained.

"I promised Captain Karos and his girl friend a meal."

Turner opened the screen door of the cargo office. "Captain Karos, would you come in and sit down?" As the Greek carried the cigar box into the office, Turner added to me, "Your corruption of the bosun forced me to wake the skipper."

"Not corruption. Persuasion. He understands that New York sent me here to call the shots."

"Yes. Absolute power corrupts absolutely. What other corruption did you think I meant, Captain Schuster?"

Before I could think of a comeback, he had followed Karos into the cargo office.

I went up to the skipper's quarters. The door was on the hook. I knocked, got a groaning "Come in," and did so.

Skinny Eggerton, his pipe-cleaner body in singlet and shorts, was slumped on the settee with a wet towel around his head.

"Hello, Bob," he said weakly. "I don't know what hit me at the noon meal. I just saw you bringing that Greek aboard. It's the beginning of the end, I suppose."

"You know me better than that, Skinny. You got VHF?"

He gestured to the desk telephone. "Tell the spark what you want. Nobody else can get through on the damned equipment."

I picked up the phone and eventually located the radio officer in the chief engineer's cabin. I hoped he was sober. I said, "This is the supercargo. Buzz the agent, will you, and find out when he can get stevedores out here. Five gangs to the holds. We'll use our own crew on the booms. Soonest, hey?"

"Okay, instanter."

I hung up. Skinny was shivering. "Will I always be talking into the wind? Will mankind never see beyond its nose?"

"See what? The vermin are under control," I said. "You know every grain shipment swarms with rats. When you walk at night past the Baltimore grain elevators, you walk through rats like scuffing through autumn leaves. But the flour is okay. The flour mills deliver a pure product.

"Or take this cargo. It looks like nothing but bugs and roaches and rats. By the time it's screened, sterilized and refined, it will be completely wholesome. In three months people will be eating it in non-dairy dessert topping and feeling no ill effects."

"But the waste, Bob, the waste! The rats killed off the dinosaurs by eating their eggs. Nil population growth. They're killing us off by eating our food. Why all the yelling for birth control? Because the world is crowded? No! Dammitall, the world is empty! Travel around it—fly over it. Except for a few large cities, do you see any ant hills?

"Population explosion is a statistical myth. Did you know that the world's entire population could be contained in North Norway alone? The problem is not overpopulation but undersupply of food. Who is eating the food? The rats and mice and cockroaches! Enough food to feed the world twice over.

"It's funny, isn't it, Bob? When humans run out of food, they kill their own unborn young. They never think about killing off the rats. And scientists claim the dinosaurs were stupid! At least they didn't step on their own eggs!

"For God's sake, open that locker and get me a drink!" he finished. "Nil population growth! The vermin don't believe in nil population growth!"

I thought of the barbiturate. "Try coffee. Maybe you're too sick for alcohol."

He eyed me. "Sick with what?"

"Sunstroke. Heat prostration. Arteriosclerosis. How the hell do I know? Besides, I want coffee. I think the Greek is brewing his own moonshine in a rusty boiler."

He indicated the phone again. I ordered up a pot of coffee and sat at the table, opposite him. After a moment he said,

"What's the real condition of the Greek's derricks and grabs?"

"In good working order, of course. He hustled me inside the ship so I wouldn't see that his derrick wires are slick-greased. Before you came on the scene, he had been selling the cargo wholesale. I doubt that there's 4,000 tons left."

"You can't compel him to use his grabs? The coolies may sink through that mess like buckshot into rice pudding."

"Oh, it's not all that sloppy, inside a sun-baked hull. The coolies will dig it out all right. We can't force Karos to do anything at all with legal delays. He'll go to the last ditch before admitting his equipment was in condition to load the copra into other ships."

The messman brought the coffee. It tasted good to me, but Skinny could not swallow it. He unwound his wet turban, unkinked himself from the settee and walked unsteadily to the desk phone. He dialed and said,

"Turner? I'm half-croaked and hitting the sack again. Let Schuster bring the ship alongside and direct the rigging—I know, but there's no law against a guy being insufferable. If you ask me, there's not much to choose between the pair of you!"

He slammed down the phone and held onto the desk. "What did that kid slip me? Chloral hydrate?"

"Were you that far off the rails?"

"Probably. It's tough being an endangered species."

I saw he was in bad shape, so I got up and helped him to his bunk. He faded out as soon as his head dropped on the pillow. I switched on the bedroom fan and looked around. He had a screen fitted into his opened porthole. I made sure it was tight. I checked his bathroom and dayroom. I thought of the plumbing lines and closed the bathroom door. Finally I closed his dayroom door.

I was thinking about Leda the cockroach. She was a gal who was used to sleeping with the captain. You get that type, and they do not stay in any cargo office.

I went hunting for Turner and found him once more working on the tabulation in his typewriter. He said, "Karos has a bottle of whiskey, a pile of comic books and some plate scraping for his pet. He won't leave the cargo office because he thinks it's the best place for the cockroach—not too recently sprayed."

He paused and looked thoughtful. "How would you have got Karos to do what you wanted if the cockroach hadn't been there?"

"I play these things by ear, Mr. Turner. A slob like Karos always has a weakness—if not a cockroach, liquor or something else. I was pretty sure I would find an unbalanced man over there. He can't go off the ship without being served with writs and subpoenas. He's a prisoner, in a vulnerable mental state."

There was a hoarse shout from below. Karos came charging up the companionway. "Leda! Leda!"

I blocked his hysterical rush. He grabbed me. "She is gone! I am talking to the messman and suddenly I see the door is open and she is gone! They will kill her!"

"Calm down," I told him. "She's not wandering loose. She ducked down the first drain she found. Bring the cigar box, and we'll get her back."

He let go of me, and a different hysteria shook him. "You mean—she is climbing through the drains to Eggerton? She has throwm me aside because he is higher class, his food is better?"

I thought that was exactly what she was doing, but I said, "She's climbing topside because she wants to get back to her own bailiwick. She don't know we changed ships. She was shut up in a box."

"Yes, yes!" His face brightened. "I get the box."

Turner bulled past us with an exclamation and raced topside. I smiled to myself and lumbered after him. I caught up to him in Eggerton's bedroom. He was staring at the closed bathroom door. He said,

"I was afraid—if that thing crawled on the skipper—" He looked at the sleeping man. "But you'd already shut it out."

"Yeah. Any time I can't out-think a cockroach—"

Eggerton gave a weird, humming cry. He thrashed in the bunk, his neck muscles corded, his sleep-blind eyes rolling, and that strained noise inside his mouth.

I shook him and yelled, "Skinny! Wake up!"

His heavy lids trembled, his eyes focused on me. He relaxed. "Oh—just a nightmare, thank God! A roach—a horrible roach—"

He could not keep awake. His head fell back and he sagged into unconsciousness. I felt his pulse. It was rocking round the clock. I stood with my fingers on his wrist until sleep quieted his heartbeat.

"You made two mistakes, Mr. Turner," I said. "You gave too big a dose to a man already exhausted by anxiety. And you told me about it. I won't make trouble for you, but I know men who would."

He studied me a moment. "There are ramifications, aren't there?"

Karos was banging on the dayroom door. I let him in. He was carrying the cigar box. He rushed into the bedroom but paused at the sight of the unconscious Eggerton.

"Malarial attack," I said. "Close yourself into the bathroom and don't open the door until that cockroach is in the box."

He disappeared into the bathroom. I went into

the dayroom and stretched out on the settee. I said to Turner, "When the rustbucket is on an even keel, kindly put a note on a silver salver and—"

I paused. "Mr. Turner, why do I associate you with silver?"

"I have no idea." He walked to the door and faced me again. "Maybe just my sterling worth."

He slid out and closed the door quietly. Once again loud-mouth Schuster was caught flat-footed for a comeback. I chortled to myself before falling into a half-doze.

I was roused by Karos, talking a blue streak in the bathroom. He came out with the cigar box in his hand and a radiant expression on his face. After he left I checked the doors again and slept until the telephone rang. The main engine was throbbing, and Turner was on the bridge, ready to roll.

It was a clear, tropical twilight. In the distance, over Singapore's skycrapers, a jet angled upwards, blinking red, green and white against the pale lavender sky.

There was no wind and only a steady, predictable current. In half an hour we were tied up to the Greek, a solid padding of fenders protecting *Miss Jane*'s clean hull from contamination. Karos and Leda returned to their own ship, with a case of beer, several bottles of whiskey and a box of food stores.

The radioman relayed the message that the stevedoring company would be sending the coolie gangs the first thing the next morning. I made sure Turner and the bosun knew how the booms should be rigged, and when I saw the work well-begun under the cargo lights, I said to Turner,

"Any reason I can't leave you guys, check into a hotel room and get the first plane out tomorrow?"

Turner's face was pale. "I was hoping you would join the volunteers."

"Volunteers for what?"

"For saving the planet from vermin. The copra bugs will die, the cockroaches can be sprayed away. The rats have to be trapped. We have one hundred traps. We intend to set them in Karos' holds—and keep re-setting them all night."

"Karos is already short-loaded 3,000 tons. He's not gonna let you guys take more weight out of his ship. All right, all right," I grumbled. "If Karos agrees, find me sea boots and gloves."

I figured the whole thing was a pipe-dream. I ambled into the officers' pantry and made myself a sandwich with the left-overs in the fridge, washing the sandwich down with a bottle of beer from Skinny's stores. I felt pleased with myself. I had done my job. The trans-shipping would not proceed on its own momentum. I ambled out on deck.

Turner was coming toward me with boots and gloves. Something didn't jibe. Karos would have to answer for every ton of missing cargo. From now on, he would be breeding rats, not killing them. Wharf rats are as big as rabbits. If Turner's gang worked those traps all night, they could take out a ton of weight. Karos was not letting Turner add a ton of liability to his charge sheet.

I said nothing. I pulled on the boots and gloves and followed Turner to the other ship. The Greek had rolled back the cover on No. 1 hatch. Once again it didn't jibe. All the hatch covers should have been rolled back. Karos was forcing a card on the kid.

We looked into the hold under the glare of a cargo light. It was a third loaded, but what we saw through the stench was a low veil of flittering black bugs. The waves of motion under the veil were rats.

"We'll start with twenty traps in this hold," said Turner, letting a trap-loaded sack fall into the cloud of bugs. He threw a leg over the hatch coaming.

Karos looked at him and smiled.

"Come out of there," I said to Turner. He hesitated, and I snapped, "That's an order, Mister!"

He swung off the coaming, "What—?"

There was a sharp crack and a grinding wrench. We looked over the coaming. The hatch ladder, broken loose at one side, was twisting away. The second side cracked, and the ladder plunged into the hold. It knifed through the bugs and the rats and the copra and disappeared in the rotten swamp. Turner would not have had a chance.

The Greek crewmen bunched near Karos. They were outnumbered by our gang, who looked to Turner. He stepped up to Karos and said,

"You filed the rusted ladder too deep. It fell of its own weight. But you meant it for me, didn't you? You this-and-that son-of-a-thus-and-so-forth—"

I could not have expressed it better myself. Really good going for a kid born with a silver spoon—. There was that damned silver again. Silver?

Suddenly I had it. A heavy silver photo frame. His keen schoolboy face had looked at me from a silver frame angled on top of an office cabinet. I had noticed the photograph while his maternal grandfather—a hard nut named Alderman—was banging on an age-darkened mahogany desk and yelling, "Schuster, you're fired!"

The kid paused, having run out of breath, if not words. Karos bared his yellow teeth like one of his rats.

"You think I do not know who you are?" he spat at Turner. "You think I do not know your grandfather? Who is majority stockholder and Board Chairman of your shipping company? Alderman. Who heads the consortium that owns the copra? Alderman. Who refused to declare the cargo a dead loss? Alderman. Who wants to arrest me because I am a little short-loaded? Alderman.

"But it is more than that. Who sends Schuster here? Alderman. Because of Schuster, my nice copra business is finished. My nice home life is finished. Leda, she walks round and round, wanting to get back to Eggerton. I understand. I do not kill her. I am a poor man, a low-class man. Naturally she wants better. She breaks my heart, but I do not kill her.

"No. I think, everything is Alderman's fault. It is his heart that should break, as mine is broken. And I know how to break it. When you tell me about the rat-killing, I know you will be first down the ladder. The young gentlemen—the proud young gentlemen—they do not send, they lead. They go first into what is dirty.

"If it had not been for Schuster—!" He paused and laughed. "I am not mad at Schuster. He just works for the buck. He is a tramp, a sea lawyer, a dirty fighter. He is like me."

The kid swung and connected with Karos' front teeth. Karos threw a haymaker, but the kid ducked under it and came up with a left across the face, a right to the jaw, a left to the body.

Karo's knees wobbled. The kid followed through with a sharp uppercut. Karos' head jerked back and he folded to the deck.

The young gentleman waved his bruised hand at Karos and said to the three Greek crewmen. "Take him away." In the same breath he said to our bosun, "Rig the pilot ladder into the hold and roll back the other hatch covers."

So I had to spend all night in a fog of copra bugs, re-setting traps that sprang so often they sounded like small arms fire. I should not have said the rats were as big as rabbits. They were as big as foxes. I lost count of how many sacks of dead rats we dumped to the sharks. A ton would be an under-estimate.

About 0400 hours Eggerton returned to con-sciousness. We agreed I would leave the ship on the launch bringing the coolie gangs at 0700. Skinny was pleased with our night's work. Maybe the dinosaurs disposed of a ton of rats now and then, too.

At 0630 Skinny, Turner and I were sitting in Skinny's dayroom, having coffee. I was now eating up left-overs from the crew mess. The ship was quiet, the working day not having begun. I heard a click-scrabble and looked around.

A shiny six-inch cockroach was coming from the bedroom. Eggerton had left his bathroom door open, and Leda had crossed from the rustbucket and found her way up.

Skinny got white as death. "My God, what's that?"

Leda came purposefully across the worn carpet—not to Eggerton but to me. She stopped, twiddled, lifted her shiny wings, Turner smiled,

"Looks like she's chosen her new boy friend, Captain."

My throat went dry and I pulled my foot away from her. I always get embarrassed when some female sets her sights on me.

"I'm flattered," I told her, "but I can't afford a cockroach on my salary. Go back to Karos."

Skinny jumped up, an old news magazine rolled in his fist. "Are you out of your mind, Schuster? Talking to a cockroach!"

He swung the magazine, and Leda died in a single sickening crunch.

There was a silence. I felt pity and guilt, some-how.

"She was vermin, but she had good taste, Skinny," I said. "Even a rat is somebody's mother."

"Vermin are vermin. Do you want the planet to belong to them or us?"

Turner asked him, "From the viewpoint of Proxima Centauri, does it matter?"

We heard the toot of the approaching launch. Eggerton shook my hand, and Turner escorted me below to the accommodation ladder. He said,

"I fooled you completely, Captain. You thought I was just an ordinary ship's officer."

"I thought you were an excellent ship's officer. I still think so."

"Do you know what pleases me most? Your

manner to me has not changed since Karos blew the gaff."

"Oh, I had you placed before he spoke. Why should my manner change? The worst you can do to me is to say, 'Schuster you're fired!' and I've heard that before."

He grinned. "You specialize in being fired—in sticking your neck out—in being the fall guy. But when were you last unemployed?"

I gave him my Captain Bligh up-and-down. "Mr. Turner. If you did not have brains and guts and callused hands, you would be just another smart alec."

I caught the afternoon jet to Bangkok and points west. In 24 hours I was back at Kiel. The agent said my ship would be entering the eastern end of the Canal that afternoon. Because of the time-jog I had a few hours to live over again. I hung around Holtenau drinking beer until the ship loomed out of the Baltic fog.

When I got on board I went directly to the bridge. The chief mate, second mate, pilot and quartermaster were in the wheelhouse.

"Well, everything looks shipshape, mate," I said. "How did the discharging go?"

"Great, Cap'n. I wasn't a bit nervous about the soloing. And afterwards the flight hostess came and pinned little silver wings on my jacket."

There were snickers. I barked, "That's enough, Mister!"

I mean, he was no Turner. He was just another smart alec.

Chapter 7

January 3 . . .
Signs of Life?

The next morning Ms. Delaney—like a murderer anxious to get rid of the corpse—hurried into Operations ten minutes early so that she could replace the Rec-Pak. Alas, Mickleberry was ahead of her. She had no more than put her purse in her desk than his summons buzzed.

She reflected that the habit of thirty-six years had betrayed her. She should have gone straight from the elevator to the filing room instead of homing in to her desk. Really, she had become as much of a robot as the computers and telex.

However, what was done could not be undone. She tried to forget the Rec-Pak in her purse as she grabbed her dictation Rec-Pak and entered the office. From Mickleberry's terse 'good morning' she knew something was wrong, but her conscience was (otherwise) clear. She returned his greeting cheerfully and waited.

"Last evening, Ms. Delaney," he began, "I was astonished to find that Captain Schuster's files were not locked. After I had located a duplicate key—"

"Oh, but the cabinet *was* locked!" exclaimed Ms. Delaney. "I never would have left—" She caught herself and floundered, "Mr. Xavier and I made quite sure. I mean, it was *locked*, Mr. Mickleberry!"

His austerity softened a bit. "Perhaps the lock is defective. But you should not have let Mr. Xavier walk off with the key."

"Oh, I have the key. I'm so sorry! You never consult the files at night, so I took that one key home with me—"

"Well, fortunately the cabinet holds nothing of value. I ventured to borrow three of the shells. One moment—perhaps I should make a note in case Xavier—"

He wrote several lines on a memo sheet, gave it to her and said, "Will you put that in the file, please?"

Feeling rather giddy she said, "Yes, Mr. Mickleberry," and hastened from the office. She took key and shell from her purse and went to the filing cabinet. As soon as she opened the drawer she noticed that the whiskey was gone, but she assumed Mickleberry had removed it. He was fanatical about not contributing to anybody's delinquency. The way he had been nagging her for thirty-six years to lock her desk—!

She returned the Rec-Pak she had taken, plus Mickleberry's memo. She did not bother to count the stack. The black shells fitted so neatly into a smooth column that the eye did not immediately divide them. In thirty-six years nothing had been stolen from Operations—the possibility of theft never entered her head.

When she got back to her desk the keyboard was flashing. She dove for the phone and said breathlessly. "Operations—"

"Ms. Delaney," cut in a tired-sounding baritone voice, "Holloway here, at the ALC. Could I—?"

Space Mining's Executive Director! She switched him to Mickleberry—and was perhaps a *little* slow about switching herself out. She heard, ". . . apparently that damned fool Jardin had lost control of the entire situation . . ."

Of *what* situation? Did it mean hope for Schuster?

"Uh—excuse me—my name is Pruitt, and I had an appointment—"

She came out of her tense thoughts. The bespectacled winter-bundled man in front of her desk must be the dockyard consultant. She began, "Yes, Mr. Pruitt—"

LOCO was humming to her desk, riffling abstractedly, its circuits programmed to sort and disgorge. A chunk of mail slapped onto her blotter. "The day's loaves and fishes," said Howie Lind.

Her phone keyboard began flashing . . .

The daily rat race. She could hear the warm-up murmur within the railed enclaves. It traveled the planet, from one shipping office to the next, in a vital, life-giving wave. *Ten thousand tons soy beans out of new Orlelans . . . Vancouver needs a self-loader for sulphur . . . fifteen thousand tons titanium slag out of Fremantle . . . copper cargo, Mauretania . . . general cargo, Hong Kong . . . clean tanker for palm oil, Legaspi . . . coffee, Buenaventura . . .*

She remembered Rudyard Kipling's tribute to

the cargo ships . . . *And if any one hinders our coming you'll starve!*

She set vigorously to work, separating (as Howie would have said) the loaves from the fishes, and typing up the work that Mickleberry had put in her tray. Interchangeable robot phrases that slid easily into any context. *Thank you for . . . beg to inform you . . . regret to state . . .*

Fai k'y Atur, Khadir of Bungl'a Cush, appeared (as it were) by degrees, like the rising sun. At nine-thirty the aloof secretary phoned to request that the building's lobby be cleared and one elevator reserved for the use of the Khadir's party. Ms. Delaney referred him to the building's Security chief.

At ten o'clock the secretary again phoned, to request that there be no Drenalin and no liquor visible on the premises. "Also, the Khadir will eat only dairy and vegetable foods at the luncheon."

"What luncheon?" demanded Ms. Delaney. "The Khadir was supposed to be here an hour ago. Mr. Mickleberry is lunching out."

(This was a lie. Mickleberry always lunched at his desk, on food prepared for him by Ames and re-heated in the microwave oven in Mickleberry's private dressing room off his office.)

The haughty voice was saying, "We naturally assumed you would wish to extend the usual courtesies—"

Ms. Delaney was not taking any of *that* nonsense. She snapped, *"We* didn't call *you—you* called *us*. If *your* boss wants to see *my* boss, he'd better pick up his feet and get over here!"

She slammed down the phone, feeling better than she had felt for a month.

At ten-thirty an elevator emitted two Security guards, who stationed themselves in front of the fire doors at each end of the corridor. After a few minutes the elevator came up again and ejected a roly-poly individual in colorful robes (Ms. Delaney was reminded of her high school presentation of *The Mikado*) and a thin, dark-suited man carrying an attache case.

The murmur in Operations stopped dead. Ms. Delaney buzzed Mickleberry. "The Khadir just arrived—with a secretary."

"I have not concluded my business with Mr. Newton. Tell the Khadir to wait. If the Third World intends to pick both our brains and our pockets, they must learn that our time is their money. And, Ms. Delaney, perhaps you had better take written shorthand notes during the Khadir's interview."

Directed by the receptionist, the robe-swathed butterball and his thin secretary were bearing down upon her. They paused at her desk, and the secretary said, "His Excellency, Khadir Fai k'y Atur."

"It's unfortunate that His Excellency was delayed," said Ms. Delaney coldly. "Mr. Mickleberry is in conference. Please be seated a few moments."

The Khadir drew himself up to his full height, with the help of his jeweled platform sandals. "Dear lady, I was not kept waiting in the Kremlin!"

"Maybe they're not as busy as we are, Khadir."

Mickleberry's door opened. He ushered out Mr. Newton, looked at the theatrical get-up and said, "Khadir, come in. Ms. Delaney, if you could find a suitable chair for the Khadir—"

The Space Sharing pair preceded Mickleberry

into the office. Ms. Delaney dashed to a nearby enclave—"Oh, Mr. Sheppard, if we could have that large oak chair—" and while Mr. Sheppard gallantly lugged the chair into Mickleberry's office, she switched her calls to the receptionist, took notebook and pencil and joined the conference.

The oak chair was set in front of the desk. One of the heavily carved straight-back mahogany chairs that flanked the breakfront was moved forward for the secretary. Mickleberry shifted the interview chair away from the desk and nodded her toward it.

The Khadir settled into the oak frame, the secretary perched on the mahogany chair, Mickleberry resumed his place at the desk, Ms. Delaney sat on the sidelines in the interview chair ("the hot seat", as Schuster used to call it) and the conference was off and running.

"Please observe at the outset," said Mickleberry, "that Ms. Delaney is taking shorthand notes. In these days when the alteration—indeed the entire falsification—of tapes is commonplace, I prefer personally written records."

The secretary, who had switched on his Rec-Pak, said, "We request a copy of those notes. Shorthand can also be falsified."

Mickleberry might have been a blue-glinting iceberg. "That remark deserves no answer. However you will receive a copy of the record. Now, what is the substance of your complaint?"

The secretary began, "For the record I should like to review the terms of Space Sharing. The measurement for the tax base begins as soon as the asteroid is staked out and assayed. It is at that point that it disappears as a resource for all mankind—"

As if Space Mining could in ten thousand years make a dent in the 400 planets, 1,600 asteroids, and 50,000 lesser spheroids within the 340,000,000-mile Belt, thought Ms. Delaney, inscribing swift strokes and loops.

"—and subsequent loss due to transportation or manufacture must be borne by the research-user. The procedure is for the Q-Pod to seek out assay, and label the desired asteroids. This assay is checked by Space Sharing monitors aboard the Headquarters Wheel. Whereupon the tugs maneuver the asteroids into towing position.

"Now, Mr. Mickleberry," continued the secretary in a more severe tone, "at the time the Q-Pod broke off communication, Schuster had assayed and piton-tagged what he referred to as a string of minor spheroids in the heavy-metal range. He gave the Space coordinates and said he would—and I quote—'jockey the string into position' for the tug.

"He then ceased transmission. Several Wheel-days went by, as the Wheel waited for Schuster's 'jockeying' to conclude. Finally, at the insistence of the tugs—which had been maintaining non-official contact with the Q-Pod—the alarm was raised and the search was begun.

"When the probes and tugs went to the designated area, they found only four tagged speroids, none of them corresponding to Schuster's measurements—and all of them grossly under-assayed. At the time of his disappearance, Schuster was engaged in a shocking fraud."

"Nonsense!" snapped Mickleberry. "Only an absolute idiot would falsify measurements which would come under immediate control. The distortion and Q-Pod disappearance are part and parcel of the same problem. There must be an unexplained factor—"

"Then let Dr. Jardin and his scientists explain it."

Mickleberry put his fingertips together. "What does the Khadir—and the UN—propose to do?"

"Double the monitoring. The Khadir and his committee will travel to the Moon this summer and re-assay such speriods as the tugs have brought to Moon orbit. If their value, also, has been distorted upwards, a tax increase must be made."

"The Moon Residence is overcrowded as it is."

"You have six months to enlarge it. The Khadir will require a suite for himself, stalls for his personal dairy cattle, and cages for the sacrificial fowl."

Ms. Delaney broke the point of her pencil. Mickleberry said, "I am not competent to discuss what must be Mr. Holloway's decision. If there is nothing further—?"

The Khadir rose to his feet and gave voice. "We are not Colonials, Mickleberry, not aborigines hoodwinked by mission schools. No more rice and hallelujah."

His thick sandals glittered with gem-facets as he bounced from the office. The secretary followed him.

Ms. Delaney drew a wrath-shaky breath. "Sacrificial fowls—!"

Mickleberry smiled a dry little smile. "I doubt if it matters to the fowl whether he is sacrificed or—uh—eaten."

He sounded just like Schuster. A nervous giggle spurted tearfully from Ms. Delaney. Mickleberry continued, "Four copies of your notes, please. Mr. Holloway can pick up his copy this afternoon. The Space Mining jet is bringing him here—hopefully, at five o'clock. Since something seems to have gone awry on the Wheel, I would like the information taken in shorthand. Can you arrange to work over-time?"

"Yes, Mr. Mickleberry."

Ms. Delaney set the office to rights again, returned to her desk and dealt machine-gun fast with her shorthand notes. She wondered what had brought Holloway haring up from Canaveral.

It was precisely five o'clock when Howie Lind guided LOCO into Operations. Ms. Delaney said, "Honestly, Howie—!" Howie's sharp eyes narrowed. "Gonna work overtime on them letters? How long?"

"That does not concern *you*, Howie."

A tall executive-type man got off an elevator and bucked the stream of departing personnel. Ms. Delaney (absently thinking Howie was *such* a dawdler) buzzed Mickleberry, "Mr. Holloway—"

LOCO ingested the Out mail and hummed his guide away from the desk.

Ms. Delaney, noticing that the Space boss seemed drawn and tired around the eyes, returned Holloway's greeting and ushered him into Mickleberry's office.

She resumed her typing and suddenly was—afraid. One after another the fluorescent tubes over the enclaves had gone dark. It was *so* important to save Energy—yet she was *afraid*, sitting spotlighted under the one bright glow. She seemed to feel eyes watching her from the darkness.

Mickleberry buzzed for her, and she felt almost

hysterical relief. She took up her notebook and
pencil, switched off her light and stepped (more
quickly than usual, with those eyes at her back) into
Mickleberry's office.

(Howie Lind, intent on beating the Security patrol, raced noiselessly into the filing alcove, pin-
pointed the cabinet with his pencil-flash, unlocked
it, buried the stolen shell inside the stack, slid the
drawer shut and raced away.)

Ms. Delaney (happy to close the solid door between herself and the darkened department) saw
that Mickleberry had mixed a martini for his visitor and himself. The men were talking in a relaxed manner across the desk. At Mickleberry's
gesture she moved a mahogany chair to join the
group and sat down, pencil at the ready.

Holloway sipped the martini, set down the glass
and said, "I'll begin from my first intimation—!
Yesterday I received a phone call from Mrs.
Compton, wife of the senior astronaut on Space
Tug 4. Mrs. Compton said that their son Wendell
had received a long, rambling—and expensive, of
course—message from Compton. She thought her
husband must have been either drunk or Space-
crazed, but young Wendell realized that all messages had to clear the Headquarters operators. He
knew his father had no confidence in Dr.
Jardin—and he suspected the message concerned
the Q-Pod. He took the first number off the message's date and went through the message for a
code. He found it."

Holloway drew a notebook from his pocket,
"What young Wendell had deciphered was, 'S - C -
O - K - N - E - E - D - L - B - E - T - A - M - O - O - N.'

Which, after a little study became 'Schuster okay. Needs L (or 1) B upon arrival (ETA) Moon.' In fact, 1B is the ALC loft where the Asteroid physicists have been working. So the message is that Schuster is on his way to the Moon and will need help from the physicists on arrival.

"Immediately—time-lag permitting—I called the Wheel and demanded to know if the Tugs had received a message from Schuster. Jardin said he has a psychopath in sick bay—a technician from Space Tug 4 who claimed to have received a Morse message from Schuster via the water recycler. The man himself could not decipher Morse, and Compton was on the Wheel, so the technician suited up and beat it over there—"

Mickleberry interrupted, "Is such reception possible?"

"Apparently the usual laws of physics are not applying very well up there."

Ms. Delaney burst out, "Oh, Mr. Mickleberry, I recall distinctly my old uncle saying he used to get KDKA through the glass flower vase on the door frame of his Hupmobile!"

The men smiled. Holloway remarked, "Radio reception has been claimed for tooth fillings, also. But it's easy to picture the details of the Wheel incident—Jardin dismissing the technician as mentally unstable, while Compton grimly kept his mouth shut and returned to the Tug—and the water recycler—as soon as he could."

"Were you able to speak to Compton?"

"No. Space Tug 4 had lit out—AWOL—as soon as Compton's message to his son had cleared the Wheel transmitter. Headquarters monitors discovered that Tug 4 had scrounged extra supplies from the other Tugs before blasting off what seems to be an informal and insubordinate rescue mission. They are a month behind Schuster—but a Tug can easily overtake the Q-Pod, which is designed for Wheel-based local work."

"Can their navigating be that exact?"

"Well, they're both heading for the same dot in Space—and both Schuster and Compton are navigation wizards."

There was a silence. Mickleberry remarked, "I wonder why Schuster did not return to the Wheel, instead of attempting a Moon journey in a Q-Pod."

"I assume the physical anomalies—whatever they are—simply drove him out of the Belt. Mars is off-limits. His only recourse was to ration supplies and attempt the Moon. The other Tugs are, naturally, refusing to make any mining probes."

"And Dr. Jardin?"

Holloway lifted his hands in a helpless gesture. "You know Jardin—more concerned about the insubordination—and about covering his own inadequacy—than researching the trouble. We should never have taken a chance on him—but he's superb with protocol and handling theorists and politicians—"

Mickleberry asked, "Your conversation went through scramblers?"

"Of course. My God, we can't let a hint of mutiny or unknown forces get to the media! I've spoken to the wives of the men on the Tug and the Q-Pod— emphasized that ill-timed publicity could start a lot of irresponsible Space probes that would interfere with our communications and perhaps cost their

husbands their lives. The women understood—
they know Space conditions. Schuster is still missing, believed dead—and Space Tug 4 is still at the
Wheel, officially."

Mickleberry coughed. "By the way, Schuster has
recorded some confidential Rec-Paks. I noticed a
label concerning Jardin. Perhaps you would be
interested—?"

"Very interested."

Mickleberry turned to Ms. Delaney. "Would you
fetch the Jardin shell? And Mr. Holloway's copy of
our interview with the Khadir?"

Ms. Delaney rose and left the office. Switching
on lights as she went, she arrived at the cabinet,
turned her key—

The cabinet was unlocked!

Ice water ran down her spine. She opened the
drawer. Had the stack been that high in the morning? She remembered Xavier had counted eight
shells. She counted five—Mickleberry had taken
three. So nothing was missing. Was the lock really
defective?

She found the Jardin shell, took the pencil from
her chignon and added the label to Mickleberry's
memo, closed—and locked—the cabinet.

She decided not to mention the lock in front of
Holloway. Later, she could report it to Mickleberry. It was not that anything had been *taken*—

Chapter 8

January 3 (cont.) . . .
Holloway Reads Aloft

At seven-thirty that evening Charles Holloway felt the Douglas jet level off its climb. He had been deep in thought—so deep that his features seemed to recede in sympathy. His eyes gleamed dully from concave shadows. His cheekbones stood out against pallid, strained cheeks. He unfastened his seat belt and watched the lights of Long Island slide out of sight under the night clouds. He had burned a lot of Space Mining fuel to speak to Mickleberry personally.

He realized it had been the need for personal contact that had driven him to New York. For six months he had been talking into a void—with the time lag getting longer and longer. Yesterday it had taken forty-five minutes between question/answer with Jardin. He had flown to New York—and would be back at Canaveral—in less time than his total conversation with Jardin.

The Space lag was wearing him down—pulling him out like taffy. Schuster had the right idea—go out into Space and be where the action was. Do the immediate job—cope with the immediate problem—let the other guy be stretched like taffy. Waiting was always worse than acting.

Schuster could have had the Executive Director job at Space Mining—and had refused it. He wanted to quarterback on the field, not coach on the sidelines. And he could never look at Jardin without wanting to drown him in a bucket.

Holloway smiled as he took his Rec-Pak unit and the Schuster tape from his briefcase. He in-shelled the cartridge that had been in the unit and inserted the Jardin tape. Above his head the cabin air nozzle was whining. He reached up and modified it.

Schuster's voice—as if the troubleshooter and Holloway were shoulder-to-shoulder—began, "If I was the guy calling the shots for my shipowners . . ."

● ● ●

ACTIONS SPEAK LOUDER

If I was the guy calling the shots for my shipowners, I would keep myself working at sea, year in and year out. Schuster, the Flying Dutchman. But the docs have to get into the act and haul me ashore once a year for a vacation.

Sometimes I can finagle Mickleberry in Operations into keeping me afloat a few weeks longer.

On this particular winter day, I was optimistic because Mickleberry himself had called me to his office after I had finished my troubleshooting assignment aboard a liquid gas tankship. I figured he had another job too dirty for anybody else.

I was right—but not in the way I had thought.

I dropped my suitcase beside the receptionist's desk and barged into Mickleberry's office. He waved me to a chair. His parched face gave me a thin smile. He began,

"I assume, Captain Schuster, you are aware of the Company's recent investment in Space Mining, Incorporated?"

"Yeah, sure," I said cautiously. I plow a percentage of my salary back into Company stock, and I had read about Space Mining in the latest quarterly report.

"The investment was made on the assumption that Space Mining would move into action on the Moon, as soon as the various government licenses were granted," continued Mickleberry in his dry voice, "but all licenses were in order several weeks ago, and no action has been forthcoming."

"They're developing difficult real estate."

"They are nowhere near an approach to the real estate." Mickleberry placed his fingertips together. "Since our medical department has recommended that you be relieved of sea employment for six weeks, Captain Schuster, Mr. Bennington is requesting that you look into the Space Mining delay."

"Me!" I barked, surprised. Bennington was the Company's Chairman of the Board. Until that moment, I had thought he was a smart businessman. I went on, "I don't know a god-damned thing about space!"

"The issue is not space but a bureaucratic bottle-neck. The launching site at Cape Canaveral—and you will kindly, while in Florida, refer to the Cape as Canaveral, not Kennedy—as I say, the launch-ing site is ready and waiting. The subcontractors are meeting their delivery deadlines—"

I interrupted, "NASA is providing a dockyard?"

He winced. "Not dockyard, captain. Space Min-ing has leased ground on the government reserva-tion for their ALC."

"ALC?"

"Assembly/Launch Complex"

"And Bennington thinks I can get the SOBs off their ASS?"

Mickleberry choked briefly. "You are an expert in—uh—expediting desired results. Will you ac-cept the assignment?"

I thought it over. If I had to take a winter vaca-tion, I could just as well spend it at Cape Canaveral. Besides, as a Company stockholder, I was kind of pleased at being able to shove my oar into a Com-pany investment.

If the job stretched out longer than I wanted, I could always get myself fired. I was also an expert in getting fired.

I said finally, "Okay, I'll give it a whirl. How do I get down there?"

Mickleberry handed me an airline envelope. "You can catch the next Orlando flight from LaGuardia. I will phone Dr. Jardin about your flight time."

"Who's Dr. Jardin?"

Mickleberry disregarded this. "Your flight leaves in one hour. Clear jets, captain!"

Whatever that meant. I took it as dismissal, grabbed my suitcase and was lucky enough to hail a cab at the building entrance.

On the flight to Orlando I reviewed what I knew about mining on the Moon. There had been a very handsome color spread of future operations in that quarterly report. The kilometer-wide space wheel in Moon orbit . . . the magnetized ore-carts docking at the wheel with their Moon-cargoes of bauxite, titanium, iron, silicates, crust-oxygen . . . the hub factories and the spoke farms terraced with Moon dirt. (Apparently hydroponics was Out and Moon dirt was In) . . . the bat-wing space shuttle on this Janus/Double-Thrust rockets . . .

I had never in my life heard of anything quite so screwy.

I deplaned at Orlando. Nobody was waiting for me in the airport terminal, and no message had been left at the airline desk.

One hell of an outfit, I reflected. They were planning to put The Big Rock Candy Mountain into orbit, but they could not lift a guy from Orlando to Canaveral/Kennedy.

While I debated about renting a car a hand touched my sleeve and a friendly voice asked, "Are you Captain Schuster?"

I turned to look at a shipshape young chap—ruddy face, healthy eyes, curly brown hair foaming over his forehead. He wore a white cotton pullover and college-boy jeans. I said,

"Yeah, I'm Schuster. Did Dr. Jardin send you?"

"No. I'm extemporizing. I'm a CRM, and your flight data transited my panel. When Dr. Jardin event/cancelled, I knew he was stonewalling, so I put a rec on a car. This your suitcase?"

I nodded. He picked the suitcase up and led me to a car illegally stationed in the Arrivals lane. He slung the suitcase into the rear seat, I tossed my overcoat on top of it, and we dived into the car and pulled away fast before we got a cop astern.

I had not understood a single damned thing the young guy had said. As I eased the seat-belt straps around me, I began.

"You say you're a CRM. Got a name?"

"Yes, but you won't want to clutter your brain-banks with it. In a project of this size, the function and not the identity is important. For example," he continued as we bowled along the wide, flat toll road, toward the oncoming night, "I'm a Communication Relay Master, working Time Phase 2. An event in my reference frame is coded CRM2."

In other words, I reflected, the kid was like a ship's radio officer. I went on hacking through the word jungle. "Who's Dr. Jardin?"

I thought the kid would run off the road. "Why, Dr. Jardin ideated/implemented the entire project! How can you be ignorant of his identity?"

"I figured it was the function that was important, not the identity."

This playback stopped him cold.

He activated the headlights. I said nothing more. I had already pegged CRM2 as a well-meaning young fellow. In the matter of my arrival he had acted with initiative and good sense. I was betting he would level with me faster if I did not push him too hard.

I had read him rightly. We drove for a while. Then he said, "Dr. Jardin is a sensitive man—a genius—but I feared he was not considering the consequences of refusing Mickleberry's call. I told Mickleberry that Dr. Jardin was in conference, and I took the message about your flight time. Ordinarily Dr. Jardin would have met you with his private helicopter. The best I could do was to find a CRM to finish my shift while I scrounged a car from the pool and drove over here.

"Don't get me wrong, Captain Schuster. I'm not criticizing Dr. Jardin. He's a terrific scientist. This project is like—well, Instant Utopia. A space colony planned for perfection—a place without disease or crime or poverty—"

He took a deep breath at the beauty of it all. He was young, of course. He would learn the hard way, like the rest of us. He went on,

"Perfection can't be built piecemeal in space. It's like a jigsaw puzzle put together on Earth, carefully separated and lifted into space, and reassembled in orbit.

"But after Bennington's takeover, this orderly process was disturbed. Bennington wants to hurry the Moon mining so the Company will make money. Dr. Jardin hates commercialism."

"Oh? A guy who can meet guests with his private chopper ain't giving away his services."

Another silence. I was dog tired, fighting for a toehold on a bureaucratic ALC. The way I figured it, if Jardin was dodging the Company, it was because he was deliberately responsible for the work-lag. If the foul-up had been inadvertent, beyond his control, he would have jumped at the chance to justify himself.

Probably Jardin was, as the kid had said, a terrific scientist. Bennington would go slow about removing him, especially since other key men might quit in protest. I had to outflank Jardin—put a wedge between him and those key men—isolate him so that he could not block our countermeasures.

The only wedge I had so far was the young man sitting beside me, I began honing him down. I asked, "What's your name? I can't keep calling you CRM2."

"Herbert Douglas. Mostly, just Herbie."

"You gonna get the heave-ho for meeting me?"

"No. When Jardin event/cancels, the CRM can make an assessment/decision. Refusing calls is a genius-reflex. Dr. Jardin expects the CRM to utilize existent directives. There was no directive on Schuster, and Dr. Jardin is opposed to sequential logic. He wants every event to be handled as a discrete space/time segment."

"Spell that out, will you, Herbie?"

"Sequential logic would have said, 'Since Dr. Jardin does not want to talk to Company executives, he naturally will not want to have Captain Schuster at the ALC.' But discrete analysis assesses Company/executives/Schuster without connecting them in any way."

No wonder the project was not moving. Each unit was like a train of disconnected freight cars.

I gave the problem more thought. Despite the double-talk, Herbie had stepped way out of line in meeting me. In issues like power politics, Jardin's logic probably was as sequential as the next guy's. Of course, maybe Herbie was the kind of secretary/assistant who can save an impulsive boss from embarrassment without being hauled over the coals later.

The closer Herbie was to Jardin, the more leverage I would need to get him on my side. I remarked,

"You're really all fired up about putting this space colony in orbit, hey?"

He said quickly, "But I don't want a botch job because of the profit motive."

"Well, Herbie, when I say the Company wants a productive investment, I'm not talking about ripoffs. I'm talking about Moon ore being mined as quickly and efficiently as possible. The result will, we hope, improve the quality of Earth life, but it will not bring Instant Utopia."

I paused, then said seriously, "If you demand Utopia, this project will never be anything but a bankrupt boondoggle."

He kept his eyes on the road. I went on, "I was sent here because Jardin is not delivering the goods. He is not mining Moon ore."

Herbie asked uncertainly, "Does that mean the ALC personnel have to choose up sides? The Company versus Dr. Jardin?"

"You're utilizing sequential logic," I reminded him. "Let's take the action in discrete space/time segments. To begin with, all I want is a conference with the department heads—and with Jardin, if he'll come. Can you arrange it?"

He thought it over. "As a CRM I can relay your request to the relevant function/persons. Should they bring data files?"

"If each guy wants to hand me a summary, I'll glance through it. But it's gotta be short."

He drove steadily through the headlight-sculptured darkness. I thought about the paper-work, and naturally I went to sleep. When I woke up, the car was stopped. I was slumped uncomfortably, the shoulder sling of the seat belt was digging into my collarbone, and my mouth was as dry as Moon dirt.

I straightened up. The car was parked in front of a motel office, and Herbie was gone. I unfastened the car belt and unfroze my stiff muscles.

Herbie came back, opened the car door and handed me a room key. He smiled, "We're just south of the Kennedy Center. I took the liberty of checking you into a room."

I uncrammed myself from the seat and accepted the motel key. I stood, kind of groggy, and watched Herbie drag my suitcase and coat out of the car. I remarked, "I must have been sawing wood pretty hard."

He grinned. "Well, if I ever go into orbit with you, captain, I hope your sleep-tank is sound-proofed."

The Old Man in orbit? That would be the day. Thirty thousand feet was my ceiling.

Herbie went on, "I'll do my best to promote the conference. A car will pick you up at nine tomorrow morning."

I asked, "Can you be detached from your CRM panel? I need a guy like you to take soundings for me."

He said slowly, "I'm really a Jardin man, Captain Schuster. I just about worship the guy."

"All the better. I don't want to fight with Jardin. I want to help him get this show on the road."

Herbie smiled, "Since you put it that way, I can

formulate a replacement request through PP. Dr.
Jardin does not demand any specific function/
person on CRM2."

Jardin was shaping up as a real educated idiot, I
reflected. I took my suitcase and overcoat from
Herbie, found my Earth-level sleep-tank and hit
the hay. I felt that if I had to listen to any more
space jazz, I would blow my stack.

Cape Canaveral is imposing, of course—a vast
pancake crisscrossed with cement roads and dot-
ted with launching sites. Space Mining Inc. had
been allotted what looked like a handkerchief as
Herbie drove us toward it the next morning. The
nearer we came, the bigger it got, and we were
ant-sized by the time we stepped into the multi-
staged assembly hangar.

On the ground stage was a plywood-and-glass
room that apparently was used for jawboning. Battered folding chairs were set out on the cement
deck. They faced a slightly raised platform with a
table and more chairs. Behind the table was a
blackboard on an easel.

That I had achieved a conference right off the
bat must have been due to Herbie's persuasions.
He could not let his idol Jardin get in trouble with
the takeover management.

Herbie ushered me into the empty room and
said, "Group coordination of assessment procedures may necessitate a temporal readjustment."

"Herbie, do me a favor and knock off the pig-
Latin."

"But, captain, the sea also has a work-related
language!"

"Work-related, yes. It gets space-cute only in small-boat marinas. I once heard the owner of a fifteen-foot motorboat yell to his wife to freshen her nip, and I didn't know which way to look. All the guy meant was that the boat's mooring line was chafing at the bow."

Herbie clutched his curly mane and stuttered out an unpracticed laugh. It looked as if humor was in short supply at Space Mining. From what Herbie had said about Dr. Jardin, I wondered if I was getting into a cult-bureaucracy. If so, my first step would be to shake the cultists until their teeth rattled.

About a dozen guys in white boiler suits were trooping into the hangar, three of them bearing solid chunks of paperwork. Herbie pulled himself together and surveyed the gang through the glass. "The chiefs—but not Dr. Jardin, yet."

As the chiefs filed into the conference room, the three leaders piled their data chunks on the table. Herbie introduced these three first, by function not name, "PPC—MBFC—TTAC—"

The rest of the crowd was more alphabet soup. They shook my hand and sat on the scattered chairs. I realized I would have to put the operation on a name basis as soon as I could. I suspected that part of the work-lag had come about because Jardin had reduced his team to human hardware.

A small vehicle like a golf cart puttered into the hangar and stopped. The driver got out and came into the conference room.

Even in a white boiler suit, Jardin had presence. Although he was not really stout, there was a softly benevolent plumpness to the skin on his face and hands. His cheeks were apple red, and his eyes were the dreamy amber of a satisfied cat.

He favored his team with a gracious nod. He gave me a condescending smile and a space sermon. "Captain Schuster, previous data exchanges between the Company and ourselves have obviated the necessity for verbalization of our common goal of space penetration according to the principles of Human Rights. Across the relevant horizontal levels—"

I let him rave while I watched his team. If they all agreed that it was the Company versus Human Rights, I was up the creek. I had intended to hit the Space Mining line like Ohio State rolling over Indiana, but I saw I would have to pull my punches. Most of the team were, like Herbie, giving Jardin all their respectful attention. Some were poker-faced, taking a wide-angle view.

And one guy—TTAC— was watching me watching them.

Jardin was droning on, "—further breakdown of the vertical structure. The data sheets have been supplied you."

I woke up and looked at the paperwork on the table. I remembered that TTAC had put his chunk on top of the others. I lifted it off and said, "Well, Dr. Jardin, if I knew how to read and write, I'd be applying for a better job. What's this stuff? Anybody care to verbalize?"

As I had expected, TTAC spoke up. "That's the data for a torus."

I grinned, "Jeez, I didn't ask for my horoscope!"

Nobody cracked a smile. Jardin's benevolence got a little tight. He said, "Torus Technology/

Assembly! The space wheel! The colony satellite!"

"Yeah, but why do we have to build a satellite?" I interrupted. "What's wrong with the satellite that's already up there?"

They all stared at me. Jardin said, "Captain, there is no satellite—!"

"Since when is the Moon not a satellite?"

"The Moon can't be colonized!" exclaimed Jardin. "It should be held open for common use by all nations able to reach it! The Moon can't be adjusted to simulate Earth gravity, in the manner of a torus! The Moon has a darkness phase! It can't be sunlight oriented! It can't—"

"It can't be shot down."

They stared at me again. I said, "You bleeding-heart Utopians can talk about Human Rights and Common Use—but over my dead body is the Company gonna invest my hard-earned dough in a billion-dollar clay pigeon!

"A space wheel a kilometer in diameter is a sitting duck," I went on. "A real setup as a military target. Vulnerable on all sides to meteors and space debris. Making no sense economically. The ore is on the Moon. The dirt for agriculture is on the Moon. Use them on the Moon."

TTAC spoke up. "It's not Utopian to wonder about the Russian reaction to a western usurpation of Moon territory."

"Nuts. The Russians would welcome an American colony as a precedent for their own Moon expansion—if the time ever comes when they can put a man on the Moon—and if he doesn't defect the minute he lands there. Forget the Reds. They can't do a damned thing except bang their shoes on the table and try to outbluff us."

This got a mixed reception. I figured I would rather deal with hawks and doves than function/robots.

Again, the TTAC recovered the ball. "Leaving politics aside, captain, gravity was a factor in the choice of the torus. Space workers should not be asked to live in uncomfortable, debilitating environments."

"Well, Mr. —? Can I have a name?"

"Holloway."

"Mr. Holloway. I admit that human muscles will need training to work on the Moon—just as they need training to work at sea—but they won't atrophy. The Moon-walks have already proved that it takes as much muscular skill to keep from falling up as to keep from falling down. The old idea that muscles would grow flabby in Moon gravity has gone by the board. They have to be used a different way, that's all."

"What about the Moon's dark phase?"

"Well, what about it?" I returned. "As I understand it, any space structure will have to be completely shielded against cosmic rays. Even on a wheel, nobody will be sunbathing."

An amused murmur loosened up the gang, but Herbie reddened at my dumb remark. Holloway explained, "I was referring to the storage of solar energy during the Moon's long night."

"Solar energy! It's all over the damned place! Is the Sun any brighter next to a torus than next to the Moon?"

"And where would you place the solar energy station?"

"The Company is not paying me to interpolate a Nautical Almanac and decide where to moor a Moon energy station. That's your department. How much station hardware have the subcontractors delivered?"

There was an uneasy pause. I saw I had hit upon a divisive issue. Jardin seemed to go on the defensive. He said, "Delivery must mesh with in-siloing. We cannot build a space colony one piece at a time."

I had always supposed everything—including Rome—had been built one piece at a time. I sense my comments were not wanted, so I let the matter rest and skimmed the next section off the data pile. "What's this?"

The MBFC answered. "Medical/Biological Factors. Physical requirements for colony members—space hygiene—pathogenic precautions. I would advise strongly against cutting corners in MBF."

"Are you a medical man or an engineer, Mr.—?"

"Dr. Grant. Medical."

"Dr. Grant, for all I've ever read about the Moon trips—especially from the astronauts' own accounts—95% of NASA's physical and mental vivisections were unnecessary and had no bearing whatsoever on the work that was done."

"That's a narrow view, captain. The NASA tests provided a wealth of research material."

"Maybe so. But Space Mining has a narrow budget. We can't afford to subsidize medical research. MBF's job will be to make sure that employees are fit. A space worker must be sound in wind and limb. No heart trouble, ulcers or hernias.

"But—," I paused for emphasis and included the whole group, "—if you guys think it is possible—or advisable—to keep the common cold out of your Instant Utopia, you are absolutely dead wrong, criminally wrong."

They were staring at me again. I went on, "The best way to destroy a space colony is to make it germ-free, disease-free and sterile. A guy living in that sort of artificial atmosphere will die in a week if he returns to the Earth.

"I know what I'm talking about—know damned more than the high-domed theorists—because I roam around the planet on a man-in-the-street basis. Seamen like me have every germ on the planet inside them, continually immunizing them. A very smart port doctor in Madras told me once, 'It takes a lot to kill a seaman.'

"But just one breath of nonsterile air will send an American tourist grabbing for his paregoric. American cruise tourists, coming from their hygienic, plastic-wrapped, supermarket milieu, go ashore in countries where oven-warm bread is delivered hand-to-hand, the meat is sold with a layer of flies, and the streets are sewers. As long as these tourists go from their air-conditioned sterile ships to their air-conditioned sterile Hilton in their air-conditioned sterile limousines, they're okay.

"But the first time they step onto the street, they come down with nausea, diarrhea, common virus infections—and blame the local water instead of recognizing that their own overprotected isolation is what has made them sick. Sterility is not natural to this planet."

Before Jardin's team could fall on me like a ton of bricks, I added, "Now, I want to make two qualifications. First, I agree that Earthmen should not bring Earth diseases to other space life. The Polynesians were nearly wiped out by the smallpox brought to the Pacific by European whalers. That was a tragedy that must not be repeated in space.

"But the Moon colony will have just ordinary germ-filled Earthmen. They'll catch colds and minor and major diseases—like the rest of us—and maintain the immunities built up since all of us apes came down from the trees.

"The second qualification I want to make is that I'm not—repeat not—saying that smallpox is good for us. I'm all for eradicating every disease as smallpox finally has been eradicated—*provided the eradication is species-wide in scope.* Then everybody is on the same immunity level. It would be a terrible mistake to make a space colony into an isolation chamber where a sneeze would kill the colonists like flies."

Dr. Grant asked, "Will the Company erase our psychiatric program?"

"I don't know the extent of your program. We have a staff psychologist who interviews guys who suddenly start putting their pants on backwards, but I can't see the need for in-depth head-shrinking. I mean, let's face it—the world's pioneers are not generally well-adjusted, rational types. Neither Dan'l Boone nor Davy Crockett would have scored high with the NASA shrinks, and the West was explored by weirdos who were one step ahead of a sheriff and/or a butterfly net.

"In my book, anybody volunteering for the Moon has to be nuts from the word Go. If we start examining sanity, we won't have any work crews at all."

Herbie protested, "Oh, no, captain! Everybody working on the ALC has applied to ride the shuttles! All of us want to blast off for the Moon!"

I ducked my chin and eyed Herbie gravely. There was a burst of laughter. I grinned, "Yeah, I was overstating—to make a serious point. The psychiatric norms for suburbia are not necessarily relevant in space."

Herbie subsided, but he was not happy. I tackled the last chunk of data. "What's the rest of the bad news?"

The PPC said, "Personnel/Payroll. And my name is Lyle."

"Giving you guys the third degree, am I? Well, Mr. Lyle, why so many Personnel tabulations? Has there been a check on redundancies?"

Lyle said stolidly, "Given the traveling-unit system, our work force is barely minimal."

"What's a traveling-unit system?"

Jardin resumed the floor, beaming. I could tell he had invented the traveling unit and thought it was the cherry on top. "It coordinates the rotation of the shuttle schedules. In succession, an assembly unit, service unit, countdown unit and space unit will work the Alpha shuttle. Upon finishing the Alpha, the assembly unit moves to the Beta, the other three units traveling to the Beta in due course, according to function. Meanwhile, since the Alpha will be returning while the Beta is blasting off, we have a third intermediary set of units to service and man the second Alpha trip. When the units go from the Beta to the—"

"Hold it!" I ordered. "I seem to count twelve units niffnawing around two shuttles."

"Think of the units as a conveyor belt of discrete segments keeping the shuttles in constant operation."

I thought of it as progressive bankruptcy. I asked, "Why do we need separate units for each shuttle? Is there so much variation in technical competence?"

They looked at each other. Lyle said to me, "We don't understand your question, captain."

"One peculiarity of space research and construction is the high level of formal education demanded by all aspects of the work. I assume that the men in one unit are technically as competent as those of another. You can shift men from one unit to the next without difficulty."

Lyle considered. "An engineer tends to specialize—to know more about certain systems than others, but—yes, generally the personnel can be interchanged."

"That being the case—and accepting the fact that all of you have applied to ride the shuttles—is there any reason we can't put together an all-round team that can assemble, service, lift-off and work in space? One slightly-expanded unit instead of a conveyor belt?"

"Technically there's no barrier. But you would take great risk in eliminating the backup checks possible with the interlocking units."

"Well, Mr. Lyle, one reason why submarines have so few disasters is that the guy responsible for closing the topside hatch is inside the sub. When the skipper orders, 'Take her down,' he doesn't worry overmuch about the function/ person forgetting his duty. If a shuttle worker knew that his name was likely to be pulled from the hat for the Moon lift-off, he would be double-checking to save his own skin and would not be so likely to goof off and let the next guy find the errors.

"But personnel is a kinky problem I have to go into later." I restacked the data files with a pleasant sense of relief and accomplishment. "I want to thank all of you for coming and clueing me in. You've been a big help."

TTAC Holloway doubled over with a haw-haw. Some guys smiled, but the rest looked poleaxed. Herbie's bewildered eyes were begging Jardin to set the meeting to rights, but Jardin apparently was not at his best with the in-fighting. All he could say was,

"Captain, I am amazed that the Company would send a spokesman who knew so little about this space project."

"Dr. Jardin, the Company doesn't give a damn about your project. They sent me here to channel your resources into mining Moon ore—a limited, specific, economically feasible operation."

I faced the department chiefs and went on, "A financial takeover is tough, I admit, but are you and the Company really at cross-purposes? Would a compact, productive Moon colony be such a bad first step into space? Would it violate any basic

Human Rights or anybody's Pursuit of Happiness?

"I don't say a torus will always be a lot of bull. To spin a future colony to Mars—fine and dandy. But not now."

Herbie had anti-Schuster feelings written all over his pan. I still wanted him as my liaison man with the departments. I said to Jardin,

"Thanks very much for your cooperation—and for letting me commandeer a CRM who must be one of your most loyal and most valuable assistants."

"I'm a Judas," blurted Herbie, red as a beet, to Jardin. "Schuster said all he wanted was a conference. He said he wanted to help you get the show on the road. Now he can find another CRM."

Even Jardin's fan club smiled at Herbie's whole-hearted devotion to a lost cause. With more humanity and less jargon, the plump scientist said to Herbie,

"We all assessed the Company's takeover motives wrongly, and you are no more at fault than the rest of us. Had I accepted Mickleberry's call—or had you refused to aid Captain Schuster—the result would have been the same. This conference would have been inevitable."

Herbie brightened. Jardin went on, "We must now work within Company framework to ensure that mercantile ethics do not override human ethics. No need for further disorientation, CRM2. You have established a familiarity basis for future assessment/decision and ideate/implement more effectively than a replacement."

This rebuttal scored a point for the Utopians, but I figured I still had managed to get between

Jardin and his department heads. It was not only that I reminded them of the Company's financial clout. I had proposed an alternate program to get the shuttles into space. Men can become so frustrated over a logjam that a stick of dynamite looks like salvation.

The meeting broke up with another round of handshaking. Herbie trailed me out to our car. I said matter-of-factly, "I gotta send a coded telegram. Where's the nearest Western Union office?"

Herbie struggled with his ideals and decided he could not make the grade. "Even for Dr. Jardin's sake, I can't work with you, captain. You lied to me and used me. I think you're contemptible."

"You're not looking at the whole picture," I told him. "I warned you, you know, that you could not demand Utopia. Yes, you smoothed my path to Jardin—but you smoothed Jardin's path even more. If he had continued stonewalling, he would have been O-U-T. You were his best friend in the matter, not his Judas.

"Bear with me, Herbie," I went on. "When the first shuttle lifts for Moon orbit, maybe you won't take such a negative view of the Old Man."

He was thoughtful. "What do you want to send in code? What's so important?"

"Bennington has to lease an unused NASA pad so that we can begin preshipping the nuts and bolts into Moon orbit. The energy station has to be positioned above a lunar pole before the shuttles go out there."

"But, Captain Schuster, you heard Dr. Jardin say the station hardware had been in-siloed!"

"Then we'll just have to out-silo it. With a second

launch pad and a transfer of a few niffnawing shuttle units—"

"But how can you be sure that one all-round team can build and work the shuttles?"

"Because generalization—not specialization—has been the historical pattern for all successful pioneering. Do you know who the old Vikings really were, Herbie?" As he shook his head, I continued, "They were just a bunch of guys who lived around the same *vik*—another word for *fjord*. During the winters they all tramped into the forest, cut down trees, dragged the logs home, split them into boards and built longboats. In the spring they launched the boats and piled aboard, every man-jack of them able to sail, row, repair, fight, and cook *lapskaus*."

"But, captain, you can't compare half-savage boatbuilders and raiders with men trained in the subtleties of modern engineering!"

"Herbie, ask any naval architect to name the most brilliantly engineered vessel. He'll tell you it was the longboat. No hull before or since has combined such strength, elasticity, or speed through heavy seas. And it was built with dull iron, and stone whittlers. Assembling a space colony from premanufactured hardware is like falling off a log, compared to the skill demanded by that half-savage engineering.

"The all-round Viking teams erupted into a world of specialists—warriors, scribes, peasants—and they took that world like Grant took Richmond. Before the Black Death wiped them out, the Vikings ruled the seas from Greenland to the West to Constantinople in the East.

"When men go into space, they must go as an all-round, self-contained gang, or else they won't survive in a totally hostile environment. Although why they have to leave a pretty good planet for a lunar ash heap," I added, "I will never know."

"You are including yourself out of space travel?"

"That's a ten-four, kid. In a pinch I might consider flying Concorde. But the Janus/Double-Thrust booster? No way!"

Herbie laughed. As I had hoped, he was a good-natured guy and was willing to believe the best of everybody—even of that sly old bastard, Schuster.

For a week, SpaceMining Inc. lay hove-to, with backed sails. I had made my report to Bennington, and I assumed Jardin had done the same. Because I liked Herbie too much to pull another rug out from under him, I was glad I could hold off asking for Jardin's removal. I had seen at the conference how I could bypass Jardin and work with the department heads. Jardin was a nitpicker in practical matters, but he was a prestige asset. Investors like a big name as a company director. I decided there was no urgent reason for getting rid of Jardin.

It was a bad, almost fatal decision. Yet I made it according to the best evidence I had at the time.

During that week of waiting for Bennington's word, Jardin kept aloof—a genius-reflex, maybe. I hustled around the ALC buildings like a grass-root politician, selling the Moon colony.

I had to sell it. I could not build those shuttles myself. By the end of the week I had found out the technical changes necessary to the new program.

The winged shuttles were strictly Earth orbit vehicles. We would need small jet-dollies to discharge the shuttle cargo and jockey it down to the Moon.

The torus components would have to be reworked into surface structures. The entire wheel was of interchangeable parts, so I foresaw no expensive alternations. The farm-area spokes could be laid down as they were, wherever a Moon sea could be bulldozed into a spoke contour. I was in favor of decentralizing all areas, to spread the risk in case of a meteor strike or other catastrophe.

Bennington issued the go-ahead for the Schuster Plan and leased the required NASA pad. I immediately called for a parts inventory to determine how soon we could shoot up the orbiting energy station.

The inventory computers replied NO PARTS AVAILABLE. The Space Mining warehouses were jammed to the rafters and insured for more than Fort Knox—and there were no parts available?

The time had come for me to find out if the department chiefs were for me or against me. I buttonholed TTAC Holloway and said, "We gotta talk. Someplace away from these damned phones."

He eyed me. "Will the Company pay for the drinks?"

"Yeah, Mickleberry is used to my representation tabs. Is your car here? Will you drive?"

"With pleasure."

We wound up in a Cocoa Beach bar. Holloway turned out to be a congenial rye-drinker, intrigued by the idea of a space wheel but not closed to other colonization methods. He explained about the nonavailable parts.

"Jardin was computer-programming the shuttles to deliver optimum loads at specific time periods. Having stowed ships, you understand stowage problems—as when Port A's cargo is underneath Port B's, so you have to move Port C's in order to move B's in order to get at A's."

I laughed, and Holloway went on, "Jardin intended that the wheel spokes, the hub, and the power satellite would be assembled simultaneously. Thus, theoretically, it would be more efficient to have each shuttle cargo contain the spoke, hub, and power components needed simultaneously at that time/stage.

"Well, captain, the entire project ran to several million components, from microscopic transistors to steel girders. The computer obligingly gave a time/stage breakdown, but this implied that each of the several million components would be delivered according to plan. The subcontractors are not able to do so. It would be, I believe, humanly impossible. There we sat, while the silos filled and the components piled up—'inconsequentially', as Jardin complained—and nothing got off the ground."

I remarked, "Jardin could have finished the shuttle, at least."

"Not even that. Except for the control cockpits, which are factory-finished, the shuttles are being delivered in sections to be modified and fitted up as per our requirements. These modifications use some of the same components as similar fittings on the wheel. Once the computer had in-siloed a component for a time/stage, it had to stay there. No borrowing from Peter to pay Paul.

"And then, of course, the discrete time/space segments make coordination difficult. In my own department, a TTAC3 could be one of the half-dozen assistants. Jardin is fanatical about erasing identity from scientific processes."

"For what reason?"

Holloway took a swig of rye. "The wheel represented a kind of Nirvana. It would be a heaven of selflessness and harmony. People were biological cogs. The idea of stating 'John Doe worked this shift' is completely repugnant to Jardin."

It seemed to be the old story—the guys who yell the most about Human Rights are exactly the ones who want to clamp down hardest on Human Freedom.

After I talked to Holloway, I set about unfreezing the time/stage in-siloing. It broke Herbie's heart, seeing the computers disgorge the stray pieces for our nuts-and-bolts preshipments.

I had decided to put unmanned cargo canisters in a string-of-beads orbit around the Moon. A jet-dolly fore-and-aft would berth each canister on the Moon as neatly as a gull landing on the beach. The basic mine-camp structures, the transformer, the air and water recyclers, food and machines—the complete package would be waiting for the workers on the first shuttle.

My contribution to all programs was legwork—and finagling. If we had been forced to wait our turn with the space subcontractors for the canisters, jet-dollies, and other extra equipment, I would have had a long white beard before the first canister went into Moon orbit. So I cheated. I paid "rush bonuses" so that Space Mining hardware would get priority. I browbeat and swore and waved the Company flag.

The bonuses eventually were leaked to the newspapers, and I got a bad press from holier-than-thou columnists who thought nothing of bribing a headwaiter. By that time we had got what we needed, and no harm was done. A lot of dough would be riding on that Alpha shuttle, and I could not afford any Alphonse/Gaston dithering.

One day I woke up to the fact that the month was now June. Six months had whizzed by without my noticing. I was in the hangar cubbyhole I used as an office. On my desk were the work-progress sheets. They looked good—I was proud of them—but suddenly I was so fed up with space hardware and space jargon, so homesick for a deck under my feet, that I phoned Mickleberry.

"We're pretty well organized now," I told him. "the solar cells are in lunacentric orbit, the cargo canisters are shooting up on schedule, the Alpha shuttle goes onto her Janus rocket tomorrow, the Beta shuttle is on Standby in the upper loft, the astronauts are in simulator training—and I want to get back to the ships."

"Have you any more surprises for our Public Relations department? We would rather be prepared for your—uh—flamboyant departures from rectitude," said Mickleberry.

"Those yapping columnists can't pin a thing on us," I assured him.

"Whom would you place in your job? Jardin?"

"Hell, no. Jardin is a visionary. Nirvana Or Bust. Keep him as a figurehead for investors, but give my job to Holloway."

"We have no openings in the fleet at present, Captain Schuster. We assumed you would be aboard the Apha shuttle on her maiden voyage."

"If that's your joke of the year, Mickleberry, it isn't very funny. I'm like a fish out of water on this damned ALC."

"To the contrary, you have done such an excellent—if unorthodox—job that we are considering a permanent position for you with Space Mining. We'll keep in touch."

"Hey, you can't do that to me!" I bellowed into a dead phone. I hung up, reflecting that I would have to quit or be fired.

As if Mickleberry had not already ruined my day, Jardin came into my cubbyhole. The last time Jardin had wanted to see me, it was because I had written "The data *is*" instead of "The data *are*."

He now had something more important on his mind. He pinched his plump earlobe and began, "I note from the bulletin board that your Alpha soap-box derby team is drawing lots tomorrow for the initial lift-off. I'd like very much to be aboard, Schuster."

I was surprised, of course. I said, "Well, Dr. Jardin, I was kind of hoping you'd wait till the colony was a going concern. We've been planning an official ceremony with ribboncutting and so forth."

"My dear captain! If I thought your jury-built, jerry-rigged one-piece-at-a-time Moon ghetto would actually materialize—"

"Jury-*rigged*," I muttered. Him and his damned data-*are*.

"—I would not be requesting this ride on the Alpha. But your method has no possibility of success, and the initial Alpha is the only chance I will have to go into space for a very long time."

"I have nothing against you going into space," I said honestly, "but the Alpha has been stowed and fitted out for a Moon crew of eight cargo handlers. We can't discharge the canisters properly with fewer—in the same manner as a ship can't discharge cargo in normal time with fewer than a full longshoreman gang.

"Take my word for it, Dr. Jardin, the initial Alpha trip will be a success, and the Beta will be right along after her. We can't restow the Alpha for an extra passenger at this late date."

He took my refusal with strained courtesy and left.

I had not realized that the Alpha draw was on the cards already. I legged it out to where the Janus booster was positioned. A notice board had been posted next to the conference room. One of the sheets read:

ALPHA CREW
Pilot . . . Astronaut Col. G. Fairweather
Co-pilot . . . Astronaut Col. F Compton
8 Orbit/Moon crew to be chosen by lot,
Wednesday, 1300 hours

I felt tired but pleased. The Moon colony would soon be off the drawing board.

At 1300 hours the next day, all hands knocked off work and swarmed into the hangar. The Alpha gang had crammed themselves into the conference room. Herbie Douglas had scrounged a lottery cage from someplace and put it on the raised table.

As I ambled into the crowd outside the conference room, I became aware of grins and nudges. TTAC Holloway called me over to the notice board. The Alpha sheet now had "Schuster" scrawled in big letters, under "Compton," and the crew number had been reduced to seven.

For once my loud mouth had nothing to say. The guys haw-hawed and applauded. Holloway shook my hand and said, "You put us in orbit, captain! Go up to the Moon and sock it to 'em!"

I looked at the monster Janus, looming ten stories, a massive obelisk rising past the loft stages. I got all choked up. I said, "Gee, thanks, everybody. It's really swell of you, including me with the Alpha gang. I'll never forget this moment as long as I live."

I wished I had not added that last part, but the guys cheered and then crowded to see who would be on the first Alpha flight. I was too sandbagged to follow the proceedings closely. As soon as the drawing was over, I hustled to the MBF offices in the Administration Building.

I mean, Doc Grant would never let an old guy like me go into orbit!

MBF had my Company medical records in their files, of course. Grant gave me a brisk once-over, as if I was taking out insurance, and said,

"You're in excellent physical condition, captain—as tough as shoe leather. Blood pressure a little high—"

"On occasion it gets very high," I muttered.

"—but there's no reason you can't go into space. Momentary discomfort from the lift-off G's, of course, but otherwise all systems are Go. Mind you, under NASA rules you wouldn't be allowed up in a Piper Cub, but the Company's more liberal outlook enables us to take a common-sense approach. *Bon voyage,* captain!"

Hoist by my own petard. I reflected that there was nothing for me to do but get measured for a suit and join the briefing classes being conducted by Astronauts Fairweather and Compton.

When I got back to my cubbyhole I found Herbie waiting for me like a lowering storm. He burst out, "This is the dirtiest trick you've pulled yet! Telling Dr. Jardin the Alpha was only for the work crew—and then weaseling your way aboard yourself!"

"Will you pipe down and listen, Herbie? It was the guys themselves who put my name on that sheet. What was I gonna do? Chicken out? There's still a full work crew, with me aboard. I can handle cargo, and I know what's in every hold of those canisters. I objected to Dr. Jardin because he's not accustomed to wrestling cargo."

"Who can believe anything you say?" continued Herbie. "The newspapers are right—you'd sell your soul for the Company buck. You don't consider who you hurt! I don't care if the hangar gangs put your name on the list! A lot of Jardin's friends think you cut his throat!"

I calmed Herbie down and sent him away. I had to take action before this lift-off hassle split Space Mining in two. I sent out a call for Astronaut Fairweather, and he arrived a half-hour later.

"I got a stinking mess here," I told him. "The Alpha load had been figured to the last kilogram, but if I don't let Jardin aboard I'll have a Utopian mutiny.

"It's not only Jardin," I added. "It's the fact that he's a VIP and expects service. We can't shove him into a corner and tell him to read a book while we work."

"Oh, I doubt that Dr. Jardin expects service in a space shuttle," smiled Fairweather. "He may on occasion need help in suiting up—or grasping food utensils in weightlessness. Why don't you bump two guys and take Jardin and Herbie Douglas? Herbie would be tickled pink to look after Jardin."

Before I could protest, he went on quickly. "The shuttle will take care of herself when she's locked in orbit. Compton and I can join you guys on the jet-dollies. Frankly, we'd rather set the canisters down for you. Those dollies have been canned-up in outer space for weeks. If the retrofire jet controls are frozen, the dollies will have to be manually operated, and none of you have worked against Moon gravity. Jardin and Herbie can stay aboard the Alpha."

"Can Jardin handle a shuttle emergency?"

He grinned. "Well, it would be like asking DeForest to repair a TV, but he could do it. I don't know what emergency might arise. Holing by a meteor? Not a chance in a million."

As long as the astronauts were willing to help us on the dollies, I gave the okay for Jardin and Herbie to come aboard. This necessitated a sad little ceremony as we drew two names from the chosen Alpha 7. The two losers names went on the board for the second Alpha lift-off.

When the bat-winged long-hulled Alpha was finally poised on the Janus rocket, like a wide blunt arrow, I began to feel different about the trip. The feeling took me way back to when I was a small kid watching ships disappear over the horizon. Eventually I had run away to sea.

Standing on the top staging loft and watching the Alpha, I realized I had not needed to be pushed into space. Eventually I would have wangled my way aboard.

The day came when everything suddenly was for real. I was an awkwardly encased space traveler riding that elevator to the shuttle hatch—finding my padded tier—strapped myself down— . . . 3 . . . 2 . . . 1

We had lift-off.

A steamroller pushed me into a hole and sat on me. I guess I blacked out. I woke up fighting for breath, but the weight was gone.

I had a nosebleed I could not reach because of the helmet. I just lay there, taking an equal strain on all parts, while the other guys unstrapped, unhelmeted, and drifted around in weightlessness.

Herbie was attending to Jardin, so Co-pilot Compton assisted me up, took off my helmet and thrust a towel in my face before my nose started drifting with everything else. Meanwhile, Fairweather was checking with ground control on our Moon course.

The shuttle jets boosted us out of our Earth orbit. Next port, Moon.

The extra payload made possible by the Janus meant that we were aboard a roomy, well-fitted-out craft. The cargo hold had no bulkheads, but the passenger quarters had two cabins in addition to the control cockpit and the airlock.

"Stand by for magnetizing," came Fairweather's order.

We could not stand anywhere, but we floated while the cabin made a half-turn around us. Fairweather had trimmed the craft from rocket-vertical to airplane-horizontal. The lift-off tiers folded against the bulkheads, our boots clung to the magnetized deck, and we had dimensions. Earth was astern, the Moon was ahead, and the cabin had up, down, and sideways, like the interior of a cargo plane. As the sun-side of the hull warmed, the filter-shield ejected on spidery struts.

I grinned to Jardin, "You build a classy chassis."

"A fragment of perfection, captain. If only you had utilized your ruthless drive on the Wheel—!"

I did not want to rehash that argument, and fortunately I did not have to. Some genius had brought along magnetized card decks and poker chips in his flight bag. MBF had checked the bags for liquor, cigarettes and dope—just for the record—but had not censored the personal junk the guys had brought along.

We were in good spirits, without a care in the Cosmos. We were only a commercial construction crew, so we had no medical/scientific experiments cluttering up the cabins. Nobody was monitoring our hearts or lungs or physical processes, or telling us not to bet on filling inside straights.

Jardin was a wet blanket, of course. The rest of us, including Herbie, suited up and popped out the airlock into space. The Earth was a mottled blue agate, as everybody had said she was, but after the first awe-filled moment was over, we horsed around in the great void and rehearsed our canister/dolly routines.

Jardin went into space by himself, in a solemn, mystic way. He made Herbie feel like a roistering sinner and squelched the kid completely. Well, not completely. The first time I strapped down in my aft-cabin sleep-tier for a snooze, Herbie unstrapped from his own tier while I was sawing wood and jammed my helmet over my face. The helment drifted off, of course, but it woke me with a scare.

I started to cuss Herbie out, but I saw by the shy grin he gave me that he was just using a leg-pull to tell me he was not mad at me any more.

Hour by hour the Moon's bright pockmarks approached and expanded. On the third Earth-day of our trip the Moon looked near enough to touch, and Fairweather and Compton were calculating orbital mechanics with Earth's ground controllers.

A navigator myself, I appreciated the skill with which Fairweather maneuvered above the proposed colony site, jet-spewed the lurid dye markers directly on target, and then chased up to the orbiting canisters. Now the exciting moment had come. We were allowing one orbit for dollying down one canister. A lost orbit meant loss of valuable time.

Leaving Jardin and Herbie in the shuttle, Fairweather and Compton suited up and came out to show us how it should be done. It went like clockwork. The opening of the aft canister, the unloading of the two dollies, the positioning of a dollly fore and aft, the mooring of the rest of us along the canister-cleats, the suspense until the dye-marked site appeared, just short of the night-line, Fairweather's countdown, the dolly flares—and we were dropping like a leaf. A short retroblast that billowed the dirt under the canister—and we were on the Moon.

Weaving back and forth in the weak gravity like half-rooted seaweed, we unloaded the canister's cargo compartment and tested the seals of the residence cabin. We needed a work-break before we brought down the microwave transformer we had carried, along with space tools for spacesuited hands, in the shuttle's cargo hold.

The next time the shuttle swung overhead, the eight of us piled like circus clowns on the two dollies and returned to orbit. We moored the dollies to hull cleats on the shuttle and entered the airlock one by one.

I was the last man in. As I unhelmeted I found a discussion circulating with the food packets. Herbie was saying,

"There must be something Dr. Jardin and I could do!"

I answered at once, "Sit here and jaw with the ALC. You're passengers."

Jardin objected, "But, captain, none of the work crew has been in space before! We all are on the same function level. We all have a right to participate."

"That's the trouble with you guys who work only with your brains," I declared. "You have no understanding of the timing of physical labor. You know the world only two-dimensionally, through your imagination. That's why all your Utopias end up on the rocks.

"The Alpha gang and I have actually worked with this hardware—picked it up, moved it around, fitted it together. We can take the hardware for granted and concentrate on space safety. We can estimate timing."

Dr. Jardin looked unfairly hurt, and his half-baked right-to-work argument was okayed by the gang. I felt in my bones that I would now regret not having asked for his removal the day I arrived at the ALC.

Everything went fine, at first. We all rehelmeted, since two guys had to be detailed to convoy Herbie and Jardin, and the rest of us were needed to unload the transformer. We filed out of the shuttle in good order, cracked the cargo hatch and began to unsecure the transformer.

A crate of space tools was in the way. Herbie was the nearest. He unlashed the crate and tried to push it aside. Of course, the damned thing took off and looked like it was going to plow us all down. Herbie dove after it to grab something—anything—

He caught the safety bar of a laser-beam cutter. The beam needled a zigzag path through the microwave transformer and sliced through the shuttle hull.

Just a split-second of carelessness.

The escaping jet of air from the shuttle cabin blew us and the cargo around like leaves inside an empty oil drum. I hooked a boot on a hatch brace and grabbed Compton, who managed to hook Jardin. Three crewmen were safely anchored at the other side of the hatch, but four guys and the hardware were blasted into space. Each suit had an emergency jet-pistol for maneuvering in space, and I hoped everybody knew how to use it.

When Compton had a handhold on the brace, I let go of him and climbed over the shuttle to the moored dollies. A crewman from the other side of the hatch had the same idea. We activated the dollies and headed for the sparks that told us the missing crewmen were trying to jet to the shuttle. We picked up Fairweather and two crewmen in a hurry, but Herbie had disappeared.

I knew he was alive and in the vicinity because I could hear a hopeless whimper on my suit radio. Nobody else was saying a word. They were waiting for orders, and I realized that as project boss I had to make the big decisions. I said,

"Herbie! Use your flash gun!"

Weakly, "Let me die. It's all my fault!"

"Dammitall!" I roared. "You come back here and help us collect the hardware you blew all over the Sirius sector! We need every man on the job!"

The whimper sniffled out. I heard a murmur of "There!" as several guys spotted Herbie's jet-flash. I dollied over to him, nearly ramming the ruined transformer, which I swooped up on my way.

Herbie was still holding the edge of the tool crate with one hand, in his shock and utter misery. I dragged my assorted finds back to the shuttle and said,

"Okay, so we've holed the shuttle and have to repair the transformer. And we're marooned. But nobody's hurt, so we can continue with what we came to do—establish a colony. If we had been working with a single in-siloed time/stage, we'd be in trouble because we would have no alternatives.

However, the cargo canisters have been stowed for general use and are as specialized as a hall closet.

"Now, we're gonna divide into two groups. Colonel Compton, you take charge of the work crew and continue the canister work while stockpiling oxygen cylinders from all the canisters. Colonel Fairweather, with Dr. Jardin, Herbie, and I will reenter the shuttle. If her rockers are still operable—and loss of air should have no effect on them—we will pick up the solar energy station and bring it here so that it can be dollied to the surface."

I heard the surprise and the muttered comment. I said, "It will be nearly two weeks before the colony site will be in shadow. We can use the solar cells directly for power and can start the recyclers almost at once. If we succeed in repairing the transformer, we'll put the station back where we found it."

Dr. Jardin's voice: "The solar cells cannot be used directly without readaptation of Moon residence circuitry."

"Fine. It'll give the guys something to do until we get back."

An easy laugh brought things to normal. I said, "The Fairweather gang will switch to radio channel B. The Comptons keep A. Over and out."

The shuttle cabin looked as if a Texas tornado had hit it, but the reserve oxygen tank still had a full supply for our suits. We had lost Earth contact, but I saw no sense to wasting time on that circuitry. The cutoff was Mayday enough, and we could not hold our breaths until ALC answered it. We had power and propulsion. Fairweather and I took a celestial fix, and then we gave a short spurt to where we expected to find the solar station.

The multiple-section honeycomb was clearly visible against outer space. I suppose we could have detached a section, in the same manner as remote control had put them together in orbit, but I figured the dollies could handle the whole station in Moon gravity. As we slowed into the satellite's higher orbit, I stood on the shuttle's hull, wound up like a fast-ball pitcher and threw a nylon-line monkey-fist into the satellite's work-base struts. The line caught, I hauled her home, and—like a tugboat towing the QE2—we spurted back to canister orbit, where Compton and his gang—with two more dollies from the second canister—were waiting for us.

Within six hours the Moon-moored solar station was giving direct power to the Moon residence. When the lights went on the recyclers started up, the residence was as comfortable as a well-built house-trailer. We showered in the needle-mist stall and hit the sack for eight hours of recuperation.

When we woke up, we unfroze some lobster thermidor and had a policy council. First on the agenda was patching the shuttle hull. The patch would not resist reentry burn—we would be as marooned as ever—but it would allow us to restart the shuttle's air recycler. If necessary, we could survive in the shuttle after the shadow-line had fallen across the Moon's solar cell station.

Naturally, we hoped the Beta would come after us within that deadline. Jardin doubted that the ALC would respond immediately to the communication cutoff.

"If you recall," he explained, "the last time we talked to ground control, we were nowise in a hazardous situation—merely about to unload the cargo hold. Since Captain Schuster has tried every trick in the book—and invented new ones—to hasten the Moon colonization, ALC may assume he deliberately sabotaged communications to force the Beta into space sooner than planned. You recall also, both astronauts were away from the cockpit—ALC certainly will note that fact."

Herbie was gray with guilt and despair. Jardin glanced at him and added, "Of course, fire departments answer even false alarms—"

The tone rang hollow. We all knew the newspapers would be yelling, "Another Schuster gimmick!" Public opinion might keep the Beta on the ground until its scheduled lift-off the following month.

We put the Beta from our minds and made the best of being marooned. Jardin was working over the mangled transformer. The guys decided they needed more room. They locked the air-seal door to the galley, reduced the galley to vacuum, cut away the aft bulkhead (fusing tight the seam in the insulation-packed double hull) and welded the second cargo canister to the breach.

All the canisters were double-hulled to protect food cargoes from cosmic-ray contamination. In the event of a meteor strike, the viscous insulation flowed to the pressure-escape point and gummed it up. By adding the second canister, the guys had a messroom and gym.

By the fourth day we were living in style, and the guys began wondering how they could get a few dames up there. I glared at them and barked, "If the dames come, Schuster goes!"

They chorused, "Bye, Schuster! Nice to have known you!"

My one worry was Herbie. He was in a suicidal mood from guilt and continuing shock. I kept him going by dinning into him the truth that we needed work from every man. His suicide would harm us and would not change what had happened.

After a pep talk Herbie would perk up for a few hours, but fatigue would make him sag again and begin whimpering, "But I might have killed somebody! I might have killed all of you! What if the laser beam had swept the other way! What if—!"

"A miss is as good as a mile," I would say. I wondered how I could get him back to Earth alive. He had to be suited-up to jet-dolly to a shuttle, and if he got a suicidal impulse on the way, nobody could stop him from wrecking his suit.

On the fifth Earth day of our marooning, we stopped talking about the Beta. This was the day the Beta would come, if the ALC had begun the two-day fueling of the Janus as soon as they had lost contact with us. We dared not hope for action that fast, implying as it did the elimination of careful backup checking.

That night after supper, a few of us began a poker game. The body-beautiful nuts retired to the gym to do pushups. Jardin kept Herbie busy with plans to enclose the work area with a ray-repelling magnetic field. Jardin may have been a science-idiot, but I could not fault his treatment of Herbie.

The airlock buzzer sounded, and the hatchway

light began blinking. We just sat. The blinking stopped, the hatchway opened, and a clean new white spacesuit entered the residence. The suit's occupant unlocked his helmet, removed it and gave us a smile.

TTAC Holloway!

He gave me a nod. "Dr. Livingstone Seagull, I assume."

"What kept ya?" I deadpanned.

"You think you're kidding, but Mickleberry was bucking everybody from the *New York Times* to The Leauge of Women Voters when he ordered immediate fueling of the Beta without the usual countdown checking."

"But the Beta gang was willing to lift off?"

"Sure. They built that shuttle with their own hands. They knew she would fly. We have spare hull plates in our cargo hold," he added. "Mickleberry figured you had run into a meteor shower, and he wanted us to salvage the Alpha even though—as he expressed it—her personnel had perhaps succumbed."

Old profit-and-loss Mickleberry. Holloway went on, "We saw your Moon spread before we went into orbit, so the slashed Alpha did not worry us. What happened, anyhow?"

Herbie wailed, "It was my fault! I did it!"

I explained, "Apparently in stowage the On-switch of the laser cutter was flicked back. When Herbie accidentally pulled the safety bar, we had a laser squirt until the bar snapped in place again. Just one of those things."

To change the subject I continued, "If you care to step up to orbit and invite your minions to inspect our country club, we'll tidy up a bit and bake a cake."

That night was more fun than a picnic. The way the Alpha gang, as Moon natives, lorded it over the Beta visitors was a sketch. The next day we got to work again. The repair of the Alpha coincided with Jardin's completion of the rebuilt transformer, so we used the Alpha to put the solar satellite back where we had found it.

When the time came for the Alpha gang to blast Earthward, I think they were almost sorry to leave. Holloway was going with them, and I was staying with the Betas to mastermind the ore surveys.

Herbie's face got tighter and tighter as departure time approached. I could see he intended to kill himself as soon as he was out of the residence. I said to Jardin, "We gotta shoot some emergency morphine into the kid. You can keep him sedated on the Alpha."

"My dear captain, are you mad?" fussed Jardin. "Three days under morphine sedation could give the lad an addiction! Why, I wouldn't think of it!"

I could see only one way out. I did not like it, but I knew I would never forgive myself if I backed off and let Herbie die.

He had been slow about getting his suit, like a guy who looks at a pistol for hours before he blows his head off with it. I said to him, "Hurry it up, will ya?"

He was too depressed to hurry, and he was bewildered at the sudden harshness of my voice. I strode over to him and grabbed the front of his sweat shirt, as if I intended to shake him. In the weak Moon gravity it was easy to pretend I had shaken too hard, and I sent him crashing into the bulkhead. Blocking him out from the others, I leaned over, quickly grabbed his forearms and twisted them inward with a sharp jerk. I could feel the elbows dislocate and then jar into place.

As I lifted and supported the unconscious kid, Jardin exclaimed, "What is the meaning of that uncalled-for brutality? Never in my life—!"

I ignored him and said to Holloway, "Help me get Herbie suited up and into orbit. With two sprained elbows, he won't be able to kill himself— at least, not by scuttling his suit or sneaking into the Alpha's airlock. We'll get him down."

Herbie came to, while we were stuffing him into his suit. His elbows were already swollen and discoloring, and I saw that I had bumped his head harder than I had intended. He gave me that bewildered look again. I told him,

"Sorry, Herbie. I had to keep you alive. Someday you'll thank me for it."

He was still giggling helplessly when we locked his helmet in place.

After the Alpha gang went home, we had four days of peaceful and productive work, although the residence was now in the darkness phase. We could have lighted ten football fields with the solar power from the satellite—and no bills from Con Edison.

The next day the guy who had the Communications watch handed me a curt message. Mickleberry wanted me, and the Alpha was blasting off immediately to bring me home.

I reflected that Mickleberry must want me awful bad, to send the Alpha back as soon as she had arrived.

Three days later I was on my way Earthward,

with two newly-hired astronauts I did not know.
All they could tell me was that Jardin was giving me
a bad press over Herbie Douglas. It did not seem
like sufficient reason to send the Alpha. I would
have expected Mickleberry to fire me and tell me
to walk home.

On orders from the ALC, the Alpha held an
orbiting pattern until Earth time at Cape Canaveral was 0100. Then we skipped into the atmosphere, the aero-jets roared to life, and we landed
at the Canaveral air base as casually as a New
York-Miami commuter jet.

I sure was happy when the Alpha's wheels hit
terra firma. We cracked the hatch, and I took a deep
breath of warm, soggy, wonderful Florida air. As I
walked down the ladder, a limousine came racing
across the runways and screeched to a halt in front
of me. The security guard beside the driver
jumped out and said, "Captain Schuster?" and
opened the rear door.

I squeezed into the seat and dimly perceived a
familiar figure. A precise voice said, "Good morning, Captain Schuster."

"Mickleberry!" I returned weakly, as the guard
slammed the door and got back into the car, and
we accelerated away from the shuttle. I went on,
"Who unchained you from your desk?"

"I came down here this evening in the Company
jet and will be in Operations at my usual time, after
our conference."

Before I forgot it in the rush of other business,
like getting fired, I said, "Thanks for the quick
Beta lift-off. The guys wondered if you would

think the communication cutoff was just a Schuster trick, what with the media—"

"We judge you by your actions, not by the media's words. Never once have you sent us a distorted report. That a licensed master mariner would fabricate an emergency—for any reason whatsoever—was beyond belief. I ordered the Beta fueling at once.

"And speaking of the media—" He handed me a newspaper and pencil flash.

I played the flashlight over thick black letters: JARDIN CALLS SCHUSTER BRUTE. The article started out, "Company executives are remaining silent in face of demands for the repatriation and arrest of Captain Robert Schuster for his allegedly brutal treatment of Alpha crewman Herbert Douglas. 'Captain Schuster's deliberate maiming of this man is in direct violation of all Human Rights,' stated Dr. Claud Jardin, . . ."

"Sonofabitch," I muttered.

"Yes," agreed Mickleberry. "Young Douglas has admitted, both to NASA investigators and Mr. Bennington, that he would have killed himself if you had not lamed his arms. He is recovering very nicely in the ALC clinic.

"However, the incident, on top of the previous publicity, forces us to remove you temporarily from Space Mining and employ you in a fleet matter which has coincidentally arisen."

"That so?" I murmured. A great, happy wave washed over me—a blue, salt-fizzy breaker I could feel, smell, taste—

". . . outward-bound from Cadiz," Mickleberry

was saying, "rammed and sank a Liberian tank-ship. The Spanish authorities have impounded our ship and put our captain in jail. Damages and oil clean-up are mounting toward the half-billion mark. Our captain insists the Liberian was at fault and we expect you to prove him right."

"Half-billion, hey? So that's what was worth shooting up a Janus. Otherwise you would have told me to walk home."

"We would have let you hitchhike. But, captain, the next time you wish to be relieved of an assignment, kindly do not resort to mayhem."

"Mayhem! For Gods' sake, Mickleberry, you don't think I'd rough up a kid—!"

I could feel his austere glare. "Need we review the previous ploys by which you have made yourself eligible for severance pay and unemployment insurance?"

I had to admit my record in that department was not so hot. Besides, maybe an in-depth head-shrinker would say that I had gone off the rails with Herbie because of subconscious frustration at being kept away from my natural element, the sea.

The limousine stopped at the ALC clinic. Mickleberry handed me an envelope. "Your airline ticket. The Spanish flight leaves Miami this afternoon. We arranged for your belongings to be moved here from the motel. A clinic room has been prepared for you. Safe voyage, captain."

I climbed out of the car—definitely feeling Earth gravity—and slogged up the clinic steps. The night orderly let me in and showed me to a staff room. My suitcase and overcoat were beside the bed.

Before I hit the sack, I opened the airline envelope to look at the ticket. A second envelope was beside it, holding a nice bonus check signed by Bennington himself. I was glad to get it, but I figured I had earned it as the founder of the moon colony.

The next morning I went to find Herbie Douglas. He was sitting in a sunroom chair, in bathrobe and slippers, his arms still in casts. His depression seemed gone, and he smiled at me. I said,

"Can you forgive me, Herbie?"

"Oh, I forgave you on the way up to the shuttle. I guess I really didn't want to die, but I would somehow have felt honor-bound to rip away my airpack—if my arms had not been too lame and painful to move. I'm sorry Dr. Jardin is making trouble."

"No trouble," I smiled.

"And I'm sorry, too, I didn't understand what you were trying to tell me about programmed Utopias," he went on. "The Moon colony turned out better than we had planned, exactly because it was improvised and open to new ideas. When you have a rigid, programmed mold, like the Wheel, you can't expand it or improve it. When you build one piece at a time, the construction is open-ended, with no limit. You can build and build—all the way to the stars.

"Dr. Jardin was always talking about the perfection of Nirvana, or the perfection of heaven. But you can't improvise in heaven. Heaven doesn't seem so desirable to me any more."

I agreed emphatically. According to a usually reliable source, the main deal about heaven is that it has *no more sea*. I, for one, am not gonna sign up for a place with no sea.

Not that Anybody is gonna offer me a job there, I reflected as I left to connect with my Miami flight to Spain—and the ships.

Chapter 9

January 3 (cont.) . . .
Xavier Wants to Know

At eight o'clock that evening, Philip Xavier was still at work in the Company's law library, researching precedents on a complicated dispute within international waters. The telephone on the heavy walnut table chirped discreetly. As he answered the call, Xavier thought *Mickleberry.* Only the old boy and himself worked so late.

His guess was correct. The dry, precise voice said, "Excellent! I caught you before you left. Holloway has paid us a flying visit. Space Tug 4 received a message from Schuster, could not get Jardin to act upon it—and has gone AWOL on a frankly mutinous rescue mission."

"The presumption-of-death formalities—"

"Must be suspended, but without—uh—making waves. We can risk no media hysteria—no tangle or prestige-oriented Space probes by other agencies. Schuster must remain dead, to all intents and purposes, until the Q-Pod arrives safely in Moon orbit."

Xavier remembered Schuster's confidential Rec-Paks. "Our PR Department is being requested—even being bribed—for sensational material on Schuster. Those eight Rec-Pak shells ought to be locked in a bank vault. No telling what those tapes contain."

A small chuckle interrupted him. "They don't spare *me* at any rate."

"Legally, you should not have listened—"

"Oh, come now, Xavier. The labels clearly indicated the tapes concerned Company business. That is undoubtedly why Schuster kept them at Operations instead of in a bank deposit box with his private papers. I agree his comments should be kept confidential—"

Xavier sighed. "Would it trouble you too much to bring the lot up here before you leave? I expect to be some hours yet—"

"No trouble at all. The collection is not—uh—complete—"

Xavier reflected he was glad he had spoken up, before the shells vanished altogether.

A quarter hour later Mickleberry laid the shell stack on the walnut table, bade Xavier a courteous *good night* and withdrew.

Xavier pushed aside the legal tome. He really had not time to listen, yet if Schuster had recorded any indiscretions—and discretion was not in the Old Man's vocabulary—the Company's legal counsel ought to *know*—

Xavier rose from his chair, picked the top shell off the stack and inserted it into the audio built into the bookshelves. He heard the unit slide the cartridge from the shell, and he returned to his chair. Schuster's voice—engaging though gruff and vigorous—began, "Even before the bulkship *Ceres* slid down the ways . . ."

The *Ceres!* Xavier straightened in his chair. His fingers slid a small flat Drenalin case from a pocket in his blue watered-silk vest. He sniffed a careful pinch into his nostrils as the tape went on.

". . . she killed two men. . . ."

● ● ●

GRIGGS AND THE EINSTEIN FALLACY

Even before the bulkship *Ceres* slid down the ways, she killed two men. A dockyard crane cable slipped, unloading steel plates on workmen at her bow.

During her first year at sea she added a third victim, via a sliced power cable on a wet deck. The Company felt lucky that the year's toll had not been higher. *Ceres* had survived a collision, an engine-room fire, and an accidental discharge of CO_2.

The second year claimed the life of a cook lost overboard, an incident written off as par for the course. The Company was more concerned about the continual foul-ups of the ship's derricks and grabs.

The third year seemed uneventful until a

routine insurance survey revealed a skeleton (male) in a ballast tank. Probably a stowaway who had squeezed into the temporarily unsecured deck hatch, not realizing the tank would be filled with water as soon as the ship was trimmed.

A horrible way to die, come to think of it.

Even while the survey was continuing in the Baltimore drydock, *Ceres'* bosun plunged from the dockyard catwalk. Broke every bone in his body, including his neck.

The crew walked off the ship, swearing "Jinx!"

At this point Mickleberry in Operations telephoned me on a chemical tanker loading liquid chlorine at Freeport, Texas, and ordered me back to New York.

I packed my suitcase, left the tanker in charge of my chief mate, got the ship's agent to drive me to the Houston airport and was in Mickleberry's office that same afternoon.

I sat down in the smooth-worn chair beside his desk, and he began, "Captain Schuster, we do not believe in jinxed ships."

I thought, uh-oh, I'm slated for *Ceres*. I said, "Well, you gotta admit that certain ships are accident-prone."

"A level-headed skipper could be a step in the right direction. *Ceres* has had six skippers in three years."

"Why have you taken Captain O'Neal off the ship? The skeleton was in the tank long before he came aboard. And why drag me into it? Scraping the bottom of the barrel, are you?"

Mickleberry puckered a smile at me. "Applying

you to a problem, captain, is a case of the cure being worse than the disease. However, when Chief Mate Griggs notified us that the crew would go back to work under your command—"

"Griggs? You've got Tom Griggs on *Ceres?*"

"O'Neal asked for him, and we have left him aboard." Mickleberry cleared his throat. "Griggs is a very intelligent man."

"Yeah, and he's wasting his intelligence at sea. He should have quit years ago."

Mickleberry lowered his voice discreetly. "His unfortunate indebtedness to the Company—"

"His wife still has him in hock to the eyebrows, hey? Mink-mad Mary. How's young Tommy?"

Mickleberry brightened. "Quite well. The leukemia seems completely arrested. The boy is back in school."

"Fine." I smiled at the thought of Griggs, Jr. and got back to *Ceres*. "What's Griggs up to now?"

"Pending the arrival of a new skipper he is commanding *Ceres*. He looks at the problem mathematically. E equals Schuster squared away."

"Nuts. Griggs just don't want a jinxed ship as his first command. I told you, the guy is smart."

"Captain, this irrational concept of a jinx—"

"Won't matter a hill of beans to me. I'll still run the ship my way, with no back talk from you or Griggs or the goddamned jinx. Is that clear?"

"Standard Schuster procedure," sighed Mickleberry. He ripped a page from his memo block and held the page out to me. "Your flight number to Baltimore. Pick up the ticket at the airline desk. Do you require expense money?"

I rose, took the page and glanced at the flight time. "Not as long as I can catch the airport bus. I'll buy my own Scotch."

"The Baltimore agent will meet the plane. Good luck, captain."

Later than night I boarded *Ceres* in a Baltimore drydock, under the cold glare of work lights and welding torches. A seaman ran down the ladders of the access-staging to take my suitcase. Apparently Griggs had persuaded the crew to go back to work.

Griggs himself was on the top catwalk. Thirty-odd, well set up with finely-honed features and cool analytical eyes. He smiled, "Welcome aboard, captain!"

"Thanks, mister!" I barked. "but no thanks for passing the buck to me on this jinxed hooker!"

He laughed. I went on, "All the ship's papers are in your office, hey? Let's go there first."

Three years had worn the newness off, but the mate's quarters were roomy and comfortable. Taped to a bulkhead was the photo of a freckled-faced smart-looking kid. I asked, "How's the boy, Tom?" as I pulled off my coat and dumped myself on the settee.

"Recovered and holding steady, sir." He restrained his fatherly pride. "Scotch? There's no ice. The workmen have disconnected the refrigerating systems. Captain O'Neal ordered the checkup. Nobody has ever found the bugs."

"The real jinx of *Ceres* is the wiring," I commented. "That collision at sea was due to a fuse blackout. During maneuvering at close quarters the wheel went dead. And, of course, the derricks and grabs are always haywire."

Griggs took a bottle of Scotch and a glass from the locker. "The ship is out of phase."

"Out of phase with what?"

"You think relatively. Everybody does." Griggs set the Scotch and glass on the table in front of the settee. "It's the Einstein fallacy."

I poured a slug of Scotch, which I figured I would need if Griggs began upon Einstein. I am a low-velocity Newton man, myself.

"Einstein was concerned with the interaction of mathematically calculable phenomena within a specific time dimension," continued Griggs. "It was the How of the universe. A horizontal survey, in other words.

"Relativity is measurement, not causation. It is position, not meaning. It can explode the atom with poisonous fallout—but not unlock it harmlessly. It cannot explain the Why of gravitational fields or electromagnetic energy. It does not touch the inherent nonrelative qualities of phenomena. It makes no vertical survey."

"Yeah, but the Why of phenomena is way over our heads, Tom," I objected. "Who can hope to know the Why of gravity?"

"All of us, sir, if we can free ourselves from the How of Relativity. Things exist in-and-for themselves, not only as observed in relation to the rest of the universe. They exist, for example, in independent relation to Time.

"If we look beyond mass-velocity concepts, we find that Time has two corollary aspects. First, the universal all-points-contiguous post-Euclid configuration of past-present-future—a general field which is the background fabric of mass-energy movement, but which I will not discuss now—"

I thought, thank God for small favors.

"—and second, the aspect we call timing, which is the integration of each individual phenomenon into the general time field. It is a vertical function. The horizontal Relativity survey ignores it—and in so doing, distorts the shape and functions of the general field.

"Captain, *Ceres* is jinxed because something went wrong with her timing. That's why her electrical systems don't work properly and her human element always feels disoriented. But, I believe, by tight and constant control of all systems, we can warp her into shape again."

"You may be right, Tom, but my functions are neither horizontal or vertical. Just pragmatic. Forget the How and Why. A jinxed ship is like a lemon car. We're stuck with her until the Company scraps her."

Griggs stopped theorizing and handed me the dockyard estimates, Captain O'Neal's last reports, *Ceres'* grain charter and the Crew List. I asked Griggs, "How did you sell the crew on coming back to work? You didn't promise them anything in my name, did you?"

"No, sir," he smiled. "They agreed that having you aboard was fighting fire with fire."

I considered. I really respected Griggs' brains, and he had given some practical advice. Tight and constant control. The wiring foul-ups aside, most of the jinx items were what I would call carelessness and sloppiness. No cooks fell overboard from ships I commanded, and no stowaways found unsecured tank hatches at their disposal. I said, "Can we persuade the crew that the jinx can be licked with hard work?"

"Why not? Most people understand the fluid nature of all phenomena. That's why they always hope. That's why it's always a new ball game. The constant movement of particles is an observed fact on the horizontal Relativity plane. Change must also be immanent in the Vertical Causation line."

He continued earnestly, "Think of ships as clay vessels from a potter's wheel in an aboriginal village. Most of the vessels turn out okay, but one like *Ceres* is lopsided. The aborigines, seeing only the behavioral How aspect, say the vessel is bewitched.

"But the aborigine, without being interested in the Causative Why of the potter's wheel, might take that lopsided vessel and mold it in his hands until it was straight."

"You're assuming the clay was still unfired and malleable."

"Yes, sir. The total mass-energy field of any phenomenon is fluid and malleable. *Ceres* is steel, true, but the steel is only seemingly solid and is not the total field. The fact that the navigation officers, regardless of modern instruments, most constantly check the compasses for deviation and variation, proves the far greater importance of the electromagnetic fields within which the ship operates.

"At the time *Ceres'* keel was laid, there was a

malfunction in that electromagnetic environment. Since we are aborigines in the Why calculation, we have no understanding of the problem. We can say only that the ship is jinxed."

He tapped the grain charter. "But during this voyage we can mold our vessel and warp our timing into the general time field."

I looked the charter over and remarked, "A cargo for Belfast, hey? Northern Ireland is not a destination I would choose for a jinxed ship."

He smiled again. "Well, the IRA has not yet bombed the waterfront."

"Yeah, that's what I mean."

The next morning the repair work was finished, the shipyard refloated *Ceres* and we moved to a Baltimore grain dock. Knowing that Griggs could handle the grain tonnage the conveyors were shooting down into our holds, I turned my attention to the ship's other departments. The chief engineer and chief steward were capable men but admittedly ready to declare the ship a disaster.

"Not a goddamned thing works the way it should," complained Chief Engineer Hazeltine. "O'Neal said he was glad to get off the ship."

"Let's keep ahead of the breakdowns by constant checking and renewal," I said. "It'll cost overtime, but we'll spot a good percentage of the trouble before it peaks."

"What's the checkup area?"

"The total mass-energy field. From the main engine to the lifeboat motors—"

"Both lifeboats have brand-new marine diesels. Mickleberry threw a fit, but no crew would sign aboard *Ceres* unless they figured they could get away from her fast."

"Brand-new or not, check them. I want you and Griggs to keep tight control of all systems."

"All?"

"From the water condensing unit to the iron cow. From the radar mast to the emergency lanterns under the fo'c'sle. Every inch of mooring line, every foot of deckplate—"

"Mickleberry will have a stroke."

"All he can do is fire me, and I've been through that routine before."

Hazeltine, who knew me pretty well, glinted a look at me. "Why the sure-bet attitude? Changed your brand of Scotch, or what?"

"Griggs has found an Einstein loophole you can drive *Nimitz* through. Relativity is only half the answer—and the noncausative half, at that. We can take *Ceres* as she is, a malleable mass-energy field relative to nothing but herself, and mold the jinx out of her. We'll shape her up like the Fat Lady in a new corset."

"Yeah, it's the Scotch," muttered Hazeltine. "Hard-headed Schuster has cracked at last."

All the same, the jinx-shadow was off his face. I had given him a new angle to think about.

Modern conveyors fill a grain ship in a hurry. By mid-afternoon we were settling down on our marks. I was working in my office, waiting for Griggs to notify me that the loading was finished. There was a tap at the opened door.

I glanced up to see a sharply dressed young man with blue-black hair, blue eyes and a tightly wound expression. He said, "Captain, may I have a moment of your time? Your ship could be a godsend, if she's going where the shipping news states. My name is Cullane—"

He advanced to the desk and handed me a business card. I took it and read,

MORTON-LAND TOOL & DIE
Alex Cullane
Sales Rep.

He went on, "We have six crates of machine parts to be rushed to a customer in Belfast. It would be saving us the delay of transshipment or the expense of air freight if you would be taking the crates aboard. As deck cargo, maybe."

The pitch was as phony as a three-dollar bill. I had no time for a hassle, but I wanted to find out what the guy's racket was. I said, "What size crates? We're exclusively a grain carrier. Stowing deck cargo according to safety regulations would mean extra work that I would not authorize without urgent reason."

His voice became confidential. The hint of Irish brogue broadened. "Then I'll be putting me cards on the table. Why should there be reservations between meself and Captain Patrick O'Neal?"

I was silent. Not so much from guile as from sheer disbelief that a guy named Schuster could have a map of Ireland on his face.

Cullane continued. "We have a great gathering of Irish-American patriots. The names I could name, that are backing us! Sure and you yourself, Patrick O'Neal are an Irishman born and bred, with memories of the bloody tyranny of Cromwell.

"But I wouldn't be asking you to help us from

patriotism alone. There's money to be made in running guns into Ulster, and why shouldn't you get your share of it? Just to smuggle six crates past the British—"

Another tap at the opened door. It was Griggs in a grain-dusty boiler suit, a small memo paper in his hand. I nodded him to speak, and he began, "Captain Schuster, here's—"

Cullane drew a breath and stared at me. His glance shifted to the business card I was still holding. He had made a bad mistake, and shiny paper holds fingerprints.

I dropped the card briskly into the top drawer of the desk, shut the drawer decisively and said, "Sorry, but no deal, Mr. Cullane."

He turned around and beat it fast. Griggs looked at me uncertainly, I asked him, "Why—at that time of all times—did you address me by name, Tom?"

"I don't really know, sir," he answered, puzzled. "I was going to say, 'the draft figures, captain,' but when I saw the visitor, your name slipped out."

"It would, on a jinxed ship. The human element was sure out of phase in that minute! A few more seconds of him thinking I was Pat O'Neal, and I would have conned those crates out of him."

"What crates, sir?"

"Guns for the IRA. Get on the shore phone and tell the FBI we have information for them if they can send an agent here before we sail."

Griggs raced below on the double.

The FBI were prompt. A granite-faced gray-suited agent was on board in twenty minutes. I had not realized Baltimore was an IRA-sensitive area. I gave the agent Cullane's card and told him the whole story. I finished, "Now don't send your cloak-and-dagger boys after Captain Pat O'Neal. He has no connection whatsoever with IRA gun-running. The gang undoubtedly saw his name in the newspapers. God knows there has been enough publicity about *Ceres*' drydock troubles. These mercenary shamrocks remembered the Irish captain when they saw in the morning paper that *Ceres* was loading for Belfast.

"I would have tried to con more information out of Cullane," I added, "but the mate came and inadvertently blew the gaff."

"Bad luck," commented the agent.

"Bad luck is the only kind we have on board," I told him.

The incident loomed larger than normal in my mind because it seemed to imply that the jinx was psychic instead of electromagnetic. I said as much to Griggs later, on the bridge.

We had dropped the pilot. Griggs had the bridge watch. He looked speculatively into the night-clouded east.

"I don't dismiss psychic force from the mass-energy picture," he said slowly. "There's too much empirical proof for extrasensory phenomena. But the Cullane incident is a common example of mis-timing, like a car engine sparking too soon or too late."

"You don't believe somebody cursed the ship?"

"If it is possible to cause malfunction by psychic or psionic force—and there seems to be some evidence for the latter—the malfunction would necessarily be remodeled as the total field was warped into phase. Besides, there has never been proof that anybody cursed *Ceres* or the Company. Why would they? As companies go, it's decent enough.

I thought of the large debt the Company was carrying for Griggs, and I said no more.

All hands turned to with a will on our beat-the-jinx tune-ups. There was good sense in what Griggs had said about remolding. A jinx can only work on the material at hand. If all systems are relentlessly kept in optimum running order, the jinx is stymied.

Hazeltine's engine room gang had the most work, of course. After several days at sea he told me he could do no more checking without shutting down the main engine. The weather being favorable I told him to shut her down, and we coasted eastwards with the breeze and current.

As I sent off the noon position I wondered how Mickleberry would react to the decreased distance covered during the eight hours of drifting.

To judge from the coded message the radio officer handed me the next afternoon, Mickleberry blew his stack. The results of our work would have to be quick and convincing, if I was not to become the seventh skipper fired from *Ceres*.

The message had come during Griggs' watch. I went out to the bridge to tell him about Mickleberry's blast. He said, "The ship's morale couldn't be higher, captain, and morale is a significant factor. A jinx is a feedback mechanism. A man can be so preoccupied by impending doom that he trips over his own feet."

Assuming we had the morale and the physical plant under control, what about the rest of what Griggs would call the electromagnetic environment? What about the weather and the sea?

The wind had been kicking up. I watched the

forward deck corkscrewing through the swell. Grain was a shifty cargo at best.

But, as events turned out, I was worrying about the wrong factor.

As Griggs and I were talking, the radio officer came into the wheelhouse. He stopped short at seeing me and said, "Excuse me, captain—"

I nodded and he turned to Griggs. "Tom, your wife is on the phone."

I spoke up at once. "Take the call, Tom. I'll stand watch."

He thanked me and followed the radio officer from the wheelhouse. I felt a twinge of impending doom, myself. Mink-mad Mary was always bad news.

I ambled out to the bridge wing. In a couple minutes Griggs came out to me. He looked as if he had taken a low blow and was about to go down for the count. I asked, "Is something wrong with Tommy?"

"No—no, the boy is fine, sir. It's just that I have to ask you to authorize another salary advance. Mary needs a thousand dollars. She let a department store account ride too long—"

"You've got to put a reef in her sails," I told him.

"I can't—not without having the withdrawal go out over Tommy. Mary's psychiatrist says compulsive spending is a sickness, like alcoholism or gambling. She's got to be handled with kid gloves."

That was not how I would have handled her, but I kept my mouth shut. We watched a wave explode at the bow. Water flooded the low-riding deck and cascaded over the scuppers.

Griggs burst out, "But honestly, captain, I don't

think Mary is sick. I think she's resentful about my working at sea—not that she ever gives me a breathing space to pay my debts and look for other work. I think she's punishing me, and I know she's socking away most of her allotment and making me find the money for these credit purchases.

"If I fell off a catwalk and broke my neck, she'd be satisfied and live an easy life on the double indemnity insurance. She'd make a dime go even further than Mickleberry."

The woman was a cold greedy bitch. If Griggs died, she would find another damned fool and drain his blood, too.

I said only, "I'll authorize the salary advance. Don't worry, Tom," and I went to my quarters. It was Griggs' problem, not mine.

Or was it? *If I fell off a catwalk* . . . They were not words to say on a jinxed ship. So help me, a chill ran along my spine when I thought of them.

We had normally gusty weather until the approaches to Belfast Lough. The wind died, the sea smoothed, and dense fog muffled us up in the Lough like damp lamb's wool.

We inched into the position assigned us by the pilot station, dropped the hook, shut down the engine and waited.

I did not like that fog, although I had no reasons to be leery. We had arrived unjinxed where we were going, and everybody was glad about it. Of course, the guys were straining at the leash to go ashore, and they were beefing because the mail would be delayed in coming aboard, but generally the tension relaxed.

The next morning the fog was still dense. With the main engine shut down, the silent hollow-sounding ship got on my nerves. I cleared away some paperwork and typed up my Voyage Report, leaving it in the typewriter until we would dock.

About 1030 hours the desk phone rang. It was the third mate, who had the bridge watch. He said hesitantly, "You wanted a report on any unusual occurrence, captain. Well, there's the damndest hide-and-seek on the radar screen—"

I dropped everything and beat it to the bridge.

The fog was so thick I could not see the bow from the wheelhouse windows. From the bridge VHF came the voices of arriving skippers calling the pilot station.

The third mate moved away from the radar, and I stared into the screen. In the wide corridor of the Lough, the sweep blipped a pattern of anchored ships. A smaller vessel was cutting an arc through the pattern with proper caution in the fog.

The arc altered course. A still smaller blip shot away from the lee of an anchored ship, as if trying to keep that barrier between herself and the searcher's radar.

"You know, captain," mused the third mate, "I'm beginning to understand what Griggs means when he says all the bridge instruments are How-oriented. This radar tells How that cops-and-robbers chase is moving, relative to us and to the other ships. But it does not tell Why the chase is edging toward us."

I said absently, "Why is a different dimension."

"When a guy is a sitting duck on an anchored ship—and a jinxed ship, at that—the Why dimension is the important one. Matter of fact, it's always the important one. Where's the sense to measuring How things act, unless you can find out the reason behind them?"

As I watched the zigzag course of the smaller boat dart nearer, I shared his preference for vertical Causation instead of horizontal Relativity. For inherent meaning instead of relative position. Was the boat darting randomly to escape from a patrol, or was she coming as a threat to us? Who on Earth would be a threat to us?

My brain must have shifted into the right gear, because the answer came in a flash. Cullane. Had the FBI nabbed him through the information I had given them? If so, Schuster was now on the same blacklist as Cromwell, on both sides of the Atlantic. And when those IRA hotheads got sore, they said it with bombs.

If they had a fast radar-equipped cruiser and had heard over the VHF where *Ceres* had been advised to anchor, they might come out and throw a bomb at us, counting on escaping in the explosion and fog.

Sitting duck was the word for us, all right. I went to the bridge telephone and called Griggs' quarters. He answered and I said, "Mayday, Tom. The IRA in a fast cruiser. Lower both boats and find a couple volunteers to set up a roadblock."

"I'll take one boat myself. What's the play?"

"Block them and duck. They have a patrol boat on their tail. I wouldn't set you guys up unless I figured the British were coming."

"Let's hope they're not too little and too late."

In ninety seconds the lifeboats were lowered and

lying alongside. Griggs, with a walkie-talkie, was in the starboard boat. The life-jacketed second engineer was in the port boat, which he had brought around to join Griggs. Life jacket. Had Griggs forgotten his?

The stalking in the fog-stuffed Lough continued on the radar screen. It was obvious now that the small cruiser had no other purpose than to reach us. I thought, the stubborn Irish. At last they seemed to say to hell with dodging the patrol boat, and they came toward us like a torpedo.

I grabbed my walkie-talkie and said to Griggs, "The enemy is two points off the starboard bow and coming fast."

"Right, sir!"

I went to the bridge wing and watched the lifeboats start up and glide forward into the fog, with Griggs' boat in the lead.

Back to the radar, now switched from the general Lough-scan, to the immediate range. Griggs was on a collision course with the cruiser. The fast craft swerved. Griggs countered. The craft circled completely around, showing her heels to the slower lifeboat.

Bypassing Griggs she resumed course—and was blocked by our second boat. Another evasive swing.

The radar went black.

I roared a curse that must have blistered all How and Why dimensions, and I barged out of the wheelhouse. I jumped down the ladders and lumbered along the forward deck to the bow.

Through the mist I could see that the fast end-around rushing had brought the play to our twenty-yard line. The attacker was a flying-bridge cabin cruiser, far outclassing our dories. There was no way our slower boats could block her swivel-hipped ground-gaining.

Griggs suddenly charged full speed toward her. I saw that he meant to ram.

Those were not my orders. I had told him to block, not to commit suicide by ramming a craft which undoubtedly had high explosives aboard.

Suicide. *If I fell off a catwalk . . . the double-indemnity insurance . . .*

The heartsick fool was going to add another death to *Ceres'* score. He was going to wreck our beat-the-jinx campaign. I roared, "Stop!"

He could not hear, of course. He swung to shortcut across the cruiser's evasive turn. Just before the lifeboat's bow rammed her midships, he dove into the sea.

He surfaced and struck out for our other boat, which I could make out dimly off the port bow.

The cabin cruiser blew to glory. The bomb they had intended to lob against *Ceres'* waterline must have been a lulu. I saw the man on the flying bridge flap into the air like a rag doll and come down near Griggs in a shower of debris.

Griggs was hit. He sank and did not come up.

I ripped off my wool jacket, vaulted over the rail and splashed feet first into the drink. I thought, Mary has broken Tom down until he doesn't care if he lives or dies.

I lunged toward him underwater, grabbed him, bulled our way to the surface and held his chin clear of the water.

Something hit me weakly on the back. I looked

around and saw the disjointed but still-living rag doll from the cruiser. His eyes stared from their sockets as he flailed helpless limbs to clutch me.

I brought my arm out of the water and chopped a blow into his neck. He sank like a stone.

Griggs had been hit on his left shoulder and arm. Probably his ribs, too. He opened his eyes. They were still cool but very tired.

"Never mind," he coughed, and a pale blood bubble wheezed through his nose.

"Mind!" I yelled. "We had a jinx licked, and you tried that damnfool stunt! Shut up and live! Live for the ship! Live for Tommy! Dammitall, live for Tommy!"

His eyes showed warmth and interest. I could see strength come into his face despite the dribbling bubbles.

The second engineer was maneuvering his boat alongside us, but a white hull slid out of the fog and walled us on the other side. A clipped accent called down, "Ahoy! You chaps need assistance?"

I looked up into a spade-cut beard and braided cap. I barked, "My mate is badly hurt. Can you rush him to a hospital?"

Well, the British were not too little or too late. They hoisted Griggs aboard and shoved off fast, pausing only to put an Intelligence officer into our lifeboat to get the story. A quiet clerklike guy who I found was named Dunning, when we had time for details.

Dunning and the second engineer hauled me into the lifeboat and took me to *Ceres*. I climbed aboard by the pilot ladder. The lifeboat, under

Dunning's direction, returned to fish up identifiable pieces of the cruiser.

By the time I had changed to dry clothes and given the radio officer a message about Griggs for the Belfast agent, the lifeboat was being winched aboard. Dunning came to my quarters. I ordered a tray of coffee and gave what I thought was a clear account.

Dunning did not seem to know what the hell I was talking about. "You have said, captain, you had no prior expectation of an attack. Yet you had alerted your watch officers, and you took immediate steps when the blips appeared on the radar."

"Yes, but that was just part of the beat-the-jinx tune-up," I explained carefully. "The ship's timing was off. That is, her mass-energy field was out of phase with the universal time field."

"I see. Quite."

"No, you don't see. I don't see, either, because Griggs did not waste time trying to get post-Euclid theorems into my thick skull. But he gave me some practical advice. By forcing the ship's systems into a straitjacket of absolute control, we could bring the ship into phase. Like adjusting the spark on a car motor."

"But, according to your account, the radar went black. So the ship is still jinxed."

"To the contrary, when I got to the ship's bow I realized our timing was okay."

Well, I could not get through to him. He dropped the subject and asked if I had seen the men aboard the cruiser. I said I had seen only the one who had been blown off. I added, "He was interfering with my rescue of Griggs, so I clobbered him. He was far gone anyhow."

Dunning's puzzlement increased. "My word, captain! Did you kill a dying man? A man who was no serious threat to you?"

It was then I felt the shock of how far astray Relativity had led the world's values. All measurement—and no meaning. Nothing was evil, nothing was good. Everything was relative. I said to Dunning, "I was not working on the Relativity plane. I was not measuring How the man was, relative to health, relative to me. Inherently he was a vicious murderer. He was a malfunctioning psychic entity, and I scrapped him."

"I understand your attitude—I think—but I advise you to modify the incident when you make your official report."

I had to admit the guy had something there.

The patrol boat took Dunning off *Ceres* shortly after noon. I suspended my Relativity arguments and got back to work. I went to Griggs' quarters and packed his suitcase, so the ship's agent could take it ashore. I did not forget the photo of Tommy.

When we docked the next day and the mail came aboard, I had a letter from Mickleberry:

Please be advised that the FBI have apprehended the man named Cullane who attempted to ship six crates of weapons aboard Ceres. *He has uttered threats, so I further advise that you be alert for reprisals from his Belfast organization.*

Tightwad Mickleberry could unlimber his telex for a beef about an eight-hour engine stop, but a terrorist threat to the ship was worth only a postage stamp.

Well, that about concluded the excitement of the voyage. We were lucky enough to replace the blown-up lifeboat. In disordered Ulster, that was really luck.

I went ashore to visit Griggs in the hospital. He was doing fine, minus two crushed ribs and with his arm in a cast. The hospital planned to repatriate him by air the next week. He was back on even keel again, his depression having worked itself out.

After the grain was discharged we had an uneventful voyage back to Baltimore. And who should traipse on board after we docked, but Mickleberry!

He came into my office and remarked wryly, "I expected to find the decks paved with gold, captain, after the expense of this voyage."

While he sat and griped I mixed him a martini, took a Scotch for myself and said, "You put me aboard to unjinx the ship and I did so, thanks to Griggs and his Einstein fallacy. The job cost money, but *Ceres* will never again cost a life."

"Why do you reach that conclusion?"

"Because the radar went black, sending me to the bow where I was right at hand when Griggs went under. Instead of being killed by a jinx, Griggs was saved by a miracle. In the Why dimension—which is the operative dimension—that means all systems are go."

Mickleberry swished his drink. I added, "How is Griggs?"

"Recovering fast. We are thinking of giving him command of *Ceres* when he is medically fit."

"Good idea." I paused. "But what are you gonna do with the Old Man?"

He puckered another smile. "Don't worry, captain. We'll think of something."

Chapter 10

January 3 (cont.) . . .
Xavier Hears The Worst

The *Ceres* tape had run its course. It re-clicked into its shell and dropped to the *Hold* slot. Xavier felt rather weak at the legal complications that could result from Schuster's admission of murder. He had heard enough for one session—and yet the other tapes would hang like swords over his head until they were played.

Abruptly he got up and fed another shell to the unit. His apprehensions relaxed as the tape began, "On that hot July afternoon, swinging with the Gulf Stream past Hatteras, the bulk carrier *Sea Loader* . . ."

He reflected that the *Sea Loader* was a de-fused issue, though explosive at the time.

". . . was in dangerous water," the tape was saying, "but my much-advertised troubleshooting sixth sense never let out a yip. . . ."

● ● ●

NOW YOU SEE HER

On that hot July afternoon, swinging with the Gulf Stream past Hatteras, the bulk carrier *Sea Loader* was in dangerous water, but my much-advertised troubleshooting sixth sense never let out a yip.

The *Sea Loader* was bound for Perth Amboy with a cargo of copper slag from Venezuela. I was skipper aboard because I had given Mickleberry in Operations some advice he had taken, for once. The previous skipper had been an old ditherer named Hibbard, half-sick from a nervous stomach and unequal to the job. I told Mickleberry to pension the guy off before he made a mistake that would cost the Company real dough.

After the *Sea Loader* had been involved in a harbor collision while Hibbard was in his bunk, Mickleberry took my advice, eased the guy out and sent me aboard to tighten up the sloppiness that results when the top man is not minding the store.

That afternoon, as the bridge watch was changing at 1600 hours, the *Sea Loader's* chief engineer ambled onto the bridge wing, coming topside for air after his daily siesta. He was a pipe-smoking bookworm, named Buchanan. I had nothing against him except his indifferent cold-fish attitude.

On that afternoon he seemed to have turned out like a bear with a sore head. He gave me a curt nod, grated his pipe stem to the corner of his mouth and rested a tattooed forearm along the dodger. His heavy eyelids raised to scan the sea.

Without looking at me he commented, "You ordered the RPM's reduced," as if I had put one over on him while he was pounding his ear.

I said mildly, "Yeah, I reduced her to Half Ahead. Perth Amboy don't want us before noon tomorrow."

He chewed his pipe stem and made another comment. "I don't see the coast. We must be way out."

"Out where?" I asked, surprised. "We're right on the beam for Ambrose."

This did not seem to satisfy him. He took the pipe out of his mouth and explained, "Hibbard always cut along the coast, north of Hatteras. He said it helped him keep his bearings straight."

"Hibbard never stepped up to bat without making sure nobody had stolen the base paths."

Cold humor gleamed in the heavy-lidded eyes, and the waxy lips quirked. It suddenly occurred to me that Buchanan really disliked me very much.

"Always expect to bat a thousand, Schuster? Carrying a rabbit's foot? Maybe that's a trouble-shooter's first law of preservation."

"Nobody bats a thousand," I said shortly. I noted Buchanan's odd mood. His face had a tense pallor, the eye pouches faded to greenish white.

He clamped his teeth on the pipe again, gave me another curt nod, and ambled into the wheel-house. I saw him head for the chartroom. He generally took a once-a-day-gander at our course and position, but I wondered why the final leg of the voyage had any interest for him. He could not get to Perth Amboy faster than the ship.

He retired below after a short session in the chartroom. I went to my quarters to line up my Voyage Report. Paperwork not being my strong point, I decided to take a break around 1630 hours to see if I could catch a news report from some coastal radio station.

I caught it, all right.

". . . yachtsman allegedly run down at three o'clock this afternoon by the bulk carrier *Sea Loader* five miles off Cape Henry. Donald Claremont, aged 42 from Virginia Beach, was repairing the motor aboard his 30-foot cabin cruiser *Amelia* when the 20-thousand-ton ship allegedly ran him down, throwing him into the water and sinking the cruiser. The badly-shaken yachtsman was picked up immediately by the tugboat *Halmar Cross*, which had witnessed the incident. The *Sea Loader*'s owners have no comment, aside from stating they have no ships in the Cape Henry area. Coast Guard sources say the *Sea Loader* is due in Perth Amboy tomorrow noon."

Well, it really zonked me. At 3:00 PM we had been a good hundred and fifty miles eastwards of Cape Henry, and we sure had not run down any cabin cruisers. The incident was a damned lie. The tugboat *Halmar Cross* could not possibly have witnessed it. I knew the *Cross* line of tugs. A hard-bitten, no-nonsense bunch.

What the devil would I be doing, up under the coast? As long as there was a northward boost to be sneaked from the rim of the Gulf Stream, I was staying with it. I was no Hibbard, who got nervous prostration unless he could keep one foot glued to home base.

Hibbard. Yeah, that rang a bell. Buchanan had expected me to use Hibbard's course lines. He had expected the ship to hug the coast north of Hatteras and be in sight of land at 1600 hours. Blue water from horizon to horizon had drained the blood right out of him.

The radio officer knocked at the opened door and handed me a message from Mickleberry. I reflected that Mickleberry's ulcers had been through a bad hour and a half.

The message was: RECONFIRM NOON POSITION SUBSEQUENT COURSE

A reasonable request, everything considered. I went to the chartroom. The chief mate was taking our 1630 bearings from the radio navigation unit. He scribbled the final figure and moved aside to let me at the chart table.

A pair of dividers lay open on the chart.

Now, although there was no law about it, the mates usually closed the dividers and returned them to the long tray at the back of the chart table. Since the mate had only now jotted down the bearings, he probably had not been measuring distance on the chart. But I asked anyhow, "You been using these dividers?"

"Why no—not yet, Captain," he returned, puzzled.

"Who's been in here since the position was marked at 1600?"

He hesitated. "I saw Buchanan. Somebody else could have ducked in here while I was on the bridge, but—"

I picked up the dividers carefully, put one point on Cape Henry and swung an arc. It went through our course line as near to our 1500 position as I would expect a chief engineer to come.

Without commenting, I rechecked our noon position and course. I returned the dividers to the chart tray and said to the mate,

"The heat wave must be scrambling the wire services. They got us running down a cabin cruiser off Cape Henry."

"Cape Henry!" The mate pushed his cap off his forehead. "Sounds like a stunt Hibbard might have pulled. He always made a beeline for Hatteras and steamed hell-for-leather up the coast." He gestured to Hibbard's erased course lines, still visible on the much-used chart. "Hibbard burned up a lot of bunkers, racing around that dogleg to Ambrose."

I left the chartroom and went to my office. There was no ignoring the connection between Hibbard's usual return route and the incident off Cape Henry. The lie must be a deliberate attempt to discredit the ship. A planned fraud? A hit-and-run insurance swindle?

But how did Buchanan fit into it? The more I thought about his tense, sarcastic attitude on the bridge, the more I was convinced he had known that the Cape Henry incident was due to occur.

I wrote the message to Mickleberry and took it across the alleyway to the radioroom. As I handed it over, I asked the spark, "Anybody aboard had messages or phone calls I don't know about?"

His honest surprise could not be doubted. "No, there's been nothing, Captain."

I went back to my office and thought some more about Buchanan. Apparently he had not sent our Perth Amboy ETA to the plotters. But then, nobody needed to get the ETA from the ship. All they needed to do was to call up the charterer's agent and ask.

The agent had known about our noon arrival long before the information had been finalized and sent aboard.

Was Buchanan really framing a hit-and-run damage suit against his employers? I had not thought he was such a fathead. Aside from anything else, he must have known that squeezing even legal payments out of the Company was like getting juice from a pet rock. Trying a fraud on them would be like tangling with the *Sea Loader's* twin screws.

Well then, I figured, let's put it another way. Buchanan was no dummy. If he was trying a shakedown, he knew it would work. Therefore, most probably, it had worked before. Like, a yachtsman reports being run down by a ship—most likely from a small foreign company. Having lined up witnesses, the gang sues the ship's owners, and if the ship has been in the immediate vicinity, the owners pay up rather than drag out legal costs or have US waters closed to them. A small Scandinavian or Dutch company would not have the means to investigate perjured testimony.

I had built up quite a case, but it fell apart at that point. The newscast had said the Cape Henry incident had been witnessed by the *Halmar Cross*. None of the *Cross* tugs would be involved in fraud.

I needed more facts. I saw that a 1700 hours

bulletin was about due, so I tried the radio again.

". . . captain of the tugboat *Halmar Cross* stated there was no doubt that the cabin cruiser was run down by the bulkship *Sea Loader*. He told reporters that he had berthed the bulkship several times and recognized her in detail."

I was zonked again. The radio was continuing.

". . . account was corroborated by the steel tycoon George Festerman, whose yacht *Trident* was also at the scene. 'The ship crossed our bows after running down the cruiser and proceeded at Full Speed. Her name was clearly visible in our binoculars and there was no doubt of her identity,' said Festerman. The Coast Guard is withholding any statement until the *Sea Loader* arrives at Perth Amboy."

Yeah, the Coast Guard must be doing some head-scratching as they reviewed our noon positions. They knew I could not possibly have been five miles off Cape Henry, but like me they did not doubt the integrity of the *Halmar Cross* or of George Festerman, steel tycoon.

What, actually, had these unimpeachable witnesses seen? Not a real ship. That was absolutely out of the question—because of the astronomical expense to the swindlers, if nothing else.

The whole fraud revolved around a gimmick, and it must be so foolproof that it did not need perjured testimony. Still, if it had been used before, it must have left a trace somewhere.

I coded a message to Mickleberry: INVESTIGATE SHIP-YACHT INSURANCE PAYOFFS MIDDLE ATLANTIC STATES. It was late in the day to catch Mickleberry at the office, but I figured he would be hanging over his Telex until the uncertainty was cleared up.

It only got worse. The news item might have died a natural death, since it could be only of local interest, but the skipper of a charter schooner apparently saw a way to get some free advertising. At 1730 hours the following bulletin had been added,

". . . charter schooner *Gold Ness* reports having sighted the bulkship *Sea Loader* one hundred and fifty miles east north east of Cape Henry at three o'clock this afternoon, the exact time at which the bulkship allegedly was running down the cabin cruiser *Amelia* only five miles off the cape. The schooner ship radioed this station that all his ten passengers were on the deck of the *Gold Ness*, which charters tourist cruises to Bermuda and the Bahamas, when the *Sea Loader* crossed astern . . ."

I remembered meeting the *Gold Ness*, a neat little schooner under full sail, with the light westerly wind giving her a boost toward Bermuda despite the contrary current. I had altered course to go well astern of the schooner, so that our bow wave would not swamp her—a courtesy the skipper apparently had noted in his logbook, since fewer and fewer Masters Of Steam have any understanding of Sail.

The radio station was fading out, so I fiddled with the megahertz until I remembered that our supper would now be under way and unless I legged it down there I would find nothing left but bread and salami.

I went below to the officers' mess room. Supper

had come and gone, and all the places were cleared except mine at the head of the table and Bucanan's at my right hand.

I turned off the mess-room radio, which was squawking static, and took my place. As the messman was slinging a hot platter of hashed browns and fried eggs in front of me, Buchanan came into the room.

He paused a fraction of a second, then transferred his cold pipe from his mouth to his pocket and seated himself as usual. When the messman had gone back to the pantry I did something I usually do not do aboard—touch upon personal conflicts. As I helped myself to the platter, I said, "Whenever a guy hates my guts, I generally know the reason for it, but I'm damned if I can figure out why you dislike me, Buchanan."

He poured himself a cup of coffee. "Nothing personal, Schuster. General resentment, I suppose, that any man gets to the top in an organization without conscious effort."

"You mean, I got where I am by bull luck?"

"No. That's the most irritating part," said Buchanan, giving me a heavy appraising glance, "Luck is nothing to resent. It's just—luck. Nobody detests a man for beating the odds at the dog track. It's when luck changes to destiny that it becomes something to resent."

"I don't follow you."

"Luck evens out. It doesn't pick favorites. Lucky today, unlucky tomorrow. Chance is blind—like justice," he added, his eyelids dropping lower.

"But destiny is whimsical," he resumed. "Destiny takes a man like you, Schuster—a man with no

special talent except a dogged capacity for work—
and loads the dice. The difference between you
and a dozen smarter men in the Company is that
you are always in the right place at the right time.
You become a man who cannot do anything
wrong."

"I oughtta introduce you to Mickleberry."

He waved this aside. "Oh, I've heard Mickleberry sounding off about you. About your rough
manner, your loud mouth, your damn-the-
torpedoes attitude. Mickleberry has to fire you
once a year to give his ulcers a rest. But when you
tell him something he listens. For example, why
are you aboard the *Sea Loader* at this moment?"

I did not answer, and he went on, "Because you
stuck a knife in Hibbard's back. The old guy was
sick and just serving time until his pension. You
had Mickleberry kick him out and put you
aboard."

I gave Buchanan a heavy look of my own. "Yeah,
me being aboard kinda queered your Cape Henry
caper, didn't it?"

"Believe it or not," Buchanan said patiently, "my
irritation stems entirely from impersonal resentment about those loaded dice. Once again you
seem to be the right man at the right place. You are
still batting a thousand. For that reason and no
other, I hate your guts."

I believed him. The bookish intellectual type
gets hot under the collar about general
principles—more than personal ups and downs.

The messman came back with a refill on the
bread, so we knocked off the conversation and I
stoked up on the calories. Buchanan did not have

much appetite. Sometimes I had the same effect on Mickleberry.

I do not know how the news coverage would have gone if another more important story had broken. But it was midsummer, the politicians were at the beach, and nobody was hijacking planes, so the whereabouts of the *Sea Loader* became of intense interest to the news bureaus.

The crux of the matter was that the *Halmar Cross* and the Festerman yacht *Trident* were sticking to their guns about seeing the real bulkship *Sea Loader*.

For me, the significant item was the steadfastness of the skipper of the *Halmar Cross*, since he must have found out right away that Schuster and not Hibbard had been on the bridge. It was the first question he would ask either the Coast Guard or Mickleberry, since he knew the ship. The answer must have zonked him as much as his report had zonked me. If he was sticking to his guns, it was because he was honestly convinced he had seen us.

The gimmick! I had to figure it out, and the newscasts were only distracting me. "This looks like it's becoming one of the great sea mysteries," yapped one broadcaster, "comparable to the *Mary Celeste* and the disappearance of the steamer *Portland*. Where was the *Sea Loader* at three o'clock this afternoon? Off Cape Henry or a hundred and fifty miles at sea? How can a ship be in two places at once?

He left the question open, which did not help me a lot. But at 2000 hours came the slipup I had been waiting for. The newscast played a taped statement from the dunked yachtsman Donald Claremont, who was (quote) resting comfortably despite what looked to be a crippling back injury (unquote):

"The *Sea Loader's* bow wave lifted the *Amelia,* and as she heeled over I saw the ship's hull looming above me—black with rusty spots and a funny long dent over her port hawsepipe."

It was true that we had such a dent from Hibbard's harbor collision. However, we would show no sign of having struck the cabin cruiser, and Donald Claremont was being very careful not to claim we had. It was the *bow wave* that had done the damage.

Legally the statement warmed the heart of an old sea lawyer like me, but it made the mistake I had been waiting for. Now I knew what questions to ask the captain of the *Halmar Cross.* Now I could lower the boom on that well-read engineer, Mr. Buchanan.

To prove I could do things in an intellectual and civilized manner, I phoned his quarters and invited him up for a drink. He came, wedged himself in the settee corner, pipe in mouth, and opted for beer. I poured myself a slug of scotch, pulled up a chair and began.

"I've been thinking over the Cape Henry incident."

"Yes, it's certainly all over the radio dial," grimaced Buchanan around his pipe stem. "Claremont was lucky with witnesses—the *Halmar Cross,* especially. Kind of makes you the fall guy, doesn't it?"

"Well, now, the Coast Guard has the *Sea Loader's* course and noon positions since we left Venezuela. They knew my course is nowhere near Cape Henry."

"And what is their evidence worth?" Buchanan

took the pipe out of his mouth. "A civil damage suit is not a Coast Guard hearing. A civil jury believes eyewitnesses, not official documents or navigation figures they don't understand."

"As you know to your profit."

He took a slow drink of beer. I went on,

"I'm not trying to trap you with a bluff. I'll bet one thousand dollars—and you know I'm no welsher—that I can describe what you would call the *modus operandi*. Take me up on it?"

He considered a long moment. "No. I was betting that Donald Claremont would end your perfect record today. I won't throw good money after bad."

"Yet you must have known I would not follow Hibbard's course."

"Well, we assumed you would part company with the Gulf Stream in the general vicinity of Hatteras. Distance is really not all that important. You see, Schuster, a civil jury is oriented to land speeds. To them, a discrepancy of fifty miles is nothing. They can't comprehend that fifty miles could mean five hours steaming for a small freighter.

"One hundred and fifty miles is admittedly stretching the limits," he added, "and having that damned charter skipper poke his nose into the affair—! Destiny again."

"Not at all. The skipper of that schooner logged our meeting because I changed course when I could have plowed ahead and let our bow wave punch him in the nose. He phoned the radio station to show me his appreciation by getting me off Donald Claremont's hook. It was my knowledge of

Sail and my correct maneuvering that made the
Gold Ness a factor."

Buchanan thought this over. "Yes, the *Gold Ness*
can perhaps be credited to your dogged capacity
for knowing your job. But when all is said and
done, if Claremont brings suit the issue will boil
down to the personal testimony of the two most
technically impressive witnesses—you and the
skipper of the *Halmar Cross.*"

"But it wasn't meant to be my testimony," I
pointed out. "The plot was laid when Hibbard was
skipper. With his indefensible courses, sloppy log-
books and the recent harbor collision, Hibbard
could be torn apart before a jury.

"I'm no ready-made fall guy like Hibbard," I
continued. "I run a tight ship and my record is
clean as a whistle. This caper should have been
aborted when I replaced Hibbard. That it was not
aborted, Buchanan, would seem to indicate that
personal spite overcame your normally good
judgment. You had to take that chance of doing
me dirt."

Buchanan sealed his lips over his pipe.

I went on, "Cockiness—the cool nerve of chal-
lenging the Company's legal powerhouse—was
what first struck me about the caper. The fraud
had what the swindlers believed to be an unbeat-
able gimmick—a duplicate ship that could make
eyewitnesses swear to her on a stack of Bibles.

"But, you know, any con game, no matter how
ingenious, works only against weakness. If this
gimmick had worked over and over—as I was betting it had—then the victim-ships were carefully
chosen. Badly-run ships, captains like Hibbard,

drunken officers, other collisions against the ship's record. So, at least one member of the gang was in shipping."

Buchanan was watching me with ironic detachment. I continued,

"The difficulty is, a working officer does not get aboard the very large variety of ships that the scheme needs. After all, companies worth suing don't have all that many badly-run ships. So the man who cased the victims must have been a shipping agent who went aboard scores of ships in the normal course of his work. He spoke with the officers and could size up the conditions on board.

"Now, here's where I got the cart before the horse," I said, and Buchanan shifted his pipe. "I assumed that the agency man was the Master Criminal. But that could hardly have been the case. The fraud is nothing without the gimmick, and a ship's agent would have a hard time finding a scientist who would duplicate ships for him.

"So let's turn the picture around and say that a scientifically-inclined guy invented a way to duplicate sizable objects. Probably he can duplicate just about anything—Bedloe's Island, a diesel locomotive, the Taj Mahal. If he decides to duplicate ships, it's because he works on ships—with his scientific background, probably as an engineer. It was the engineer who masterminded the fraud and found a shipping agent to help him.

"I'd suppose," I said conversationally, "a three-dimensional duplicator of that scope would be worth more on an honest market than used in an insurance swindle."

Buchanan snorted and took the pipe from his

mouth. Dull color darkened his cheeks. "You know damned little about it, Schuster! Do you know what happens to an independent inventor today? The big corporations rob him blind! They reject his patent—and build the same thing themselves, using a staff of lawyers to invalidate his claim. Or they pay him a few hundred dollars plus royalties, with so many contract loopholes that they can make millions without giving him a cent.

"If an inventor has a new idea," Buchanan finished more calmly, "he had better make the millions any way he can—and to hell with being an honest sucker."

I wondered what patent deal had burned Buchanan so badly that he had decided to use his duplicator gimmick outside the law. I went on,

"When I came to think about the fake *Sea Loader,* a couple of things were obvious. First, she could not be a solid ship. The whole fraud is based on the fact that only one *Sea Loader* exists. The ringer appears at the collision site and disappears immediately, leaving the real ship to take the rap.

"Next, the captain of the *Halmar Cross* said he recognized the details of the *Sea Loader.* The fake ship was the spitting image of the real. That implied photocopying. Something like a Xerox copy blown up three-dimensionally.

"When I got that far I realized I was trying to pin down an optical illusion. How could it be created out of thin air? Well, from a ship's bridge I see plenty of solid-looking illusions—rainbows, islands where no islands ever were. And, generally, nature's effects can be imitated.

"Especially in these days of films, slides, tapes. A

few years ago, when I couldn't finagle myself out of the compulsory vacation the docs order now and then, I took a bus to Florida and moseyed around the tourist places. I saw the 360° movie screen at Disney World, where the audience is in the middle of the action.

"I remember it," I added parenthetically, "because in one scene we were standing on the forward deck of a ship. I could see the guys making ready the mooring lines on the focsle, and I could turn around and look up at the bridge. It was so real that I got the hell out of there, phoned Mickleberry and told him if he didn't put me on a ship soonest, I would sign aboard the first rustbucket that would take me.

"So the 360° screen stuck in my mind, and I thought of it in connection with a fake *Sea Loader*. Suppose the technique could be reversed. The movie is the 360° center and the audience is outside it."

Buchanan stirred. "But the spherical screen? On the open sea?"

"I think the gimmick uses the same screen that nature uses––waterladen atmosphere. Only, the water molecules have to be fogged."

"A time-consuming process, even for nature."

"Not necessarily. I remember a voyage through the Straits of Magellan, when a full hurricane hit us out of a clear blue sky. The wind whipped the sea and air together. In a few seconds—literally seconds, Buchanan—we were floating in a homogenized mist, a three-dimensional screen of shattered molecules.

"I don't know because I never tried it, but I

believe a field of high-speed particles would break the sea atmosphere into the same screen of fog. On a hot summer day, the fog would continually evaporate upward, like the heat shimmer off an asphalted dock.

"So there's your hollow screen—cigar-shaped, probably, since a ship is much longer than she is high. The generating machinery could be very small in relation to the area covered. The difficulty, in fact, would be in keeping the electromagnetic activity from seriously disturbing radio and telephone communications within the entire horizon area.

"In the center of the three-dimensional fogged shell would be the tape projectors, gimballed to keep the image steady at sea. They would throw a solid-looking copy of the ship on the insides of the screen. From the outside the projection would look like a solid ship, from any angle."

"Not with a cigar-bulge field," frowned Buchanan. "You'd get a projection like a Fun House mirror."

"Okay, okay. All I want to make clear is that the technique of the 360° screen could be applied from within to the vapor field, giving an image as sharp and valid as a rainbow." And I went on,

"Well, when the Master Scientist has the gimmick ready, the shipping agent starts casing likely ships. He could build up a file of descriptions and photos without knowing which ship will satisfy all conditions.

"Then he stalks the likelies through ordinary shipping channels. Eventually one of them is going to be due along the Continental Shelf during the

midsummer yachting season. The scientist prepares the duplicator tapes from the photos, and
the pair of swindlers start looking for a yachting
stooge.

"Now, this scheme has implied a scientist and a
shipping agent. It also implies a crooked lawyer for
the courtoom work, and the lawyer now comes into
the act. He looks through his pending bankruptcy
files—at least, a bankrupt would be easiest to
persuade—"

Buchanan's eyelids lifted a little, and he smiled.

"—until he finds a guy with a boat. If the guy also
has an old whiplash or back injury, so much the
better, but the important thing is that he really can
handle small craft.

"The lawyer and the yachting stooge come to
terms, the yacht is equipped with the necessary
remote-control devices, the other gadgetry is
loaded aboard a sturdy workboat—probably a rebuilt fishing trawler—and the plotters wait for the
agent to pick up the victim's one dependable
time-message—the 48-hour ETA required before
arrival at an American port.

"From this ETA and the ship's position the
swindlers plot on a chart the most convenient
point—convenient from the aspect of traffic and
water depth—that the victim will be passing in
daylight. They move their two boats to a nearby
marina and wait.

"During the next dark hours both boats go out to
the chosen site, which will be far enough offshore
to avoid most of the small boat traffic. From the
trawler they assemble the long narrow pontoon
raft that will hold the control machinery and the

banks of gimballed projectors. They attach the gadgetry to the raft and add the outriggers that will generate the field screen."

Buchanan muttered around the pipe, "He even guessed the outriggers!"

"You don't give me credit for having a brain in my head, do you?" I demanded. "The field generators have to be outside the projector core, right? Where else can they be, except on the outriggers?"

Buchanan shrugged, and I went on,

"Now, all this equipment has been built to withstand underwater pressures, so they anchor it and sink it with submerge-and-recall controls. A sea mile along a course parallel to the one the victim will be using, they anchor and submerge a homing base.

"They go back to the marina. A couple hours before the countdown the stooge takes the yacht out alone, finds the anchored units with his sensors and stations himself between them. Naturally his engine is working, since he can't let himself be carried away by wind or current.

"What he is waiting for is a clear sea in the area. He may have to wait an hour or so, though the shipping lanes are not as crowded as they used to be. When he is alone, he recalls the projector unit to the surface and switches on the field and the projector tapes. If the illusion is fuzzy, he can undoubtedly fine-tune it from the yacht.

"Now he's ready for the eyewitnesses—and the more the merrier. As soon as they start coming over the horizon, he recalls the homing base to the surface, uncouples the illusion from its mooring buoy and sends it homing to the base. As the illusion passes him, looking exactly like a real ship—and being avoided by other craft, exactly like a real ship—he kicks out a prepared hull panel in the yacht, which capsizes and sinks.

"The rescuers pick up the yachtsman, and he impresses upon them the fact that the *bow wave* has sunk him. While he keeps the witnesses busy, the illusion finishes its run, shuts itself off, couples itself to the homing base; and resubmerges. If the witnesses don't find the ship when they look for her again, they assume she has proceeded over the horizon."

Buchanan removed the pipe. "Don't be an ass, Schuster. The illusion can't go out like a light. She reduces over the base, keeping in scale. Trick perspective can fool the keenest eye. People have been known to walk through walls painted to lead to distances."

I was willing to take his word for it. I continued, "Well, after dark the trawler goes out, recalls and dismantles the gadgetry and hauls it home. The lawyer brings suit, and several months later the poor slobs aboard the victim-ship are being torn apart in a courtroom. The nearer they have been to the scene of the swindle, the less defense they have against perfectly honest and well-meaning eyewitnesses, and the stooge is awarded the million or so he is demanding.

"Because of the scientific preparation and legal aftermath, the swindlers probably can handle only one victim a year. But after a few years the routine goes so smoothly that the two shore men and the current stooge handle the actual trap. The inventor continues in his job as a chief engineer.

"Now, he has not tackled his own company because he knows they would be tough. But he is put aboard the *Sea Loader,* and after a while the temptation to scuttle Hibbard is too much. I don't know when he prepares the duplicator tapes. Maybe he stops ashore one voyage, maybe the tapes are already on file. Anyhow, at this last turnaround in Perth Amboy the trap is finalized with the new stooge Donald Claremont. Then, unexpectedly, Schuster replaces Hibbard. For the first time, they are facing a strong skipper instead of a weak one. But the inventor gives the go-ahead."

Buchanan said quickly, "Why not? We had no way of knowing your course would lie so far off Cape Henry."

"You should not have sold me short as a navigator, Buchanan. If you've heard Mickleberry sounding off, you know I use less bunkers than any skipper in the Company. That's because I ride the currents the way an astronaut rides his orbit before letting it spin him onto his next course.

"The difference is this—a space orbit is a mathematical certainty, but a sea orbit shifts continually. Only a master mariner knows how to find the fast rim of the Gulf Stream. Too far west, he's in the strong southward current. Too far east— unless he's going that way—he's got to fight the Stream to get out of it.

"Until 24 hours ago I did not know where I would be steaming. But the rate of the current, the color and feel of the water, told me where the rim had shifted. So I slid onto it, cut the speed to Half Ahead and coasted, ready to spin off to Ambrose.

"You can call it luck or destiny. I call it hard work

and experience. Whatever it is, it means you're all washed up."

Buchanan opened his eyes wider. "On what evidence? The so-called gadgetry will no longer be at the site of the caper."

"Yeah, but the *Amelia* with all those remote controls is still wrecked on the Continental Shelf, and I can make the Coast Guard dive for her by asking the captain of the *Halmar Cross* just one question: how long after the collision did the bow wave hit his tug?

"When he thinks back, he will realize *there was no bow wave*. And there goes the old ball game."

Buchanan sucked the pipe. "How can you identify the plotters?"

"Wake up, man! Mickleberry will come aboard tomorrow with a list of big-money ship-yacht settlements. Donald Claremont and all those other stooges are definitely not going to take the rap alone."

A pause. Buchanan asked, "How did I give myself away?"

"You came to the bridge on the muscle about trifles, and you were cocky enough to bait me. But even if you had controlled your feelings, you would have made the one real mistake."

He opened his eyes and held his breath. I told him, "You went into the chartroom to find out how far the ship had been from the trap at Cape Henry. Stunned by those hundred and fifty miles, you left the dividers lying open on the chart. The distance they measured gave you away."

"Now what?"

"You'll be confined to quarters," I said shortly. I rose and got my passkeys from my desk. "But not your own quarters. God only knows what escape-artist gadgetry you have in there. You can spend the night in the pilot's cabin on this deck."

"I'm no Houdini," Buchanan seemed calm, but his lips were wax and his eye pouches were greenish again.

I motioned him to his feet. "Come over here and dump your pockets. I want your knife and belt. You intellectual types tend to go off the rails when your pride is crushed."

Buchanan stood up and moved slowly towards me. His eyes were wide open, the pupils like blank ball bearings. He put his fist over the pipe bowl, and I saw that the knuckles were white.

As his wrist turned, I punched him in the belly and chopped a hand below his ear. He fell like a stone.

The pipe lay in two pieces on the deck. Inside the stem was a glass hypodermic unit. No wonder the pipe had always been cold. I refitted the stem carefully so as not to break the glass tip, stepped out on deck and tossed the pipe over the side.

Then I phoned the mate's quarters and told him, "The heat must have got to Buchanan. He went berserk up here. I'm putting him in the pilot's cabin. Get a guard in the alleyway, right away, will you?"

Buchanan returned to the land of the living while I was taking his knife and belt. He choked hoarsely, "You're a real son of a bitch Schuster, you know that?"

"Yeah," I agreed. "that's the big difference between me and a dozen smarter men in the Company."

I hoisted Buchanan off the deck and propped

him onto the settee. "Why self-destruct?" I asked him. "Spent all the chicken feed you got from the capers?"

"Chicken feed?" he flared. "I have a million dollars socked away where nobody can get their hands on it!"

"Fine. If the judge gives you ten years for grand larceny, you'll be earning a hundred thousand a year for sitting in jail. Most guys would be glad to have half your troubles."

"Glad to be taken ashore in irons? To be ashamed, humiliated—!"

"Irons?" I snorted. "For a two-bit con artist? Who do you think you are? Jack the Ripper? Look, Buchanan, if you don't give me any trouble tonight, I'll let you clean up and make a decent appearance in shore clothes tomorrow—under supervision, of course. A lot of guys have cussed me out, but none of them ever said I kicked a man when he was down."

Buchanan could not meet my eye, but he began to perk up. By the time the mate and an AB came to the office, he was pretty much his old ironic self.

Well, we berthed at noon the next day as per orders. The pier was a mob scene. We managed to repel all but official boarders, and eventually four of us convened in my office—Mickleberry, an insurance investigator, a Coast Guard commander and myself.

I had the bridge logbook on my desk, ready for Coast Guard scrutiny, but red tape always bugs me, so I said to the commander, "Jeez, you guys know me from way back! What went through your heads when you heard I was as far off course as Cape Henry?"

"As I understand it," said the commander, straight-faced, "there was some talk about flying out a psychiatrist."

Mickleberry liked that one. He and the insurance investigator were feeling good. They had a list of six ship-yacht settlements in eleven years and had already reasoned through to the shipping agent who must have been common to all of them.

I took a look at the sums involved and realized Buchanan had not been kidding about his million. Somehow I did not begrudge it to him. He had got a raw patent deal from some big corporation and had been turned a little haywire.

I told Mickleberry and the others the story, beginning from Buchanan's tension on the bridge, and the carelessly dropped dividers. I finished, "I don't know how much of Buchanan's admissions to me can be used, but there should be enough evidence available without it."

I stepped into the alleyway and told the guard to bring Buchanan to the office. Buchanan came quietly. He was clean-shaven and neatly dressed in a good shore suit. He nodded at us and said evenly, "I admit nothing and won't talk until I consult my attorney."

This being fair enough, the commander left the officer to arrange for Buchanan's formal arrest.

The insurance investigator said to Mickleberry, "It was lucky that your ace troubleshooter happened to be aboard this ship."

Buchanan spoke up irritably, "It's not luck!" Everybody looked at him, and he went on, "I remember a .400 hitter complaining about an outfielder who always hauled in his home runs. He said, 'It ain't that the bastard covers the outfield—

it's that he stands there and makes the hits come to him.'"

There was a short laugh. Buchanan went on, "It's something psychic. Schuster stands there and makes the action come to him. Maybe that's why he's an ace troubleshooter.

"The thing that was bull luck," he added, "was that Schuster caught onto the basics of the duplicator. The guy hasn't opened a book since he finally crammed his way past his shipmaster exams."

There was another laugh, and I grinned, "Yeah, I had horseshoes all over me."

I was not about to discuss what I know or do not know. When you come right down to it, keeping 'em guessing is really a troubleshooter's first law of preservation.

* * *

The *Sea Loader* tape followed the *Ceres* into *Hold.* Two tapes remained. Xavier reached again for his Drenalin box, changed his mind, rose and went into what his clerks called "the judge's chambers." He brewed a cup of coffee and carried the cup back to the walnut table.

He looked at the remaining two labels. He could not remember any serious problem—any *public* problem—with the *Ocean Wanderer,* so he laid that shell aside. On the other hand, the Space Mining tape . . .

Five minutes later, listening with shocked horror to the genial voice, he blotted the sweat from his forehead. Thank God *that* tape had not got away! The terrible—far-reaching—consequences, if *that* tape had got away . . .

Chapter 11

The Q-Pod Tape Continues

I do like to recall that first hour after the adhering/cohering spheroids had engulfed us. I could visualize us being found a million years later, like a fossil engulfed by the La Brea tar pits. However, my job was not to speculate but to react to the emergency in a proper manner.

What saved our lives had been my insistence that the Q-Pod, like all our Space vehicles, should have internal thermionic/atomic power. The Space engine is taken for granted today, but when we were developing it, I had to battle against proponents of the external solar-cell propulsion systems. I had argued, first, that the solar cell would inevitably suffer efficiency-losses as we moved ever outwards from Sol. And second, the only safe power is *internal*.

I mean, Nature is still the best designer. A human being's power center is inside his body. We don't really wear our hearts on our sleeves.

With an external solar-cell system, we would have been dead within seconds of being overwhelmed by the avalanche. The alternative, of course, did not seem so hot to us at the time—an environment system that would be functioning flawlessly long after we were dusty skeletons on the deck.

When the initial Mayday was running through the transmitter, I called the meeting to order and said, "I hope—and expect—us to be rescued sooner, but we hafta base our plans on our own resources, which will get us to Moon orbit in a year."

I could see Lieutenant Worthing smile sarcastically, but he did not interrupt. I continued, "We will go on half-rations at once. We will also maintain a strict work/leisure routine. There will be no talking except at meal times—and on neutral subjects. Anybody with a complaint against another guy will come to me with it and not express it directly. I want us to be good friends after this trip is over."

They could see the sense to this arrangement. Dr. Loft and Grimes even looked cheerful. They could not know, of course, of the inevitable navigation errors.

My first order of business was to devise a signal that might get through the ore mass. Since our stern tube and jets were clear, we might be only partially covered. Any signal, however weak, might save our lives. However, it would have to be as distinct as possible.

I thought immediately of Morse, though the Morse code has pretty much gone by the board with the development of audio/video systems. Still, its definite dit-dah-dits could be separated out from the cosmic static, put on tape and deciphered by old bastards like me who had been drilled in it before the modern systems had come into general use.

Not wanting to waste time rigging a telegraph key, I took the ordinary mate's whistle that travels everywhere with me—like my chronometer watch and the Company code book—and blew long-short-long onto a transmitting tape. My message was, *Q-Pod buried in dangerous cargo estimate fifty thousand tons proceeding Moon alert Loft 1B*.

I then set our station to transmit/receive at irregular intervals—as a fog-bound ship whistles at irregular intervals, to avoid inadvertent synchronization with another signal.

It was then time for supper, and we foregathered in the main cabin. I will say at once that half-rations did not especially bother us. Since we had been reduced to half-activity—and were plenty solid to begin with—half-rations were exactly what the doctor would have ordered.

We were maintaining silence, but I saw that Dr. Loft had something on his mind. Finally he smiled at me, "Permission to speak?"

"Permission granted."

"It seems to me," he said slowly, "we're overlooking a chance-of-a-lifetime to test the Laws of Probabilities. Now, the textbooks tell us that if we flip a coin, the ultimate result will be an equal number of heads and tails. But it has never worked out that way for me, personally."

"Yeah, but the joker is the word *ultimate*," I

grinned. "We could flip a coin all day, every day, from here to the Moon, and have it come up heads all the time—but at some future date it would reverse itself and even up the score."

"But the fact is," he insisted, "that over the short run, the odds do not apply."

"Of course they apply!" I barked. "A gambling house makes its profit by playing the odds."

"A gambling house makes its profit by rigging the wheels, marking the decks, and hiring croupiers with fast rakes. Let's not be naive, captain. And despite the rigging, people occasionally break the bank.

"Matter of fact," he continued, "life is based on the fact that the odds can be beaten. You yourself, captain, rose from a deckhand to a shipmaster *against the odds*. The Company went into Space *despite the odds*."

There were maybe a few marked decks in both those accomplishments, so I said, "*Rigging* the odds and *beating* the odds are two different things. Are you claiming that—over the short term—you can outguess the Probabilities?"

"Take the heads/tails problem. Think of its sequence as being the circumference of an infinite circle. We can never follow the whole circumference—but we can study the action along a certain arc and recognize *patterns*. And short-term patterns do not necessarily follow the odds.

I could see that the others were interested in our argument. Grimes said, "Successful crap players are telekinetic—they *will* the spots to turn up."

"Ah! That's a still further aspect!" beamed Dr. Loft. "Now, what I propose—since we have a year without other employment—is that we investigate the Probabilities. If we cannibalize the ore centrifuge, we can build a roulette wheel. We can test coins and playing cards. We can divide the research into Mechanical Odds and Telekinetic Odds. And when we get back to Earth, we can break every bank in Las Vegas!"

I did not know whether he was serious—or whether, like me, he was concerned about keeping our minds constructively occupied. It did not matter. Grimes and Worthing were eager to begin, and we drew up our research schedule.

As soon as the roulette wheel was spinning, gambling fever took over the Q-Pod. The guys grudged the necessity for the daily chores. They would have shortened the meal/sleep times when there seemed to be a Mechanical/Telekinetic divergence.

I had to slow them down. I decreed Saturday night to be Music Night. (Eventually the music Rec/Paks were supplanted by a Barber Shop Quartet.) Sunday morning was earmarked for non-denominational divine service, presided over by Dr. Loft. As skipper, I had started the services but my congregation complained I was addressing the Almighty as if He were Mickleberry—an attitude they feared might be taken amiss.

I found out, anyhow—on using the Bible that had been put aboard as standard equipment—why Sunday School teachers use those big black markers. A slip of the page—and the reader is into some pretty hot stuff, let me tell you!

We had been on this schedule for about six weeks—and I had been posting our dead-reckoned course every noon, just as if I knew what I was doing—when the monotonous cosmic fizzle from our receiving station was broken by a faint chatter of static. Being so used to maintaining silence between meals, we just lifted our heads from our "work".

Unbelieving, I listened to the chatter form words in my mind—*calling Q-Pod . . . do you read me . . . do you read me . . .*

I had always thought I was pokerfaced—but the guys looked at me and went wild. I shouted them down and went into the cockpit to answer directly into the transmitter mike. My bones were jelly, I was so afraid the rescuer would give up and go away before I could reach him.

But he was still there. (We did not find out exactly *where* he was for another five months.) It was Compton in Space Tug 4. We tried to switch to voice transmission, but the tones bleached and faded, so we had to stick to Morse.

He said he was alongside, herding us home, and we figured our troubles were over. I wondered, though, when he requested assistance of our stern jets in correcting our course. A Space Tug should have been able to take care of that maneuver by herself.

However, I trimmed as per his instruction, and we were Moonward bound at Full Speed. I took satisfaction from Compton's course data, which indicated I would have missed the Earth/Moon system by a mere Moon-orbit diameter.

Constant Q-Pod/Tug communication made all the difference. We relaxed our ground rules and lived in a more normal manner. We hooked the

Tug guys into our Mechanical/Kinetic Probabilities, and I could see that Las Vegas was gonna be in for a hard time.

The next hint that all might not be well with the Tug came when I received Compton's instructions for the deceleration. Instead of a straightforward retro-blast, he was planning a series of zig-zag trim maneuvers. When I started puzzling out his reasons, I saw there could be only *one* reason—*he had no retro-blast!*

It was lucky that nobody was watching my face at that moment. I understood that Compton had come too close to the massed spheroids—and was bogged down, like us.

I said nothing. The nearer we got to the Earth/Moon system, the more likely a probe would note that we were maneuvering oddly, for a stray chunk of ore.

I had forgotten that stray chunks of ore were exactly what Fakey Atur's Space Sharing Committee wanted to intercept. Other probes were looking for the Q-Pod and a Tug, but Fakey Atur was looking for easy graft. A thin dime would not have got past him. Fifty thousand tons of ore could hardly escape his monitors. While Space Mining screens were patiently tracking us as a "meteor", Fakey was yelling about illegal shipments and penalty payments.

So everybody was looking at us when we began our deceleration zig-zag and we got Instant Reaction.

Inside the Q-Pod, of course, we were aware only that our radio reception had increasing background noise. Compton, now in contact with a

Moon rescue party, was under orders not to trigger an emotional disturbance inside the Q-Pod by rousing hope prematurely. Day after day went by with routine Morse from Compton—although our own Chart Reader showed we must be in Moon orbit.

Finally we felt physical vibration within the Q-Pod. I thought the dummies were trying to drill us out of the ore, and I yelled, "Quick—suit up—before they hole our hull!"

We suited up in record time—but the vibration had stopped. I unhelmeted and coded to Compton, "What the hell is going on?"

He admitted at last that we were in Moon orbit—that he had been mired to within a meter of his viewscreen and sensors since his approach to us—and that a power-drill team on jet-dollies had failed to free him. The vibration of the attempt had traveled through the ore and shaken our hull.

"Like quicksand," he coded back. "Inner tension draws everything. Nearly lost dollies. Must find disruptive force."

We took off our Spacesuits and had yet another Vita/Carbo meal. Dr. Loft said, "Maybe when they assay the ore—"

Worthing flared, "They can't assay it until they can reach it without falling in!"

Our nerves had taken all they could take. We had to get out, or somebody would go berserk. I thought, *a disruptive wedge . . . a substance too alien to be absorbed by the mineral molecules . . .*

I jumped up and tapped a Mayday to Compton on the transmitter mike. When he answered I coded, "Try organic materials in a pressure hose. Repeat, organic."

"Will do . . . will do . . ." came back fast.

I explained my theory to the guys. They were interested, but Worthing said, "The Moon has no organic materials that can be pulverized for a pressure hose. What they need is sawdust. It'll take a week for Holloway to load a shuttle with sawdust and send it up here."

"Okay, so you guys have another week to work out your gambling system. What's a week?"

I got no answer, but I already knew it. A week would be the straw that broke the camel's back. We sat aimlessly, silently. After a while I meandered out to the cockpit and sat by the transmitter. We all were in shock—the shock of being home and yet held fast in our coffin. I suppose hours elapsed.

I heard a soft noise on the hull, like snow sweeping over it. I could see it sweeping over the viewscreen, a mist that obscured the glare of the daylit Moon.

"The Moon!" I bellowed, and the guys came stumbling into the cockpit. "We're free!"

Now we could see the jet-dolly hanging "upside-down" over the Q-Pod. The hose and the dolly's compensating jets shut off, and the outfit floated there, in a thick mist of disintegrating ore and organic particles. I kept saying over and over, "Where did they find organic particles? There's no sawdust on the Moon! Where did they find . . . ?

Chapter 12

June 2 . . .
The Time Bomb Goes Off

Ms. Delaney lifted the pink-and-white orchids from her desk and pinned them carefully to her frilled shirt. The corsage had been lying on her blotter that morning, together with a personal note from Mr. Bennington and a *very* satisfactory cash enclosure which need not be reported to IRS.

Of course, the last week in May had been simply dreadful. The Moon Residence finally had released the fact that the Unidentified Blotch (which Fai k'y Atur had accused of being a Space Mining swindle) was actually a fifty-thousand-ton ore shipment with the Q-Pod *inside* and Space Tug 4 *outside*. The Residence had admitted knowing, since January, that Schuster's team was alive and that Compton had gone to rescue them. By June 1 they would be in Moon orbit.

Well! The media had been *furious* at the deliberate deception—not only the news networks but the

weekly and monthly magazines which had chosen
to Memorialize Schuster in their June 1 issues.
They had descended like a tidal wave upon the
Company executives, bowling the PR Department
aside.

But, reflected Ms. Delaney proudly, the secretaries had held the line—herself, Mr. Bennington's Ms. Ingram, Mr. Xavier's Ms. Dulaire,
and the lesser ladies. They had mutually resolved,
not an inch!—and the media had fumed in vain in
front of their desks.

The seige had taken its toll. Ms. Ingram had
suffered a recurrence of her migraine, and one of
the lesser ladies had gone into hysterics in the
Ladies' Lounge. But the line had held—and the
Company was now quite properly expressing its
gratitude.

Ms. Delaney guessed that Trudy Bennington
had added the orchid-touch to the cash gift. It was
so *like* Trudy. Ms. Delaney smiled a little, before
turning her thoughts to the day's business. Howie
had not yet brought LOCO to the department. He
would be late to work, of course, after the Memo-
rial Day weekend.

Ms. Delaney glanced at the TV panel that had
been hung above the Operations blackboard. As
soon as the Moon rescue team began freeing the
spacecraft from the Blotch, all Company departments would be able to watch the action.

Her musings were interrupted by a slim young
man in an open-necked short-sleeved sports shirt
and brown slacks. An oblong leather case hung by
a strap over one shoulder, and he was carrying a
rolled magazine in one hand. Ms. Delaney

thought, "the *Times*" and prepared to be graciously adamant.

The young man grinned at her, "How's Stonewall Delaney today? Honest to God—cross my press card—I'm not here about the Moon action. It's something else entirely."

"I can't believe that, Mr. Aston," smiled Ms. Delaney. "There's no other news around here."

"I deduce you haven't read your current issue of *Harpy's Bizarre*."

"Never even heard of it. What in the world—?"

Aston unrolled the magazine he was holding and displayed the cover. "It's a camp rag for the Gays and the Libs."

Ms. Delaney stared, her heart nearly stopping. Across the lurid, pornographic cover were the words, SPACE MINING EXPOSE . . . BY . . . CAPTAIN BOB SCHUSTER . . .

Her recollection flew back to the *unlocked cabinet*. She stammered through numb lips, "Schuster never—*never*—"

"Of course not. Somebody obviously got hold of confidential tapes—and waited to publish until they figured Schuster would be too dead to sue. Now, may I speak to Mickleberry? Honestly, as a friend, Ms. Delaney."

Moving as in a dream, Ms. Delaney buzzed Mickleberry, said, "Mr. Aston with—something dreadful to show you—" and admitted Aston into the sanctum.

She was still sitting in a daze when Aston came out of the office—minus the magazine—and waved her a jaunty "so long." Mickleberry buzzed. "Kindly come here a moment, Helen."

He had not called her Helen since old Alderman had dropped dead. It was the sign of grievous stress. Automatically, feeling oddly weak, she fumbled out her dictation Rec-Pak and went into his office.

He glanced at her, rose from his chair and guided her wavering steps to the chair beside his desk. "Sit down—it was a shock, of course."

He stepped into his dressing room. She heard the clink of a glass—the whoosh of a soda siphon. He came out carrying a drink, which he pressed firmly into her icy hand. "I did not summon you to blame you. I myself was remiss about the files."

She gulped the fizzing whiskey. Steadying warmth ran along her veins. She put the glass on the desk, beside her Rec-Pak, and faltered, "Schuster couldn't have taped anything—pornographic."

"No, naturally not. But the stolen tape—we must face the fact that it was stolen—dealt with a controversial theme, which Schuster attacked with his usual irreverence."

"Oh, Mr. Mickleberry, who *could* have opened that cabinet?"

"Between us, we should be able to deduce the answer." Mickleberry put his fingertips together. "Let us cast back to the day of that particular Board meeting. You and Xavier locked the cabinet in the morning—"

Ms. Delaney took a deep breath. "I—I locked it again at five o'clock."

His eyebrows twitched slightly, but he went on, "I found the cabinet unlocked at eight. Was there nothing—no disturbance—you noticed the following morning when I asked you to put that memo with the shells?"

"No—not really—I didn't count the shells. The only thing missing was the whiskey bottle you removed—"

The eyebrows shot into his parched forehead lines. "Whiskey bottle *I* removed—?"

"But I assumed—" she stammered. "You worry so much about—temptations—suspicions—"

"I follow your reasoning," he said dryly, "but I assure you my zeal does not extend to—uh—hijacking Captain Schuster's whiskey."

She giggled, and he continued, "The next time the files were opened—"

"The very next night, when I got the Jardin shell for Mr. Holloway. And the cabinet was *unlocked*. I was so upset I counted the shells—and none was missing. I remember—" she shuddered in retrospect, "how I thought I could feel eyes watching me as the department went dark—"

"So we have narrowed the time limit significantly. The cleaning staff is nowhere near Operations before eight. Our culprit is someone who knew about Schuster's files—knew the Operations schedules—the Security routine—"

"But, Mr. Mickleberry, none of the nine-to-five workers know the Security routines! My goodness, I work more overtime than most, but I wouldn't know when it was safe to steal from any specific department. And I'm sure none of *us* in Operations—! I mean, even if one of us wanted to steal a tape, we wouldn't call attention to the theft by taking the whiskey too!"

"Yes, a certain lack of wit is evident. Who do we have—inconspicuous and slightly stupid—who can wander freely from department to department—"

"*Howie Lind!* I remember, he hung around my desk—wanted to know how long I would be working—! He never gets LOCO to the mail room before five—he would know how the guards begin their patrols—"

"And he has unsavory friends in the pools racket. I have never liked Personnel's indifference to his betting slips."

"But can we accuse him? Would there be proof—fingerprints—?"

"Accusation would be a waste of time. I shall simply fire him. Would you please have Personnel send down his records?"

She rose, feeling recovered and competent again.

Mickleberry's phone rang. He answered, "Yes? Thank you." He turned to Ms. Delaney. "The special Moon telecast—"

She hurried from the office. The TV screen had activated. The old-fashioned window shades had been lowered at that end of the room. All work had stopped—all heads were tilted to look up at the screen.

Glare-lit by the sun, the rough-surfaced Blotch seemed like an enormous, swollen-headed whale. Atop the head sat a fly—no, a Space Tug! Where the Whale's tail dwindled into Space was the glitter of metal—stern tubes!

The commentator was saying excitedly, "They got here—they got here! Wait! There goes the drill-hammer team on the jet-dollies—they've got metal shields—"

A swarm of gnats approached the whale and attacked a protuberance near the Space Tug. The protuberance shivered into a dusty cloud, which thickened, darkened. The gnats backed away, like men fighting off a cloud of angry bees. The bees clung to them—covered shields and helmets— drew the jet-dollies inwards—

Rescuers with personal power packs zoomed to the team, uncoiling lines around them and dragging them away. The Blotch was as solid as before.

Transmission switched to Moon Residence and the physicists. "We have here a phenomenon analogous to that of the living sponge," said a worried-looking scientist. "If the sponge's living cells are shaken apart, they re-form in the same pattern as if they *remembered*. Now, there are two schools of thought about the Asteroid Belt—one claiming the fragments to be part of an exploded planet, and the other claiming the area to be in *pre*-planetary form. Both schools may be right.

"At this time I don't want to discuss the factors which hold a planet together—I daresay they are familiar to all of you—but apparently one unsuspected factor does *not* disappear when the planet is blown apart. The fragments retain *molecular memory* and the tendency to re-unite and cohere. Hence the simultaneous effects of explosion and pre-planetary groupings.

"Apparently, when Captain Schuster decided to assemble a scattering of adjacent mineral spheroids, the molecular memory/cohesion process was accelerated, and the Q-Pod found itself in molecular quicksand. Whether the stern tube and jets burned themselves clear—or whether there was expert last-minute maneuvering—the Q-Pod had navigation possibilities, which Captain Schuster used to head home, by dead reckoning.

"When Colonel Compton—having received a Morse report from Captain Schuster—overtook the Q-Pod with the Space Tug, the navigation could be corrected—but in the process, the Tug also was caught."

A media man interrupted, "The Tug crew can be cut out of their craft, if necessary, but how are you going to blast out the Q-Pod?"

A hesitation. "We don't know—yet."

The transmission next switched to the decontamination canister, a check-point made necessary by the new atomic engines. The media anchorman reported that the jet-dolly team and their rescuers were clean, and that no suits had been pierced by the mineral cloud.

"But I want to show you something—an idea relayed from Schuster, he went on, as a discarded suit was lobbed to him from out of camera range. "See those residual clumps on the helmet? No metal will scrape them off. But watch what happens when I take a piece of paper—"

He tore a leaf from a memo pad and sawed at the base of a clump. Within a few seconds the clump lifted and tumbled slowly in the Moon gravity toward a second clump. The anchorman deftly slipped the paper between them—and there was no cohesion. The loose clump drifted away.

"Has Schuster got the answer—or has he got the

answer?" grinned the reporter. "Take it away, physicists!"

At that point the Moon transmission signed off, and the Operations screen went dark.

Ms. Delaney became aware that Mickleberry was standing beside her. She asked, "What did he mean? Would it work?"

"I assume he means that an organic substance—pulp, for example—would interfere with the molecular attraction. I doubt that they can try the theory before Holloway can ship organic materials to the Moon."

He added, "After you speak to Personnel, get me Xavier," and went back to his office.

Ms. Delaney reflected that Xavier would have his work cut out for him, with the article in *Harpy's Bizarre,* whatever the subject was.

Operations limped absent-mindedly through the working day. At four o'clock Mickleberry said to Ms. Delaney, "Phone the mail room and tell them to send Howie here after he has finished work."

While she was relaying the message, the TV screen again came to life. Once more, the whale-like Blotch and the trapped craft. The anchorman was saying, "Here they come with the pressure hoses!"

Again, all work stopped. A murmur went around Operations. Where had they found suitable organic materials?

The TV camera zeroed in on the team jet-dollying toward the Space Tug. The pressure hose spewed a fog with cutting edges. Within a few

minutes the Tug lifted free in a shower of debris
which dissipated outwards. It took longer to free
the Q-Pod—careful, well-directed spurts of the
hose, not wasting any of the organic particles.

Even before the Q-Pod was fully clear, the anchorman was saying, "We've got Compton out of
the Tug—there he is, on a dolly, coming to greet
Schuster. A historic moment, folks!"

There were several minutes of a Spacesuited
figure on a jet-dolly. A voice said, "Could you wave
to the folks, Colonel?" and the figure waved.

The camera shifted to a view of the Q-Pod's
airlock. "They're about ready to let us in—you
first, Colonel—"

The camera emerged into the main cabin of the
Q-Pod. Four men stood at attention, proud and
glad, as if they were in new uniforms and shiny
braid—*proud*—not realizing they were Space-
haggard scarecrows in threadbare tatters. Ms. Delaney burst into tears. It was cruel of the media to
show up their pitiful delusions—to mock at their
innocent pride—

Colonel Compton had removed his Space helmet, and the awkward media-conscious greeting
proceeded. Compton and Schuster shaking hands.
Schuster's voice, careful, slightly hoarse, "Thanks,
Colonel. You've done a great job." "You made it
easy for us, Captain."

One after another the Q-Pod men were induced
to send stilted greetings to their families. The
media voice—in the tone of one wanting to liven
the meeting—asked, "Captain Schuster, how did
you happen to think of the organic fog?"

"I figured, in the Asteroids the most alien and

disruptive force would be *life*." He hesitated. "What the hell did they grind up for the pressure hoses—some of the goddamned red tape?"

A snort of laughter ran around the Operations enclaves.

The media man replied, "Haven't they told you? The Khadir of Bungl'a Cush brought his private cow barn to the Moon. There were several tons of cattle fodder and poultry feed, plus the straw on the barn floor, with its—uh—digestive residue—"

Schuster threw back his head with an uninhibited *Haw Haw*. The voice pursued, "You don't find the situation—repulsive?"

"Oh, I'm no stranger to the digestive residue in cow barns." The engaging grin lit up his haggard face. "I started life as a country boy."

This caused another flood of tears from Ms. Delaney's eyes. Mickleberry's voice said, "Surely nothing to cry over!"

She looked up to see him standing beside her desk. She scrubbed at her cheeks and said angrily, "Oh, Mr. Mickleberry, the media shouldn't have been *allowed*—! The poor men looked so pathetic!"

"To the contrary. I thought they trailed clouds of glory."

He turned and went into his office. The TV screen had gone dark again. Ms. Delaney blew her nose and resettled the pencil in her chignon. Howie Lind's voice said, "So the old bastard made it, after all."

"Howie!" chided Ms. Delaney. She looked at the clock. Five already! Howie and LOCO hummed away.

Having accomplished so little during the day,

Ms. Delaney continued to work as Operations emptied. The department was still light from the summer sun.

Howie, by himself, came ambling up to her desk. "They said downstairs that Methuselah wants to see me. What's up?"

"Go right in and find out."

Scowling, the youth entered the office. Ms. Delaney tried to concentrate, but her mind was spinning off in all directions. Schuster was home safe—but what would happen when he learned about *Harpy's Bizarre?*

Chapter 13

Howie Lind Departs the Premises

Howie approached the desk, and Mickleberry waved him into the interview chair. "One moment—while I read your employment record."

Howie sat down. "I ain't in your jurisdiction, Mickleberry."

Mickleberry reviewed the sheets in an unperturbed manner. "Few things in the Company are not in my jurisdiction, Howie."

"You say to this one, 'Come,' and he cometh?"

"And to the other one, 'Go,' and he goeth." Mickleberry neatly assembled the sheets. "I regret that I must now tell you to go, Howie. You're fired."

Howie straightened up indignantly. "Why?"

"For one thing, habitual tardiness. And for another, your brisk trade with the betting slips."

"Considering the lousy money you pay me, you can't fire me for moonlighting!"

"But you are moonlighting on Company time."

"Collecting for the pools don't interfere with my work."

"Howie, no man can serve two masters. You had better go to the master you find most profitable."

The youth glowered, "I know why you're firing me. You're the most subtle of all the beasts of the field, Mickleberry."

"I try to be, certainly."

"Yeah, well, suppose I tell the reporters that Schuster really did tape the Rec-Pak for that stinker of an article in *Harpy's Bizarre?* That's why you wanta get rid of me—so's you can sue the magazine for faking the tape and taking Schuster's name in vain! You and Schuster can slap a big damage suit on them and bankrupt them and drive them outta business. But I can bear witness that the story came off of a genuine Schuster tape."

Mickleberry indicated his desk phone. "If you are so eager to confess yourself into a prison term—"

"Prison! A first offender for petty larceny gets off easy."

"Opening locked files, stealing from them and fencing the loot is not petty larceny. However, if you think the editor will thank you for your zeal—"

Howie paused. "Seems to me that using a swiped tape wouldn't cost the editor as much as the kind of damage suit you'd come up with."

"The editor's choice is between being a receiver of stolen property—or countering a civil damage suit with the defense that the tape had been submitted through the mail in the ordinary manner. It's not much of a defense—editors are expected to doublecheck carefully the sources of libelous material—but it's better than the admission of criminal guilt."

Howie thought this over. "I'm still fired, huh?"

"Definitely. You may apply at the Payroll Office tomorrow for any wages that may be due."

Howie rose from the chair. "You wormed *that* story outta me slick enough, didn't you?"

"I never mentioned the Schuster Rec-Pak. The wicked flee when no man pursueth."

"I oughtta report you to Unfair Employment Practices," grumbled Howie, shuffling to the door. It was occurring to him that—for some reason he did not understand—he was no match for this elderly powerhouse, and he had better throw in the towel while he was in condition to do so.

After Howie had left, Mickleberry tidied and locked his desk, fetched his Glare/Visor summer hat, attache case and ivory-headed cane from his dressing room and walked briskly from the office.

He paused beside Ms. Delaney's desk, and she ceased her quick rat-a-tat on the typewriter keys. He said, "Working late? I shall be in the law library with Mr. Xavier for an hour—but I require nothing further here."

Ms. Delaney said, "Very well, Mr. Mickleberry. Good night," and resumed the rat-a-tat.

When he had vanished into the elevator, she stopped typing, waited a moment, and went into his office. He had probably read the Schuster story by now—and would not be taking *Harpy's Bizarre* home with him. If a copy of the magazine was needed as evidence, the legal department must have secured their own.

What would Mickleberry have done with the

magazine—? Ms. Delaney reviewed her boss's tastes—and went directly to the wastebasket. Yes, the magazine was there.

She took it out, returned to her own desk, sat down and began to leaf through the pages. There was a double-page spread of news photographs of various Schuster milestones. The story began in a red-rimmed inset. "There comes a time when a guy—"

Her keyboard flashed urgently. An outside line. She reflected that an overseas caller must have miscalculated New York time, and she lifted the handset. "Operations—Ms. Delaney."

Against the hollow ship-to-shore band, a male voice said, "The tankship *Sea Naphtha*. A call from Second Mate Fiske. One moment please."

Ms. Delaney was utterly amazed. Junior officers did not make direct calls to Operations. And a second mate, of all people, should be able to calculate time zones!

"Ms. Delaney—Fiske here" said a hard female voice. "I wanta ask—"

"But Ms. Fiske, it's five o'clock! Everybody has gone!"

"I know, I know. That's why I called. I figured you'd still be slaving away and could talk freely. Tell me—is the news broadcast true?"

"You mean, about the Q-Pod? Yes, everybody's safely on the Moon by now—"

"I don't mean *that* broadcast! I mean the news that an anti-female Schuster Rec-Pak has been transcribed in *Harpy's Bizarre!*"

"I know no more about it than you do, Ms. Fiske," lied Ms. Delaney stoutly. "I understand that

several magazines, among them *Harpy's Bizarre,*
have been featuring Captain Schuster in their June
issues—"

"Then it *is* true!"

"If it claims to be a Schuster Rec-Pak, it's certainly false!"

"Oh, come off it, Ms. Delaney! Aggie got somebody to swipe a Rec-Pak for her—and I say, good
for her! Now maybe we'll find out who's been
stabbing us in the back! When's Schuster due back
in Operations?"

"I doubt if anybody knows. The matter of
assaying the ore on the Moon—"

"Well, you can make a guess, for Godsake, can't
you? All your years in the department—"

"Not within the next two weeks," said Ms.
Delaney helplessly.

"Great! I'll be off this damned rustbucket and
waiting for him. And you can tell him so!"

Ms. Delaney laughed. "Oh, Ms. Fiske, take care!
Operations is full of whitened bones of second
mates who thought they could tangle with Schuster!"

"But none of them have been *women!*" snapped
Ms. Fiske, and the band cut out.

Ms. Delaney glanced down at her orchid, still
fresh and blooming from its tiny stem-vial, looked
softly amused and began again on the tape transcription,

"There comes a time when a guy likes to loosen
his belt a notch . . ."

● ● ●

MORE DEADLY THAN THE MALE?

There comes a time when a guy likes to loosen his belt a notch, put his feet on the desk and make like an Elder Statesman. For years I had been a hard-driving master mariner and troubleshooter aboard the Company's sea-going fleet, and just when I would have liked to slow down, the Company took over Space Mining, Inc.

The takeover employed me—intermittently—in planting a Moon colony and mining Moon ore. When I was not unscrambling a problem aboard a Company rustbucket, I was shuttling up to Moon orbit to listen to beefs from Space Mining crews.

It was Moonlighting with a vengeance. So when Mickleberry in Operations once more pulled me off a Company ship and summoned me to his New York office, I groused plenty.

The old fellow was amused. "In other words, Captain Schuster," he said in his thin wry voice, "you feel either at sea or up in the air."

"Yeah, that's about the size of it," I agreed, "and it ain't all that funny."

Mickleberry put his fingertips together. "Your impending assignment is merely to—uh—hold a watching brief at Space Mining's Assembly/Launch Complex at Cape Canaveral during Mr. Holloway's absence abroad."

Holloway was Space Mining's Executive Director, a very smart Space engineer and a good guy. It was always hard for me to refuse Holloway. He was under enormous pressure—and a roughneck like me could just as well knock heads together on the Moon as on the ships.

However, I knew Mickleberry had not called me home for my "watching brief." I said, "Well, what's the problem now?"

He hesitated. "Although in the forefront of technical progress, scientists are hidebound about procedure. They tend to form in-groups, cliques."

I did not know what he was driving at. "So what? Any long-seniority group develops cliques. We have 'em among our sea officers."

"But our sea operations are not vulnerable to attack from minority groups. We hire and advance officers according to merit. One of your functions, captain, has been to advise us on this matter."

"Yeah, and I'm surprised to hear that Space Mining has minority trouble. They have a typical American Mix at the ALC."

"Their caste system is on a different plane," smiled Mickleberry "A cast of mutually-held theories, of mutually-attended status universities—what the British call the Old Boy network—and of other factors you will find when you get down there."

"I ain't said I'm gonna go," I growled. I did not see how a lowbrow like me could persuade the Ivy Leaguers to install Cowtown U. grads on their teams.

Mickleberry gave me what he thought was his winning smile. "The Medical/Biological Clinic now has a swimming pool. Therapy for rotating Moon personnel."

"You pulled me off clean blue water two miles deep—and expect to bribe me with a tub of chlorine?"

Mickleberry coughed. "It's possible that the Company's medical department will accept the Space Mining assignment as your compulsory vacation from your sea job, and you will be able to return immediately to the ships."

The old fox knew I hated to be drydocked. I grinned, "That's a bribe I'll accept!" I added, "Who's trying to fill Holloway's shoes down there?"

"The various departments are—uh—free-wheeling, but Mr. Lyle of Personnel/Payroll is interim coordinator." Mickleberry handed me an airline envelope. "Your flight for Orlando leaves Kennedy in two hours. Mr. Lyle will send the helicopter to meet you at Orlando. Enjoy the pool, captain!"

I deplaned in Orlando in the afternoon. An airline luggage truck gave me a lift to where the Space Mining chopper was waiting. I was tired and preoccupied, so I hoisted my suitcase aft of my seat, climbed aboard as I would have climbed into a taxi, and grunted to the young pilot wearing Space Mining's white jumpsuit, "Full Ahead to the ALC."

I had not really looked at him—just registered that he was smooth-faced, kinda handsome, with half-long, glossy dark hair.

The control tower let us rise, and we thrashed into action. All of a sudden I got a whiff of light perfume.

I looked around hard. The jumpsuited figure was a young woman. For a split-second it threw me. I mean, I had been conned into sitting next to a woman driver!

I commended my soul to God and discovered I was trying to hold the chopper in the air with my ankle bones.

To my relief the flight proceeded routinely, and I could stop holding my breath. We made a beeline across the flat Cape to the area leased by the Assembly/Launch Complex, and circled above the towering assembly hangar before setting down on the front lot of the Administration Building.

When we were on the ground and the girl had cut the blade-clatter I said, "Thanks for the lift."

She said in a clear but ironic voice, "Don't thank me. I get paid to do it."

A chip did not look good on her shoulder. She was clean-cut, with that immaculate dark hair and intelligent hazel eyes. She seemed wholesome and straight—but uptight.

I felt better as I walked towards the Administration entrance, but I wondered what was the girl's resentment.

Before I reached the building's front mall, a procession of cars cut me off and blockaded the entrance. I could see large placards protruding from tied-down trunk lids.

Picketing? Mickleberry had not hinted at labor trouble! I stood there, sandbagged. Women began erupting from the cars, like ants swarming to a picnic.

Young dames in jeans. Old dames in pant-suits. The leader seemed to be a husky old biddy who never should have thrown away her corset. She began snapping orders. I had not heard a voice like hers since Casey Stengel had last charged from a dugout.

She distributed the signboards and marshalled

the pickets, who began their chain-gang procession. I read, MAKE SPACE FOR WOMEN! MARIE CURIE WAS ONE OF US! IQ, IQ! JOBS NOT JIBES!

So this was the minority that was attacking Space Mining! I cussed Mickleberry but good. If I had known—!

No time for recriminations. A car had braked and disgorged a TV Mini-Cam unit and reporters. The activists sure knew their PR ropes.

The fog-voiced old battle-ax headed for the media—and spotted me. She thundered up like a tank. She had a long, strong-jawed face, the moustache spikes of the elderly, and eyes she must have inherited from Attila the Hun.

She pointed a bony finger at me and crowed, "I know you! You're Schuster—the Company's triggerman!"

I get a fair amount of media coverage. A lot of people know me by sight.

The feisty old girl dug a police whistle from her pocket and shrilled a blast that drew the Security guards out of the building—and alerted the media. It also drew a trio out of another car—two men and a girl.

When I saw the small, shabby guy with the long envelope, the slick pouchy-eyed Lothario, and the model-slim girl, I said to myself, *looks as if a broad and a shyster have horned into the equality racket.*

As everybody converged on us, the old girl bellowed to the shyster, "Dumont! What's taking you so long to get moving? To hell with Lyle! Serve the papers on Schuster! He's the high-echelon bastard!"

I squared my shoulders. The reporter with the TV Mini-Cam zeroed in. The shyster did not seem enthusiastic, but he nodded. The shabby process server handed me the envelope, gabbled a formula and effaced himself.

I ignored the media men and opened the envelope. I saw that Space Mining, its owners, directors, and executives, were being sued for noncompliance with the equal-employment laws *re* Ms. Christina Copps. The preliminary legal bout was scheduled for three weeks hence.

As I folded up the summons, I told the clamoring press, "No comment. I gotta investigate first."

The lukewarm Lothario stepped forward and offered me his hand. "Blaine Dumont, attorney for Ms. Copps."

I put the summons in my pocket, shook hands with Dumont, nodded at the girl and said genially, "Is this young woman the plaintiff?"

Dumont presented the girl to the cameras. "Ms. Christina Copps."

Ms. Copps was wearing oversized steel-rimmed eyeglasses, and her blonde hair was wound into a flat bun on top of her head. The intellectual pose was not all put-on. There were sharp eyes behind the glasses, and the face had the well-modeled bone structure I had noted before in brainy people.

But she had not been brainy enough to follow through on her image. Her red, mobile lips were a sensual giveaway, as were the dangling ear-hoops, skin-tight pants and half-unbuttoned blouse.

She probably did not consider herself a whore, but I could see she was a ringer for the types that hang around piers. Looking mad as a wet hen, she gave me a cold handshake and a "How d'y' do!"

Her counselor allowed no more. He took her arm, drew her away and said to me, "Will you excuse us, captain?"

"Sure," I grinned. "See you in court."

The old female activist did not like their quick retreat, but Dumont shook her off, and they drove away with the process server. In the course of my work I had learned how to make a reasonable "No Comment" stick, so the media dispersed.

As if feeling that the show was over, now that the main act had hotfooted away, the pickets also began to disperse. The old hard-line activist grumbled to me,

"Dumont must be a fool, losing his nerve just because you're here, Schuster. Space Mining can't possibly beat this rap. Christina was entitled to the job. A brilliant Ph.D. in Physics. If she'd been a man—"

"It can't be that simple," I said shortly. I added, "If Copps has a real case, how come she had to hire a male shyster?"

Carrie Nation had no answer to that one. I strode through the pickets—who were re-stacking the signboards in the car trunks—went past the Security guards and into the building.

Personnel/Payroll chief Lyle had been watching the proceedings from his second-floor window. When I emerged from the elevator and walked into his office, he sighed, "Thank God you kept them out!"

Lyle was a medium-sized guy with high cheekbones and black-rimmed glasses, a good administrator of somewhat plodding manner.

I tossed the summons onto his desk. "Better transmit a copy of this to New York. Your local lawyers may need coaching. What's the story?"

We sat down, and he began, "As you know, captain, we've been laying workers off, paring away waste and redundancy. The hiring of women—or of men—has not been relevant.

"However, since we are receiving an increasing number of applications from women for jobs in the engineering labs and in Space, our legal advisers said we should make some sort of token conformation to the equal-opportunity laws."

I remembered the female chopper pilot. "So the Ellerdown girl is a token?"

"Leslie Ellerdown applied for research work on the basis of a B.S. *summa cum laude* in math. She had stopped at the B.S. level, worked a year as an airline flight attendant, then taken a job with a Midwest cargo/taxi airline. She stayed with the outfit six years, while getting commercial piloting licenses and learning the cargo business.

"What struck us about her application was her obvious willingness to work at all aspects of a job. If we had to hire a woman for Space research, she seemed most likely to be an asset.

"The trouble was, we had no research openings for a math/aeronautics capability. The Space-project teams tend to bypass Personnel. The team leader will come to me and say, 'There's been a breakthrough doctoral thesis by a Princeton man named Zilch. Since our man Filch is retiring in June—"

As Mickleberry had said, the Old Boy network. Lyle resumed, "While we were mulling over Leslie's application, the Transportation job suddenly became vacant. We wrote and offered it to her, with a promise to fit her into one of our research departments later.

"She came, her licenses were in order, and she handled the helicopter and the Douglas jet like an old pro. Because we had no math/aerospace opening, we enrolled her in the shuttle program and have been letting her take cosmo-navigation and simulator training with the astronauts."

"Why is the girl so uptight?"

Lyle spun the summons on his desk. "Now we come to this whole unfortunate hassle. Old Amtland on the Mars Thermionic team dropped dead. The thermionic engine is still delayed by math inconsistencies. Amtland had to be replaced, so I sent Leslie Ellerdown to be interviewed by project leader Jorkins.

"Jorkins wouldn't say Ah Yes or No. He's a pettifogger, anyhow. But both Leslie and I assumed she would be hired. A week went by and then Jorkins came and told me he had offered the job to a Berkeley man highly recommended by the grapevine.

"I argued Leslie's case but got nowhere. The project leaders have the final say on their teams. The Berkeley man was In, and Leslie was Out."

I commented, "The girl took it hard, hey?"

"She didn't blame us here in Personnel. She knew I had offered her the job in good faith and had gone to bat for her. But she is bitter about the Company ruling that permits autonomy to an ass like Jorkins. I'm surprised she didn't slice your head off with the chopper blade."

"Yeah, I saw that something rankled, but she got

over it. A nice, straightforward girl. How did the Copps bitch get into the picture?"

"The women activists were laying for us. Old Amtland was still in *rigor mortis* when we got Christina Copps' application for that specific job. Christina looked very good on paper, but I never considered her over Leslie. Besides the *summa* in math, Leslie has had seven years in aeronautics. All Christina had were college degrees.

"We replied carefully to Christina's application, stating that Amtland's vacancy had been filled in accordance with a prior committment to Dr. Jorkins. We explained that we would consider training Christina for Space if she proved qualified for a related job in Transportation, Communications, Programming or Secretarial.

"The girl had absolutely no skills or practical training, nor any desire to cooperate. Whereas Leslie gritted her teeth and kept her foot in the Space Mining door, Christina went to Holloway with a lawyer and made threats."

He spun the summons again. "I personally believe Christina is a limousine-liberal troublemaker with no sincere interest in the job. But it may be hard to bat down the sex-discrimination charge. Jorkins' man has nowhere near Copps' brilliant university record."

"Brilliance ain't everything," I told him. "Courts weigh motives and actions pretty carefully where injustice is the issue." I pushed myself to my feet. "When you transmit the summons, add a copy of Christina's job application and tell New York to get their best detectives on the girl."

Lyle balked. "An inquiry into the girl's personal

life could be construed as a smear campaign. I couldn't authorize—"

"I'll authorize it. The person who has the true case against us is Leslie Ellerdown. This Copps action is just dirty pool by a power lobby, and as far as I'm concerned, our defense should have no holds barred. If that shyster Dumont is taking his fee out in trade—"

"The court undoubtedly will rule it irrelevant to the issue."

"Ha, Ha, now I'll tell one. Any time a woman goes to court on a good-faith issue, she had better take an unsullied reputation with her. If Copps has been—as her looks and dress imply—a cheap campus tart, her application for Space Mining employment is frivolous harrassment, and her brilliant Ph.D. ain't gonna save her.

"I'm not saying a double moral standard is equable or desirable. I'm only saying it exists and I intend to use it." As Lyle chewed his lip doubtfully, I added, "Whose desk can I swipe while I'm here?"

"Use Holloway's. I assume you would like a copy of Christina's application. I'll send one down."

I thanked him and beat it below to Holloway's first floor offices. They were under the command of Holloway's secretary Ms. Neems, who, as the highest-paid Girl Firday, was on top of Space Mining's female pecking order. She was middle-aged, in good trim, always smartly dressed.

Since the last time I had seen her, she had added what my grandmother used to call a 'rat' to her hair-do. I have no idea what women call that stuff nowadays. Girls will be girls.

However, Ms. Neems was attractive and on her toes, so I shook her hand cordially, asked her to get me the Company's legal department in New York, and entered Holloway's office with a feeling that everything would soon be under control.

While I was on the phone, authorizing the check on Christina Copps, the girl's job application was relayed to me by Ms. Neems. When I was through talking to New York, I studied the application.

Christina was twenty-five years old. I did not know if this was par for the Ph.D. course. Her address was a flossy Boston suburb, so I figured— as Lyle apparently had figured—that she was living home and her old man had dough.

I wondered if Leslie Ellerdown had 'quit at the B.S. level' because she could not afford the graduate work. I decided that a girl who had managed a commerical pilot's training would have managed the graduate degrees, had she wanted them.

There was no evidence that Christina Copps had done anything except study. Probably she could not boil water, either.

I inspected Holloway's phone console, which had more buttons than a Polish accordion, and decided not to take the risk of pressing one that might connect me with the White House. I walked to the door and asked Ms. Neems to come in and bring me up to date on the scuttlebutt.

She picked up notebook and pencil, jabbed a button on her own phone console, and sailed into Holloway's office. I told her to take a chair and fill me in on the activist jazz.

She sat down, sprightly but correct, and said,

"Well, Captain Schuster, I was aware we had activists on the payroll, but Space Mining didn't seem a likely target. Women have to be more than just women to qualify for Space employment. Mr. Holloway and Mr. Lyle were at their wits' end when finally Leslie Ellerdown's job application arrived.

"I mean," she went on, "it's all very well for the lawyers to say, 'hire women', but you can't hire inexperienced people for Space research! Leslie was a godsend!"

"Do you like her?"

Ms. Neems bridled a little. "I don't really know her—except meeting her in the Employee Cafeteria and so on. A corn-fed type. She's an only child, and her parents probably wanted a boy—her father owns a Sales and Service for farm machinery—so Leslie grew up being a son more than a daughter."

The things women do not know about other women is a caution.

Ms. Neems continued, "Leslie keeps to herself and seems too businesslike and—unfeminine. I think women can work and still be—feminine."

If she expected a compliment, she did not get it from a wary old bachelor like me. I remarked, "Christina Copps seems feminine enough."

This galvanized Ms. Neems. "Don't mention Christina Copps in this office! Poor Mr. Holloway had to take four aspirin after she and that smarmy lawyer were here to demand Amtland's job!

"Of course, I don't want to be unfair to the girl herself," she amended. "Young girls get brainwashed with so much nonsense from these pressure groups! When older women tell a pretty girl that she's striking a blow for female freedom by sleeping with every man she meets, it's hard for her to realize she's being used and deceived."

I was getting plenty of viewpoints. I asked curiously, "What's your opinion of equal rights?"

"It's a rip-off for the men, as usual!" she said indignantly. "Let me tell you, I'm glad I got my divorce in the days when women were unequal! I took my two-timing son-of-a-bitch to the cleaners, and got the house and bank savings and car, plus alimony and child support. God knows how I would have made it otherwise, with three small kids to support and not wanting to deprive them of home care. Child day-care centers are not homes, Captain Schuster."

I had never thought a boy's best friend was his shrink, so I gave her no argument. I thanked her for clueing me in and asked how I could reach Leslie Ellerdown.

"Through Transportation," said Ms. Neems, rising from her chair. "I'll connect you."

A moment after she had left the office, one of the phone buttons lit up. I lifted the receiver, pressed the button, and a male voice—there were still some of us left!—muttered, "Transportation."

"This is Schuster, from Holloway's office," I said. "Is Miss Ellerdown free to come here for a conference?"

"Free and free," was the laconic reply. "She's tuning up a Beechcraft for Astronaut Fairweather. A spare-time job—Fairweather's paying her for it."

I was uncertain about the temper of a dame slaving over a hot Beechcraft. I said, "I'll call her tonight. Have you got her home phone?"

"She's our stand-by man, so she's bunking in Transit Staff, captain. Oughtta be there by six."

That was that. It was too late in the day for me to go over to the Assembly hangar and fraternize, so I ordered a pool car and drove south to Cocoa Beach for a seafood dinner.

A warm, humid tropical night had settled over the ALC by the time I had returned. The new Transit Staff quarters were across a palm-planted mall from the Clinic. The brightly-lit swimming pool area was in the middle of the mall and seemed to be enjoying optimum utilization.

The Transit clerk gave me a key and directions to my room off the upper balcony. I beat it up there, showered, changed to khakis and mentally rolled up my sleeves. Leslie Ellerdown had Space Mining over a barrel. I could not understand why she was sitting with a royal flush and not trying to claim the pot.

I phoned her via the desk. She said, "Yes, captain, Transportation said you wanted to see me."

I said heartily, "I'm kinda stymied, Miss Ellerdown. Aboard ship I can ask crew members to report to my quarters, but I don't think much of businessmen who invite female employees to hotel rooms."

"For once the Company and I are in agreement," came her cool voice. "I have a couple chairs on the balcony—south corner. As good as a park bench?"

I said it was fine. I hung up and barged south on the balcony. Her corner had plant boxes, a table and two folding chairs. The nook was off the direct path of the overhead lamps, as restful as anything could be, in the center of an industrial complex.

Leslie, wearing pale gold slacks, a white shirt and white sandals, was standing at the balcony balustrade, looking towards the pool. I caught a whiff of the nice floral scent I had noticed in the chopper.

She turned and waved me to a chair. I lowered myself cautiously into the webbed aluminum and remarked, "Have the Transportation guys stopped changing-off the stand-by work?"

"With me here, yes," she answered, sitting in the second chair and wedging her sandals into the balustrade fretwork. "They are married men with families."

"As a single girl, you feel you've drawn the short straw?"

"No—because I made my own terms. I told Mr. Lyle I had no objection to being on permanent stand-by, provided the Transit accomodations and the overtime pay equaled what a male employee would receive. Actually, the deal suited me very well—until Jorkins slammed the Thermionic door in my face.

"I shouldn't have been so surprised," she added ruefully. "After I had got my math degree, I found nothing but slammed doors."

Since she obviously had a rational approach to the problem, I began, "Well, Miss Ellerdown, I think you oughtta realize that a lot of scientific research is being funded by limited grants which can't afford the extra expense of hiring women. A woman can break an employment contract by getting pregnant, yet her inconvenienced employer is seldom able to fire her outright and is increasingly being forced to shell out paid pregnancy leaves and other perqs which small funding can't afford. If women get lower wages, it's partly because of the higher expense of having them on the payroll.

"As a matter of fact, the total cost to the taxpayer of putting family women to work is astronomical beyond belief. Pregnancy welfare, child-care centers with overpaid shrinks, the crime rate of neglected juveniles who become adult criminals—and for what? So that housewives can become industrial robots?

"That's all the majority become, you know," I added. "For every college-educated woman in a creative field, like you or Christina Copps, there's a hundred—a thousand—women who are today's slaves. They lift-that-barge-and-tote-that-bale in a world that has become poorer, uglier and more violent since women are insisting on their so-called rights and are letting their home responsibilities go hang."

Leslie was looking at the pool, giving me her pokerfaced profile again. I concluded, "It's okay by me if women wantta exchange a home and kids for a time-clock, an assembly line, male hangers-on and abortions. That life-style makes it all the easier for the men who can—and do—prey on them."

"So stipulated, captain," came the irony. "Can we get down to the nitty-gritty?"

"Sure. I see by Holloway's schedule that the next Moon lift-off is a week away. Could you hold out a month on the Moon?"

She looked at me a moment, her eyes narrowed. "You disappoint me, captain. You can't suppose I'll throw away a pat hand and let you kick me upstairs?"

"No, my girl," I countered, "but you're way off the beam if you think the Company is gonna let you milk Space Mining while Christina Copps pulls your chestnuts out of the fire!"

She kept her face straight, but her hazel eyes brightened in the lamplight. The confounded minx was having fun with the Old Man! She repeated, ". . . milk Space Mining?"

"Yeah. You knew damned well Lyle promised you the Moon because your qualifications fit Space Mining like a glove. The timing was sheer luck, but you've made the most of it. Top wages in Transportation—expensive shuttle training we usually reserve for Air Force Colonels—permission to use ALC equipment on private jobs like Fairweather's plane. What the hell were you gonna demand next?"

"If the Copps case went against the Company, I thought I could force a general showdown with the research labs. Naturally, when I was told that Schuster was coming, I knew all bets were off. Mickleberry had sent his shock troop."

"Your pat hand don't look so good now, hey?"

"Oh, the hand is still a winner, but what's the use of winning one pot if the bouncer is going to throw me out of the game?

"That's what I warned Christina against, when she asked me to be co-plaintiff with her," Leslie continued. "Christina could possibly win a judgment against the Company, but it would be her last triumph. By just bringing suit, she's putting her name on a quiet blacklist throughout the industry.

"Christina is confusing employment rights with civil rights. Business is give-and-take, wheeling-

and-dealing. Legal confrontation is a dead end. Granted, women are an underpriveleged minority—but an underprivileged ghetto male does not expect to succeed in business or engineering without a long hard pull and plenty of setbacks. Why should girls think the Constitution guarantees them Instant Satisfaction?

"I realized as a college senior that my academic world was too narrow for a job basis. A year as a flight attendant enabled me to extend my horizons, and I saw that a small-town cargo airline, where everybody was wearing three hats and doubling in brass, was my best opportunity for training, experience, and advancement.

"Subsequently, with a good basis in practical aeronautics, I threw my hat into the aerospace ring, applying once more as a math/aerospace researcher—but with seven years of experience. Captain Schuster, I've worked too long and hard to lose my Space Mining chances by what you would call a bonehead play."

I had to laugh, and she went on, "I don't think I've milked the Company. As a man would do in the same situation, I've made the optimum deal for my services."

After a pause she said, "My second reason for refusing to go along with Christina is that Jorkins' discrimination against me is really clique-oriented, not sex-oriented. A male Midwesterner would have received exactly the same brush-off."

I relaxed and also braced my feet against the balustrade. "You know, Miss Ellerdown, the Company seldom briefs me on these troubleshooting assignments. They don't want to define the situation beforehand and lead me to prejudiced observations. Disfunction is like an iceberg—the visible part can be the minor part.

"For me, the most disquieting thing I've heard today is that the thermionic engine still has serious bugs. The engine is the key to opening the Mars jackpot. Moreover, a stall in Thermionics induces a plenty-of-time let-down in related Mars projects.

"There are two ways to deal with the Thermionics lag. One of them, obviously, is to fire Jorkins. The other is to go deeper into cause. The idea of giving a project leader full autonomy is great if he is on the right track and his hiring policy reinforces his theory-implementation.

"However, if the leader is a petty tyrant on the wrong track who hires only yes-men, the initial error is feedback-reinforced, and no breakthrough is possible.

"So I find that you and Christina are only the top of a great disfunction iceberg. If Thermionics had been on schedule, the other Mars projects would be expanding so fast that qualified women would be getting their share of research jobs regardless of chauvinism in a few leaders.

"Now, I've learned through experience that brains are a fragile commodity," I explained. "A genius behaves erratically because the usual incentives are secondary to him. We can't treat our genius teams in such a way that top scientists and university labs refuse to cooperate with us because we have flouted time-honored procedures."

Leslie asked, "Then how can you work with these chauvinists without capitulating?"

"By creating a new situation with no precedents.

By insisting that part of the Thermionics work be done on the Moon."

She considered a moment. "I don't understand, captain. Let's say, you put three men on the Moon and keep three men on Earth. The team members alternate the Moon work—and where's the new situation?"

"In the fact that not all the men will be okayed by Medical/Biological for Moon lift-off."

"You don't know that!"

"Knowing Doc Grant as I do," I said gravely, "I feel fairly sure of it."

She stared at me and then laughed so hard that the loungers on the mall below looked up at us. Finally she said, "I wish you well, captain, but I doubt that you can break the Old School Tie that binds. If Jorkins is a genius, he'll think of something."

"Then the Old Man will think of something else," I grinned. "Let's shake Thermionics up and see what falls out. A fluid situation always has possibilities. But can you blast off for the Moon next week?"

"Certainly. I have my Spacesuit and am fully briefed. It's short notice for Transportation, though."

"I'll speak to Lyle tomorrow."

We sat for a moment, mutually preoccupied. I realized that Leslie felt no need to play up to me in what Ms. Neems would call a feminine manner. Of course, a tough old bastard like me would not arouse interest in a girl of Leslie's generation. Or of any generation, come to think of it.

I extracted myself from the chair. Another aspect occurred to me. I said, "I'm gonna sling mud at Christina Copps. I hope there's nothing on your slate for Dumont to sling back at us."

She looked up at me and grinned. "Plenty of time-clocks and robot-work, but no hangers-on or abortions."

I was relieved, although her work-record and wholesome appearance spoke for themselves. Because she was a straight-shooter, I was uneasy about letting her bunk in the Moon Residence with a bunch of wolves. I wondered how I could face her dad if some jerk lost his head and attacked her.

If a girl wants to work in a male field, okay. But her being physically equal to a man is a lotta tripe, as any police blotter will testify.

The next morning I got busy on sending Leslie to the Moon. I warned Lyle he would need a new Person in Transportation. From Holloway's office I phoned the Assembly hangar and told them to hold final stowage of the shuttle until they had the weight of the Thermionics hardware/personnel.

Then I phoned the Thermionics lab and asked Jorkins to come to the office for a conference. He sounded touchy and irritable, and he went off half-cocked with, "Captain Schuster, I will tolerate no more badgering over the Ellerdown issue. Without intellectual freedom to choose my associates—"

"Even with that freedom, Dr. Jorkins," I interrupted, "your productivity ain't overwhelming. We hafta get together and straighten a few matters out. The financing of the Thermionics program—"

"Oh, all right, all right," he grumbled. "I'll be over there presently."

I knew the financing would bring him. No research chief ever got as much funding as he thought he needed.

After about an hour—during which I browsed through the Thermionics data in Holloway's files—Jorkins turned up. He was an uncombed, pallid-faced, sedentary type who seemed to make his clean white boiler suit look untidy.

We shook hands. He sat down impatiently and waited for my first pitch. I began, "What I wanta talk about is the way the Thermionic program has stalled. The Mars engine is strictly a Space engine, and I feel the research would get along faster if the components were tested under Space conditions."

"The usual lay ignorance!" he snorted. "Absolutely nothing can be achieved by researchers fumbling around in orbital weightlessness!"

"I wasn't thinking of an orbiting lab. There's too much junk in Earth orbit already. As you know, we've been expanding the Moon Residence by the addition of surplus cargo canisters, and the Residence has a number of extra rooms, one of which could be a Thermionics lab."

"The present funding—"

"Is enough. Think of the Moon lab as an extension of the Earth lab, with constant telecommunication. On the Moon you can use the local gravity—or the Earth gravity of the magnetized deck—or the zero gravity of shuttle orbit. You can have all degrees of solar radiation, temperature and types of atmosphere."

"The personnel—"

"Split 'em up any way you want. In one-month hitches, as for the other Moon workers."

"No," said Jorkins definitely. "Absolutely nothing would be accomplished by such frenetic commuting. In six months—in a year, for engine trials—"

He hunched forward and went on, "I cannot but assume that your suggestion is further harrassment of Thermionics because I would not let Personnel foist that boondocks girl-graduate upon us—a harrassment which will be viewed very negatively by the entire scientific community!"

I reflected that Leslie Ellerdown had been right about Jorkins. The situation was gonna get more fluid than I had intended. I said quickly. "Thermionics is not being singled out. We hope to move all Mars research to the Moon, eventually. I started with Thermionics, Dr. Jorkins, because of its urgent priority."

The old priority oil mollified him somewhat. He sniffed and commented, "I doubt that you can make Moon-participation a job-requisite for research personnel. The hazards are unreasonably high. Quimberly in Dynamics even refuses to travel by air!"

A Mars expert who had never left the ground? Well, it figured.

I said casually. "I expect the Medical/Biological check-ups to reduce further the Space-potentials. We'll probably have to re-integrate the teams on a Moon/Earth basis."

Jorkins quivered as if I had sent an electric current through him. "Re-integrate? You mean, an exchange of team personnel if there is no Moon/

Earth balance? Captain, nobody in Dynamics or Logistics could possibly qualify for Thermionics!"

"Why not? All of them are aerospace physicists. They're more familiar with our Thermionics than the guy you brought in cold from Berkeley. If one of your Groundhogs goes to Quimberly in exchange for one of his Spacemen, so what? After a week on the job, both of them will be squared around.

"Whenever there's trouble down here," I went on, doing some beefing of my own, "it's because of the specialization syndrome that means our right hand don't know what our left hand is doing. I'm not asking you to exchange biologists for chemists. I'm asking all you leaders to reassign scientists of a common physics/aerospace background who ought to have been keeping tabs on the general Mars progress anyhow.

"One thing is sure—we gotta do something drastic. Moving the projects to the Moon oughtta provide a sense of immediacy, if nothing else. Why horse around with lab-induced gravities and atmospheres, when you can step outside the Moon Residence—or jet-dolly up to Moon orbit—and fine the real McCoy?

"Before we can determine how much team exchange is needed for Earth/Moon rotation, we hafta check the guys through M/B. If you, Dr. Jorkins, could make arrangements today—"

"And you'll speak to Quimberly and Dyers?"

"Right now. But Thermionics retains priority over the Moon lab."

Once again the spoonful of priority made the shake-up go down, and Jorkins left.

Having unexpectedly painted myself into a corner, I spent the rest of the day getting out of it. There was no real reason why the other teams needed Moon labs, but both Quimberly and Dyers were quick to resent what they considered Jorkins' one-up score. For once, the team jealousies worked in my favor, and by the end of the day, the teams were filing into M/B for classification.

I had phoned Doc Grant at M/B after Jorkins had left. When I hinted rather broadly that I wanted a maximum of team rejections, the doc said, "Well, captain, having compromised medical ethics by allowing an apoplectic old bastard like yourself to lift off, I suppose I can compromise further by keeping borderline hearts on the ground. These research teams are mostly middle-aged men who would be better off on *terra firma* anyhow."

The final M/B returns would not be ready until the next day. Once again I drove off the reservation for dinner and arrived back at Transit Staff after dark.

I recognized our Senior Astronaut, Colonel Fairweather, among the swimming pool gang. I dragged a chair from the rustling black shadows of the palms, sat down and gave Fairweather the high sign. He climbed out of the pool, sopped his graying head in a towel, lifted another chair and came over to me. I asked,

"Are you scheduled for the next shuttle? How come you flew here a week early?"

"Yes, Jones and I drew this Alpha trip." He mopped himself more extensively and sat down. "Dynamics wanted to run me through some velocity tests this week." He paused, then added with a grin, "You really set off a bomb, captain, with the proposed Moon labs."

"Well, something had to get those guys off their duffs," I growled. "If it's not expedient to fire 'em, we can at least shuffle 'em and have a new deal."

"I stopped by the hangar and found they expected a Thermionics cargo. Has Thermionics anything to test?"

"A few components are off the drawing board. All I expect on the shuttle, though, is equipment to outfit a canister—air and water recyclers, a couple bunk units. The Thermionics guys can bunk in their lab-canister and fit somehow into the staggered messroom hours."

I saw Fairweather look past me, grin, and wave. I turned and saw Leslie cycling up to Transit Staff. I commented, "She can't scrounge a pool car?"

"Hell, she's all over the lot," said Fairweather. "A bicycle suits her better."

"I'm sending her on this lift-off to start the Moon lab," I told him. "The Moon crew had better not give her a hard time."

"Don't worry. She's everybody's sister—the small-town smarty-pants who gets straight A's, builds drag racers from scrap, hits the softball out of the park, and marries into the blue chips."

I personally thought Leslie liked the wheeling-and-dealing too much to tie herself down, but I do not comment unduly about employees. I went up to my room to plan the next day's moves against Jorkins.

It soon became apparent that the Space teams had joined common cause despite their jealousies. I spent the next morning at the hangar, watching the lift-off crew move the Janus/Alpha unit onto the launching pad. Not all the Thermionics gear was aboard the shuttle, but the small stuff could be taken up the pad elevator and stowed later. When I got back to Holloway's office after noon, Jorkins was waiting for me.

He was hunched over eagerly and pleased with himself. I sat down at Holloway's desk, and Jorkins handed me a schedule.

"Medical/Biological mowed us down with a scythe," he reported, "but the combined teams have a two-thirds Space potential. Now, in Thermionics I see no need for more than a two-man subsidiary on the Moon, so that four men can alternate the mission. If I exchange one man with Quimberly—"

I remembered too late that all these guys were mathematicians. They had cut their teeth on the hen-and-a-half who had laid an egg-and-a-half, not to mention the guy who had rowed upstream at two knots while his hat had floated downstream at four. A combined Moon-rotation schedule had been duck soup for them.

I was painted into another corner, and I saw I would have to pull rank to get out of it. I said casually, "It's too late for any of you to be briefed for the coming lift-off, but I'll put a qualified person aboard to start the Moon lab."

Jorkins snapped up the 'person' like the genius he was. He squeaked, "Miss Ellerdown? I object! I resign! I will not be hampered—!"

I asked patiently, "Is there anything wrong with Miss Ellerdown's math qualifications? With her work-record in aeronautics?"

He sputtered, "I'd hardly expect you to

understand—varying quality of college degrees
—women always an unstable element—" He took a
deep breath as a further point occurred to him,
and burst out.

"The Company has no women among its sea
officers—that is, not in command posts! Reform
the fleet before you come down here and try to
force women into places they're equally not
wanted!"

I explained, "Women will not be viable as Senior
Merchant Marine officers until the crews are as
strictly disciplined as Navy crews—or as severely
policed as the Communist-bloc crews who have
female mates and skippers. Only a two-fisted male
can cope with the rowdyism and violence that continually erupt in crew quarters. A ship's safety depends on command officers who can maintain discipline physically, if necessary.

"But a science lab has no Donnybrooks to be put
down by force. Two guys bickering over the square
root of x don't slug it out toe-to-toe or carve each
other up with switchblades. Nothing physical is
involved, and physical strength is the only factor
where women are inferior—and I mean average
women, not hormone-altered Olympic athletes.

"Dr. Jorkins, this may seem to you like a case of
the tail wagging the dog, but I'm sticking to my
guns. A clique that is blind to Miss Ellerdown's
ability is probably blind to a lot of scientific truths
as well."

I indicated the schedule. "I should have thought
sooner of reshuffling the teams. It's the only way
new ideas are gonna circulate. If there still is no
thermionic breakthrough, you won't have to
resign—you'll be fired. Space Mining is a profit-

making institution, not an endless boondoggle for mediocrities."

He was paralyzed by this insult. I went on, "It is my decision that Leslie Ellerdown, who has been fully trained for Space, will begin the installation of the Thermionics lab, and I'll send her to Thermionics tomorrow for briefing. If, after a fair trail, you find she is not competent, we'll discuss the matter further."

He was still stirred up over 'mediocrity'. He said, "No other lab is as near to a thermionic engine as we are! Your attitude is uncalled for!"

"I'm leaning over backwards to be fair to all parties, Dr. Jorkins. I'm letting you continue as Thermionics leader, and I'm assuring you that if Leslie is incompetent, you can fire her. She has to make good on her own.

"The Thermionics budget can be increased to cover her salary until a comparable job opens for the odd man out. You may actually find you want to retain Miss Ellerdown and transfer somebody else."

The funding increase put Jorkins one-up again, and he was fairly happy as he left the office.

I immediately phoned both Lyle and Transportation to warn them that Leslie would be a Thermionics researcher as of the next day. Transportation was understandably teed off. I agreed, "Yeah, it's short notice. If you need an extra man for the Douglas, call in an astronaut. They all swipe the Douglas when they can get away with it."

Ms. Neems and her Underground were listening in, of course, and the announcement about Leslie spread over the ALC like wildfire.

I waited to tell Leslie until my return to Transit

Staff that evening. After I had showered and made myself comfortable in khakis, I phoned her room and said, "I gotta borrow your park bench again, Miss Ellerdown."

"Come ahead, captain," she replied cheerfully, and I barged along the balcony as before. She was wearing her chopper jumpsuit and said, "Transportation gets hectic before Moon lift-off. Visiting firemen and such."

We sat down, and I reflected that a male Transit could never have made the balcony nook so cosy. I said, "Well, Miss Ellerdown, I've bulldozed your way into Thermionics. You report to Jorkins tomorrow for instructions about the Moon lab. You gotta make it on your own, though."

"I know I'll have to be twice as good as any man on the team—but women are smarter than men," she said calmly. "The reason the men catch up, in the late teens, is that the environment slows the girls down. If a girl opts out of the dating-sex-marriage trap, she keeps her advantage. As Kipling wrote, 'Down to Gehenna or up to the Throne, he travels fastest who travels alone.'"

"Yeah, but luck has a lot to do with anybody staying single," I objected. "When I was of a marrying age, I was working on all-male rustbuckets. Jeez, I mighta been snagged right off the bat, if I'd been working the passenger ships. How come you think you can stay single?"

"Because girls are less dependent on sex-satisfaction than men. My goodness, captain, if you hadn't stayed on the rustbuckets, you would have been married ten times over by now!"

I did not know whether she was implying that I

was unusually dumb or unusually sexy, but I joked,
"All the women would have thrown me back, once
they had hooked me, hey?"

"When they dragged you on deck, you would
have spit out the hook into the scuppers, wiggled
overboard and swum away."

I haw-hawed, and the loungers below looked up
at us again. I recollected that I was high-echelon
and Leslie was a female employee, and I went back
to my room to study the new team switchovers.

During the next two days the ALC was peaceful,
though agog over Leslie's advance into Thermionics. There was general optimism about the
changes I had made in order to give the girl the job
she had earned. I reflected that Leslie's constructive, positive attitude had been a catalyst giving a
new quality to Space Mining research. I had
started out to do justice to the girl—and had ended
by giving a shot in the arm to the whole research
program.

No such constructive results could be expected
from Christina Copps' "Gimme—or I'll sue!"

The following evening the Janus fueling began,
and the Transit Staff quarters filled up with Moon
personnel and visitors. The next day, as I was
looking over some audits in Holloway's office,
Ms. Neems buzzed me and asked if she could
discuss something with me. I told her to come in, sit
down and sing out.

She came and sat, sprightly and correct as before, and said, "I thought it best that I was spokesman for our ladies. Some of them are really upset,
captain, about where Leslie Ellerdown is going to
live."

I thought she was referring to the Moon, and I interrupted, "Since Miss Ellerdown will be the only Thermionics worker, she'll have the lab-canister to herself."

"Oh, I don't mean the Residence, captain! I mean, the ladies don't think it's fair that she's continuing to live free at Transit Staff, now that she's in Thermionics. All of us have had a dreadful time finding places to live near the reservation, and the ladies feel that Leslie should be asked to move from Transit Staff and live like the rest of us!"

I was irked by this pettiness. "Naturally the girl won't wanta live on top of her work."

"But, really, captain, the ladies think she should be given formal notice to move, as Company policy!"

I had supposed the women would be pleased that Leslie had cracked the clique barrier. Instead, they were envious. I temporized, "She's lifting off tomorrow night. She has no time—"

"It's the principle, captain! Of course, to you it's a minor point—and I agree completely," Ms. Neems added with bright insincerity, "but we can't have ignorant people saying that Leslie is living in Transit Staff as a Company favorite—perhaps even as an executive's protégée—!"

If I had subscribed to equal rights, Ms. Neems would have got a fat lip. I said shortly, "Miss Ellerdown understands the ramifications of her job transfer. I have no intention of throwing her out during the Moon briefings. You know very well, Ms. Neems, that Moon workers are accommodated at Transit Staff prior to lift-off and after return."

She rose in a huffy manner. "I only wanted to

explain the ladies' consensus, captain. I'm sure Leslie Ellerdown is nothing to me!"

She marched out. I reflected that women still had a long way to go, baby.

I had no sooner simmered down than Colonel Fairweather phoned from the Assembly hangar. He said uncertainly, "Sorry, captain, but I must refuse to take the 80-kilo overload on the Alpha."

"Nothing to be sorry about, Colonel," I assured him. "Safety comes before anything else. What's the specific overload item?"

"Why, it's Dr. Jorkins!" said Fairweather. "Didn't you know he was scheduled?"

"Scheduled!" I bellowed into the phone. "The damned son-of-a-bitch has no Space training! He don't even have a suit! Who the hell told him he could lift off?"

"He must have made his own arrangements to borrow a suit from M/B. Then it's okay if I bump him?"

"Of course. No—wait a minute," I muttered. "It's that damned one-upmanship again! Jorkins won't let Leslie Ellerdown go to the Moon ahead of him. I swear, this place is worse than a banana republic!"

Fairweather laughed. I revved up my brain. There was no such thing as non-essential shuttle cargo, unless the Thermionics—? I saw at once what could be—what oughtta be—removed. I suggested,

"Colonel, instead of bumping Jorkins, let's unload the Thermionic bunk units and personal lockers. For now, Jorkins and Miss Ellerdown can bunk with another Moon team. Okay?"

Fairweather agreed, and I felt I had forestalled trouble. Better that Leslie should bunk with several guys together than in the lab-canister with Jorkins alone.

The day's hassles were not over. When I got back to Transit Staff that evening, a group of women politely but firmly ganged up on me. In the Transit area, they would have to be wives of Moon personnel. By the light of the mall lamps, riffle-shadowed by palm fronds, I could see taut faces and glittering eyes. The natives were restless.

A woman stepped forward and began, in a nervous, almost hysterical voice, "Captain Schuster, we've just found out that you're sending a girl to the Moon with our husbands. It's not enough that this equality rip-off is breaking up our homes—not enough that whores walk every street, and topless bars and porno movies get police protection—but Space Mining is sending these liberated hussies to the Moon!

"Captain, you're not a harebrained ivory-tower liberal! You know the hanky-pankying that goes on with a mixed crew aboard a ship! While we're staying home with their kids, our husbands are bunking with girls who take men's jobs and have no decency or self-respect!"

There were murmurs of agreement. Another woman cried out, "We'll stop the lift-off—we'll sit down on the launch pad—we won't let our husbands work on the Moon!"

I answered, "Now, let's get the right focus, ladies. I hafta agree that the media's hard sell of drugs and pornography is wrecking homes and ruining kids—but Space Mining don't concur with any part of that campaign. We're proud to have decent folks working for us.

"Moon work is hazardous," I went on. "Life is very valuable up there—personal integrity is held in deep respect. Living with constant reminders of the vastness of the cosmos, men tend to behave better on the Moon than in their everyday Earth lives. But when all is said and done, it's up to the guy himself. Being an isolated group don't make all that much difference. A decent guy is a decent guy—on a ship or on the Moon.

"And I want to emphasize that Miss Ellerdown is not a liberated hussy. Seven years of hard work are behind her Space Mining job. She did not ask to be sent to the Moon—but that's where we've decided to use her. As you ladies know—and sometimes complain over—we're ruthless about squeezing the last ounce of value from our talents. When we need a specific Moon worker, we don't care if the person is male, female or a little green Martian."

This rang so true that involuntary giggles bubbled from the women. I added, "Miss Ellerdown was hired on merit, not because of activist pressure. It'll be a cold day in hell when Space Mining lets pressure groups do its hiring and firing!"

The tension had dissolved, and the faces had half-smiles. I concluded, "When the Alpha comes back next month, you'll find all your worries were unnecessary. So relax and trust the Old Man, hey?"

They agreed and let me go. I went up to my room and phoned Leslie. "There's something damned wrong with this equality jazz," I barked. "You're getting all the equality, and I'm getting all the fallout!"

I heard a gasp of suppressed laughter. "Striking your colors, captain?"

"Hell, no. But you could defuse a torpedo aimed at us both."

"How?"

"By making clear that you intend to find ordinary housing after you return from the Moon. Your Sisterhood is stabbing you in the back."

"What! Why would anybody choose to live inside this rat race? And how could it involve you, captain?"

"It's a hell of a thing to explain, but maybe you'll get a laugh out of it. The word *protégée* is being slung around."

"Oh, cripes." A pause. "Anything else? That protest meeting just now, on the mall—are they raking our tops or holing our waterline?"

"That depends on your evasive tactics and broken field running."

"Old swivel-hips Ellerdown," she murmured.

I had to haw-haw again, and I could hear her chortling to herself. I said finally, "Well, keep your spirit and your sense of humor, Miss Ellerdown. You have only yet begun to fight."

I hung up and opened the bottle of scotch I had smuggled in my suitcase, liquor being an unwanted commodity at the ALC. I turned on the TV, sat down and eased off my shoes, hoping a rock group or sit-com would lower my blood pressure.

What I had push-buttoned, of course, was a round-table discussion of Space Mining chauvinism, featuring Ms. Christina Copps. Taped a couple days previously, it gave me an indication of Attorney Dumont's strategy.

He had toned down his client's sex-radiation by several decibels. Christina was wearing small pearl earrings, a high-necked shirt and a conservative pant-suit. Her eyeglasses gleamed intellectually and her spiel was the usual low-key, multi-syllable, university double-talk.

Her interviewers had done their homework, and they had not missed Leslie Ellerdown's entirely different tack toward the Space Mining goal. The mention of *work* and *cooperation* roused Ms. Copps to a fanatical fever. She spat out. "Uncle Tomism!" as if only confrontation and hate could serve the female cause.

I had to admit that plenty of people might agree that she had been unfairly deprived of Amtland's job, but I did not intend the case to go to court.

I sorta dozed off until a knock at the door woke me up. I padded over to see who it was, and I was surprised to find Astronaut Fairweather.

"I noticed a light behind your curtains," he smiled, "and decided to stop and tell you that Leslie has moved out."

"What!" I craned my neck around the door and saw that Leslie's balcony corner was as empty as if a wave had swept it clean. I asked, "What happened?"

"The Transportation guys are letting Leslie stash the bike and her luggage in a parts shed. I drove her and a small suitcase to a motel south of the Kennedy Center."

"But she's lifting-off tomorrow night!" I exclaimed. "She has every right to be here as Moon personnel!"

"Since when have those liberation broads thought of any rights but their own?"

I could not get over it. I wondered aloud, "Why the hell did Leslie yield without a fight?"

Fairweather hesitated. "She said Mickleberry was too old for unexpected shocks."

A laugh busted out of me. If anything could jolt Mickleberry's pokerfaced precision, it would be a rumor that Schuster had a protégée.

Fairweather continued to his room. I put on my shoes and took a turn around the mall. I am not generally superstitious, but I did not like all this niffnawing before a shuttle lift-off. When I glanced at Leslie's vacated premises, I felt no good would come of the dislocation and strife.

The next day we went into high gear, readying the Janus countdown and coping with the tourists. Being a tourist attraction had helped our Image, but some damned camera nut would always try to sneak too close to the launch pad.

At 1800 hours I went into our command bunker, a redundant NASA post we had leased and renovated. We had built a small semicircular gallery for the press and any Moon relatives who wanted to watch. As the Janus boosters continued to shoot up flawlessly month after month, the press coverage had trickled away, but the wives and kids visited more frequently.

On this lift-off, because of the Jorkins/Ellerdown/Copps wrangle, the press again had come in force.

The launch was starting as routinely as all the others, but my hunch about trouble would not go away. I looked at the cheerful gallery crowd—the wives exchanging recipes and the kids eating popcorn and bouncing around—and I said to the PR chief, "Be ready with emergency procedures. Up to now, our batting average has been too damned good."

He eyed me seriously, nodded, and moved away to alert his crew.

Five minutes to countdown. Quiet tenseness at the tracking and control consoles. The large viewing screen came to life, and the gallery hushed with anticipation. The boarding elevator had been retracted, and the Janus/Alpha stood alone, a gigantic arrow pointing skyward.

Launch control began relaying the voices of Astronauts Fairweather and Jones. Routine technical stuff. All systems Go.

Countdown. I clamped my teeth together and wished to God I was on the bridge of a ship I could control. . . . 3 . . . 2 . . . 1 . . .

A heart-stopping moment while the Janus sat on a cushion of exploding fire. Then the steady rise of the Double/Thrust system into the brief sunset sky. The Janus had lifted—and the gallery relaxed. I still felt leery.

Fairweather's voice was droning, ". . . one minute from lift-off . . . two minutes . . . in orbit . . . guess we can take off our hats and stay awhi—"

Twunk—Scree . . .

My hunch had been right, dammit. The shuttle had been holed, and the air recycler alarm was blasting.

Over the alarm I heard a gallery kid wail and begin crying. I thought, *the shuttle is in orbit—she can't fall back.* I hoped nobody had dehelmeted.

The alarm broke off, and Fairweather's voice

resumed coolly, "The main cabin has been punctured by what looks like a rod from a communication satellite. Nobody hurt—the entry missed the lift-off tiers. Stand by, ALC."

We did not permit media transmissions inside the bunker, so the relay-men were stampeding to their outside vans. I saw that PR was on the hot line to M/B, which had the next-of-kin data. The gallery wives and kids were staring desperately at me. As if I could do anything.

Fairweather again. "Repeat, everybody is okay. We're still on our suit airpacks, but the shuttle's double-hull insulation has flowed around the rod, blocking the breach. The air recycler has stopped up from the reserve tank and shows normal readings. Captain Schuster, I advise that we proceed to the Moon."

They could not risk re-entry burn with a punctured hull, and they could reach the Moon quicker than the ALC could position and fuel a reserve shuttle. I picked up my mike and answered, "The Moon is probably your best bet, Colonel, but let's check hull integrity first. How well is the insulation blocking the breach?"

Astronaut Jones took over communication while Fairweather went out the airlock. From the corner of my eye I could see PR damping down the press clamor for a direct shuttle interview.

Fairweather reported, from outside the hull, "This is the damndest thing I've ever seen! We collided with a burnt-out satellite about two meters in diameter. And I mean, this is real old junk!"

I remembered telling Jorkins there was too much junk in orbit. I asked Fairweather, "One of Ours, or one or Theirs?"

"God knows. It's jabbing into us like a lollipop on a stick."

I heard a nervous titter from the gallery. Fairweather went on, "We have a problem with the insulation plug. It stays molten on the sun side, and I can see it continuing to extrude from cabin pressure. Unless we keep the shuttle trimmed so that the rod is on the right side, the insulation will bleed out of the hull."

Fairweather re-entered the shuttle, and the trim maneuver was carried out. A second inspection confirmed that the extrusion had congealed in direct contact with the cold of Outer Space.

Jones had been inspecting the inner damage. He reported, "The rod has cancelled the tier mechanism. There's no possibility of folding the lift-off tiers against the bulkheads and magnetizing the deck for simulated gravity. We'll just have to endure null gravity all the way to the Moon."

This was a minor item. The air recycler was still holding steady so the Moon personnel unstrapped from their tiers, dehelmeted and floated around.

I was worried about the equilibrium of the hull damage. As long as the rod remained fixed, the viscous hull insulation could plug air-escape. Probably the thinness of the rod and the angle of penetration was minimizing pressure effect, but I would not bet on that fatal spear remaining unjiggled for the three days of the Moon trip. I said,

"Colonel, the Beta shuttle has gotta blast from Moon orbit and meet you guys halfway. Stand by for course coordination."

ALC picked up their cue and alerted the Moon Residence, which may or may not have been monitoring us. Three days before their own blast-out, the Moon workers generally were too busy winding up their month's reports to care what was happening at the ALC.

As far as I was concerned, the initiative had now passed to the technicians and computers. A Deep Space meeting between two speeding shuttles was gonna be trickier than coordinating a trapeze act.

Fairweather had gone on Stand-By while we spoke to the Moon. Within an hour the Beta astronauts, with their rescue crew, extra oxygen and fuel, had jet-dollied up to Moon orbit and boarded their shuttle.

As I paced behind the command table and waited, I reflected that *drift factor of solar wind* was another navigation giveaway. Leslie definitely had primed her boss and sent him to the cockpit. Our corn-fed Machiavelli was still wheeling-and-dealing through proper channels.

It was lucky that Jorkins had immediately grasped the validity of her observation. Well, I had never denied the guy was a genius. Lots of geniuses are s.o.b.'s.

At last came a pause. Fairweather said "Blasting," and like an echo we heard "Blasting" from the Beta.

I felt as if I had been put through a wringer. Both shuttles were now on course. A navigator myself, I trusted the astronauts more than any lag-hobbled computer. There would still be 36 hours of anxiety about the speared hull, but I decided I could call it a night. Until I saw the pale, shiny faces of the waiting wives, and the small kids sleeping across laps and chairs, I did not realize how much time had passed.

I left the table, went over to the gallery and said, "You Moon families are welcome to stay at Transit Staff. The situation has stabilized. Put the kids to bed and get some rest."

Numbly, they gathered up the kids. Other Space Mining personnel had reported to the bunker, and they helped the shocked women.

Until now the media had behaved with sense and restraint. With the worst danger over, they rustled to life, and I was hemmed in by a scuffle of reporters. In chorus came the question, "Captain, do you think the Alpha is jinxed because a woman is aboard?"

"Of course not," I growled. "Plain human carelessness is responsible for the Earth's junk-strewn orbit. The Alpha had horseshoes all over her, to sustain minimum damage."

PR tunneled a path for me through the crowd outside the bunker, blocked me into a pool car and drove me to Transit Staff. Safely in my room, I showered, gave my face a scrape in case I would be summoned in a hurry, and hit the sack.

I awoke at 0600 hours and checked immediately with ALC control. They said there had been intermittent air leakage from the plugged hole, and Fairweather had gone topside again. I cussed them out for not calling me sooner, threw on my clothes, ordered a car and was driven to the bunker.

The jam of media vans and tourists was being handled by federal troops, since the ALC was on federal land. The guards rushed me into the bunker, and I got on the mike to Fairweather. He reported,

"The contraction of the insulation, after several

hours exposure to Space cold, causes a slow leak until the still-viscous insulation between the double hull flows into the crack. By trying slow rotation—"

"You would still be like a guy bleeding to death from a razor nick. We've gotta remove that damned satellite—but lash it to the hull so our next shuttle don't wade into it."

Fatigue in his voice, Fairweather said, "The break would be the diameter of a gas pipe."

"Yeah, but the leak is the reverse of a leak in a ship's hull. The pressure is working with you, not against you. What can you rig that would conform to the inner hull, like a compress over a wound?"

A pause. "A section of tier cushion might do it."

"Use plastic—anything—to collar the rod as it's being pushed out. When the end is even with the inner hull, slap the patch against it. The guy steadying the rod on the outside of the hull can complete pulling it through."

"We'll try it, captain."

The media were breathing down the back of my neck. We heard Fairweather and Jones talking to the Moon workers. An experienced cargo handler was sent outside to steady the rod.

Jones' voice: "How the hell can we collar the rod? Nobody's hand can fit between these tier struts! We'll lose a barrel of air before the pressure sucks a patch tight!"

A general murmur, with a distinct, "Hey, lookit Leslie! She can reach it!"

Once again Leslie Ellerdown was taking up the slack, her smaller but strong hand fitting into a space where a big male fist could not go.

I sweat blood while Leslie held the collar tight

against the hull and Fairweather pushed the rod back through the entry hole, centimeter by centimeter. Finally he said, "Okay, Leslie, ready with the cork!" And he ordered the outside man. "Pull!"

There must have been terrific suction as the rod was pulled free, but the cushion-wad choked the breach. A moment later the outside man, lashing the satellite to a hull cleat, reported a new insulation plug flowing into place and congealing. As soon as plastic sealer had been slapped over the patch, the inner hull would be airtight despite occasional cracks in the insulation.

It had been a risky maneuver. Air pressure might have ripped open that entire hull section. And more than 24 hours before the Beta could come alongside. I asked Fairweather, "How's your reserve air?"

"Half gone," he admitted. "But the recycler is steady, and we should have no more loss."

I paced the bunker until 0900. The news still being good, I went directly to Holloway's office. Business had to go on, regardless of what was happening in Space. I had missed breakfast, so I asked Ms. Neems to duck down to the cafeteria and bring me some sandwiches and coffee.

She hurried off and came back with a loaded tray. As she put it on my desk she said, "The new girls don't fetch and carry for their bosses, but I know you've had a terrible siege, so I'm only too glad to help."

"Thanks very much," I said, meaning it.

She preened and returned to her office. I wolfed down the sandwiches and coffee and tried to do a day's work. In the back of my mind was the dread of a domino effect on the delicately posed shuttle mechanism. The unsafe hull, the cracking insulation. I asked myself, *what next?* Somehow, the anxiety was worse when a woman was involved.

I guess I was experiencing instinctive male anxiety over mankind's preservation. Up until this generation, the motto had been, "Women and children first."

I would not expect a resident of Tokyo or Manhattan to believe me, but the "overpopulation" fear was a lot of statistical crap. Except for a few high-concentration areas, the world was fast depopulating, as every seaman knew from direct observation. Communist Europe was offering family bonuses—and their birthrates were continuing to drop. Sweden was importing workers from Itay, Jugoslavia, Greece—and predicting that the Swedish "race" would be extinct by the year 2000.

Africa, not content with its endemic cholera and a dozen other plagues, had embarked on systematic genocide—of which Idi Amin was the most publicized but not the only proponent. India's trouble was poor management. She had a potentially rich sub-continent, but even if she sterilized half her population, the other half would starve to death while she fragmented into political and economic chaos.

When statisticians reported that the USA's population had "stablized", what they meant was that fewer children were being born than were necessary for the USA to exist past the next generation. If we lost a woman on the Alpha, we lost her potential children as well. That was why woman had no business in hazardous work—on ships, in

Space, in front-line trenches. Male chauvinist or not, I believed women should be kept safe—that is, young women of childbearing age.

Older women could take any risks they damned pleased. For all I cared, that gravel-voiced, fat-fannied picket-organizer could sit on a Janus and be blasted to Kingdom Come.

But Leslie was different. If she strangled to death on bad air in that shuttle, the species would lose her talents unto the third and fourth generation. The goddamned Libbers and Abortionists were not thinking of the species. They were acting as if a woman produced a million offspring a year, like codfish, whereas she produced a mere handful in a lifetime.

If the inner cities were decaying shells, it was because the family had decayed first.

In the afternoon, the red button on Holloway's console lit up. Well, I had been half-expecting it. I answered, and a voice from the bunker said, "A deterioration, captain. Continued air loss. Here's Fairweather."

The line hummed as they spliced me into the shuttle transmission. Fairweather's too-even voice said, "The unbalanced flow of insulation apparently has induced metal fatigue in the inner hull, and we're losing infinitesimal amounts of air through weld areas—the viewscreen ports and so on. Jones was outside and detected slight bulges in the outer hull where air pressure was forcing insulation fluid outwards."

"What have you done to counter this effect?"

"Slapped liquid sealer on the weakened seams—just a delay, but any loss-stoppage helps.

We've also switched off the automatic topping from the reserve tank. We're breathing substandard air and topping up manually when absolutely necessary."

"Still have air in the suits?"

"Yes, but I think we'll gradually release it to be recycled. The recycler is still the most efficient way to use the air we've got."

"Heard from the Beta?"

"Yeah. So near and yet so far. We need that thermionic engine." A hesitation, then, "Captain, we could let Leslie keep her suit air. If the gap is narrow, maybe she could survive, even if the rest of us conked out."

"No!" I barked immediately. "She wanted equality in a man's field, and she has to take the consequences. Treat her exactly like a man."

"She'd sure chew me out if I didn't," said Fairweather, "but I had to ask for orders. In my book, women still aren't men."

"Well, don't try telling them that," I advised. "Jeez, I've got a hornet's nest around my ears! Dames nowadays wouldn't give a drowning man a drink of water!"

Fairweather laughed and cut off transmission. I naturally phoned for a pool car to take me to the bunker at once. The driver was prompt, but instead of heading straight for the bunker, he took a swing around the perimeter of the ALC's land. I asked, "What's the big idea?" and he handed me a battery shaver. He smiled. "PR wants only clean-shaven, spruce executives talking to the media."

I meekly rubbed the shaver over my shadowed jaw, but 'spruce' I was not.

When I arrived at the bunker, I found there was good news. The Apha now had visual contact with the Beta. This did not thrill me as much as it thrilled the media. The Apha also had visual contact with Canopus.

There was now sixteen hours until the Beta could come alongside. Never have hours seemed so long or time so short. To conserve air use, the Alpha ceased all transmission and the crew strapped themselves to the lift-off tiers. Fairweather said they had knocked themselves out with sleeping pills. I wondered what kind of dreams they were having.

The seconds, minutes, hours ticked away. At last the Beta was alongside. I listened dully as the Beta captain reported from his view-screens, ". . . rescue crew now entering the Alpha with oxygen. As soon as their suitpacks can be filled, the Alpha crew will be carried . . ."

Maybe some of them were still alive. A guy could be unconscious a long time and still survive.

"Wait! An Alpha suit is emerging!" said the Beta skipper. "The first man is okay . . . here he comes, under his own power . . . out of the airlock . . . Leslie Ellerdown! How was your giant step into Space?"

The media told me later that I banged my fist on the table and said, "I knew it!" and they asked me what I had known. I said I had known that the Alpha crew would survive, but what I really had known was that the rescuers would save Leslie first. Whether women liked it or not, they would always have priority in the lifeboats.

Leslie's low voice answered the skipper, "The

step was fine, Colonel, but it left me a little breathless."

A huff of laughter gusted from the gallery. The tension was over. One after another, all the Alpha guys entered the Beta, unlocked their helmets and told the listening planets that they felt fine, okay, swell, great, splendid (Jorkins)—lying in their teeth but reassuring their families.

From here on out, the communication belonged to the engineers. How to salvage the Alpha? Restructure her on the Moon? Piggyback her home to the ALC?

I extricated myself from the media, returned to the Administration Building, fetched my own breakfast and decided to look at the just-arrived mail before catching up with my sleep at Transit Staff.

Topmost was a thick envelope marked, *Confidential—Captain Schuster*. I slit open and found that our New York legal department had sent us a gumshoe report on Christina Copps. There was a lot of dirt, and apparently people had been eager to spill it. Girls who are not 'nice' make enemies on both sides of the street.

Christina was openly shacked up with her Florida attorney, Dumont. She probably thought she was 'glamorous' because she had a 'live-in love'. The media terms were so seductive—with-it, swinging, liberated—and at forty the swindled women were alcoholic hags. I had seen them on the cruise ships—face-lifted, bewigged, lonely.

I forgot about sleep and decided to strike while the iron was hot. The invaluable Ms. Neems got me Attorney Dumont on the phone. He said, "Ah, yes, captain. Congratulations on the Space rescue."

"Thanks," I said amiably. "A great relief to us all. Mr. Dumont, could you bring Ms. Copps here this afternoon? I think a conference is now in order."

He agreed, cautiously. He knew damned well I was not about to throw in the towel. We made the appointment for 1500 hours. I scanned the rest of the mail, beat it to Transit Staff and slept out the morning.

Dumont brought his client as per my request. and they sat in Holloway's executive-type chairs. I leaned back in the swivel chair behind the desk and began mildly.

"Ms. Copps, your scholastic record shows you have a good head on your shoulders, and it's about time you used it. So far, you've been digging yourself into a hole instead of laying foundations."

Christina's face got the ugly scowl of a spoiled brat. "My purpose is to undermine a rotten system, not build it up."

"You're just parroting an emotive phrase, but I won't argue semantics. I only wanta point out that you can't have it both ways. Either you undermine—or you support. You can't expect to be given a job in a building you're trying to tear down. I don't mean a job in Space Mining, but participation in society generally. You're like a baseball rookie who demands that the base paths be shortened, the outfielders eliminated, and every batter be put on first base on a walk."

I had Christina's file on my desk, and I took out her job application. "I find, Ms. Copps, that Mr. Lyle did, in fact, offer you Space training in several fields."

Dumont interrupted, "Fields irrelevant to Ms.

Copps' job request. She did not apply for steno-
graphic work."

"Mr. Lyle was not hiring her as a stenographer
but as a Space-trainee whose practical skills might
give direction to her academic background. As a
physicist, could she also do statistical analysis of the
Mars data? Collate, edit and publish departmental
reports? Had she, perhaps, practical engineering
experience with aeronautic or electronic systems?
Space Mining, in short, was willing to tailor Ms.
Copps' talents to our Space needs. Surely we can't
be required to do more! An employer can't retool
his plant to fit the demands of every Ph.D. who
applies for a job!"

Dumont smiled, "You are at liberty to plead that
line before the court—"

Christina lashed out, "Of course he'll plead that
line—with Miss Goody Two-Shoes Ellerdown as
Exhibit A!" She spat at me, "Luck! You were just
lucky that Leslie was already on that payroll—
lucky that she could be one of your Space heroes!"

"Well, now," I countered, "it was the kind of luck
that built the free and prosperous society in which
we live. I'm no social scientist, but as I look at
history I find a well-defined process of human
interaction which has carried mankind forward
and upward despite unceasing wars and natural
holocausts. That process is the mutual cooperation
of hard-working constructively-oriented individuals who hope that the world is somehow better for
their strivings. Not important or powerful people.
Working people who grow the grain and drive the
trucks and sail the ships.

"Like a coral reef building up cell by cell, despite surf and storms crashing over it, until a vast, fruitful island is formed. The interaction/cooperation of individuals builds towards the stars. When constructively-inclined men like Holloway and Lyle had hired a hard-working girl like Leslie, only good luck could have come of it—*because that is the way the law of human interaction works.* I don't know *why* it works that way—any more than an individual cell of coral knows why the reef keeps growing.

"I *do* know," I added, "that Leslie played her cards very cleverly, confident she had Jorkins beat six ways from the ace."

"You chauvinists are all alike!" said Christina spitefully. "Just because a virtuous little daddy's girl bats her eyes at you—!"

"Yeah, that's what really gripes you, don't it?" I grinned. "Leslie is also clever *as a woman.* You've been on more beds than a mattress and you can't even find a job. Leslie not only has a fine future with Space Mining—she's also got all of us wrapped around her little finger."

Dumont said to me, "If you continue on that line, Schuster, we'll sue for defamation of character in addition to the job suit."

"I doubt very much that you'll sue at all, Mr. Dumont," I answered, indicating the report from the detective agency. "I am prepared to expose your job suit for what it is—a malicious, unprovoked, activist-incited attack. If you sue, you'll unleash an overkill response that will destroy both you and your client.

"The issue is not only Jorkins' chauvinism," I went on, "but Ms. Copps' true motives. The court may well wonder at her good faith when it learns that her campus years were a series of flagrant sex adventures and political demonstrations, that she had never worked or applied for a job, until Amtland's job became vacant, and that she is openly cohabiting with her attorney."

Christina jumped up and tongue-lashed me with four-letter invective that would have burned the ears off a bucko mate.

When she paused for breath, I said, "Yeah, I'm a tough bastard and a dirty infighter. You got a tiger by the tail when you tackled Space Mining."

Dumont motioned the girl to sit down. He said to me, "I dispute that Ms. Copps' private life is at issue."

"Depends on the balance," I argued. "If Leslie Ellerdown had sued us, we would have no defense, even if her private life had been an open scandal. Her job record proved she had worked earnestly and single-mindedly to qualify for aerospace, and we did not treat her fairly in the Amtland matter. In contrast, Ms. Copps' extra-curricular activity was limited to sex and demogoguery. Her application for Amtland's job was presumptuous and frivolous."

She lashed out at me again. "And I suppose you'll try the case in the newspaper before you try it in court."

"If you force Space Mining into a defense, this private-eye report will be sent to our PR department, and we'll have public opinion on our side. Right now you're enjoying the excitement of what you call 'total liberation', but someday you'll wake up and find that the middle-of-the-road majority has quietly closed ranks against you. A single standard of immorality is never gonna beat the double standard of morality, no matter how wrong the double standard may be.

"If you didn't have a remarkable brain, I couldn't care less about letting you be shouldered aside, but you must have colossal mental ability to make high college grades despite the turmoil of your life. I would be genuinely sorry if the mud of this court action forever mired you down.

"So I'm asking you directly, Ms. Copps, to use your intelligence, to think straight, to admit that you are being used by a pressure group that has not thought for your welfare."

Dumont began to speak, but Christina's scathing voice cut him off. "Can't you see we've been shafted?" she yelled at him. "You know we never meant to buck Mickleberry! Holloway was the perfect set-up, a nuts-and-bolts character out of his depth with legal matters. He or Lyle would have caved in!

"It was just our damned luck that Mickleberry sent Schuster down here—and that the old Action bitch forced our hand! Instead of hairy-eared engineers, we're battling the New York brain trust! Well, I'm not letting Schuster tar and feather me in the media. Overkill, he says! I should damn well think so!

"Leslie Ellerdown was right when she warned me I couldn't fight City Hall. Space Mining looked like a fat cat, but it's turned out to be a wounded grizzly. So, my dear counselor, you can withdraw the suit and tell the Action committee to case the next joint better!"

In the same breath she whirled on me and said, "Not that I'll stop politicking against a man's world—not that I think Space Mining is in the right—not that I'm ashamed of my ideas or my liberated sex—but that you have the power to distort and smear and destroy—and little Christina is no martyr! That much brain I *do* have!"

She raged out of the office like a tornado. Dumont got up and said sarcastically, "Thanks a lot, Schuster."

"Cheer up," I told him. "You can always go back to chasing ambulances."

"Hell, I was talking about my sex life. There's no sex object like a liberated college kid." He gave me a slow wink. "It's a matter of degree."

He strolled out. I closed Christina's file and put the gumshoe report in my pocket so that it would not fall into Ms. Neems's hands before I got it to a shredder. I figured I could wind up my Space Mining assignment and return to the ships.

I had to wait, of course, until the rescued Alpha crew could settle down to their work on the Moon. About a week after they had arrived up there, I dropped into Thermionics. The large wall-TV transmitting from the Moon lab made the two units seem next door to each other. Jorkins was alone in the Moon lab when I spoke to him. He said Leslie was up in orbit, testing expansion/contraction factors—something he called null-gravity flexibility.

I did not understand it, so I asked the Thermionics man who was monitoring the transmission. He explained, "There is considerable evidence that the rigidity of the conventional jet engine is the wrong principle for the thermionic heat/energy flow. We suspected this in Dynamics but somehow never could get through to Jorkins."

I eyed him. "You're the man Jorkins got from Dynamics? And still a Quimberly man?"

"Null-gravity flexibility is a Quimberly idea. I like to give credit where credit is due."

The team shake-up was producing the idea-exchange I had hoped for. I had not made a mistake in going all-out to secure Leslie her rightful place in Thermionics.

Wanting to return to the ships as soon as possible, I hustled around the ALC, spending a day in each division and dictating my conclusions into Holloway's recorder. I hit my stride over the hiring issue and thought my description of Jorkins was just right.

Being in a hurry, I signed each batch of reports as they leafed out of the copier. I did not know until later that Ms. Neems had upgraded, pruned and deleted the stuff before sending it along to the steno pool. The Company's Board of Directors, who knew my style pretty well, said the reports sounded as if I had made a pit-stop to change hormones.

The reports being cleared away, I phoned Mickleberry and asked for the ship assignment he had promised me.

He gave his temporizing cough. "Since you are doing such an excellent job, Captain Schuster, we are extending Mr. Holloway's mission and sending him to Japan, to negotiate certain electronic contracts. If you could remain at Space Mining for three more weeks—"

It sounded to me as if Holloway was flying to Japan via the beach at Waikiki, but as the girls had said, you can't fight City Hall. I told Mickleberry what I thought of his tub of chlorine, hung up and resigned myself to the wait.

So I was still at Space Mining when the Alpha team returned to Earth in the Moon-repaired shuttle. As was customary, I met the crew on their release from the M/B check-up. Leslie seemed thinner and somewhat tired, despite three days of rest on the home trip. I had time for just a 'hello,' since there were matters I had to discuss with the mining team, about the manganese cargoes and the crust-oxygen extracting unit.

I managed to talk to Astronaut Fairweather before he left Transit Staff, and he said, "Leslie got along fine on the Moon, but we noticed she was staying her distance from Jorkins. The most unlikely guys turn out to be skirt-chasers, don't they?"

"I dunno. Guys who think women are second-class citizens are the likeliest to give them a hard time." I added, "I noticed Leslie hitched a ride from M/B to Cocoa Beach. Did she find a place to live?"

"Yes, a Moon miner rented her his garage apartment. Said his wife could use the extra dough."

I had planned to stop by Thermionics and talk to Leslie myself, but Mickleberry phoned on that Saturday morning and said I could board an ore-carrier at Perth Amboy on Sunday night.

I could not leave Space Mining without some gesture of appreciation to the staff, so I hired a private dining room at a beach resort and threw a party Saturday night for the division chiefs and their wives. I figured I had better invite Ms. Neems if I expected cooperation from her area of expertise the next time I came, but I made sure that the Lyles picked her up and took her home. Ms. Neems was not gonna be a two-time winner at my expense.

Sunday morning the Space Mining chopper clattered down, forward of the Transit Staff lot. Having had a good time at the party, I was tired—in fact, very tired. I plodded out of Transit Staff, boosted my suitcase into the chopper and growled, "Orlando—and stay outta air pockets."

As I dumped myself into my seat, a familiar pleasant fragrance wafted towards me. I focussed my bleary eyes and saw Leslie Ellerdown, fresh and brisk in her Space Mining jumpsuit. I said, "Holy Cats!"

She smiled, "I asked Transportation to let me fly you to Orlando. A symbolic trip—for me, anyhow."

Her eyes were bright, and there was shy color on her cheeks. No female had looked at me like that since I was ten years old and had clobbered Stinker Gooley at the Fourth of July picnic. I realized Leslie was like a high-school kid who has a crush on her history teacher. She had opted out of the dating race, and Nature was now making itself felt, transforming gratitude into a long-delayed kid-yearning.

I said, "Gee, I appreciate your thoughtfulness, Miss Ellerdown. If you knew how many guys I've helped up the ladder of success—! But did any of 'em powder his nose and put on an ironed jumpsuit, just to say 'thanks' to the Old Man? I can't tell you how much—"

It broke her up, and her hearty laughter raised Sunday morning echoes all over the mall. When she had recovered, she gave me her old grin and spun the chopper. Everything was back to normal.

Nevertheless, I am not in a hurry to be assigned to Space Mining in the near future. I mean, a bachelor of my obvious charm and culture cannot be too careful!

Chapter 14

Schuster Tapes the Last Word

When we finally left our Q-Pod and jet-dollied down to Moon Residence, I found I had gone from the frying pan into the fire. The minute I unsuited in the Residence, the media were all over me, trying to prise a sensational statement out of me while I was still Space-weak.

Fortunately, their questions never even registered. The noise of a normal environment had put all us Q-Pod guys into shock. We had been living in a sardine can with only the hum of the support systems and the deliberately restrained sound of our own voices. To make the Q-Pod seem roomier we had unconsciously keyed down even our Barber Shop Quartets, as those tapes later showed.

Compton and the Tug crew felt the same effect to a lesser extent, and Compton thought it was more a psychological reaction to being physically bound to the spheroid mass. During the trip out to

331

the Asteroids, when the guys had the choice of being on the Wheel or on their docked Tugs, they had stayed more often on the Tugs.

The Moon medics rushed us into the hospital canisters. Over a week's time they weaned us off our Vita/Carbo diet onto normal food—bland stuff like mashed potatoes and creamed fish, but it sure tasted good. At the end of the week the other guys took the shuttle home to their families, but I stayed to get the Assay results—and to argue over the scrambler with Mickleberry on how *Harpy's Bizarre* ought to handled.

My view was that the public knew damn well the Rec-Pak had been stolen—or had been put together with stolen Space Mining data. I wanted to nab Howie Lind and the editor on a theft/receiving charge and put them behind bars. A forced retraction or forced bankruptcy would not erase the tape and would only make the editor a Lib heroine who had got away with murder.

Mickleberry—and to a greater extent Xavier—were concerned about the Company's legal position *re* damage suits for those mentioned on the tape. Mickleberry pointed out, also, that jailing the editor would turn her from a Lib heroine into a Lib martyr. Needless to say, Mickleberry's view prevailed, and I set about disassociating myself entirely from the Rec-Pak—in other words, lying my head off.

Three weeks after I had come out of the Q-Pod, I was bound for Earth. Because of the *Harpy's Bizarre* mess, I flew directly from Canaveral to New York. Bennington's man Cartwright met me at the Space Mining jet and drove me to the penthouse, which was the best refuge from the media.

The next morning Bennington and I went together to the Company offices. He said, "Better report first to Operations. If Mickleberry doesn't fire you, come up to the Board Meeting at ten o'clock."

Maybe he thought he was kidding, but stranger things had happened.

It was exactly nine o'clock when I stepped out of the elevator on the Operations deck. I was nearly bowled over. As one man, the Operations enclaves rose to their feet and cheered and clapped. Noise still was a shock to me, but I grinned, clasped my hands over my head and went forward to thank everybody personally. I did not feel I deserved an ovation. Compton and his crew—especially the technician who had first detected the Morse and was thrown temporarily into Jardin's looney bin—were the guys who deserved the laurels.

As I gradually made my way toward Mickleberry's office, my way was blocked by the mail-sorting machine they call LOCO. It had conked out and dumped a flood of letters to the deck. Scooping them up was a cute, copper-curled young dame who belonged in a shipping office about as much as I belonged in a chorus line. She wore a sleeveless denim shirt that had an orangey smear around the collar, denim knickers and thin black slippers.

She straightened up with an armful of mail and said, "Oh, gosh, I'm sorry—but LOCO spit up! I think the sudden noise jarred his circuits."

Well, it had jarred my circuits, too. I said genially, "You the new office boy?"

"Only until I get the walk-on part that's promised me in a new musical. And don't *look* at my collar—it's greasepaint, not dirt. Oh, how can I move poor LOCO?"

"You could try re-activating him," I said, finding the imbalance button and pushing it.

LOCO hummed to life. The girl said, "Thank heavens!" and guided LOCO aside to re-charge him.

Ms. Delaney was standing behind her desk, smiling at me. I reflected, as always, what a good-looking woman she was and how kindly the years had treated her. She had left her thick white hair natural, with just a touch of blue. Her eyes were clear—and gentle. Her skin was fine-textured, youthful.

Thirty years ago she had all the sea officers jumping through hoops, and in my opinion she was just as attractive now. In a different way, perhaps. More assured, more charming.

Strange, that she never had married. Well, she liked her job—and probably would rather paddle her own canoe.

She held out her hand. When I took it I could feel it was trembling, and I noted color in her cheeks. Naturally a foul-up in Operations would vex her. I gave her hand a squeeze and joshed her,

"Don't tell me you're upset, Ms. Delaney, because LOCO disgraced himself in front of the Old Man!"

"No, Captain Schuster," she laughed. "When a robot does nine-tenths of the work, it's impossible to find a human being who'll stay long enough to learn the other tenth." She added, "You're looking more like yourself again—and we're so glad to have you back."

"Thanks, Ms. Delaney," I said, feeling, as always, clumsy and tongue-tied when I looked at her. "It's sure great to be back. Mickleberry still going strong?"

"Oh, dear me, yes! Keep your guard up, captain!" With another smile at me, she opened Mickleberry's door, announced, "Captain Schuster, Mr. Mickleberry!" and gently closed the door as I stepped into the office.

The spare—somehow impelling—figure rose from his chair and gave me a firm handshake. "Good to see you, captain. That is, after drawing up a balance sheet, I decided the good news outweighed the bad news."

We sat down, and I grinned, "Yeah, I pulled a boner, leaving those Rec-Paks in Operations. What kind of news do you wanta talk about first?"

"The mining assays," he said immediately. "I can make no sense of Khadir Fai k'y Atur's statement to the press. He claims two thousand tons of the cargo is platinum—and pure platinum is not found in nature—"

"He's probably referring to the osmium assay. It'll work out to at least a billion dollars of finished platinum."

"Do our assays agree with the Khadir's?"

"The point is academic, since the UN figures form the tax base—but no, they don't." I took our Moon Lab's tabulation and handed it to Mickleberry. He scanned it quickly and murmured,

"The osmium, yes . . . rutile . . . titanite . . . iron . . . uranium . . . you were sweeping with a wide broom up there, weren't you? what's this? A misprint $FeCr_4O_4$ . . ."

"It's chromite with a double charge of chromium—a freakish twinning within the lattice. The lab men on the Moon were doing handstands. They feel the twinning implies an increase of hardness and toughness—and consequently an incredible increase in the value of the ore."

"And the Khadir's lab missed it?"

"In their damned greed they stopped at the osmium and only made a superficial analysis of the rest."

You don't feel we have an—uh—ethical obligation—"

"No, definitely not!" I said shortly. "The Third World wants everything on a silver platter. Loans they never have to pay back. Development help they can kick in the pants when they feel like it. They want to be awarded university degrees and professional licenses without working for them or qualifying for them—as if being "exploited" was enough qualification for everything, from medicine to metallurgy.

"Their heads being so goddamned full of voo-doo and astrology and tribal lore that they have no place for Space sciences, they've dreamed up this Space Sharing blackmail in the name of 'mankind's resources'—a damned fraud if there ever was one. Grifters themselves, they won't trust our assays. *Their* decision has to be the final word.

"Okay, *let* it be final. And if they squawk after-wards and demand a recount when this freak chromite comes onto the market, we'll give 'em both barrels. If the Third World is so damned smart, how come *we* never get through feeding *them*?"

Mickleberry raised his eyebrows, but he did not contradict me.

His intercom buzzed. Ms. Delaney's voice said, "Mr. Mickleberry, a delegation of women just arrived, headed by Second Mate Fiske. They are requesting to see Captain Schuster."

I muttered, "Let Fiske come in. No sense to having a riot."

Mickleberry spoke into the intercom. "If the rest of the delegation will wait elsewhere in the building, we will admit Ms. Fiske. But I cannot have Operations disrupted."

There was a pause. Mickleberry said to me, "I hope this has taught you, Captain Schuster not to record Personal Memos."

"It's taught me not to leave 'em around," I admitted.

Ms. Delaney's voice said, "The delegation has moved outside the railing, by the elevators."

"Very well. Admit Ms. Fiske—and perhaps you'd better take shorthand notes."

A moment later Second Mate Fiske strode into the room. She was gussied up with a pink-laquered hairdo and a sleeveless divided-skirt tunic with a pink-studded belt. Ms. Delaney followed her quietly. I got up and shifted the chairs into conference-formation and led off by saying,

"Ms. Fiske, I have a Board Meeting at ten, so this hasta be short and sweet. No sewing circle then-*e*-and-then-*I*-said. State what you have to state, and I'll answer it."

She gave me a mannish nod. "Short and sweet, captain, we women officers don't buy that crap about physical strength being necessary for the top jobs at sea. And don't try to deny your Rec-Pak transcription in *Harpy's Bizarre.*"

"I don't intend to discuss *Harpy's Bizarre.* What I wanta talk about may surprise you." I paused. "I wanta talk about the odds."

Ms. Delaney glanced up briefly from her transcribing, and Mickleberry looked amused. I went on, "For six months the guys on the Q-Pod and Space Tug have been figuring odds. And the fact is, certain odds can't be beaten. In any graduating class of deck cadets, only a small minority will ever command a ship—simply because of the mathematical possibilities.

"Therefore, at some stage in their careers, deck officers have to size up their chances and make a decision. Do they want to continue at sea in subordinate posts? Or do they want to use their sea training in a related job on land—as an agent, chandler, broker, insuror, and so forth. There are various reasons why junior mates don't make the grade. One undeniable factor is leadership—the *macho* quality that other men recognize and respect. It's not a common quality. The odds are against the average guy having the kind of *macho* that enforces commands.

"And the odds are against any woman having that intensely physical, masculine quality at all. You can go back in history and name Semiramis—and Boadicea—and Joan of Arc—and that's about it. Elizabeth I was a superb politican—but was smart enough to let her captains dispose of the Armada. Her old man had plenty of *macho*—but she had to rule by other methods.

"Now, since the Company is not a military organization—since we can't install troops or police aboard our ships, our senior officers have to command *respect* before they can command anything else—and that means the physical ability to wade into a scrap and knock a few thick heads together. It's something from our tribal past, I grant you—but we can't ignore it for that reason.

"So, Ms. Fiske, like your male fellow-mates, you have to face the *odds* and plan your career accordingly. You may feel the odds are unfair to you as a woman—but the Company didn't rig them. *That* was done when *homo sapiens* evolved as bisex instead of unisex. All of us are limited by that evolution. After all, neither Mickleberry nor I can become mothers."

Ms. Delaney's pencil jiggled, and I heard a gulp of laughter. Ms. Fiske turned upon her. "You *would* think it's funny! With your slave mentality—!"

Ms. Delaney looked up, round-eyed. "Slave—?"

"Why else are you satisfied with this crummy hey-you job?"

Ms. Delaney sat straighter, with dignity. "My salary is far from 'crummy', Ms. Fiske. But what I really like about my job is—the feeling of power."

"Power!"

"Why, yes. Ms. Ingram and Ms. Dulaire and I agree that we like our *power.* You see, an executive's decision has to be implemented—communicated. If this isn't done efficiently, he just sits there like—like—"

"Like LOCO," I grinned.

"Oh, I wouldn't make *that* comparison," she

laughed. "but we secretaries undoubtedly feel we're the mortar holding the Company bricks together."

Ms. Fiske jerked her thumb at Mickleberry and asked Ms. Delaney, "Do you mean to tell me you've never wanted *his* job?"

Ms. Delaney said slowly, "I've never felt that any job was worth getting involved in the male identity crisis."

I guess we all stared at her, because she colored as she went on, "A man takes his identity from his work. Another tribal thing. Or maybe medieval, when men actually took their names from their jobs—Baker, Smith, Butler, Taylor, Miller, and so on. That's why men have such a terrific drive for job status. About a woman, the question is, 'what's she like?'. But about a man, it's 'What does he *do*'?

"That's why, Ms. Fiske, it disturbs you not to reach the top in your field. It's a man's field, and you've become caught in a man's identity crisis. A woman *has* an identity—she doesn't need to seek it from a job. She is the—the life-giver—the Earth mother. Every woman is born—Somebody."

Ms. Fiske opened her mouth—and shut it again. It was so true. Without our Company jobs, Mickleberry and I would be nothing. But Ms. Delaney would always be—Ms. Delaney.

After a moment I said, "Tell your delegation, Ms. Fiske, to remove all the physical aspects of sea work—and we'll talk again about female skippers."

She got up from her chair. "Yes, I see that political action is the only answer. If other nations can have police on board—"

She strode from the office. At Mickleberry's nod

and smile, Ms. Delaney followed her. I looked at my watch, and Mickleberry said, "Just one more detail, captain. About the crews of the Q-Pod and Tug—"

I waited, and he went on, "The public undoubtedly expects a gesture from the Company—a gold medal, perhaps—"

I had been hoping for this opening. I said, "Yeah, there's something you could do that wouldn't cost much more than gold medals. The crazy fools are planning a trip to Las Vegas with their Mechanical/Telekinetic Betting System. Unless somebody restrains them, they'll bet their families into the poorhouse."

"And—?"

"I'd like to try a little psychology. I'd like to have the Company put up a stake—a Telekinetic Research Project—with strict rules as to when the betting starts and stops. Because it's research, the guys will follow the rules and get the fever outta their systems, I hope. At any rate, I'm damned sure they'd rather have a betting stake than medals. And maybe they'll quit while they're ahead, with something to divide among themselves."

"What if they—uh—break the bank?"

"As Dr. Loft would say, let's not be naive."

I got up from my chair. Mickleberry said, "The Board will want to know how another ore shipment can be brought—safely—from the Asteroids. Another multi-billion dollars of precious metals."

"Yeah, I've been turning the problem over in my mind. Let's hope I can pull my usual rabbit out of the hat."

It takes money to meet a payroll, and money

does not grow on trees. Not that gimme-gimme grifters like Fakey Atur can get the fact into their ivory skulls . . . *and let that last remark stand!* . . . *Over and out!*

PROJECT PROMETHEUS WOULD STEAL THE FIRE OF THE SUN—
BUT THE PRICE MIGHT BE TOO TERRIBLE TO CONTEMPLATE

A NOVEL OF THE NEAR FUTURE BY
HARRY HARRISON

SKYFALL

$1.95

ACE
SCIENCE
FICTION

360 PARK AVENUE SOUTH · NEW YORK, N.Y. 10010

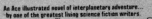